The Infidel
A Story of the Great Revival

by

M. E. Braddon

The Infidel
A Story of the Great Revival
by M. E. Braddon

ISBN: 978-93-62206-46-6

Published by

DOUBLE 9 BOOKS

2/13-B, Ansari Road
Daryaganj, New Delhi – 110002
info@double9books.com
www.double9books.com
Tel. 011-40042856

ABOUT THE AUTHOR

Victorian-era English popular novelist Mary Elizabeth Braddon. Her best-known work is the sensational novel she wrote in 1862, Lady Audley's Secret, which has been many times dramatized and staged. Mary Elizabeth Braddon, who was raised in Soho, London, attended private schools. When Mary was five years old in 1840, her mother Fanny filed for divorce from her father Henry due to his adultery. Edward Braddon, Mary's brother, departed for India at the age of twelve and then moved to Australia, where he rose to the position of Premier of Tasmania. After three years of working as an actress, Adelaide Biddle and Clara became her friends. Braddon was able to provide for her mother and herself despite their little responsibilities. In 1861, Mary moved in with publisher John Maxwell after they first met in April. But Maxwell had already tied the knot with Mary Ann Crowley, with whom he shared five kids. Crowley was living with her family, while Braddon and Maxwell were living together as husband and wife. When Braddon's "wife" status was revealed as a façade, Maxwell attempted to justify their relationship in 1864 by telling the newspapers that they were lawfully married. However, Richard Brinsley Knowles wrote to these papers, letting them know that his sister-in-law and Maxwell's real wife was still alive. Up until Maxwell's wife passed away in 1874, Mary raised his children as a stepmother. After that, they were able to tie the knot at St. Bride's Church on Fleet Street.

CONTENTS

CHAPTER I
GRUB-STREET SCRIBBLERS

Father and daughter worked together at the trade of letters in the days when George the Second was king and Grub Street was a reality. For them literature was indeed a trade, since William Thornton wrote only what the booksellers wanted, and adjusted the supply to the demand. No sudden inspirations, no freaks of a vagabond fancy ever distracted him from the question of bread and cheese; so many sides of letter-paper to produce so many pounds. He wrote everything. He contributed verse as well as prose to the *Gentleman's Magazine*, and had been the winner of one of those prizes which the liberal Mr. Cave offered for the best poem sent to him. Nothing came amiss to his facile pen. In politics he was strong—on either side. He could write for or against any measure, and had condemned and applauded the same politicians in fiery articles above different aliases, anticipating by the vehemence of his phrases the coming guineas. He wrote history or natural history for the instruction of youth, not so well as Goldsmith, but with a glib directness that served. He wrote philosophy for the sick-bed of old age, and romance to feed the dreams of lovers. He stole from the French, the Spaniards, the Italians, and turned Latin epigrams into English jests. He burnt incense before any altar, and had written much that was base and unworthy when the fancy of the town set that way, and a ribald pen was at a premium. He had written for the theatres with fair success, and his manuscript sermons at a crown apiece found a ready market.

Yes, Mr. Thornton wrote sermons—he, the unfrocked priest, the audacious infidel, who believed in nothing better than this earth upon which he and his kindred worms were crawling; nothing to come after the tolling bell, no recompense for sorrows here, no reunion with the beloved dead—only the sexton and the spade, and the forgotten grave.

It was eighteen years since his young wife had died and left him with an infant daughter—this very Antonia, his stay and comfort now, his indefatigable helper, his Mercury, tripping with light foot between his lodgings and the booksellers or the newspaper offices, to carry his copy, or to sue for a guinea or two in advance for work to be done.

When his wife died he was curate-in-charge of a remote Lincolnshire parish, not twenty miles from that watery region at the mouth of the Humber, that Epworth which John Wesley's renown had glorified. Here in this lonely place, after two years of widowhood, a great trouble had fallen upon him. He always recurred to it with the air of a martyr, and pitied himself profoundly, as one more sinned against than sinning.

A farmer's daughter, a strapping wench of eighteen, had induced him to elope with her. This Adam ever described Eve as the initiator of his fall.

They went to London together, meaning to sail for Jersey in a trading smack, which left the docks for that fertile island twice in a month. The damsel was of years of discretion, and the elopement was no felony; but it happened awkwardly for the parson that she carried her father's cash-box with her, containing some two hundred pounds, upon which Mr. Thornton was to start a dairy farm. They were hotly pursued by the infuriated father, and were arrested in London as they were stepping on board the Jersey smack, and Thornton was caught with the cash on his person.

He swore he believed it to be the girl's money; and she swore she had earned it in her father's dairy—that, for saving, 'twas she had saved every penny of it. This plea lightened the sentence, but did not acquit either prisoner. The girl was sent to Bridewell for a year, and the parson was sentenced to five years' imprisonment; but by the advocacy of powerful friends, and by the help of a fine manner, an unctuous piety, and general good conduct, was restored to the world at the end of the second year—a happy escape in an age when the gifted Dr. Dodd died for a single slip of the pen, and when the pettiest petty larceny meant hanging.

Having bored himself to death by an assumed sanctimony for two years, Thornton came out of the house of bondage a rank atheist, a scoffer at all things holy, a scorner of all men who called themselves Christians. To him they seemed as contemptible as he had felt himself in his hypocrisy. Did any of them believe? Yes, the imbeciles and hysterical women, the ignorant masses who fifty years ago had believed in witchcraft and the ubiquitous devil as implicitly as they now believed in Justification by Faith and the New Birth. But that men of brains—an intellectual giant like Sam Johnson, for instance—could kneel in dusty city churches Sunday after Sunday and search the Scriptures for the promise of life immortal! Pah! What could Voltaire, the enlightened, think of such a time-serving hypocrisy, except that the thing paid?

"It pays, sir," said Thornton, when he and his little knot of friends discussed the great dictionary-maker in a tavern parlour which they called "The Portico," and which they fondly hoped to make as famous as the Scribbler's Club, which Swift founded, and where he and Oxford and Bolingbroke, Pope, Gay, and Arbuthnot talked grandly of abstract things. The talk in "The Portico" was ever of persons, and mostly scandalous, the gangrene of envy devouring the minds of men whose lives had been failures.

The wife of Thornton's advocate, who was well off and childless, had taken compassion on the sinner's three-year-old daughter, and had carried the little Antonia to her cottage at Windsor, where the child was well cared for by the old housekeeper who had charge of the barrister's rural retreat. It was a cottage *orné* in a spacious garden adjoining Windsor Forest, and to-day, in her twentieth year, Antonia looked back upon that lost paradise with a fond longing. She had often urged her father to take her to see the kind friend whose bright young face she sometimes saw in her dreams, the very colour of whose gowns she remembered; but he always put her off with an excuse. The advocate had risen to distinction; he and his wife were fine people now, and Mr. Thornton would not exhibit his shabby gentility in any such company. He had been grateful for so beneficent a service at the time of his captivity, and had expatiated upon his thankfulness on three sides of letter-paper, blotted with real tears; but his virtues were impulses rather than qualities of the mind, and he had soon forgotten how much he owed the K.C.'s tender-hearted wife. Providence had been good to her, as to the mother of Samuel, and she had sons and daughters of her own now.

Antonia knew that her father had been in prison. He was too self-compassionate to refrain from bewailing past sufferings, and too lazy-brained to originate and sustain any plausible fiction to account for those two years in which his child had not seen his face. But he had been consistently reticent as to the offence which he had expiated, and Antonia supposed it to be of a political nature—some Jacobite plot in which he had got himself entangled.

From her sixth year to her seventeenth she had been her father's companion, at first his charge—and rather an onerous one, as it seemed to the hack-scribbler—a charge to be shared with, and finally shunted on to the shoulders of, any good-natured landlady who, in her own parlance, took to the child.

Thornton was so far considerate of parental duty that, having found an honest and kindly matron in Rupert Buildings, St. Martin's Lane, he left off shifting his tent, and established himself for life, as he told her, on her second floor, and confided the little girl almost wholly to her charge. She had one daughter five years older than Antonia, who was at school all day, leaving the basement of the house silent and empty of youthful company, and Mrs. Potter welcomed the lovely little face as a sunny presence in her dull parlour. She taught Antonia—shortened to Tonia—her letters, and taught her to dust the poor little cups and ornaments of willow-pattern Worcester china, and to keep the hearth trimly swept, and rub the brass fender—taught her all manner of little services which the child loved to perform. She was what people called an old-fashioned child; for, having never lived with other children, she had no loud boisterous ways, and her voice was never shrill and ear-piercing. All she had learnt or observed had been the ways of grown-up people. From the time she was ten years old she was able to be of use to her father. She had gone on errands in the immediate neighbourhood for Mrs. Potter. Thornton sent her further afield to carry copy to a printer, or a letter to a bookseller, with many instructions as to how to ask her way at every turn, and to be careful in crossing the street. Mrs. Potter shuddered at these journeys to Fleet Street or St. Paul's Churchyard, and it seemed a wonder to her that the child came back alive, but she stood in too much awe of her lodger's learning and importance to question his conduct; and when Antonia entered her teens she had all the discretion of a woman, and was able to take care of her father, and to copy his hurried scrawl in her own neat penmanship, when he had written against time in a kind of shorthand of his own, with contractions which Antonia soon mastered. The education of his daughter was the one duty that Thornton had never shirked. Hack-scribbler as he was, he loved books for their own sake, and he loved imparting knowledge to a child whose quick appreciation lightened the task and made it a relaxation. He gave her of his best, thinking that he did her a service in teaching her to despise the beliefs that so many of her fellow-creatures cherished, ranking the Christian religion with every hideous superstition of the dark ages, as only a little better than the delusions of man-eating savages in an unexplored Africa, or the devil-dancers and fakirs of Hindostan.

This man was, perhaps, a natural product of that dark age which went before the Great Revival—the age when not to be a Deist and a scoffer was to be out of the fashion. He had been an ordained clergyman of the Church of England, taking up that trade as he took up the trade of letters, for bread and cheese. The younger son of a well-born Yorkshire squire, he had been a profligate and a spendthrift at Oxford, but was clever enough to get a degree, and to scrape through his ordination. As he had never troubled himself about spiritual questions, and knew no more theology than sufficed to satisfy an indulgent bishop, he had hardly considered the depth of his hypocrisy when he tendered himself as a shepherd of souls. He had a fluent pen, and could write a telling sermon, when it was worth his while; but original eloquence was wasted upon his bovine flock in Lincolnshire, and he generally read them any old printed sermon that came to hand among conducted all their spiritual exercises, had won for themselves the name of "methodists." From those quiet rooms at Oxford had arisen a power that had shaken the Church of England, and which might have reinforced and strengthened that Church with an infinite access of vigour, enthusiasm, and piety, had English churchmen so willed. But the Methodists had been driven from the fold and cast upon their own resources. They were shut out of the churches; but, as one of the society protested, the fields were open to them, and they had the hills for their pulpit, the heavens for their sounding board.

George Stobart flung himself heart and soul into his work as an itinerant preacher, riding through the country with Mr. Wesley, preaching at any of the smaller towns and outlying villages to which his leader sent him, and confronting the malice of "baptized barbarians" with a courage as imperturbable as Wesley's. To be welcomed with pious enthusiasm, or to be assailed with the vilest abuse, seemed a matter of indifference to the Methodist itinerants. Their mission was to carry the tidings of salvation to the lost sheep of Israel; and more or less of ill usage suffered on their way counted for little in the sum of their lives. 'Twas a miracle, considering the violence of the mob and the inefficiency of rustic constables, that not one of these enthusiasts lost his life at the hands of enemies scarce less ferocious than the Indians on the banks of the Monongahela. But in those savage scenes it seemed ever as if a special providence guarded John Wesley and his followers. Many and many a time the rabble rout seemed possessed by Moloch, and the storm of stones and clods flew fast around the preacher's head; and again and again he passed unharmed out of the demoniac herd. Missiles often glanced aside and wounded the enemy, for the aim of blind hate was seldom true; and if Wesley did not escape injury on every occasion, his wounds were never serious enough to drive him from the stand he had taken by the market cross or in the churchyard, in outhouse or street, on common or hillside. He might finish his discourse while a stream of blood trickled down his face, or the arm that he would fain have raised in exhortation hung powerless from a blow; but in none of his wanderings had he been silenced or acknowledged defeat.

It was John Wesley's privilege, or his misfortune, at this time to stand alone in the world, unfettered by any tie that could hamper him in his life's labour. He was childless; and hard fate had given him a wife so uncongenial, so tormenting in her causeless jealousy and petty tyranny, that 'twas but an act of self-defence to leave her. In the earlier years of their marriage she accompanied him on his journeys; but as she quarrelled with his sister-in-law, Charles Wesley's amiable helpmeet, and insulted every woman he called his friend, her companionship must have been a thorn in the flesh rather than a blessing. His brother Charles—once the other half of his soul—was now estranged. Their opinions differed upon many points, and John, as the bolder spirit, had gone far beyond the order-loving and placable poet, who deemed no misfortune so terrible for the Methodists as to stand outside the pale of the Church, albeit they might be strong enough in their own unaided power to gather half the Protestant world within their fold. Charles thought of himself and his brother Methodists only as more fervent members of the Church of England, never as the founders of an independent establishment, primitive in the simplicity of its doctrine and observances, modern in its fitness to the needs of modern life.

John Wesley was now almost at the height of his power, and strong enough in the number of his followers, and in their profound affection for his person, to laugh at insult, and to defy even so formidable an assailant as Dr. Lavington, Bishop of Exeter, with whom he was carrying on a pamphlet war.

George Stobart loved the man and honoured the teacher. It was a pleasure to him to share the rough and smooth of Wesley's pilgrimage, to ride a sorry jade, even, for the privilege of riding at the side of one of the worst and boldest horsemen in England, who was not unlikely to come by a bad fall before the end of his journey. In those long stages there was ample leisure for the two friends to share their burden of sorrows and perplexities, and for heart to converse with heart.

Wesley was too profound a student of his fellow men not to have fathomed George Stobart's mind in past years, when Antonia's lover was himself but half conscious of the passion that enslaved him; and, remembering this, he was careful not to say too much of the young wife who was gone, or the love-match which had ended so sadly. He knew that in heart, at least, Stobart had been unfaithful to that sacred tie; but although he deplored the sin he could not withhold his compassion from the sinner. The Methodist leader had been singularly unlucky in affairs of the heart, from the day when at Savannah he allowed himself to be persuaded out of an engagement with a girl he loved, to the hour when he took a Zantippe for his spouse; and it may be that his own unfortunate marriage, and the memory of Grace Murray, that other woman once so dearly loved and once his plighted wife, made him better able to sympathise with the victim of a misplaced affection.

It was after Stobart had been working with him all through the summer and autumn, and when that eventful year of 1760 was waning, that Wesley for the first time spoke of Antonia.

"Your kinswoman Lady Kilrush?" he inquired. "What has become of so much beauty and fashion? I have not seen the lady's name in the evening papers for an age."

"Lady Kilrush has withdrawn herself from society. She has discovered how poor a thing a life of pleasure is when the bloom of novelty is off it."

"Aye, aye. Fashion's child has cut open the top of her drum and found nothing but emptiness in the toy. Did I not hear, by-the-bye, when I was last in London, that the poor lady had come through an attack of confluent smallpox with the loss of her beauty? If it be so, I hope she may awaken to the expectation of a kingdom where all faces are beautiful in the light that shines around the throne of God."

"No, sir, her ladyship has lost but little of her beauty. And it is not because she can no longer excel there that she has left the world of fashion."

And then Stobart took courage for the first time to speak freely of the woman he loved, and told Mr. Wesley the story of his wife's death-bed and Antonia's devotion. But when questioned as to the lady's spiritual state, he had to confess that her opinions had undergone no change.

"And can this presumptuous worm still deny her Maker? Can this heart which melts at a sister's distress remain adamant against Christ? It is a mystery! I know that the man atheist is common enough—an arrogant wretch, like David Hume, who thinks himself wiser than God who made the universe. But can a woman, a being that should be all softness and humility, set up her shallow reason against the light of nature and revelation, the light that comes to the savage in the wilderness and tells him there is an avenging God; the light that shows the child, as soon as he can think, that there is something better and higher than the erring mortals he knows, somewhere a world more beautiful than the garden where he plays? Stobart, I grieve that there should be such a woman, and that you should be her friend."

"The fabric of our friendship was torn asunder before I went to America, sir. I doubt if the ravelled edges will ever meet again."

"And you heave a sigh as you say it! You regret the loss of a friendship that might have shipwrecked your immortal soul."

"Oh, sir, why must my soul be the forfeit? Might it not be my happiness to save hers?"

"You were her friend and companion for years. Did you bring her nearer God?"

"Alas, no!"

"Abjure her company then for ever. I warned you of your peril when you had a wife, when I feared your spirit hovered on the brink of hell—for remember, Stobart, there is no such height of holiness as it is impossible to fall from. I adjured you to renounce that woman's company as you would avoid companionship with Satan. I warn you even more solemnly to-day; for at that time it was a sin to love her, and your conscience might have been your safeguard. You are a free man now; and you may account it no sin to love an infidel."

"Is it a sin, sir, even when that love goes hand in hand with the desire to bring her into Christ's fold?"

"It is a sin, George. It is the way to everlasting perdition, it is the choice of evil instead of good, Lucifer instead of Christ. Do you know what would happen if you were to marry this woman?"

"You would cease to be my friend, perhaps?"

"No, my son. I could not cease to love you and to pity you; but you could be no more my fellow worker. This pleasant communion in work and hope would be at an end for ever. At our last Conference we resolved to expel any member of our society who should marry an unbeliever. We have all seen the evil of such unions, the confusion worse confounded when the cloven foot crosses the threshold of a Christian's home, the uselessness of a Teacher whose heart is divided between fidelity to Christ and affection for a wicked wife. We resolved that no member of our society must marry without first taking counsel with some of our most serious members, and being governed by their advice."

"Oh, sir, this is tyranny!"

"It is the upshot of long experience. He who is not with me is against me. We can have no half-hearted helpers. You must choose whom you will serve, George: Christ or Satan."

"Ah, sir, my fortitude will not be put to the test. The lady for whom I would lay down my life looks upon me with a chilling disdain. 'Tis half a year since I forced myself upon her presence to acknowledge her goodness to my wife; and in all that time she has given me no sign that she remembers my existence."

"Shun her, my friend; walk not in the way of sinners; and thank God on your knees that your Delilah scorns you."

George Stobart spent many a bitter hour after that conversation with his leader. To be forbidden to think of the woman he worshipped now, when no moral law came between him and her love, when from the worldling's standpoint it was the most natural thing that he should try to win her; he, who for her sake had been disinherited, and who had by his life of self-denial proved himself above all mercenary views. Why should he not pursue her, with a love so sincere and so ardent that it might prevail even over indifference, might conquer disdain? There was not a man in his late regiment, not a man in the London clubs, who would not laugh him to scorn for letting spiritual things stand between him and that earthly bliss. And yet for him who had taken up the Cross of Christ, who had given his best years and all the power of heart and brain to preaching Christ's Law of self-surrender and submission, how horrible a falling away would it be if he were to abandon his beloved leader, turn deserter while the Society was still on its trial before the sight of men, and while every fervent voice was an element of strength. He thought of Wesley's other helpers, and recalled those ardent enthusiasts who had broken all family ties, parted from father and mother, sisters and brothers and plighted wife, renounced the comforts of home, and suffered the opprobrium of the world, in order to spend and be spent in the task of converting the English heathen, the toilers in the copper mine or the coal pit, the weavers of Somerset and Yorkshire, the black faces, the crooked backs, the forgotten sheep of Episcopal Shepherds.

But had any man living given up more than he was called upon to surrender, he asked himself? Who among those soldiers and servants of Christ had loved a woman as beautiful, loved with a passion as fervent?

He went back to London discouraged, yet not despairing. There was still the hope, faint perhaps, that he might lead that bright spirit out of darkness into light; win her for Christ, and so win her for himself. Ah, what an ecstatic dream, what an ineffable hope! To kneel by her side at the altar, to know her among the redeemed, the chosen of God! For that end what labour could be too difficult?

But, alas! between him and that hope there came the cloud of a terrible fear. He knew the Tempter's power over senses and soul, knew that to be in Antonia's company was to forget the world present and the world to come, to remember nothing, value nothing, but her, to become a worse idolator than they of old who worshipped Moloch and gave their children to the fire.

Wesley had warned him. Should he, in defiance of that warning from the best and wisest friend he ever had, enter the house where the Tempter lay in wait to destroy him, where he must meet the Enemy of Man? Call that enemy by what name he would, Satan, or love, he knew himself incapable of resistance.

He resolved to abide by Wesley's advice. He went back to his desolate home, and resumed his work in Lambeth Marsh, where he was welcomed with an affection that touched him deeply. His many converts, the awakened and believing Christians, flocked to his chapel and his schools; but that which moved him most was the welcome of the sinners and reprobates, whom he had taught to love him, though he could not teach them to forsake sin.

Before resuming his mission work in the old district he had ascertained that Lady Kilrush no longer went there. She still ministered to the Lambeth poor by deputy, and Mrs. Sophy Potter came among them often. He was weak enough to think with rapture of conversing with Sophy, from whom he would hear of Antonia. And so in the long dark winter he took up the old drudgery, teaching and exhorting, strenuous in good works, but with a leaden heart.

CHAPTER XVIII
"AS A GRAIN OF MUSTARD SEED"

John Wesley was not without compassion for a friend and disciple for whom he had something of a fatherly affection. He too had been called upon to renounce the woman he loved, the excellent, gifted, enthusiastic Grace Murray, whose humble origin was forgotten in the force and purity of her character. He had been her affianced husband, had thought of her for a long time as his future wife, lived in daily companionship with her on his pious pilgrimages, made her his helpmeet in good works; and yet, on the assertion of a superior claim, he had given her to another. That bitter experience enabled him to measure the pain of Stobart's renunciation. He watched his friend's course with anxious care, lest heart should fail and feet stumble on the stony road of self-sacrifice; and their intercourse, while the great itinerant remained in London, was even closer than it had been before.

Mr. Wesley had much to do that winter at his home by the Foundery Chapel. He had his literary work, the preparation of his books for the press, since each year of his life added to the list of those religious works, some of them written, others only edited, by himself, which were published at his risk, and which for several years resulted in pecuniary loss, though they were afterwards a revenue. He had the services of the chapel, which were numerous and at different hours, and he had his work abroad, preaching in many other parts of London.

It was in the early morning after one of his five-o'clock services at the Foundery that he was told a lady desired to see him. He had but just come in from the chapel, and his breakfast was on the table in the neat parlour where he lived and worked, a Spartan breakfast of oatmeal porridge, with the luxury of a small pot of tea and a little dry toast. It was only half-past six, and Mrs. Wesley had not left her chamber—a fortunate circumstance, perhaps, since the visitor was young and beautiful.

Mr. Wesley had many uninvited visitors, and it was nothing new for him to be intruded on even at so early an hour. He rose to receive the lady, and motioned her to a seat with a stately graciousness. He was a small man, attired with an exquisite neatness in a stuff cassock and breeches, and black silk stockings, and shoes with large silver buckles. His benign countenance was framed in dark auburn hair that fell in waving masses, like John Milton's, and at this period showed no touch of grey.

"In what matter can I have the honour to serve you, madam?" he asked, scanning the pale face opposite him, and wondering at its beauty.

It had not the bloom of health which should have gone with the lady's youth, but it was as perfect in every line as the Belvidere Apollo, and the eyes, with their look of mournful deprecation, were the loveliest he had ever seen—lovelier than Grace Murray's, which had once been *his* loveliest.

"I have come to you in great trouble of mind, sir," the lady began in a low voice, but with such perfect enunciation, such beauty of tone, that every syllable had full value. "I am a very unhappy woman."

"Many have come to me in the same sad plight, madam, and I have found but one way of helping them. 'Tis to lead them to the foot of the Cross. There alone can they find the Friend who can make their sorrows here their education for heaven."

"Oh, sir, if I believed in heaven, and that I should meet the dead whom I love there, I should have no sorrows. I should only have to wait."

"Alas, madam, can it be that you are without that blessed hope—that this world, with its cruel inequalities and injustices, is the only world your mind can conceive? Can you look upon the martyrdom of so many of your fellow creatures—diseased, deformed, blind, dumb, imbecile, or held for a lifetime in the bondage of abject poverty, never knowing respite from toil, or the possibility of comfort,—can you contemplate these outcasts, and yet believe there are no compensations hereafter, and that a God of infinite mercy can overlook their sufferings?"

"You believe in a heaven for these—a land of Beulah, where *they* will have the fat things? But what if one of these be a blasphemer? What if he curse God and die? What will be his destiny then, sir? Oh, I know your answer. The worm that dieth not—the fire that is not quenched. What of your scheme of compensations then, sir?"

"Did you come here to shake my faith, madam, or to ask for spiritual aid from me?" Wesley asked severely.

His searching gaze had taken in every detail of her appearance: the lovely face, whose ivory pallor was accentuated by a black silk hood; the grey lute-string gown, whose Quaker hue could not disguise the richness of the fabric; the diamond hoop-rings that flashed from under a black silk mitten. Dress, bearing, accent stamped the woman of quality.

"I meant no affront, sir. I talk at random, as women mostly do. I came here in weariness of spirit, and I scarce know how you can help me. I came because I have heard much of your merits, your amiable character, your willingness to befriend sinners. And I have listened to your sermons at West Street Chapel in the month last past with admiration and respect."

"But without belief in Him whose message I bring? Oh, madam, you might as well be at the playhouse laughing at that vulgar buffoon Samuel Foote. My sermons can do you no good."

"Nay, sir, if I thought that I should not be here this morning. I rose after a sleepless night and came through the darkness to hear you preach. If I cannot believe all that you believe, I can appreciate the wisdom and the purity of your discourse."

"Look into your heart, madam, and if you can find faith there; but as a grain of mustard seed——"

"Alas, sir, I look into my heart and find only emptiness. My sorrows are not such as the world pities. My heart aches with the monotony of life. I stand alone, unloved and unloving. I have tasted all the pleasures this world can offer, have enjoyed all, and wearied of all. I come to you in my weariness as the first preacher I have ever listened to with interest. Mr. Whitefield's discourse, whom I heard but once, only shocked me."

"Come, and come again, madam, and may my poor eloquence lead you to Christ. I should rejoice for more reasons than I can tell you, if, among the many souls that I have been the means of snatching from the brink of hell, Lady Kilrush should be one."

"What, Mr. Wesley, you know me?"

"Yes, madam, I remember the Bartolozzi head which was in all the printsellers' windows two years ago; and I should be more a stranger to this town than I am if I had not heard of the beautiful Lady Kilrush and her infidel opinions."

"You have heard of me from my lord's cousin, Mr. Stobart, perhaps."

"Mr. Stobart has spoken of your ladyship, deploring, as I do, the gulf that yawns between you and him."

"That gulf has widened, sir; for I have seen Mr. Stobart only once since he came from America."

"He has been travelling about England with me—and only came to London last October. I know, madam, that his respect for your person is only less than his grief at your unhappy opinions."

"We cannot change the fabric of our minds, sir."

"*We* cannot; but God can."

"You believe in instantaneous conversions—in a single act of faith that can make a Christian in a moment?"

"The Scriptures warrant that belief, madam. All the conversions related in the Gospel were instantaneous. Yet I will own that I was once unwilling to believe in the miracle of Christian perfection attained by a single impulse of the soul. But in the long course of my ministry I have seen so many blessed examples that I can no longer doubt that the Divine Spirit works wonders as great in this degenerate age as on that day of Pentecost, the birthday of the Christian Church. Instead of the miracle of fiery tongues, we have the miracle of changed hearts."

"And you think that Christian perfection attained in a moment will stand the wear and tear of life, and be strong enough to resist the world, the flesh, and the devil?" Antonia asked, with an incredulous smile.

"Nay, madam, I dare not affirm that all who think themselves justified are secure of salvation. These sudden recruits are sometimes deserters. I do not hold the tenets of the Moravians, who declare that the converted sinner cannot fall away, whereas, after our justification by faith, we are every moment pleasing or displeasing unto God according to our works, according to the whole of our present inward tempers and outward behaviour. But I have never despaired of a sinner, madam; nor can I believe that a spirit so bright as yours will be lost eternally. Long or late the hour of sanctifying Grace must come."

"Perhaps, Mr. Wesley, had you been reared as I was—taught to doubt the existence of a God before I was old enough to read the Gospel—you would be no less a sceptic than I am."

"I was indeed more fortunate—for I was born into a household of faith. Yet I have never hardened my heart against the man or woman whose education has only taught them to doubt, for I have sometimes thought, with unspeakable fear, that, had I given my mind to the study of mathematics or geometry, I too might have been one of those nice philosophers who will accept no creed that cannot be demonstrated like a proposition in Euclid. I thank God that I learnt to love Him, and to walk in His ways, before I learnt to pry into the mysteries of His Being or to question His dealings with mankind."

"No doubt that is happiest, sir—to shut one's mind against facts and believe in miracles."

And then, gradually won to fullest confidence by his quick sympathy, Antonia told John Wesley much of her life story, only avoiding, with an exquisite delicacy, all those passages which touched the secrets of a woman's heart. She told him how she had been left alone in the world with all the power that riches can give to a young woman, how she had tried all the resources of wealth, and found all wanting, even her experience of mission work among the outcast poor.

"I doubt you were happier engaged in that work than you have ever been in the mansions of the great," he said.

"No, Mr. Wesley, I will not pretend as much. While the pleasures of the great world were new I loved them dearly; but a third season brought satiety, and I sickened of it all. I know not why I sickened of my visits to the poor, for my heart was ever touched by their sufferings, and sometimes by their patience. It may be that it was because I was alone, and without an adviser, after Mr. Stobart left England."

"Will you resume that work now, madam? I doubt you are familiar with the parable of the talents, and know that to have youth and wealth, intellect and energy, and not to use them for others' good——"

"Oh, it is hateful! Be sure, sir, I know what a wretch I am. I spent last summer in Ireland, where the poor love me; but I hardly ever went near them. I did not let them starve. My steward and my waiting-woman carried them all they wanted, while I dawdled in my rose-garden or yawned over a novel. I was discouraged somehow. Those poor creatures are all Roman Catholics. They would talk to me of a creed which I had been taught to despise. There was a gulf between us."

"But you will resume your charitable work in London, where the people's religion need not offend you, since they are mostly heathens."

"Not at Lambeth! I cannot go back to Lambeth Marsh."

She knew that Stobart was spending all his days in the old places. Not for worlds could she go back to the work which she had shared with him, and which had once been so full of innocent happiness.

"Your ladyship can choose your district. The field is wide enough. Will you visit the sick poor in this neighbourhood, and will you accept my help and counsel?"

"With a glad heart, sir. I sorely need a friend."

"But you will not go as a heathen among heathens? You will carry the Gospel with you."

"Yes, sir. If it will help your views that I should read the New Testament to your people, I would as leave do so as not. Indeed, I have read the Gospel to those who have asked me; and be sure I have never been so foolish as to obtrude my opinions upon them. 'Tis only by close questioning they have ever discovered my barren creed." And then she went on with a sigh, "Ah, sir, if you knew how I envy you the faith which opens new worlds, now that I have lost all interest in this one."

"Do not despair of yourself, madam. I do not despair of you. The Lady Kilrush I had pictured to myself was an arrogant unbeliever, possessed by a devil of pride, and glorying in her infidelity. There is hope for the sceptic who has discovered how poor a thing this life is when we think it is all."

She rose to take leave, and Wesley conducted her to the street, where a hackney coach was in waiting. He begged her to call upon him as often as she pleased during his stay in London, which would not be long; and he promised to send her the names and addresses, and particulars as to character and necessities, of the invalids whom he would advise her to visit.

"On second thoughts I will not send you amongst the unconverted," he said, "but to some faithful Christians whose piety I doubt you will admire, however you may despise their simplicity."

He went back to his study full of thought. Antonia's conversation had surprised and interested him. Unlucky as he had been in his own too hasty choice of a wife, he was a shrewd judge of women, and he felt assured that this was a good woman. Would it not then be a hard measure were he to come between George Stobart and an attachment which death had legitimatised? And what better chance could there be for this woman's conversion than her union with an honest, believing Christian? The Society's stringent rule had been inspired by the evil wrought by women of a very different stamp from this one.

And yet was not this avowed infidel, so beautiful, so winning in her proud gentleness, only the Philistine Delilah in a new guise? The temptress, the lying spirit that betrayed the strong man of old, was there, perhaps, waiting to ensnare George Stobart's soul.

"I must see of what spirit she is," Wesley told himself, "and if she may yet be numbered among the children of light."

A new phase of Antonia's life began after her interview with John Wesley. All that she had done in the past, in those dens of misery and crime by the Marsh, was as nothing compared with her work under his direction. At Lambeth she had but exercised a fine lady's capricious benevolence, obeying the whim of the moment: a creature of impulse, too lavish where her heart was touched, too easily revolted by the ugliness of vice. In the squalid regions that lay around the Foundery her charities were administered upon a different system. One of Mr. Wesley's best gifts was the faculty of order, and all things done under his direction were done with an admirable method and proportion. His Loan Society, which made advances of twenty shillings and upwards to the respectable poor—to be repaid in weekly instalments—his Dispensary, his day and night-classes all testified to his power of organization. From the days when a poor scholar at Oxford, he lived like an anchorite of the desert in order that he might feed starving prisoners and rescue fallen women, he had been experienced in systematic charity. From him, in the hours he could spare her before starting on his northern pilgrimage, she learnt how to distribute her alms with an unfailing justice, and how to make the best use of her time. Her visits in those homes of sickness and penury, which might have been hopelessly dreary without his directing spirit, became full of interest in the light of his all-comprehending mind.

She sold three of her dress carriages and dismissed her second coachman. A hackney coach carried her to Moorfields every day, and she employed the greater part of the day in visiting the poor. She was often among Wesley's hearers at the evening service at the Foundery. His sermons touched her heart and almost convinced her reason. His simplicity of style and force of argument impressed her more than Whitefield's dramatic oratory. Mr. Wesley had no deep-drawn "Oh!" for Garrick to envy. His action was calm and pleasing, his voice clear and manly. He appealed to the heart and mind of his hearers by no studied effects, no flights of rhetoric, yet he never failed to hold them in the spell of that simple eloquence.

Antonia was interested in the congregation as well as in the preacher. She was moved by the spectacle of all those fervent worshippers—mostly in the lower ranks of life—men and women of scantiest leisure, who gave much when they spent their evenings in the chapel; instead of at the playhouse, or by the fireside in the cosy parlour with cards and congenial company. For the first time she began to understand what the religious life meant, the life in which all earthly things are secondary. The earnest faces, the voices of a vast concourse singing Charles Wesley's exquisite hymns, moved her deeply.

Her work took her mostly among the humble members of that Methodist Society which had begun twenty years before by the gathering together of eight or ten awakened souls, yearning for help and counsel, groaning under the burden of sin, and which was now so widespread a multitude. In the garrets and cellars, where she sat beside the bed of the sick and the dying, she found a fervour of unquestioning faith that startled and touched her. For these sufferers the Gospel she read was no history of things long past and done with, no story of a vanished life. It was the message of a living Friend, a Redeemer waiting to give them welcome in the Kingdom of the just made perfect, the world where there is no death. He who had promised the penitent thief a dwelling in Paradise was at the door of the death chamber; and to die was to pass to a life more beautiful than a child's dream of heaven.

As the days and weeks went by, that Gospel story read so often under such solemn influences, with death hovering near, took a deeper hold upon Antonia's imagination. The message that she carried to others was for her also. She learnt to love the wise Teacher, the beneficent Healer, the Saviour of mankind. That name of Saviour pleased her. From the theologian's point of view she was, perhaps, no more a Christian than she had ever been. She dared not tell John Wesley, whom she revered, and who now accepted her as a brand snatched from the burning, that her faith was not his faith, that she was neither convinced of sin nor assured of Grace.

Her awakening had been no sudden act, like the descent of the Spirit at Pentecost, but a gradual change in her whole nature, the widening of her sympathies, the growth of pity and of love. It was not of Christ the Sacrifice she thought, not of His atoning blood; but of Jesus the Great Exemplar, of Jesus who went about doing good. She would not question how it came to pass, but she believed that, in the dim long-ago, Divinity walked among mankind and wore the shape of man; to what end, except to make men better, she knew not. In all her conversation with Wesley's converts, however exalted their ideas might be, that earthly image was in her mind, Jesus, human and compassionate, the Comforter of human sorrows, the Sinless One who loved sinners.

Wesley rejoiced with exceeding joy in her conversion. He had met her from time to time in the dwellings of the poor, had sat with her beside the bed of the dying, had seen her often among his congregation; and he believed that the work of Grace had begun, and that it needed but good influences to ensure her final perseverance and justification by faith. He wrote to George Stobart the night before he left London for the North.

"You have passed through a fiery trial, dear friend, and I admire your fortitude in renouncing a passion that was stronger than all things, except your hope of salvation. The lady you love has become my friend and fellow-worker, and I dare venture to believe that she has escaped from darkness into light, and that you may now enjoy her society without peril to your soul. Let me hear by-and-by how your suit prospers. Her ladyship is a woman of rare gifts, and of a noble character.

"Yours in Christ,

"J. W."

CHAPTER XIX
"CHOOSE OF TWO LOVES"

Wesley's letter came upon George Stobart like the sudden opening of a gate into Paradise. It was a year since he had seen Antonia's face. For a year he had been the martyr of obedience to his spiritual guide, had surrendered every hope of earthly happiness, and had submitted to regard his life on earth only as an apprenticeship to the life to come.

And in a moment he was free, free to hope, free to behold the face, to hear the voice he loved. Free to win her, if he could. There was the question! He had never yet presumed, in his more thoughtful moods, to believe his love returned. How coldly she had bidden him adieu when last they met! Her manner had been without resentment, and without kindness. It seemed as if, when he offended her by his shameless addresses, he had ceased to exist. Her goodness to his wife had no relation to her friendship for him.

How could he approach her? Not in her own house, till he had some ground for hoping that her door would not be closed against him. He would steal upon her path unawares, and endeavour to regain her confidence by gentle means. He hurried to the Foundery to answer Wesley's letter in person, and found that good man busy with his preparations for leaving London. From him he heard of Antonia's progress in good works, and in her attendance at Wesley's services.

"That heart which you thought adamant has melted, George, and the Redeemer's saving Grace will be exemplified in this ransomed soul. She is so fine a creature, so generous, charitable, compassionate, that it wrung my heart to hear her, in this room, less than three months ago, boldly confess herself an infidel."

He told Stobart all that Antonia had done for his poor, and, at his request, gave him the addresses of some of the people she visited.

"They have all learnt to love her," he said, "which has not been always the case when I have sent women of exalted piety upon such missions. Her high-bred manner has a genial charm that wins them unawares. She does not attempt to teach, but she reads the Gospel to them; and I may tell you that she has an exquisite voice, and is a most accomplished reader. It was but the other day I approved of a female preacher, the first we have ever had, whose work so far has prospered. Should Lady Kilrush continue in well-doing, I should like her occasionally to address a room full of working women. A woman should know best how to reach women's hearts."

Stobart smiled at the suggestion. Antonia, the Voltairean, the friend of Lady Bolingbroke, the avowed sceptic, the woman of fashion, preaching the Gospel to a crowd of tatterdemalions in a Whitechapel kitchen! If Wesley could bring her to that pass he was indeed a miracle-worker. Could it be that she had cast a spell around the leader of the Methodists, and that his belief in her conversion was but the delusion of a kind heart, willing to think the best of so beautiful and gracious a creature?

Stobart was not an ardent believer in sudden conversions, though, in the course of his field preaching, it had been a common thing for him to see men and women fling themselves on their knees and declare that they were "saved," convinced of sin, justified, sanctified, on the instant, by one single operation of the Holy Spirit. He had seen something of the convulsionists of Bristol. The miracle of Pentecost had, in a lesser degree, been often repeated before his eyes; and among these instantaneous conversions he knew of some that had been the beginning of changed and holy lives. But he could not picture Antonia amongst Wesley's easily won converts. Had he not wrestled again and again with that stubborn spirit of unbelief, in the days when they were friends, and when he never spared hard words? All his arguments, all his pleadings, had failed to change her.

He did not allow for the influence of time, satiety, *Weltschmerz*, the aching void of a life without love.

He rode with Wesley as far as Barnet, on the first stage of his Northern journey, heard him preach there in the evening to a closely-packed audience, and rode back to London next morning. It was late in the afternoon, a mild spring afternoon, when, after visiting several houses in the neighbourhood of Moorfields, he discovered Lady Kilrush in an underground kitchen, seated by the sick-bed of a cobbler, a young man with a wife and two children, dying of a consumption. The wife sat on one side of the bed, her husband's hand clasped in hers, Antonia on the other side reading the Gospel of St. John, in those thrilling tones which Wesley had noted. She looked up as Stobart entered the kitchen, and her cheek crimsoned as she recognized him; but when she spoke her voice was cold as at their parting.

"I thought it was Mr. Wesley," she said. "Has he sent you to see our poor Morris? This gentleman is one of Mr. Wesley's helpers, Morris."

The sick man smiled faintly, and held out a wasted hand to the visitor.

"Morris and I are old friends," Stobart said gently. "No, Lady Kilrush, I was not sent here," and then seeing there was no vacant chair, he stood with his elbow on the mantelpiece, waiting for Antonia to go on reading.

"'I am the true Vine,'" she began, and read to the end of the chapter; then rose quietly, bent over the dying man, murmured a few kind words, pressed the wife's hand tenderly, and stole from the room, almost as noiselessly as if she had been indeed the good angel these people thought her. Stobart's survey of the wretched room had shown him that her charity had provided the sufferer with every comfort and even luxury that could be administered in such a home.

He followed her into the squalid street. The sky above the dilapidated red tile roofs was blue and bright, and the north-west wind blew the freshness of April flowers from the fields and gardens between Finsbury and Islington. Antonia had no carriage waiting for her.

"I forget that I am a fine lady when I come here," she said, smiling at him. "I walk from house to house, and take a hackney-coach when I have done my day's work."

"Shall I get you a coach now? It is nearly six o'clock. Or will you walk a little way?"

"I should like to walk. The fresh air is very pleasant after that warm room; that room which he will only leave for the grave, poor soul. But it is not of him one thinks most, but of the wife. She so loves him. Happily she counts on being with him again—in a better world. She has what Mr. Wesley calls vital religion."

"Mr. Wesley has told me something that has made me very happy," Stobart said in a low voice that trembled ever so slightly. "He has told me that your heart is changed, that you do not think as you once thought."

"Oh, I am changed—heart, mind, desires, fancies—yes, all are changed. But I know not if it is for the better. I have left off caring for things. I feel ever so old. Nothing in this life interests me, except sorrow and suffering. I went to Mr. Wesley when my spirits had sunk to despair, and he has been my good friend. I go home almost happy, after I have worked all day among his poor."

"And he has taught you to believe in Christ?"

"One does not learn to believe. That must come from within, I think. I have come to feel the need of God, the need of a world after death; but I doubt I am no nearer believing in miracles than I was ten years ago when first I read Voltaire. If to love Jesus is to be a Christian, why then I am a

Christian. But if a Christian must think exactly as you do, or as Mr. Wesley does, I am outside the pale."

"Oh, but the fuller light will come! 'God is light.' He will not leave a soul so precious in darkness. I knew long ago, when I saw you among those wretched creatures at Lambeth, I knew you could not be for ever lost."

They walked on a little way in silence, facing towards the setting sun. They were crossing the public garden at Moorfields, where the cits and their wives and families walked on fine evenings.

"Will you not resume your work in my district? Our people long for you. Miss Potter is very kind—and your bounty is lavish—but they all want *you*, all those whom you visited three years ago, and who remember you with affection. Cannot you spare a little time from these new pensioners for your old friends?"

"Oh, sir, I doubt they are well cared for, now they have you."

"But will you not help me a little? Ah, madam, could you but understand what your help means for me! If you avoid the old places, the old people, can I believe that you have pardoned my sin of the past? Surely that one passionate hour has been expiated by the remorse of years."

"I have long since pardoned your folly, sir. Pray suffer me to forget it."

Her cold disdain stung him to the quick. She did not even account his passion worth her anger. How could he ever hope to break through that adamant, to melt that ice?

He was persistent in spite of her coldness, and at last she promised to return occasionally to her old work at Lambeth, and to visit the people he deemed most in need of her.

"I can but give them my surplus hours," she said, "since the best part of my life is pledged to Mr. Wesley. And now, sir, be so obliging as to call a coach, and suffer me to bid you good evening."

There was a stand of coaches close by, and he handed her to her seat in one. He stood bareheaded, watching her drive away. Her serious manner, with that touch of hauteur, kept him at an immeasurable distance. The familiar confidence of her old friendship seemed irrecoverably lost.

Nearly a year had gone since that meeting in the Whitechapel kitchen. It was spring again, but early spring, and the days were still short, and the skies still grey and cold, when George Stobart walked home with Antonia after her visit to another dying bed, the bed of extreme old age this time, the gradual fading out of the vital flame, feebler, paler, day by day, the bed of boundless faith and ecstatic anticipation of a new and fairer life.

She had seen the last sands of another life run down in the autumn of the past year. She had kept her promise, and had gone back to Bellagio in September, and had watched by her Italian grandfather's dying bed—a peaceful end, in the odour of sanctity. She had followed the old man to his last resting-place, and had stayed at Bellagio long enough to make all arrangements for Francesca's wedding, and her establishment as mistress of the old villino. She was married at the New Year, handsomely dowered by her English cousin, and having chosen a worthy mate. Antonia's obligations to her humble kinsfolk had been fulfilled.

Mr. Stobart and Lady Kilrush were on friendliest terms now; but no word of love had been spoken. To be with her, to hear her voice, to know that she liked his company, was so much; and to declare himself might be the breaking of a spell. They had been together often among the homes of the poor, in the library at St. James's Square, and sometimes in the churches and chapels where Wesley, Romaine, and other lights of the evangelical school were to be heard. But in all that time Stobart had obtained no farther profession of faith from Antonia.

"If to love Christ is to be a Christian, I am one," she told him, when he tried to bring her to his own way of thinking, and that was all.

Final perseverance, sanctification, justification, conviction of sin! Those phrases seemed to her only the shibboleth of a sect. But all the strength of her heart and intellect were engaged in those good works to which the Methodists attached only a secondary merit. Her compassion for human suffering was the dominating impulse of her life. She could feel for the thief in Newgate, pity the slut in Bridewell whose life had been one long disgrace. She had gone with Stobart into the prisons of London, those dark places as yet unvisited by Howard or Elizabeth Fry. She shrank from no form of suffering, so long as it was possible to help or to console.

She had done with the world and its pleasures. The recluse is soon forgotten in the merry-go-round of society. Her duchesses had long ceased to trouble themselves about her. The princes and princesses had forgotten her existence. The new reign had brought with it new interests, a new set. Women were the top of the fashion who had been dowdies; men who had been blockheads were wits.

Lord Dunkeld had married a rosy-cheeked damsel of eighteen summers, daughter and heiress of a Lord of Session, was settled on his Scotch estate, and had come to think Edinburgh the focus of intelligence and *ton*. The people who had courted and admired Lady Kilrush had long ceased to think of her, except as an eccentric, like Lady Huntingdon, who had caught the fever of piety that had been in the air for the last twenty years—the contagion of Methodism, Moravianism, Predestinarianism—some boring and essentially middle-class form of religion which banished her from polite company.

A woman who neither visits nor gives entertainments is socially dead. Her female friends spoke of her sometimes with pity, as an unfortunate who was afraid to let the town see her altered face, and who had taken to religion as a substitute for beauty. The idea that she was disfigured having once got abroad, her old rivals were slow to believe her face unspoilt, though people who had seen her at one of Lady Huntingdon's Thursdays swore that she was almost as handsome as ever.

"If she had not a cold, proud look that keeps an old friend at a distance," said one of her admirers, who had suffered one of Whitefield's sermons in order to meet her.

"She would not have you near enough to discover the ravages of that horrid malady. I'll wager her countenance is plastered a quarter of an inch thick with white lead," retorted the rival belle.

The library in St. James's Square was in the half light of a spring evening, as it had been a year ago when Stobart entered the room with so agonized an apprehension. He came in now with Antonia, a privileged guest, coming and going as in the years gone by, taking his rest by her fireside, after the burden of the day. Her only other visitors were Lady Margaret Laroche— who was faithful to her in spite of what she called her "degeneracy," and who came now and then to pour out her complaints at the foolishness of a world whose follies were necessary to her existence—and Patty Granger, whose dog-like fidelity made her ever welcome, and who loved to talk of Antonia's girlhood, and her own free and easy life in Covent Garden, when the General was a submissive lover, and not a peevish husband.

Stobart had been unusually silent during the walk from Lambeth, and Antonia had been full of thought, impressed as she ever was by that mystery of the passing spirit, that unanswerable question, "Whither goest thou, oh, departing soul, or is thy journey for ever finished, and is man's instinctive belief in immortality a vain dream?"

Antonia sank into her fireside chair, weary after a long day in wretched rooms, hearing and seeing sad things. She was almost too tired to talk, and was glad of Stobart's silence. Sophy would come presently and make the tea—it being supposed that no man-servant's hand was delicate enough to brew that choice infusion—and their spirits would revive. But in the meantime rest was all they wanted.

It startled her from this reposeful feeling when Stobart rose abruptly and began to pace the room, for some minutes in silence, broken only by a sigh, then bursting into impassioned speech.

"Antonia, I can lock up my heart no longer! 'Tis a year since I came from America to find a desolate home. For a year I have known myself a widower. Dare I break the spell of silence? Shall I lose all in asking for all? Will you banish me in anger, as you did when it was so black a sin to speak of my love?"

He flung himself on his knees beside her chair.

"Say you will be pitiful and kind, you who are all pity; and if you cannot give me what I ask, promise not to make me an outcast from your friendship."

"I shall never again cease to be your friend, sir!" she answered gently. "I think we know each other too well to quarrel. We are neither of us perfect creatures; but I believe you are a good Christian, and that your friendship will ever be precious to me."

"Make the bond something nearer than friendship, Antonia. Let it be the hallowed tie that makes two souls seem as one. Ah, my angelic friend, seldom has woman been so worshipped as you are by me. The love that stole upon my mind and heart unawares, in this room, when it was so foul a sin to love you; the love purified by years of repentance; the love that haunted me in the wilderness, through long days and nights of toil and pain, when your following ghost was nearer and more real to me than the foe that hemmed us round or the storm that beat upon our heads—that love is with me still, Antonia; time cannot change nor familiarity lessen it. Will you be for ever cold, for ever deaf to my prayer?"

She had heard him to the end. Was it for the joy of hearing him, though she knew what her answer must be? She knew now that she loved him, and had always loved him, from those days of a so-called friendship. She knew that he took all the zest out of her life when he left her; and that the want of his company had been a dull pain, underlying all varieties of pleasure, a sense of loss coming on her on a sudden amidst the tempestuous gaiety of a masquerade, haunting her in some melody at the opera house, saddening her in the midst of a gay throng, where arrows of wit flashed fast to an accompaniment of joyous laughter.

"Can you forget what I told you years ago?" she said. "A marriage is impossible for me. I am married to the dead. I gave myself to my husband for ever. I swore in his dying moments to belong to none but him."

"'Twere madness to keep so wild a vow."

"What! Do the Methodist Christians think it no sin to break their oath?"

"They would violate no vow made in their rational moments. But your promise was given in the delirium of grief, and he to whom you gave it could not be such a self-lover as to fetter youth and beauty to his coffin."

"'Twas he who claimed the promise, and I gave it in all seriousness. I loved him, sir. I would have given all the residue of my life for one year of happiness with him. I loved him; and our lives were severed by my act, severed for years, to unite in death. If there be that other world Mr. Wesley believes in, I may see him again, may be with him in eternity. That, sir, is indeed a great perhaps. I will not hazard such a chance of everlasting bliss."

"'Tis the pagan's heaven you picture, not the Christian's—the resumption of human ties, not union with Christ. Oh, can you be so cruel as to make my life miserable, to deny the lover who adores you, for the sake of the dead man who lies in the quiet sleep that has no knowledge of you and me—must lie there unknowing, uncaring, till the Day of Judgment?"

"If ever that day come he shall not find me forsworn; no, not even for you; not even to make you happy."

He had watched the exalted look in her face as the firelight shone upon it. She had looked upward as she spoke, her eyes dilated, her lips tremulous with emotion, and a fever spot on her cheek. But now on a sudden her head drooped, and she burst into tears.

"Not even for you," she sobbed.

It was her confession of love. In the next moment she was in his arms, and their lips had met. She let him hold her there, she let her head lie upon his shoulder, and suffered his impassioned kisses in the surprise of his wild vehemence.

"You love me, Antonia, you love me! No dead man shall stand between us. You must, you shall be mine!"

She released herself from his arms, and sprang to her feet.

"I am not so weak a thing as you fancy me, sir."

"I will not let you go. Shall a profligate's pale spectre stand between me and the woman I worship? A vow made under such conditions is no vow. Can it better him that my life should be miserable, that lovers as true as you and I should pine in solitude, go down to the grave without ever having known happiness? It shall not be."

"You are very imperious, Mr. Stobart; but I am the mistress of my own fate."

"I am very resolute. You love me, Antonia. Your tears, your lips have told me that divine secret."

"Be it so. I love you, sir. But I will not break my promise to one I loved better, my first dear love, the man who brought sunshine into my life, and extinguished the sun when he left me. The man who loved me better than he thought."

"Antonia!"

"Leave me, Mr. Stobart. If we are still to be friends, you had best leave me."

"It is no longer a question of friendship. I know now that you love me, and I swear I will not lose you."

"Leave me, sir," she exclaimed. "If you ever wish to see my face again, leave me this instant."

"At least be merciful. Do not send me from you in despair. Antonia, be kind! I cannot live without you."

"Go, sir; your vehemence, your boldness, leave me no power to reason or even to think. Go; and if after a night of thought I can bring myself to believe that I am not bound, body and soul, by my promise to the dead——"

"You will be mine," he cried, with outstretched arms, trying to clasp her again to his heart, but she drew herself away from him indignantly.

He grasped her unwilling hand, covered it with kisses and tears, and rushed from the room.

The watchmen were calling "Half past eleven, and a fine night," when Lady Kilrush left her dressing-room, carrying a lighted candle and a key, and crossed the gallery to that other side of the spacious house where the late lord's rooms were situated. The household had retired soon after ten, and the great well staircase lay like a pit of darkness below the massive oak banisters. An oppressive silence, an oppressive gloom, pervaded the house, as Antonia unlocked the door that had seldom been opened since the coffin was carried out on the first stage of its long journey, on a summer night that memory recalled as if it had been yesterday. The atmosphere, the feelings of that night were in her mind as she crossed the threshold of the room which had never known the uses of human life since Kilrush occupied it. The wainscot mouse, the spider on the wall, the moth lurking in the window drapery, had been its only inhabitants.

The tall silver candlesticks, the portfolio and standish were on the table in the oak-panelled ante-room where Antonia remembered the lawyer and the doctor talking beside the empty hearth. The vastness of the bedchamber had an appalling air in the glimmer of a single candle. Antonia's hand trembled as she lighted those other candles, the candles that had burnt beside the dying man when he spoke the words that made her a peeress.

How near that night seemed, as she stood beside the bed, funereal under the dark velvet hangings, a catafalque rather than a bed. She could hear the Bishop's full-mouthed tones, and that other voice, faltering and faint, but to her the world's best music.

"Oh, my beloved," she cried, falling on her knees beside the pillow on which his head had lain. "Oh, my dearest, kindest, best, surely it is you I love and none other—you, only you, only you!"

Her arms were folded on the coverlet, her head resting on them. She remained thus on her knees, for a long time, dreaming back the past. She lived again through those hours in Rupert Buildings, those hours spent in endless talk with Kilrush. They seemed to her now the most blissful hours of her life. She looked back and wondered at that happiness. Perhaps there was some touch of illusion in that dream of the past, something of the light that never was on sea or land; but to her there was no shadow of doubt that the joy of those past days exceeded all she had known of gladness since her husband's death.

She had made her night toilet and put on a loose silken *négligé*, meaning to spend the long hours in this room. Her first night in a husband's chamber—her wedding night, she thought, with a melancholy smile.

She had come here to solve the problem of the future, to determine whether she should or should not break her promise to the dead. For her, the free-thinker, it might seem a small thing to break a vow, when her keeping it would make a good man's life desolate. But despite the vagueness of her hope in the Hereafter, despite that early teaching which had bidden her believe in nothing that her human intelligence could not comprehend, her husband's image was a living presence in that room, a living influence in her life, and she could not imagine him lying in the dust, unconscious and indifferent. Somehow, somewhere, by some mysterious unthinkable means, the dead still lived, still loved her, still claimed her fidelity.

"My first dear love," she cried, in a burst of hysterical sobs, "I am yours and yours only. I can never belong to another, never own any husband but you."

Her tears, her reiterated vow soothed her. She rose from her knees, by-and-by, and sat on the bed, as she had sat when she held her dying lover in her arms. Gradually her head sank on the pillow where his head had lain, and she fell asleep.

"Past two o'clock, and a rainy night," called the watchman in the square.

Antonia did not wake till after five. The dead man was in her dreams through those three hours of deepest sleep. It was not George Stobart's impassioned embrace that haunted her slumber. The arms that encircled her, the lips that kissed her, were the arms and lips of the lover irrevocably lost, and there was a poignant joy in that embrace. Her wedding night! The words were repeated in her dreams. It was a night of dreams that ratified her promise to the dead. Surely he was near her! The voice that sounded so close to her ear, that very voice she knew so well, the lips whose touch thrilled her, gave her the assurance of immortality; and in some dim land she could not picture, under conditions beyond the limit of human intelligence, they two would meet again, husband and wife, spirit or flesh, reunited for ever.

George Stobart was at Kilrush House before nine o'clock. His patience could endure no longer. He had spent the night as he spent that other and much more miserable night after Whitefield's sermon, wandering about the waste places between Lambeth Palace and Vauxhall. Slumber or rest was out of the question.

The hall porter was more awake than usual, and answered his inquiry briskly.

"No, sir, not at home. Her ladyship has left London. She will lie at Devizes to-night, on her way to Ireland."

"Gone! Impossible!"

"It was very sudden, sir, and as much as could be done. 'Twas nearly six o'clock this morning when the servants had their orders. Her ladyship takes only Miss Potter, her French waiting woman, and one footman, in her travelling carriage and a post-chaise."

"What time did they leave?"

"They may have been gone over half an hour, sir. I heard the clock strike eight after the coaches left the door. I have her ladyship's letter for you, sir."

Stobart took the letter, speechless with mortification, and left the house before he broke the seal. It was a miserable morning, and he stood in the rain, under the low grey sky, while he read her letter, her letter of one line —

"Farewell for ever."

CHAPTER XX
"AND CLEAVE UNTO THE BEST"

From the Revd. John Wesley to Mr. George Stobart.

"At Mrs. Berry's Lodgings, Bristol,

"May 5th, 1762.

"MY DEAR FRIEND,

"Your letter surprised and grieved me; for I had hoped that Lady Kilrush would have smiled upon your suit, and that an union between two natures so ardent in Christian charity would be not only for your happiness, but for the spiritual welfare of that dear lady, and for the greater glory of God.

"Yet though I regret your disappointment I can but honour her ladyship for the reverence in which she holds her promise to the dead; nor can I do other than admire that chaste and heavenly disposition which would dedicate a lifetime to the memory of a husband who was hers only in one dying hour. Such widows are widows indeed!

"You ask for my counsel at this so serious crisis of your life, when the nature of your future work for Christ rests on your choice of action; first, whether you should take Holy Orders, before you go to America, a voyage upon which you tell me your mind is irrevocably fixed; and next whether you should accept her ladyship's munificent gift of the major portion of her funded property, and her mansion in St. James's Square, she retaining only her Irish estate, and the family seat on the Shannon. This latter question I unhesitatingly answer in the affirmative. The fact that this noble lady had executed the deed of gift which transferred her property to you before she declared her intention, in the touching letter which you send me, would show that she had deliberately resolved upon this sacrifice, and was influenced by the desire of doing justice to her late husband's nearest kinsman. She has indeed honoured me with a letter to that effect, and has moreover told me that she intends to spend the rest of her life in Ireland, where I hope occasionally to visit her.

"I say to you, George, accept this fortune, even though, in your present temper, it may seem a burden. Lady Kilrush will be still a rich woman; and you will have a wider scope for the employment of money in the service of Christ than any woman, not even that Mother in Israel, Lady Huntingdon, could find.

"The more serious question of your ordination I must leave to your own heart and mind, and the Spirit of God directing you. As an itinerant lay-preacher your ministry has borne good fruit, and if you transfer your labours to Georgia I shall sorely miss your help; but as an ordained priest you will enter a higher sphere of usefulness, and feel yourself sent out upon a nobler mission: so, my dear brother in Christ, I bid you go on and fear not. We desire to rivet the chains that bind us to the Church of England, not to loosen them; and the idea that we are drifting apart from that Church— *injusta noverca* though she has been to us—is a source of fear and trembling to many weak spirits, most of all to my dear brother Charles.

"For myself I care but little whether we continue to belong to the Established Church or be cast out; for sure I am that we have kindled a flame which neither men nor devils will ever be able to quench. Our fundamental principles are the fundamental principles of the Church, and will suffer no change. I have no fear for the Society, which, from so insignificant a beginning, has attained so vast an influence. I remember how, less than thirty years ago, two young men, without friends, without either power or fortune, set out from college to attempt a reformation, not of opinions, but of men's tempers and lives, of vice in every kind, of everything contrary to justice, mercy, or truth. For this we carried our lives in our hands, and were looked upon and treated as mad dogs. Knowing this of me you cannot think that I should fear to stand alone, the untrammelled shepherd of my flock. Your ordination, should you meet with a bishop of liberal mind, like Whitefield's friend, that good Bishop of Gloucester, ought not to hang tediously on hand. But I hope I may have many occasions for conversing with you before you sail for America, where, supplied with ample fortune, and armed with the faith that can move mountains, you may do much to maintain those noble enterprises, the Schools, the Orphanages, and Asylums, which Mr. Whitefield initiated, and to which he ever returns with fresh vigour. Would that he had a more robust constitution, and that we might hope to see his ministry continued to a green old age; but I fear he cannot long stand against the inroads of disease, accelerated by strenuous toil, preaching three times a day, long journeys in all weathers, the rough usage of the mob, and that fiery spirit which has been always like the sword that wears out the scabbard.

"On my return to the Foundery in the autumn I shall seek for you in your house at Lambeth. Till then, esteemed friend and fellow labourer, farewell.

"JOHN WESLEY."

From the Revd. John Wesley to the Revd. George Stobart.

"At the George Inn, Limerick, Ireland,

"November 11th, 1768.

"MY DEAR FRIEND,

"It is with poignant grief that I take up my pen to write the saddest tidings it has ever been my lot to send you. Your last letter was full of enquiries about Lady Kilrush. Alas, George, that noble being, whom we have both loved and revered, no longer inhabits this place of sin and sorrow, and I dare hope that her pure and gentle spirit has taken flight to a better world, and now enjoys the companionship of saints and angels. Rarely have I met with a nature so free from earthly stain, nor have I often beheld a life so rich in good works; and although she may not even at the last have attained that unquestioning faith which I so desired to find in her, I would hazard my own hope of Heaven against the certainty of her everlasting bliss; for never did I know a better Christian.

"Her death was worthy to rank in the list of martyrs. You may have heard that this city—the filth and squalor of whose poorer streets and alleys no pen can depict—was lately visited by an outbreak of small-pox. Lady Kilrush was at her mansion by the Atlantic, a delightful spot, where I once spent a reposeful week in her sweet company, preaching in the neighbouring villages, and narrowly escaping death at the hands of a wild mob, egged on by a bigot priest. In this healthful retreat she heard of the pestilence that was mowing down the poor of Limerick, and at once hastened to the dreadful scene. Secure from the disease herself, by past suffering, she spent her days and nights in ministering to the sick, aided in this pious work by a band of holy women of the Roman Catholic faith, and by such hired nurses as her purse could command.

"For six weeks she laboured without respite, scarcely allowing herself time for food or sleep; and when my itinerant ministry brought me to Limerick I found her marked for death. She had taken cold in passing from close and heated rooms into the windy street, had neglected her own ailments in her anxiety for others, and the result was a violent inflammation of the lungs, attended with a raging fever.

"Alas, dear sir, I can give you no message of affection from those once so lovely lips. She was delirious when I saw her, and though your name was mixed with her wild ravings, 'twas in disjointed sentences of no meaning; but on the day preceding her death the fever abated, and indeed it seemed for a short space as if my prayers had prevailed, and that she would be spared still to adorn a world where by her charities and inexhaustible beneficence she shone like a star. Her senses came back to her within an hour of the last change. She knew me, and received the Sacrament from my hand, and I dare hope that in those last moments perfect faith in her Saviour was conjoined with that perfect love which had long been the ruling principle of her life.

the rubbish heap of his bookshelves. He migrated from one curacy to another, and from one farmhouse to another, drinking with the farmers, hunting with the squires; diversified this dull round with a year or two on the Continent as bear-leader to a wealthy merchant's son and heir; brought home an Italian wife, and while she lived was tolerably constant and tolerably sober. That brief span of wedded life, with a woman he fondly loved, made the one stage in his life-journey to which he might have looked back without self-reproach.

He was delighted with his daughter's quick intellect and growing love for books. She began to help him almost as soon as she could write, and now in her twentieth year father and daughter seemed upon an intellectual level.

"Nature has been generous to her," he told his chums at "The Portico." "She has her mother's beauty and my brains."

"Let's hope she'll never have your swallow for gin-punch, Bill," was the retort, that being the favourite form of refreshment in "The Portico" room at the Red Lion.

"Nay, she inherits sobriety also from her mother, whose diet was as temperate as a wood-nymph's."

His eyes grew dim as he thought of the wife long dead—the confiding girl he had carried from her home among the vineyards and gardens of the sunny hillside above Bellagio to the dismal Lincolnshire parsonage, between grey marsh and sluggish river. He had brought her to dreariness and penury, and to a climate that killed her. Nothing but gin-punch could ever drown those sorrowful memories; so 'twas no wonder Thornton took more than his share of the bowl. His companions were his juniors for the most part, and his inferiors in education. He was the Socrates of this vulgar Academy, and his disciples looked up to him.

The shabby second floor in Rupert Buildings was Antonia's only idea of home. Her own eerie was on the floor above—a roomy garret, with a casement window in the sloping roof, a window that seemed to command all London, for she could see Westminster Abbey, and the Houses of Parliament, and across the river to the more rustic-looking streets and lanes on the southern shore. She loved her garret for the sake of that window, which had a broad stone sill where she kept her garden of stocks and pansies, pinks and cowslips, maintained with the help of an occasional shilling from her father.

The sitting-room was furnished with things that had once been good, for Mrs. Potter was one of those many hermits in the great city who had seen better days. She was above the common order of landladies, and kept her house as clean as a house in Rupert Buildings could be kept. Tidiness was out of the question in any room inhabited by William Thornton, whose books and papers accumulated upon every available table or ledge, and were never to be moved on pain of his severe displeasure. It was only by much coaxing that his daughter could secure the privilege of a writing-table to herself. He declared that the destruction of a single printer's proof might be his ruin, or even the ruin of the newspaper for which it was intended.

Such as her home was, Antonia was content with it. Such as her life was, she bore it patiently, unsustained by any hope of a happier life in a world to come—unsustained by the conviction that by her industry and cheerfulness she was pleasing God.

She knew that there were homes in which life looked brighter than it could in Rupert Buildings. She walked with her father in the evening streets sometimes, when his empty pockets and his score at the Red Lion forbade the pleasures of "The Portico." She knew the aspect of houses in Pall Mall and St. James's Square, in Arlington Street and Piccadilly; heard the sound of fiddles and French horns through open windows, light music and light laughter; caught glimpses of inner splendours through hall doors; saw coaches and chairs setting down gay company, a street crowded with link-boys and running footmen. She knew that in this London, within a quarter of a mile of her garret, there was a life to which she must ever remain a stranger—a life of luxury and pleasure, led by the high-born and the wealthy.

Sometimes when her father was in a sentimental mood he would tell her of his grandfather's magnificence at the family seat near York; would paint the glories of a country house with an acre and a half of roof, the stacks of silver plate, and a perpetual flow of visitors, gargantuan hunt breakfasts, hunters and coach-horses without number. He exceeded the limits of actual fact, perhaps, in these reminiscences. The magnificence had all vanished away, the land was sold, the plate was melted, not one of the immemorial oaks was left to show where the park had been; but Tonia was never tired of hearing of those prosperous years, and was glad to think she came of people who were magnates in the land.

CHAPTER II
MISS LESTER, OF THE PATENT THEATRES

Besides Mrs. Potter, to whom she was warmly attached, Antonia had one friend, an actress at Drury Lane, who had acted in Mr. Thornton's comedy of *How to please her*, and who had made his daughter's acquaintance at the wings while his play was in progress. Patty Lester was, perhaps, hardly the kind of person a careful father would have chosen for his youthful daughter's bosom friend, for Patty was of the world worldly, and had somewhat lax notions of morality, though there was nothing to be said against her personally. No nobleman's name had ever been bracketed with hers in the newspapers, nor had her character suffered from any intrigue with a brother actor. But she gave herself no airs of superiority over her less virtuous sisters, nor was she averse to the frivolous attentions and the trifling gifts of those ancient beaux and juvenile macaronis who fluttered at the side-scenes and got in the way of the stage-carpenters.

Thornton had not reared his daughter in Arcadian ignorance of evil, and he had no fear of her being influenced by Miss Lester's easy views of conduct.

"The girl is as honest as any woman in England, but she is not a lady," he told Antonia, "and I don't want you to imitate her. But she has a warm heart, and is always good company, so I see no objection to your taking a dish of tea with her at her lodgings once in a way."

This "once in a way" came to be once or twice a week, for Miss Lester's parlour was all that Antonia knew of gaiety, and was a relief from the monotony of literary toil. Dearly as she loved to assist her father's labours, there came an hour in the day when the aching hand dropped on the manuscript or the tired eyes swam above the closely printed page; and then it was pleasant to put on her hat and run to the Piazza, where Patty was mostly to be found at home between the morning's rehearsal and the night's performance. Her lodgings were on a second floor overlooking the movement and gaiety of Covent Garden, where the noise of the waggons bringing asparagus from Mortlake and strawberries from Isleworth used to sound in her dreams, hours before the indolent actress opened her eyes upon the world of reality.

She was at home this windy March afternoon, squatting on the hearthrug toasting muffins, when Miss Thornton knocked at her door.

"Come in, if you're Tonia," she cried. "Stay out if you're an odious man."

"I doubt you expect some odious man," said Tonia, as she entered, "or you wouldn't say that."

"I never know when not to expect 'em, child. There are three or four of my devoted admirers audacious enough to think themselves always welcome to drop in for a dish of tea; indeed, one of 'em has a claim to my civility, for he is in the India trade, and keeps me in gunpowder and bohea. But 'tis only old General Granger I expect this afternoon—him that gave me my silver canister," added Patty, who never troubled about grammar.

"I would rather be without the canister than plagued by that old man's company," said Tonia.

"Oh, you are hard to please—unless 'tis some scholar with his mouth full of book talk! I find the General vastly entertaining. Sure he knows everybody in London, and everything that is doing or going to be done. He keeps me *aw courrong*," concluded Patty, whose French was on a par with her English.

She rose from the hearth, with her muffin smoking at the end of a long tin toasting-fork. Her parlour was full of incongruities—silver tea-canister, china cups and saucers glorified by sprawling red and blue dragons, an old mahogany tea-board and pewter spoons, a blue satin *négligé* hanging over the back of a chair, an open powder-box on the side table. The furniture was fine but shabby—the sort of fine shabbiness that satisfied the landlady's clients, who were mostly from the two patent theatres. The house had a renown for being comfortable and easy to live in—no nonsense about early hours or quiet habits.

"Prythee make the tea while I butter the muffins," said Patty. "The kettle is on the boil. But take your hat off before you set about it. Ah, what glorious hair!" she said, as Antonia threw off the poor little gipsy hat; "and to think that mine is fiery red!"

"Nay, 'tis but a bright auburn. I heard your old General call it a trap for sunbeams. 'Tis far prettier than this inky black stuff of mine."

Antonia wore no powder, and the wavy masses of her hair were bound into a scarlet snood that set off their raven gloss. Her complexion was of a marble whiteness, with no more carnation than served to show she was a woman and not a statue. Her eyes, by some freak of heredity, were not black, like her mother's—whom she resembled in every other feature—but of a sapphire blue, the blue of Irish eyes, luminous yet soft, changeful, capricious, capable of dazzling joyousness, of profoundest melancholy. Brown-eyed, auburn-headed Patty looked at her young friend with an admiration which would have been envious had she been capable of ill-nature.

"How confoundedly handsome you are to-day!" she exclaimed; "and in that gown too! I think the shabbier your clothes are the lovelier you look. You'll be cutting me out with my old General."

"Your General has seen me a dozen times, and thinks no more of me than if I were a plaster image."

"Because you never open your lips before company, except to say yes or no, like a long-headed witness in the box. I wonder you don't go on the stage, Tonia. If you were ever so stupid at the trade your looks would get you a hearing and a salary."

"Am I really handsome?" Tonia asked, with calm wonder.

She had been somewhat troubled of late by the too florid compliments of booksellers and their assistants, whom she saw on her father's business; but she concluded it was their way of affecting gallantry with every woman under fifty. She had a temper that repelled disagreeable attentions, and kept the boldest admirer at arm's length.

"Handsome? You are the beautifullest creature I ever saw, and I would chop ten years off my old age to be as handsome, though most folks calls me a pretty woman," added Patty, bridling a little, and pursing up a cherry mouth.

She was a pink-and-white girl, with a complexion like new milk, and cheeks like cabbage-roses. She had a supple waist, plump shoulders, and a neat foot and ankle, and was a capable actress in all secondary characters. She couldn't carry a great playhouse on her shoulders, or make a dull play seem inspired, as Mrs. Pritchard could; or take the town by storm as Juliet, like Miss Bellamy.

"Well, I doubt my looks will never win me a fortune; but I hope I may earn money from the booksellers before long, as father does."

"Sure 'tis a drudging life—and you'd be happier in the theatre."

"Not I, Patty. I should be miserable away from my books, and not to be my own mistress. I work hard, and tramp to the city sometimes when my feet are weary of the stones; but father and I are free creatures, and our evenings are our own."

"Precious dull evenings," said Patty, with her elbows on the table and her face beaming at her friend. "Have a bit more muffin. I wonder you're not *awnweed* to death."

"I do feel a little *triste* sometimes, when the wind howls in the chimney, and every one in the house but me is in bed, and I have been alone all the evening."

"Which you are always."

"Father has to go to his club to hear the news. And 'tis his only recreation. But though I love my books, and to sit with my feet on the fender and read Shakespeare, I should love just once in a way to see what people are like; the women I see through their open windows on summer nights—such handsome faces, such flashing jewels, and with snowy feathers nodding over their powdered heads——"

"You should see them at Ranelagh. Why does not your father take you to Ranelagh? He could get a ticket from one of the fine gentlemen whose speeches he writes. I saw him talking to Lord Kilrush in the wings t'other night."

"Who is Lord Kilrush?"

"One of the finest gentlemen in town, and a favourite with all the women, though he is nearer fifty than forty."

"An old man?"

"*You* would call him so," said Patty, with a sigh, conscious of her nine and twenty years. "He'd give your father a ticket for Ranelagh, I'll warrant."

Tonia looked down at her brown stuff gown, and laughed the laugh of scorn.

"Ranelagh, in this gown!" she said.

"You should wear one of mine."

"Good dear, 'twould not reach my ankles!"

"I grant there's overmuch of you. Little David called you the Anakim Venus when he caught sight of you at the side scenes. 'Who's that magnificent giantess?' he asked."

"The people of Lilliput took Captain Gulliver for a giant, and the Brobdignagians thought him a dwarf. 'Tis a question of comparison," replied Tonia, huffed at the manager's criticism.

"Nay, don't be vexed, child. 'Tis a feather in your cap for Garrick to give you a second thought. Well, if Ranelagh won't suit, there is Mrs. Mandalay's dancing-room. She has a ball twice a week in the season, and a masquerade once a fortnight. You can borrow a domino from the costumier in the Piazza for the outlay of half a dozen shillings."

"Do the women of fashion go to Mrs. Mandalay's?"

"All the town goes there."

"Then I'll beg my father to take me. I am helping him with his new comedy, and I want to see what modish people are like—off the stage."

"Not half so witty as they are on it. Is there a part for me in the new play?"

Patty would have asked that question of Shakespeare's ghost had he returned to earth to write a new Hamlet. It was her only idea in association with the drama.

"Indeed, Patty, there is an impudent romp of quality you would act to perfection."

"I love a romp," cried Patty, clapping her hands. "Give me a pinafore and a pair of scarlet shoes, and I am on fire with genius. I hope David will bring out your dad's play, and that 'twill run a month."

"If it did he would give me a silk gown, and I might see Ranelagh."

"He is not a bad father, is he, Tonia?"

"Bad! There was never a kinder father."

"But he lets you work hard."

"I love the work next best to him that sets me to it."

"And he has been your only schoolmaster, and you are clever enough to frighten a simpleton like me."

"Nay, Patty, you are the cleverest, for you can do things—act, sing, dance. Mine is only book-learning; but such as it is, I owe it all to my father."

"I hate books. 'Twas as much as I could do to learn to read. But there's one matter in which your father has been unkind to you."

"No, no—in nothing."

"Yes," said Patty, shaking her head solemnly, "he has brought you up an atheist, never to go to church, not even on Christmas Day; and to read Voltaire"—with a shudder.

"Do you go to church, Patty? 'Tis handy enough to your lodgings."

"Oh, I am too tired of a Sunday morning, after acting six nights in a week; for if Bellamy and Pritchard are out of the bill and going out a-visiting, and strutting and grimacing in fine company, there's always a part for a scrub like me; and if I'm not in the play I'm in the burletta."

"And do you think you're any wickeder for not going to church twice every Sunday?"

"I always go at Christmas and at Easter," protested Patty, "and I feel myself a better woman for going. You've been brought up to hate religion."

"No, Patty, only to hate the fuss that's made about it, and the cruelties men have done to each other, ever since the world began, in its name."

"I wouldn't read Voltaire if I was you," said Patty. "The General told me 'twas an impious, indecent book."

"Voltaire is the author of more than forty books, Patty."

"Oh, is it an author? I thought 'twas the name of a novel, like 'Tom Jones,' only more impudent."

There came a knock at the door, and this time Patty knew it was her old General.

"Stop out, Beast!" she cried. "There's nobody at home to an old fool!" upon which courteous greeting the ancient warrior entered smiling.

"Was there ever such a witty puss?" he exclaimed. "I kiss Mrs. Grimalkin's velvet paw. Pray how many mice has Minette crunched since breakfast?"

His favourite jest was to attribute feline attributes to Patty, whose appreciation of his humour rose or fell in unison with his generosity. A pair of white gloves worked with silver thread, or a handsome ribbon for her hair secured her laughter and applause.

To-day Patty's keen glance showed her that the General was empty-handed. He had not brought her so much as a violet posy. He saluted Antonia with his stateliest bow, blinking at her curiously, but too short-sighted to be aware of her beauty in the dim light of the parlour, where evening shadows were creeping over the panelled walls.

Patty set the kettle on the fire and washed out the little china teapot, while she talked to her ancient admirer. He liked to watch her kitten-like movements, her trim sprightly ways, to take a cup of weak tea from her hand, and to tell her his news of the town, which was mostly wrong, but which she always believed. She thought him a foolish old person, but the pink of fashion. His talk was a diluted edition of the news we read in Walpole's letters—talk of St. James's and Leicester House, of the old king and his grandson, newly created Prince of Wales, of the widowed princess and Lord Bute, of a score of patrician belles whose histories were more or less scandalous, and of those two young women from Dublin, the penniless Gunnings, whose beauty had set the town in a blaze—sisters so equal in perfection that no two people were of a mind as to which was the handsomer.

Tonia had met the General often, and knew his capacity for being interesting. She rose and bade her friend good-bye.

"Nay, child, 'tis ill manners to leave me directly I have company. The General and I have no secrets."

"My Minette is a cautious puss, and will never confess to the singing-birds she has killed," said the dodderer.

Tonia protested that her father would be at home and wanting her. She saluted the soldier with her stateliest curtsey, and departed with the resolute *aplomb* of a duchess.

"Your friend's grand manners go ill with her shabby gown," said the General. "With her fine figure she should do well on the stage."

"There is too much of her, General. She is too tall by a head for an actress. 'Tis delicate little women look best behind the lamps."

Thornton was fond of his daughter, and had never said an unkind word to her; but he had no scruples about letting her work for him, having a fixed idea that youth has an inexhaustible fund of health and strength upon which age can never overdraw. He was proud of her mental powers, and believed that to help a hack-scribbler with his multifarious contributions to magazines and newspapers was the finest education possible for her. If they went to the playhouse together 'twas she who wrote a critique on the players next morning, while her father slept. Dramatic criticism in those days was but scurvily treated by the Press, and Tonia was apt to expatiate beyond the limits allowed by an editor, and was mortified to see her opinions reduced to the baldest comment.

She talked to her father of Mrs. Mandalay's dancing-rooms. He knew there was such a place, but doubted whether 'twas a reputable resort. He promised to make inquiries, and thus delayed matters, without the unkindness of a refusal. Tonia was helping him with a comedy for Drury Lane—indeed, was writing the whole play, his part of the work consisting chiefly in running his pen across Tonia's scenes, and bidding her write them again in accord with his suggestions, which she did with equal meekness and facility. He grew a little lazier every day as he discovered his daughter's talent, and encouraged her to labour for him. He praised himself for having taught her Spanish, so that she had the best comedies in the world, as he thought, at her fingers' ends.

It was for the sake of the comedy Tonia urged her desire to see the *beau monde*.

"'Tis dreadful to write about people of fashion when one has never seen any," she said.

"Nay, child, there's no society in Europe will provide you better models than you'll find in yonder duodecimos," her father would say, pointing to Congreve and Farquhar. "Mrs. Millamant is a finer lady than any duchess in London."

"Mrs. Millamant is half a century old, and says things that would make people hate her if she was alive now."

"Faith, we are getting vastly genteel; and I suppose by-and-by we shall have plays as decently dull as Sam Richardson's novels, without a joke or an oath from start to finish," protested Thornton.

It was more than a month after Tonia's first appeal that her father came home to dinner one afternoon in high spirits, and clapped a couple of tickets on the tablecloth by his daughter's plate.

"Look there, slut!" he cried. "I seized my first chance of obliging you. There is a masked ball at Mrs. Mandalay's to-night, and I waited upon my old friend Lord Kilrush on purpose to ask him for tickets; and now you have only to run to the costumier's and borrow a domino and a mask, and see that there are no holes in your stockings."

"I always mend my stockings before the holes come," Antonia said reproachfully.

"You are an indefatigable wench! Come, there's a guinea for you; perhaps you can squeeze a pair of court shoes out of it, as well as the hire of the domino."

"You are a dear, dear, dearest dad! I'll ask Patty to go to the costumier's with me. She will get me a good pennyworth."

CHAPTER III
AT MRS. MANDALAY'S ROOMS

Mrs. Mandalay's rooms were crowded, for Mrs. Mandalay's patrons included all the varieties of London society—the noble, the rich, the clever, the dull, the openly vicious, the moderately virtuous, the audaciously disreputable, masked and unmasked; the outsiders who came from curiosity; the initiated who came from habit; dissolute youth, frivolous old age, men and boys who came because they thought this, and only this, was life: to rub shoulders with a motley mob, to move in an atmosphere of ribald jokes and foolish laughter, air charged with the electricity of potential bloodshed, since at any moment the ribald jest might lead to the insensate challenge; to drink deep of adulterated wines, fired with the alcohol that inspires evil passions and kills thought. These were the diversions that men and women sought at Mrs. Mandalay's; and it was into this witch's cauldron that William Thornton plunged his daughter, reckless of whom she met or what she saw and heard, for it was an axiom in his blighting philosophy that the more a young woman knew of the world she lived in, the more likely she was to steer a safe course between its shoals and quicksands.

Antonia looked with amazement upon the tawdry spectacle—dominos, diamonds, splendour, and shabbiness, impudent faces plastered with white and red, beauty still fresh and young, boys still at the University, old men fitter for the hospital than for the drawing-room. Was *this* the dazzling scene she had longed for sometimes in the toilsome evenings, when her tired hand sank on the foolscap page, and in the pause of the squeaking quill she heard the clock ticking on the stairs and the cinders crumbling in the grate? She had longed for lighted rooms and joyous company, for the concerts, and dances, and dinners, and suppers she read about in the *Daily Journal*; but the scenes her imagination had conjured up were as different from this as paradise from pandemonium.

Dancing was difficult in such a crowd, but there was a country dance going on to the music of an orchestra of fiddles and French horns, stationed in a gallery over one end of the room. The music was a *pot-pourri* of favourite melodies in the "Beggar's Opera," and the strongly marked tunes beat upon Antonia's brain as she and her father stood against the wall near the entrance doors, watching the crowd.

A master of the ceremonies came to ask her if she would dance. Her father answered for her, somewhat curtly. No, the young lady had only looked in to see what Mrs. Mandalay's rooms were like.

"Mrs. Mandalay's rooms are too good to be made a show for country cousins," the man answered impudently, after a flying glance at Thornton's threadbare suit; "and Miss has too pretty a figure under her domino to shirk a dance."

"Be good enough to leave us to ourselves, sir. Our tickets have been paid for; and we have a right to consume this polluted atmosphere without having to suffer impertinence."

"Oh, if you come to that, sir, I carry a sword, and will swallow no insult from a beggarly parson; and there are plenty of handsome women pining for partners."

He edged off as he spoke, and was safe amongst the crowd before he finished his sentence.

"Let's go home, sir," said Antonia. "I never could have pictured such an odious place."

"'Tis one of the most fashionable assemblies in London, child."

"Then I wonder at the taste of Londoners. Pray, sir, let's go home. I should never have teased you to bring me here had I known 'twas like this; but you have at least cured me of the desire to come again—or to visit any place that resembles this."

"You are pettish and over-fastidious. I came here for your amusement, and you may stay here for mine. I can't waste coach hire because you are capricious. I must have something for my money. Do you stay here quietly, while I circulate and find a friend or two."

"Oh, father, don't leave me among this rabble! I shall die of disgust if any one speaks to me—like that vulgar wretch just now."

"Tush, Tonia, there are no women-eaters here; and you have brains enough to know how to answer any impudent jackanapes in London."

He was gone before she could say anything more. She had hated to be there even with her father at her side. It was agony to stand there alone, fanning herself with the trumpery Spanish fan that had been sent her with the domino. She was not shy as other women are on their first appearance in an assembly. She had been trained to despise her fellow-creatures, and had an inborn pride that would have supported her anywhere. But the scene gave her a feeling of loathing that she had never known before. The people seemed to her of an unknown race. Their features, their air exhaled wickedness. "The sons of Belial, flown with insolence and wine." She hated herself for being there, hated her father for bringing her there.

They had come very late, when the assembly was at its worst, or at its best, according to one's point of view. The modish people, who vowed they detested the rooms, and only looked in to see who was there, were elbowing their way among fat citizens and their wives from Dowgate, and rich merchants from Clapham Common; while the more striking figures in the crowd belonged obviously to the purlieus of Covent Garden and the paved courts near Long Acre.

Tonia watched them till, in spite of her aversion, she began to grow interested in the masks and the faces. The faces told their own story; but the masks had a more piquant attraction, suggesting mystery. She began to notice couples who were obviously lovers, and to imagine a romance here and there. Her eyes passed over the disreputable painted faces, and fixed on the young and beautiful, secure in pride of birth, the assurance of superiority. She caught furtive glances, the lingering clasp of hands, the smile that promised, the whisper that pleaded. Romance and mystery enough here to fill more volumes than Richardson had published. And then among the people who came in late, talked loud, and did not dance, there were such satins and brocades, velvet and lace, feathers and jewels, as neither the theatres nor her dreams had ever shown her. She was woman enough to look at these with pleasure, in spite of her masculine education.

She had forgotten how long she had been standing there when her father came back, smelling of brandy, and accompanied by a man whom she had been watching some minutes before, one of the late arrivals, who looked young at a distance, but old, or at best middle-aged, when he came near her. She had seen him surrounded by a bevy of women, who hung about him with an eager appreciation which would have been an excuse for vanity in a Solomon.

The new-comer's suit of mouse-coloured velvet was plainer than anybody else's, but his air and figure would have given distinction to a beggar's rags, and there needed not the star and ribbon half hidden under the lapel of his coat to tell her that he was a personage.

"My friend and patron, Lord Kilrush, desires to make your acquaintance, Antonia," her father said with his grand air.

She had heard of Lord Kilrush, an Irish peer, with an immense territory on the Shannon and on the Atlantic which he never visited; a man of supreme distinction in a world where the cut of a coat and the pedigree of a horse count for more than any moral attributes. While he had all the dignity of a large landowner, the bulk of his fortune was derived from his mother, who was the only child of an East Indian factor, "rich with the spoil of plundered provinces."

Antonia had been watching the modish women's manoeuvres long enough to be able to sink to the exact depth and rise with the assured grace of a fashionable curtsey. The perfect lips under the light lace of her mask relaxed in a grave smile, parting just enough to show the glitter of pearly teeth between two lines of carmine. Her flashing eyes and lovely mouth gave Kilrush assurance of beauty. It would have taken the nose of a Socrates, or a complexion pitted with the smallpox, to mar the effect of such eyes and such lips.

"Pray allow me to escort you through the rooms, and to get you a cup of chocolate, madam," he said, offering his arm. "Your father tells me that 'tis your first visit to this notorious scene. Mrs. Mandalay's chocolate is as famous as her company, and of a better quality—for it is innocent of base mixtures."

"Go with his lordship, Tonia," said her father, answering her questioning look; "you must be sick to death of standing here."

"Oh, I have amused myself somehow," she said. "It is like a comedy at the theatres—I can read stories in the people's faces."

She took Kilrush's arm with an easy air that astonished him.

"Then you like the Mandalay room?" he said, as he made a path through the crowd, people giving way to him almost as if to a royal personage.

He was known here as he was known in all pleasure places for a leader and a master spirit. It suited him to live in a country where he had no political influence. He had never been known to interest himself about any serious question in life. Early in his career, when his wife ran away with his bosom friend, his only comment was that she always came to the breakfast-table with a slovenly head, and it was best for both that they should part. He ran his rapier through his friend's left lung early one morning in the fields behind Montague House; but he told his intimates that it was not because he hated the scoundrel who had relieved him of an incubus, but because it would have been ungenteel to let him live.

He conducted Antonia through the suite of rooms that comprised "Mrs. Mandalay's." There were two or three little side-rooms where people sat in corners and talked confidentially, as they do in such places to this day. The confidences may have been a shade more audacious then, an incipient intrigue more daringly conducted, but it was the same and the same—a married woman who despised her husband; a married man who detested his wife; a young lady of fashion playing high stakes for a coronet, and baulked or ruined at the game. Antonia glanced from one group to the other as if she knew all about them. To be a student of Voltaire is not to think too well of one's fellow-creatures. She had read Fielding too, and knew that women were fools and men reprobates. She had wept over Richardson's Clarissa, and knew that there had once been a virtuous woman, or that a dry-as-dust printer's elderly imagination had conceived such a creature.

One room was set apart for light refreshments, coffee and chocolate, negus and cakes; and here Kilrush found a little table in a corner, and seated her at it. The crowd in this room was so dense that it created a solitude. They were walled in by brocaded sacques and the backs of velvet coats, and could talk to each other without fear of being overheard. This was so much pleasanter than standing against a wall staring at strange faces that Antonia began to think she liked Mrs. Mandalay's. She took off her mask, unconscious that an adept in coquetry would have maintained the mystery of her loveliness a little longer. Kilrush was content to worship her for the perfection of her mouth, the half-seen beauty of her eyes. She flung off the little velvet *loup*, and gave him the effulgence of her face, with an unconsciousness of power that dazzled him more than her beauty.

"I was nearly suffocated," she said.

He was silent in a transport of admiration. Her face had an exotic charm. It was too brilliant for native growth. The South glowed in the lustre of her eyes and in the sheen of her raven hair. He had seen such faces in Italy. The towers and cupolas, the church bells, the market women's parti-coloured stalls, the lounging boatmen and clear white light of the Isola Bella came back to him as he looked at her. He had spent an autumn in the Borromean Palaces, a visitor to the lord of those delicious isles, and he had seen faces like hers, and had worshipped them, in the heyday of youth, when he was on his grand tour. He remembered having heard that Thornton had married a lovely Italian girl, whom he had stolen from her home in Lombardy, while he was travelling as bear-leader to an India merchant's son.

Antonia sipped her chocolate with a composure that startled him. Women—except the most experienced—were apt to be fluttered by his lightest attentions; yet this girl, who had never seen him till to-night, accepted his homage with a supreme unconcern, or indeed seemed unconscious of it. Her innocent assurance amused him. No rustic lass serving at an inn had ever received his compliments without a blush, for he had an air of always meaning more than he said.

"Your father told me he had reared you in seclusion, madam," he said, "and I take it this is your first glimpse of our gay world."

"My first and last," she replied. "I do not love your gay world. I did wrong to tease my father to bring me here. I imagined a scene so different."

"Tell me what your fancy depicted."

"Larger rooms, fewer people, more space and air—a *fête champêtre* by Watteau within doors; dancers who danced for love of dancing, and who were all young, not old wrinkled men and fat women; not painted grimacing faces, and an atmosphere cloudy with hair-powder."

"But is not this better than to sit in your lodgings and mope over books?"

"I never mope over books; they are my friends and companions."

"What, in the bloom of youth, when you should be dancing every night, gadding from one pleasure to another all day long? Books are the friends of old age. I shall take to books myself when I grow old."

Tonia's dark brows elevated themselves unconsciously, and her eyes expressed wonder. Was he not old enough already for books and retirement? The man of seven and forty saw the look and interpreted it.

"She knows I am old enough to be her father," he thought, "and that is the reason of her *sang froid*. Women of the world know that mine is the dangerous age—the age when a man who can love loves desperately, when concentration of purpose takes the place of youthful energy."

They sat in silence for a few minutes while she finished her chocolate, and while he summed up the situation. Then she rose hastily.

"I have been keeping you from your friends," she said.

"Oh, I have no friends here."

"Why, everybody was becking and bowing to you."

"I am on becking and bowing terms with everybody; but most of us hate each other. Let me get you some more chocolate."

"No, thank you. I must go back to my father."

They had not far to go. Thornton was at a table on the other side of the room, drinking punch with one of his patrons in the book trade, a junior partner who was frivolous enough to look in at Mrs. Mandalay's.

"Miss Thornton is so unkind as to fleer at our solemnities," said Kilrush, "and swears she will never come here again."

"I told her she was a fool to wish to come," answered Thornton. "Your lordship has been uncommonly civil to take care of her. What the devil should a Grub Street hack's daughter do here? She has never had a dancing-lesson in her life."

"She ought to begin to-morrow. Serise would glory in such a pupil. Give her but the knack of a minuet, and she would show young peeresses how to move like queens, or like a swan gliding on the current."

"Oh, pray, my lord, don't flatter her. She has not the art to *riposter*, and she may think you mean what you say."

Kilrush went with them to the street, where his chairmen were waiting to carry him to St. James's Square, or to whatever gambling-house he might prefer to the solitude of his ancestral mansion. He wanted to send Antonia home in his chair, but Thornton declined the favour laughingly.

"Your chairmen would leave your service to-morrow if you sent them to such a shabby neighbourhood," he said, taking his daughter on his arm. "We shall find a hackney coach on the stand."

CHAPTER IV
A MORNING CALL

Tonia worked at the comedy, but did not find her idea of a woman of *ton* greatly enlarged by the women she had seen at Mrs. Mandalay's. Indeed, she began to think that her father was right, and that Mrs. Millamant—whose coarseness of speech disgusted her—was her best model. Yet, disappointing as that tawdry assembly had been, she felt as if she had gained something by her brief encounter with Lord Kilrush, and her pen seemed firmer when she tried to give life and meaning to the leading character in her play, the *rôle* intended for Garrick. She had begun by making him young and foolish. She remodelled the character, and made him older and wiser, and tried to give him the grand air; evolving from her inner consciousness the personality which her brief vision of Kilrush had suggested. Her ardent imagination made much out of little.

Of the man himself she scarcely thought, and would hardly have recognized his person had they met in the street. But the ideal man she endowed with every fascinating quality, every attracting grace.

Her father noted the improvement in her work.

"Why, this fourth act is the best we have done yet," he said, "and I think 'twas a wise stroke of mine to make our hero older——"

"Oh, father, 'twas my notion, you'll remember."

"You shall claim all the invention for your share, if you like, slut, so long as we concoct a piece that will satisfy Garrick, who grows more and more finical as he gets richer and more fooled by the town. The part will suit him all the better now we've struck a deeper note. He can't wish to play schoolboys all his life."

It was three weeks after the masquerade when there came a rap at the parlour door one morning, and the maid-servant announced Lord Kilrush.

Thornton was lying on a sofa in shirt-sleeves and slippers, smoking a long clay pipe, the picture of a self-indulgent sloven—that might have come straight from Hogarth. Tonia was writing at a table by an open window, the June sunshine gleaming in her ebon hair. Her father had been dictating and suggesting, objecting and approving, as she read her dialogue.

The visit was startling, for though Thornton was on easy terms with his lordship, who had known him at the University, and had patronized and employed him in his decadence, Kilrush had never crossed his threshold till to-day. Had he come immediately after the meeting at Mrs. Mandalay's, Antonia's father might have suspected evil; but Thornton had flung that event into the rag-bag of old memories, and had no thought of connecting his patron's visit with his daughter's attractiveness. He was about as incapable of thought and memory as a thinking animal can be, having lived for the past fourteen years in the immediate present, conscious only of good days and bad days, the luck or the ill-luck of the hour, without hope in the days that were coming, or remorse for the days that were gone.

Kilrush knew the man to the marrow of his bones, and although he had been profoundly impressed by Antonia's unlikeness to other women, he had waited a month before seeking to improve her acquaintance, and thus hoped to throw the paternal Argus off his guard.

Tonia laid down her pen, rose straight and tall as a June lily, and made his lordship her queenly curtsey, blushing a lovely crimson at the thought of the liberties that rapid quill had taken with his character.

"He is not half so handsome as my Dorifleur!" she thought; "but he has the grand air that no words can express. Poor little Garrick! What a genius he must be, and what heels he must wear, if he is to represent such a man!"

Kilrush returned the curtsey with a bow as lofty, and then bent over the ink-stained fingers and kissed them, as if they had been saintly digits in a crystal *reliquaire*.

"Does Miss Thornton concoct plays, as well as her gifted parent?" he inquired, with the smile that was so exquisitely gracious, yet not without the faintest hint of mockery.

"The jade has twice her father's genius," said Thornton, who had risen from the sofa and laid his pipe upon the hob of the wide iron grate, where a jug of wall-flowers filled the place of a winter fire. "Or, perhaps I should say, twice her father's memory, for she has a repertory of Spanish and Italian plays to choose from when her Pegasus halts."

"Nay, father, I am not a thief," protested Tonia.

Kilrush glanced at the hack-scribbler, remembering that awkward adventure with the farmer's cash-box which had brought so worthy a gentleman to the treadmill, and which might have acquainted him with Jack Ketch. He glanced from father to daughter, and decided that Antonia was unacquainted with that scandalous episode in her parent's clerical career.

After that one startled blush and conscious smile, the cause whereof he knew not, she was as unconcerned in his lordship's company to-day as she had been at Mrs. Mandalay's. She gave him no *minauderies*, no downcast eyelids or shy glances; but sat looking at him with a pleased interest while he talked of the day's news with her father, and answered him frankly and brightly when he discussed her own literary work.

"You are very young to write plays," he said.

"I wrote plays when I was five years younger," she answered, laughing, "and gave them to Betty to light the fires."

"And your father warmed his legs before the dramatic pyre, and never knew 'twas the flame of genius?"

"She was a fool to burn her trash," said Thornton. "I might have made a volume of it—'Tragedies and Comedies, by a young lady of fifteen.'"

"I'll warrant Shakespeare burnt a stack of balderdash before he wrote *The Two Gentlemen of Verona*, poor stuff as it is," said Kilrush.

"Is your lordship so very sure 'tis poor stuff?" asked Tonia.

"If it wasn't, don't you think Garrick would have produced it? He loves Shakespeare—a vastly respectable poet whose plays he can act without paying for them. Be sure you let me know when your comedy is to be produced, madam, for I should die of vexation not to be present at the first performance."

"Alas! there is a great gulf between a written play and an acted one," sighed Tonia. "Mr. Garrick may not like it. But 'tis more my father's play than mine, my lord. He finds the ideas, and I provide the words."

"She has a spontaneous eloquence that takes my breath away. But for the machinery, the fabric of the piece, the arrangement of the scenes, the method, the taste, the scope of the characters, and their action upon one another, I confess myself the author," Thornton said, in his grandiloquent way, having assumed his company manner, a style of conversation which he kept for persons of quality.

"I doubt Miss Thornton is fonder of study than of pleasure, or I should have seen her at Mrs. Mandalay's again——"

"I hate the place," interjected Tonia; "and if women of fashion are all like the painted wretches I saw there——"

"They all paint—white lead is the rule and a clean-washed face the exception," said Kilrush; "but 'twould not be fair to judge the *beau monde* by the herd you saw t'other night. Mrs. Mandalay's is an *olla podrida* of good and bad company. Your father must initiate you in the pleasures of Ranelagh."

"I have had enough of such pleasures. I had a curiosity—like Fatima's—to see a world that was hid from me. But for pleasure I prefer the fireside, and a novel by Richardson. If he would but give us a new Clarissa!"

"You admire Clarissa?"

"I adore, I revere her!"

"A pious simpleton who stood in the way of her own happiness. Why, in the name of all that's reasonable, did she refuse to marry Lovelace, when he was willing?"

Tonia flashed an indignant look at him.

"If she could have stooped to marry him she would have proved herself at heart a wanton!" she said, with an outspoken force that startled Kilrush.

Hitherto he had met only two kinds of women—the strictly virtuous, who affected an Arcadian innocence and whose talk was insupportably dull, and the women whose easy morals allowed the widest scope for conversation; but here was a girl of undoubted modesty, who was not afraid to argue upon a hazardous theme.

"You admire Clarissa for her piety, perhaps?" he said. "That is what our fine ladies pretend to appreciate, though they are most of them heathens."

"I admire her for her self-respect," answered Tonia. "That is her highest quality. When was there ever a temper so meek, joined with such fortitude, such heroic resolve?"

"She was a proud, self-willed minx," said Kilrush, entranced with the vivid expression of her face, with the fire in her speech.

"'Twas a woman's pride in her womanhood, a woman fighting against her arch enemy— —"

"The man who loved her?"

"The man she loved. 'Twas that made the struggle desperate. She knew she loved him."

"If she had been kinder, now, and had let love conquer?" insinuated Kilrush.

"She would not have been Clarissa; she would not have been the long-suffering angel, the martyr in virtue's cause."

"Prythee, my lord, do not laugh at my daughter's high-flown sentiments," said Thornton. "I have done my best to educate her reason; but while there are romancers like Samuel Richardson to instil folly 'tis difficult to rear a sensible woman."

"That warmth of sentiment is more delightful than all your cold reason, Thornton; but I compliment you on the education which has made this young lady to tower above her sex."

"Oh, my lord, do not laugh at me. I have just learnt enough to know that I am ignorant," said Tonia, with her grand air—grand because so careless, as of one who is alike indifferent to the effect of her words and the opinion of those with whom she converses.

Kilrush prolonged his visit into a second hour, during which the conversation flitted from books to people, from romance to politics, and never hung fire. He took leave reluctantly, apologizing for having stayed so long, and gave no hint of repeating his visit, nor was asked to do so. But he meant to come again and again, having as he thought established himself upon a footing of intimacy. A Grub-Street hack could have no strait-laced ideas—a man who had been in jail for something very like larceny, and who had educated his young daughter as a free-thinker.

"She finds my conversation an agreeable relief after a ten years' *tête-à-tête* with Thornton," he told himself, as he picked his way through the filth of Green Street to Leicester Fields. "But 'tis easy to see she thinks I have passed the age of loving, and is as much at home with me as if I were her grandfather. Yet 'twas a beautiful red that flushed her cheek when I entered the room. Well, if she is pleased to converse with me 'tis something; and I must school myself to taste a platonic attachment. A Lovelace of seven and forty! How she would jeer at the notion!"

Lord Kilrush waited a fortnight before repeating his visit, and again called at an hour when Thornton was likely to be at home; but his third visit, which followed within a week of the second, happened late in the afternoon, when he found Antonia alone, but in no wise discomposed at the prospect of a *tête-à-tête*. She enjoyed his conversation with as frank and easy a manner as if she had been a young man, and his equal in station; and he was careful to avoid one word or look which might have disturbed her serenity. It was unflattering, perhaps, to be treated so easily, accepted so frankly as a friend of mature years; but it afforded him the privilege of a companionship that was fast becoming a necessity of his existence. The days that he spent away from Rupert Buildings were dull and barren. His hours with Antonia had an unfailing charm. He forgot even twinges of gout, and the burden of time—that dread of old age and death which so often troubled his luxurious solitude.

She grew more enchanting as she became more familiar. She treated him with as cordial a friendship as if he had been her uncle. She would talk to him with her elbows on the table, and her long tapering fingers pushing back those masses of glossy hair which the ribbon could scarcely hold in place. Stray curls would fall over the broad white brow, and she had a way of tossing those random ringlets from her eyes that he could have sworn to among a thousand women.

He told her all that was worth telling of the world in which he lived and had lived. He had been a soldier till his thirtieth year; had travelled much and far; had lived in Paris among the encyclopedists, and had entertained Voltaire at his house in London. He had seen every dramatic troupe worth seeing in France, Italy, and Spain; had dabbled in necromancy, and associated with savants in every science, at home and abroad.

All his experiences interested Antonia. She had a way of entering into the ideas of another which he had never met with in any except the highest grade of women.

"Your kindness makes me an egotist," he said. "You ought to be the mistress of a political *salon*. Faith, I can picture our party politicians pouring their griefs and hatreds into your ear, cheered by your sympathy, inspired by your wit. But I doubt you must find this prosing of mine plaguey tiresome."

"No, no, no," she cried eagerly. "I want to know what the world is like. It is pleasant to listen to one who has seen all the places and people I long to see."

"You will see them with your own young eyes, perhaps, some day," he said, smiling at her.

She shook her head despondently, and waved the suggestion away as impossible.

One day in an expansive mood she consented to read an act of the comedy, now finished, and waiting only Thornton's final touches, and that spicing of the comic episodes on which he prided himself, and against which his daughter vainly protested.

"My father urges that we have to please three distinct audiences, and that scenes which delight people of good breeding are *caviare* to the pit, while the gallery wants even coarser fare, and must have some foolery dragged in here and there to put them in good humour. I'll not read you the gallery pages."

He listened as if to inspiration. He easily recognized her own work as opposed to her father's, the womanly sentiment of her heroine's speeches, her hero's lofty views of life. He ventured a suggestion or two at that first reading, and finding her pleased with his hints, he insisted on hearing the whole play, and began seriously to help her, and so breathed into her dialogue that air of the *beau monde* which enhances the charm of contemporary comedy. This collaboration, so delightful to him, so interesting to her, brought them nearer to each other than all their talk had done. He became the partner of her ideas, the sharer of her hopes. He taught her all that her father had left untaught—the mystery of modish manners, the laws of that society which calls itself good, and how and when to break them.

"For the parvenu 'tis a code of iron; for the fine gentleman there is nothing more pliable," he told her. "I have seen Chesterfield do things that would make a vulgarian shudder, yet with such benign grace that no one was offended."

Thornton was with them sometimes, and they sat on the play in committee. He, who professed to be the chief author, found himself overruled by the other two. They objected to most of his jokes as vulgar or stale. They would admit no hackneyed turns of speech. The comedy was to be a picture of life in high places.

"Begad, my lord, you'll make it too fine for the town, and 'twill be played to empty benches," remonstrated Thornton.

"Nothing is ever too fine for the town," answered Kilrush. "Do you think the folks in the gallery want their own humdrum lives reflected on the stage, or to look on at banquets of whelks and twopenny porter? The mob love splendour, Mr. Thornton, and when they have not Bajazet or Richard, they like to see the finest fine gentlemen and ladies that a playwright can conceive."

Thornton gave way gracefully. He knew his lordship's influence at the theatres, and he had told Garrick that Kilrush had written a third of the play, but would not have his name mentioned.

"'Tis no better for that," said the manager, but in his heart liked the patrician flavour, and on reading *The Man of Mind* owned 'twas the best thing Thornton had written, and promised to produce it shortly.

By this time Kilrush and Antonia seemed old friends, and she looked back and thought how dull her life must have been before she knew him. He was the only man friend she had ever had except her father. She found his company ever so much more interesting than Patty Lester's, so that it was only for friendship's sake she ever went to the parlour over the piazza, or bade Patty to a dish of tea in Rupert Buildings. Patty opened her great brown eyes to their widest when she heard of Kilrush's visits.

"You jeer at my ancient admirers," she said, "and now you have got one with a vengeance!"

"He is no admirer—only an old friend of my father's who likes to sit and talk with me."

"Is that all? He must be very fond of you to sit in a second floor parlour. He is one of the finest gentlemen in town, and the richest. My General told me all about him."

"I thought that Irish peers were seldom rich," Tonia said carelessly, not feeling the faintest interest in her friend's fortune or position.

"This one is; and he is something more than an Irish landowner. His mother was an East India merchant's only child, and one of the richest heiresses in England. Those Indian merchants are rank thieves, the General says—thieves and slave-traders, and they used to bring home mountains of gold. But that was fifty years ago, in the good old times."

"Poor souls!" said Tonia, thinking of the slaves. "What a cruel world it is!"

It grieved her to think that her friend's wealth had so base a source. She questioned her father on their next meal together.

"Is it true that Lord Kilrush's grandfather was a slave-trader?" she asked.

"'S'death, child, what put such trash in your head? Miss Lavenew was the daughter of a Calcutta merchant who dealt with the native princes in gold and gems, and who owned a tenth share of the richest diamond mine in the East. 'Tis the West Indian merchants who sometimes take a turn at the black trade, rather than let their ships lie in harbour till they ground on their own beef-bones."

It was a relief to know that her friend's fortune was unstained by blood.

"I do not think he would exist under the burden of such a heritage," she said to herself, meditating upon the question in the long summer afternoons, while she sat with open windows, trying not to hear street cries, as she bent over an Eastern story by Voltaire, which she was translating for one of the magazines.

Kilrush came in before her task was finished, but she laid her pen aside gladly, and rose to take his hat and stick from him with her dutiful daughterly air, just as she did for her father.

"Nay, I will not have you wait upon me, when 'tis I should serve you on my knees, as queens are served," he said.

It was seven o'clock, and he had come from a Jacobite dinner in Golden Square—a dinner at which the champagne and Burgundy had gone round freely before it came to drinking the king's health across a bowl of water. There was an unusual brightness in his eyes, and a faint flush upon cheeks that were more often pale.

"I did not expect to see your lordship to-day," Tonia said, repelled by his manner, so unlike the sober politeness to which he had accustomed her. "I thought you were going to Tunbridge Wells."

"My coach was at the door at ten o'clock this morning, the postillions in their saddles, when I sent them all to the devil. I found 'twas impossible to leave this stifling town."

"A return of your gout?" she asked, looking at him wonderingly.

"No, madam, 'twas not my gout, as you call it, though I never owned to more than a transient twinge. 'Twas a disease more deadly, a malady more killing."

He made a step towards her, wanting to clasp her to his breast in the recklessness of a long suppressed passion, but drew back at the sound of a step on the stair.

She looked at him still with the same open wonder. She could scarcely believe that this was Kilrush, the friend she admired and revered. Her father came in while she stood silent, perplexed, and distressed at the transformation.

Kilrush flung himself into an armchair with a muttered oath. Then looking up, he caught the expression of Tonia's face, and it sobered him. He had been talking wildly; had offended her, his divinity, the woman to win whom was the fixed purpose of his mind—to win her at his own price, which was a base one. He had been tactful hitherto, had gained her friendship, and in one unlucky moment he had dropped the mask, and it might be that she would trust him no more.

"Too soon, too soon," he told himself. "I have made her like me. I must make her love me before I play the lover."

He let Thornton talk while he sat in a gloomy silence. It wounded him to the quick to discover that she still thought of him as an elderly man, whose most dreaded misfortune was a fit of the gout. 'Twas to sober age she had given her confidence.

Thornton had been with Garrick, and had come home radiant. The play was to be put in rehearsal next week, with a magnificent cast.

"But I fear your lordship is indisposed," he said, when Kilrush failed to congratulate him on his good fortune.

"My lordship suffers from a disease common to men who are growing old. I am sick of this petty life of ours, and all it holds."

"I am sorry to hear you talk like one of the Oxford Methodists," said Thornton. "It is their trick to disparage a world they have not the spirit or the fortune to enjoy."

"They have their solatium in the kingdom of saints," said Kilrush. "I dare not flatter myself with the hope of an Elysium where I shall again be young and handsome, and capable of winning the woman I love."

"Nor do you fear any place of torment where the pleasing indiscretions of a stormy youth are to be purged with fire," retorted Thornton, gaily.

"No, I am like you—and Miss Thornton—I stake my all upon the only life I know and believe in."

He glanced at Tonia to see how the materialist's barren creed sat on her bright youth. She gave a thoughtful sigh, and her eyes looked dreamily out to the summer clouds sailing over Wren's tall steeple. She was thinking that if she could have accepted Mrs. Potter's creed, and believed in a shining city above the clouds and the stars, it would have been sweet to hope for reunion with the mother whose face she could not remember, but whose sweetness and beauty her father loved to praise, even now after nineteen years of widowhood.

"Your lordship is out of spirits," said Thornton. "Tonia shall give us a dish of tea."

"No, I will not be so troublesome. I am out of health and out of humour. Miss Thornton was right, I dare swear, when she suggested the gout—my gout—an old man's chronic malady. I have been dining with a crew of boisterous asses who won't believe the Stuarts are beaten, in spite of the foolish heads that are blackening on Temple Bar. *J'ai le vin mauvais*, and am best at home."

He kissed Antonia's hand, that cold hand which had never thrilled at his touch, nodded good-bye to Thornton, and hurried away.

"Kilrush is not himself to-day," said Thornton.

"I'm afraid he has been taking too much wine," said Antonia. "He had the strangest manner, and said the strangest things."

"What things?"

"Oh, a kind of wild nonsense that meant nothing."

She was not accustomed to see any one under the influence of liquor. Her father was, by long habit, proof against all effects of the nightly punch-bowl, and however late he came from "The Portico," he had always his reasoning powers, and legs steady enough to carry him up two flights of stairs without stumbling.

CHAPTER V
A SERIOUS FAMILY

Lord Kilrush posted to Tunbridge Wells the day after the Jacobite dinner, and found a herd of fine people he knew parading the Pantiles, or sauntering on the common, among Jews and Germans, pinmakers' wives from Smock Alley, and rural squires with red-cheeked daughters. He drank the waters, and nearly died of *ennui*. He would have liked the place better if it had been a solitude. Wit no longer aroused him, not even George Selwyn's; beauty had ceased to charm, except in one face, and that was two and thirty miles away. That chronic weariness which he knew for the worst symptom of advancing years increased with every hour of fashionable rusticity. The air at the Wells was delicious, the inn was comfortable, his physician swore that the treatment was improving his health. He left the place at an hour's notice, to the disgust of his body-servant, and posted back to town. He preferred the gloom of his great silent house in St. James's Square, where he lived a hermit's life in his library when London was empty. In years gone by he had spent the summer and autumn in a round of country visits, diversified with excursions to châteaux in the environs of Paris, and a winter at Florence or Rome, everywhere admired and in request. Scarce a season had passed without rumours of his impending marriage with some famous beauty, or still more famous fortune. But for the last five or six years he had wearied of society, and had restricted his company to a few chosen friends, men of his own age, with whom he could rail at the follies of the new generation—men who had known Bolingbroke in his day of power, and had entertained Voltaire at their country seats in the year '29.

Were Tonia's violet eyes the lodestars that drew him back to town? He was singing softly to himself as he walked up Shooter's Hill, being ever merciful to the brute creation, and loving horses and dogs better than he loved men.

"Thine eyes are lodestars and thy breath sweet air," he sang, twirling his clouded cane; and the thought that he would soon see those lovely eyes made him gay. But his first visit was not to Rupert Buildings. He knew that he had shocked and disgusted Antonia, and that he must give her time to recover her old confidence. It had been but an impetuous movement, a waft of passionate feeling, when he stretched out his arms towards her, yearning to clasp her to his breast; but her fine instinct had told her that this was the lover and not the friend. He must give her time to think she had mistaken him. He must play the comedy of indifference.

He ordered his favourite hack on the day after his return from the Wells, and rode by Westminster Bridge, only opened in the previous autumn, to Clapham, past Kennington Common, where poor Jemmy Dawson had suffered for his share in the rebellion of '45, by pleasant rustic roads where the perfume of roses exhaled from prosperous citizens' gardens, surrounding honest, square-built brick houses, not to be confounded with the villa, which then meant a demi-mansion on a classic model, secluded in umbrageous grounds, and not a flimsy bay-windowed packing-case in a row of similar packing-cases.

Clapham was then more rustic than Haslemere is now, and the common was the Elysian Fields of wealthy city merchants and some persons of higher quality. The shrubberied drive into which Kilrush rode was kept with an exquisite propriety, and those few flowering shrubs that bloom in September were unfolding their petals under an almost smokeless sky. He dismounted before a handsome house more than half a century old, built before the Revolution, a solid, red-brick house with long narrow windows, and a handsome cornice, pediment, and cupola masking the shining black tiles of the low roof. A shell-shaped canopy, richly carved, and supported by cherubic brackets, sheltered the tall doorway. The open door offered a vista of garden beyond the hall, and Kilrush walked straight through to the lawn, while his groom led the horses to the stable yard, a spacious quadrangle screened by intervening shrubberies.

A middle-aged woman of commanding figure was seated at a table under the spreading branches of a plane with a young man, who rose hurriedly, and went to meet the visitor. The lady was Mrs. Stobart, the widow of a Bristol ship-owner, and the young man was her only son, late of a famous dragoon regiment. Both were dressed with a gloomy severity that set his lordship's teeth on edge, but both had a certain air of distinction not to be effaced by their plain attire.

"This is very kind of your lordship," said George Stobart, as they shook hands. "My mother told me you were at Tunbridge Wells. She saw your name in the *Gazette*."

"Your mother was right, George; but the inanity of the place wore me out in a week, and I left before I had given the waters a chance of killing or curing me!"

He kissed Mrs. Stobart's black mitten, and dropped into a chair at her side, after vouchsafing a distant nod to a young woman who sat at a pace or two from the table, sewing the seam of a coarse linen shirt, with her head discreetly bent. She raised a pair of mild brown eyes, and blushed rosy red as she acknowledged his lordship's haughty greeting, and he noticed that Stobart went over to speak to her before he resumed his seat.

There were some dishes of fruit on the table, Mrs. Stobart's work-basket and several books—the kind of books Kilrush loathed, pamphlets in grey paper covers, sermons in grey boards, the literature of that Great Revival which had spread a wave of piety over the United Kingdom, from John o' Groat's to the Land's End, and across the Irish Channel from the Liffey to the Shannon.

Mrs. Stobart was his first cousin, the daughter of his father's elder sister and of Sir Michael MacMahon, an Irish judge. Good looks ran in the blood of the Delafields, and only two years ago Kilrush had been proud of his cousin, who until that date was a distinguished figure in the fashionable assemblies of London and Bath, and whose aquiline features and fine person were set off by powder and diamonds, and the floral brocades and flowing sacques which "that hateful woman," Madame de Pompadour, whom everybody of *ton* abused and imitated, had brought into fashion. The existence of such women is, of course, a disgrace to civilization; but while their wicked reign lasts, persons of quality must copy their clothes.

Two years ago George Stobart had been one of the most promising soldiers in His Majesty's army, a man who loved his profession, who had distinguished himself as a subaltern at Fontenoy, and was marked by his seniors for promotion. He had been also one of the best-dressed and best-mannered young men in London society, and at the Bath and the Wells a star of the first magnitude.

What was he now? Kilrush shuddered as he marked the change.

"A sanctimonious prig," thought his lordship; "a creature of moods and hallucinations, who might be expected at any hour to turn lay preacher, and jog from Surrey to Cornwall on one of his superannuated chargers, bawling the blasphemous familiarities of the new school to the mob on rural commons, escaping by the skin of his teeth from the savages of the manufacturing districts, casting in his itinerant lot with Whitefield and the Wesleys."

To Kilrush such a transformation meant little short of lunacy. He was indignant at his kinsman's decadence; and when he gave a curt and almost uncivil nod to the poor dependent, bending over her plain needlework yonder betwixt sun and shade, it was because he suspected that pretty piece of lowborn pink-and-white to have some part in the change that had been wrought so suddenly.

Two years ago, at an evening service in John Wesley's chapel at the Old Foundery, George Stobart had been "convinced of sin." Swift as the descent of the dove over the waters of the Jordan had been the awakening of his conscience from the long sleep of boyhood and youth. In that awful moment the depth of his iniquity had been opened to him, and he had discovered the hollowness of a life without God in the world. He had looked along the backward path of years, and had seen himself a child, drowsily enduring the familiar liturgy, sleeping through the hated sermon; a lad at Eton, making a jest of holy things, scorning any assumption of religion in his schoolfellows, insolent to his masters, arrogant and uncharitable, shirking everything that did not minister to his own pleasures or his own aims, studious only in the pursuit of selfish ambitions, dreaming of future greatness to be won amidst the carnage of battles as ruthless, as unnecessary, as Malplaquet.

And following those early years of self-love and impiety there had come a season of darker sins, of the sins which prosperous youth calls pleasure, sins that had sat so lightly on the slumbering conscience, but which filled the awakened soul with horror.

His first impulse after that spiritual regeneration was to sell out of the army. This was the one tangible and irrevocable sacrifice that lay in his power. The more he loved a soldier's career, the more ardently he had aspired to military renown, the more obvious was the duty of renunciation. The treaty of Aix-la-Chapelle had but just been concluded, and the troubles in America had not begun, so there seemed no chance of his regiment being sent on active service, but his conduct seemed not the less extraordinary to his commanding officer.

"Do you do this to please your mother?" he asked.

"No, sir; I do it to please Christ."

The colonel rapped his forehead significantly as Stobart left the room.

"Another victim of the Oxford Methodists," he said. "If they are allowed to go on, England will be peopled with hare-brained enthusiasts, and we shall have neither soldiers nor sailors."

Mrs. Stobart was furious with her son for his abandonment of a career in which she had expected him to win distinction. For some months after his "call" she had refused to speak to him, and had left him to his solitary meditations in his own rooms at Stobart Lodge. In this gloomy period they had met only at meals, and it had vexed her to see that her son took no wine, and refused all the daintier dishes upon the table, all those ragouts and salmis that adorned the board in sumptuous covered dishes of Georgian silver, and which were the pride of cook and dinner-giver.

"I give myself a useless trouble in looking at the bill of fare every morning," Mrs. Stobart said angrily, as the side dishes were removed untasted, breaking in upon a melancholy silence that had lasted from the soup to the game. "God knows I need little for myself; but you used to appreciate a good dinner."

"I have learnt to appreciate higher things, madam."

"I might as well order a leg of mutton and a suet pudding every day in the week."

"Indeed, my dear mother, I desire nothing better."

"With a cook at forty guineas a year!"

"Dismiss her, and let the kitchen wench dress our simple meals."

"And make myself a laughing-stock to my friends."

"To your idle acquaintances only—friends esteem us for deeper reasons. Ah, madam, if you would but hearken to the voices I hear, court the friends I love, you would scorn the worldling's life as I scorn it. To the heir of a boundless estate in the Kingdom of Heaven 'tis idle to waste thought and toil upon a trumpery speck of earth."

"Oh, those Oxford Methodists! You have caught their jargon. I am a good Churchwoman, George, and I hate cant."

"You are a good woman, madam. But what is it to be a good Churchwoman? To attend a morning service once a week in a church where there is neither charity nor enthusiasm, upon whose dull decorum the hungry and the naked dare not intrude—a service that takes no cognizance of sinners, save in a formula that the lips repeat while the heart remains dead; to eat a cold dinner on the Sabbath in order that your servants may join in the same heartless mockery of worship; to listen to the barren dogma of a preacher whose life you know for evil, and whose intellect you despise."

Mother and son had many such conversations—oases in a desert of sullen silence—before Mrs. Stobart's conversion; but that conversion came at last, partly by the preaching of John Wesley, whom her son worshipped, and partly by the influence of Lady Huntingdon and other ladies of birth and fortune, whose example appealed to the fashionable Maria Stobart as no meaner example could have done. She began to think less scornfully of the Great Revival when she found her equals in rank among the most ardent followers of Whitefield and the Wesleys: and within a year of her son's awakening she, too, became convinced of sin, the firstfruits of which conversion were shown by the dismissal of her forty-guinea cook, her second footman, the third stable servant, and the sale of a fine pair of carriage-horses. She had even contemplated dispensing with her own maid, but was prevented by a sense of her patrician incapability of getting into her clothes or out of them without help. She made, perhaps, a still greater sacrifice by changing her dressmaker from a Parisienne in St. James's to a woman at Kennington, who worked for the Quaker families on Denmark Hill.

After about ten minutes' conversation with this lady, of whose mental capacity he had but a poor opinion, Lord Kilrush invited her son to a turn in the fruit garden—a garden planned fifty years before, and maintained in all the perfection of espaliered walks and herbacious borders, masking the spacious area devoted to celery, asparagus, and the homelier vegetables. High brick walls, heavily buttressed, surmounted this garden on three sides, the fourth side being divided from lawn and parterre by a ten-foot yew hedge. At the further end, making a central point in the distance, there was a handsome red-brick orangery, flanked on either side by a hothouse, while at one angle of the wall an octagonal summer-house of two stories overlooked the whole, and afforded an extensive view of the open country across the river, from Notting Hill to Harrow. Established wealth and comfort could hardly find a better indication than in this delightful garden.

"Upon my soul," cried Kilrush, "you have a little paradise in this *rus in urbe!* Come, George, I am glad to see you look so well in health, and I hope soon to be gratified by seeing you make an end of your crazy life, and return to a world you were created to serve and adorn. If the army will not please you, there is the political arena open to every young man of means and talent. I should like to see your name rank with the Townsends and the Pelhams before I die."

"I have no taste for politics, sir; and for my crazy life, sure it lasted seven and twenty years, and came to a happy ending two years ago."

"Nine and twenty! Faith, George, that's too old for foolery. John Wesley was a lad at college, and Whitefield was scarce out of his teens when he gave himself up to these pious hallucinations; and they were both penniless youths who must needs begin their journey without scrip or sack. But you, a man of fortune, a soldier, one of the young heroes of Fontenoy, that you could be caught by the rhapsodies that carry away a London mob of shop-boys and servant-wenches, or a throng of semi-savage coal-miners at Kingswood, in that contagion of enthusiasm to which crowds are subject— that *you* could turn Methodist! Pah, it makes me sick to think of your folly!"

"Perhaps some day your lordship will come over and help us. After my mother's conversion there is no heart so stubborn that I should despair of its being changed."

"Your mother is a fool! Well, I don't want to quarrel with you, so we'll argue no further. After all, in a young man these follies are but passing clouds. Had you not taken so serious a step as to leave the army I should scarcely have vexed myself on your account. By the way, who is that seamstress person I saw sitting on the lawn, and whom I have seen here before to-day?"

His eyes were on George's face, and the conscious flush he expected to see passed over the young man's cheek and brow as he spoke.

"She is a girl whose conscience was awakened in the same hour that saw my redemption; she is my twin-sister in Christ."

"That I can understand," said Kilrush, with the air of humouring a madman, "but why the devil do I find her established here?"

"She is the daughter of a journeyman printer, her mother a drunkard and her father an atheist. Her home was a hell upon earth. Her case had been brought before Mr. Wesley, who was touched by her unaffected piety. I heard her history from his lips, and made it my duty to rescue her from her vile associations."

"How came you by the knowledge of your spiritual twinship?"

"She was seated near me in the meeting-house, and I was the witness of her agitation, of the Pentecostal flame that set her spirit on fire; I saw her fall from the bench, with her forehead bent almost to the floor on which she knelt. Her whole frame was convulsed with sobs which she strove with all her might to restrain. I tried to raise her from the ground, but her ice-cold hand repulsed mine, and the kneeling figure was as rigid as if it had been marble."

"A cataleptic seizure, perhaps. Your Brotherhood of the Foundery has much to answer for."

"It has many to answer for," George retorted indignantly—"thousands of souls rescued from Satan."

"Had that meek-looking young woman been one of his votaries? If so, I wonder your mother consented to harbour her. It is one thing to entertain angels unawares, but knowingly to receive devils——"

"Scoff as you will, sir, but do not slander a virtuous girl because she happens to be of low birth."

"If she was not a sinner, why this convulsion of remorse for sin? I cannot conceive the need of self-humiliation in youth that has never gone astray."

"Does your lordship think it is enough to have lived what the world calls a moral life, never to have been caught in the toils of vice? The fall from virtue is a terrible thing; but there is a state of sin more deadly than Mary Magdalen's. There is the sin of the infidel who denies Christ; there is the sin of the ignorant and the unthinking, who has lived aloof from God. It was to the conviction of such a state that Lucy Foreman was awakened that night."

"Did you enter into conversation with her after the—the remarkable experience?" asked Kilrush, with a cynical devilry lighting his dark grey eyes as he watched his young kinsman's face.

It was a fine frank face, with well-cut features and eyes of the same dark grey as his lordship's, a face that had well become the dragoon's Roman headgear, and which had a certain poetical air to-day with the unpowdered brown hair thrown carelessly back from the broad forehead.

"No, it was not till long after that night that I introduced myself to her. It was not till after my mother's conversion that I could hope to win her friendship for this recruit of Christ. I had heard Lucy's story in the mean-time, and I knew that she was worthy of all that our friendship could do for her."

"And you persuaded your mother to take her into her service?"

"She is not a servant," George said quickly.

"What else?"

"She is useful to my mother—works with her needle, attends to the aviary, and to the flowers in the drawing-room——"

"All that sounds like a servant."

"We do not treat her as a servant."

"Does she sit at table with you?"

"No. She has her meals in the housekeeper's room. It is my mother's arrangement, not mine."

"You would have her at the same table with the granddaughter of the seventeenth Baron Kilrush?"

"I have ceased to consider petty distinctions. To me the premier duke is of no more importance than Lucy Foreman's infidel father—a soul to be saved or lost."

"George," said Kilrush, gravely, "let me tell you, as your kinsman and friend, that you are in danger of making a confounded mess of your life."

"I don't follow you."

"Oh yes, you do. You know very well what I mean. You have played the fool badly enough already, by selling your commission. But there are lower depths of folly. When a man begins to talk as you do, and to hanker after some pretty bit of plebeian pink-and-white, one knows which way he is drifting."

He paused, expecting an answer, but George walked beside him in a moody silence.

"There is one mistake which neither fate nor the world ever forgives in a man," pursued Kilrush, "and that is an ignoble marriage; it is an error whose consequences stick to him for the whole course of his life, and he can no more shake off the indirect disadvantages of the act than he can shake off his lowborn wife and her lowborn kin. I will go further, George, and say that if you make such a marriage I will never forgive you, never see your face again."

"Your lordship's threats are premature. I have not asked your permission to marry, and I have not given you the slightest ground for supposing that I contemplate marriage."

"Oh yes, you have. That young woman yonder is ground enough for my apprehension. You would not have intruded her upon your home if you were not *épris*. Take a friendly counsel from a man of the world, George, and remember that although my title dies with me, my fortune is at my disposal, and that you are my natural heir."

"Oh, sir, that would be the very last consideration to influence me."

"Sure I know you are stubborn and hot-headed, or you would not have abandoned a soldier's career without affording me the chance to dissuade you. I came here to-day on purpose to give you this warning. 'Twas my duty, and I have done it."

He gave a sigh of relief, as if he had flung off a troublesome burden.

As they turned to go back to the lawn, Lucy Foreman came to meet them—a slim figure of medium height, a pretty mouth and a *nez retroussé*, reddish brown hair with a ripple in it, the pink and white of youth in her complexion; but her feet and ankles, her hands and her ears, the "points," to which the connoisseur's eye looked, had a certain coarseness.

"Not even a casual strain of blue blood here," thought Kilrush; "but 'tis true I have seen duchesses as coarsely moulded."

She had come at her mistress's order to invite them to a dish of tea on the lawn. Kilrush assented, though it was but five o'clock, and he had not dined. They walked by the damsel's side to the table under the plane, where the tea-board was set ready. Having given expression to his opinion, his lordship was not disinclined to become better acquainted with this Helen of the slums, so that he might better estimate his cousin's peril. She resumed her distant chair and her needlework, as Kilrush and George sat down to tea, and was not invited to share that elegant refreshment. The young man's vexed glance in her direction would have been enough to betray his *penchant* for the humble companion.

Mrs. Stobart forgot herself so far as to question her cousin about some of the fine people whose society she had renounced.

"Though I no longer go to their houses I have not ceased to see them," she said. "We meet at Lady Huntingdon's. Lady Chesterfield and Lady Coventry are really converts; but I fear most of my former friends resort to that admirable woman's assemblies out of curiosity rather than from a searching for the truth."

"Her *protégé*, Whitefield, has had as rapid a success as Garrick or Barry," said Kilrush. "He is a powerful orator of a theatrical type, and not to have heard him preach is to be out of the fashion. I myself stood in the blazing sun at Moorfields to hear him, when he first began to be cried up; but having heard him I am satisfied. The show was a fine show, but once is enough."

"There are but too many of your stamp, Kilrush. Some good seed must ever fall on stony places; yet the harvest has been rich enough to reward those who toil in the vineyard—rich in promise of a day when there shall be no more railing and no more doubt."

"And when the lion shall lie down with the lamb, and Frederick and Maria Theresa shall love each other like brother and sister, and France shall be satisfied with less than half the earth," said Kilrush, lightly. "You have a pretty little maid yonder," he added in a lower voice, when George had withdrawn from the tea-table, and seemed absorbed in a book.

"She is not my maid, she is a brand snatched from the burning. I am keeping her till I can place her in some household where she will be safe herself, and a well-spring of refreshing grace for those with whom she lives."

"And in the mean time, don't you think there may be a certain danger for your son in such close proximity with a pretty girl—of that tender age?"

"My son! Danger for my son in the society of a journeyman's daughter—a girl who can but just read and write? My good Kilrush, I am astounded that you could entertain such a thought."

"I'm glad you consider my apprehensions groundless," said his lordship, stifling a yawn as he rose to take leave. "Poor silly woman," he thought. "Well, I have done my duty. But it would have been wiser to omit that hint to the mother. If she should plague her son about his *penchant*, ten to one 'twill make matters worse. An affair of that kind thrives on opposition."

CHAPTER VI
A WOMAN WHO COULD SAY NO

Lord Kilrush allowed nearly a month to elapse before he reappeared in Rupert Buildings. He had absented himself in the hope that Antonia would miss his company; and her bright smile of welcome told him that his policy had been wise. She had, indeed, forgotten the sudden gust of passion that had scared her by a suggestion of strangeness in the friend she had trusted. She had been very busy since that evening. Her father's play was in rehearsal, and while Thornton spent his days at Drury Lane and his nights at "The Portico," she had to do most of his magazine work, chiefly translations of essays or tales by Voltaire or Diderot, and even to elaborate such scraps of news as he brought her for the *St. James's, Lloyd's,* or the *Evening Post,* all which papers opened their columns to gossip about the town.

"What the devil has become of Kilrush?" Thornton had ejaculated several times. "He used to bring me the last intelligence from White's and the Cocoa Tree."

He had called more than once in St. James's Square during the interval, but had not succeeded in seeing his friend and patron. And now Kilrush reappeared, with as easy a friendliness as if there had been no break in his visits. He brought a posy of late roses for Antonia, the only offering he ever made her whom he would fain have covered with jewels richer than stud the thrones of Indian Emperors.

"'Tis very long since we have seen your lordship," Tonia said, as he seated himself on the opposite side of the Pembroke table that was spread with her papers and books. "If my father had not called at your house and been told that you were in fairly good health we should have feared you were ill, since we know we have done nothing to offend you."

Her sweet simplicity of speech, the directness of her lovely gaze smote him to the heart. Still—still she trusted him, still treated him as if he had been a benevolent uncle, while his heart beat high with a passion that it was a struggle to hide. Yet he was not without hope, for in her confiding sweetness he saw signs of a growing regard.

"And was I indeed so happy as to be missed by you?"

"We missed you much—you have been so kind to my father, bringing him the news of the town; and you have been still kinder to me in helping me with your criticism of our comedy."

"'Twas a privilege to advise so intelligent an author. I have been much occupied since I saw you last, and concerned about a cousin of mine who is in a bad way."

"I hope he is not ill of the fever that has been so common of late."

"No, 'tis not a bodily sickness. His fever is the Methodist rant. He has taken the new religion."

"Poor man!" said Tonia, with good-humoured scorn.

She had heard none of the new preachers; but all she had been told, or had read about them, appealed to her sense of the ridiculous. She had been so imbued with the contempt for all religious observances, that she could feel nothing but a wondering pity for people whose thoughts and lives could be influenced by a two-hours' sermon in the open air. To this young votaress of pure reason the enthusiasm of crowds seemed a fanatical possession tending towards a cell in Bedlam.

"Unhappily, the disease is complicated by another fever, for the fellow is in love with a simpering piece of prettiness that he and his mother have picked out of a Moorfields' gutter; and my apprehension is that this disciple of Evangelical humility will forget that he is a gentleman and marry a housemaid."

"Would you be very angry with him?"

"Yes, Miss Thornton; and he would feel the consequences of my anger to his dying day—for, so far as my fortune goes, I should leave him a beggar."

"Has he no fortune of his own?"

"I believe he has a pittance—a something in the funds left him by an uncle on his father's side. But his mother's estate is at her own disposal; she is a handsome woman still, and may cheat him by a second marriage."

"Do you think it so great a crime for a gentleman to marry his inferior?"

"Oh, I have old-fashioned notions, perhaps. I think a man of good family should marry in his own rank, if he can't marry above it. He should never have to apologize for his wife, or for her kindred. 'Tis a foolish Irish pride that we Delafields have cherished; but up to this present hour there is not a label upon our family tree that I am ashamed to recall."

"I think my father told me that your lordship's wife was a duke's daughter."

"My wife was a— —"

He had started to his feet at Tonia's speech, in angry agitation. He had never been able to forgive the wife who had disgraced him, or to think of her with common charity, though he had carried off his mortification with a well-acted indifference, and though it was ten years since that frail offender had come to the end of her wandering in a cemetery outside the walls of Florence.

"Miss Thornton, for God's sake let us talk of pleasant things, not of wives or husbands. Marriage is the gate of hell."

"Sure, my lord, there must be happy marriages."

"Enough to serve as baits to hook fools. I grant you there are marriages that seem happy—nay, I will say that are happy—but 'tis not the less a fact that to chain a man and woman to each other for life is the way to make them the deadliest enemies. The marriage bond was invented to keep estates together, not to bind hearts."

Tonia listened with a thoughtful air, but gave no sign of assent.

"Surely you must agree with me," he continued—"you who have been taught to take a philosophical view of life."

"I have never applied my philosophy to the subject; but my comedy ends with a happy marriage. I should be sorry to think that 'twas like a fairy tale, and that there are no lovers as noble as Dorifleur, no women as happy as Rosalia."

"It *is* a fairy tale, dear madam; 'tis the unlikeness to life that charms us. We go to the play on purpose to be deluded by pictures of impossible felicity—men of never-to-be-shaken valour, women of incorruptible virtue, shadows that please us in a three-hours' dream, and which have no parallels in flesh and blood."

"For my own part I am disinterested, for 'tis unlikely I shall ever marry."

"Do not. If you would be virtuous, remain free. It is the bond that makes the dishonour."

Antonia looked at him with a puzzled air, slow to follow his drift. He saw that he had gone too far, and was in danger of displeasing her.

"What curious creatures women are!" he thought. "Here is an avowed infidel who seems inexpressibly shocked because I decry the marriage ceremony. What formalists they are at best! If they are not in fear of the day of judgment they tremble at the notion of being ill-spoken of by their neighbours. I'll warrant this sweet girl is as anxious to keep her landlady's good opinion as George Whitefield is to go to heaven."

He talked to her of the comedy. It was to be acted on the following Monday.

"I have secured a side-box, and I count upon being honoured with the company of the joint authors," he said.

Tonia's eyes sparkled at the thought of her triumph. To have her words spoken by David Garrick—by the lovely Mrs. Pritchard—to sit unseen in the shadow of the curtained side-box, while her daydreams took form and substance in the light of the oil lamps!

"My father and I will be proud to have such good places," she said. "We usually sit at the back of the pit when Mr. Garrick is kind enough to give us a pass. Father has given me a silk gown from Hilditch's in the city, the first I have had."

"If you would suffer me to add a pearl necklace," cried Kilrush, thinking of a certain string of Oriental pearls which was almost an heirloom, and which he remembered on his mother's neck forty years ago. He had taken the red morocco case out of an iron coffer not long since, and had looked at the ornament, longing to clasp it round Tonia's throat. The hands that held the case trembled a little as he imagined the moment when he should fasten the diamond clasp on that exquisite neck.

"You are too generous, sir. I take gifts from no one but my father, except, indeed, the roses you are so kind as to bring me."

"Happy roses, to win acceptance where pearls are scorned! The necklace was my mother's, and has been wasting in darkness for near half a century. She died before I went to Eton. Would you but let me lend it to you—only to air the pearls."

"No, no, no; no borrowed finery! I should hate to play the daw in peacocks' feathers."

"You are a contradictory creature, madam; but you would have to be more cruel and more cutting than a north-east wind before I would quarrel with you."

His lordship's visits now became more frequent than at first; and Tonia received him with unvarying kindness, whether he found her alone or in her father's company. Her calm assurance was so strangely in advance of her years and position that he could but think she owed it to having mixed so little with her own sex, and thus having escaped all taint of self-consciousness or coquetry. She listened to his opinions with respect, but was not afraid to argue with him. She made no secret of her pleasure in his society, and owned to finding the afternoons or evenings vastly dull on which he did not appear.

"I should miss you still more if I had not my translating work," she said; "but that keeps me busy and amused."

"And you find that old dry-as-dust Voltaire amusing!"

"I never find him dry as dust. He is my father's favourite author."

The comedy was well received, and Thornton was made much of by Mr. Garrick and all the actors. No one was informed of Antonia's share in the work, or suspected that the handsome young woman in a yellow silk sacque had so much to do with the success of the evening. Patty Lester triumphed in her brief but effective *rôle* of a tomboy younger sister, an improvement on the conventional confidante, and was rapturously grateful to Mr. Thornton, and more than ever reproachful of Antonia for deserting her.

"You have taken an aversion to the Piazza," she said with an offended air.

"On my honour, no, Patty; but I have been so constantly occupied in helping my father."

"I shall scold him for making a slave of you."

"No, no, you must not. Be sure that I love you, even if I do not go to see you."

"But I am not sure. I cannot be sure. You have grown distant of late, and more of a fine lady than you was last year."

Antonia blushed, and promised to take tea with her friend next day. She was conscious of a certain distaste for Patty's company, but still more for Patty's casual visitors; but the chief influence had been Kilrush's urgent objections to the young actress's society.

"I aver nothing against the creature's morality," he said; "but she is a mercenary little devil, and encourages any coxcomb who will substantiate his flatteries with a present. I have watched her at the side-scenes with a swarm of such gadflies buzzing round her. On my soul, dear Miss Thornton, 'twould torture me to think of you the cynosure of Miss Lester's circle."

Tonia laughed off the warning, swore she was very fond of Patty, and would on no account desert her.

"I hope you do not think I can value fools above their merits when I have the privilege of knowing a man of sense like your lordship," she said, and the easy tone of her compliment chilled him, as all her friendly speeches did. Alas! would she ever cease to trust him as a friend, and begin to fear him as a lover?

"It is my age that makes my case hopeless," he thought, musing upon this love which had long since become the absorbing subject of his meditations. "If I had been twenty years younger how easily might I have won her, for 'tis so obvious she loves my company. She sparkles and revives at my coming, like a drooping flower at a sprinkle of summer rain. But, oh, how wide the difference between loving my company and loving me! Shall I ever bridge the abyss? Shall I ever see those glorious eyes droop under my gaze, that transcendent form agitated by a heart that passion sets beating?"

Again and again he found her alone among her books and manuscripts, for Thornton, being now flush of money, spent most of his time abroad. He sported a new suit, finer than any his daughter had ever seen him wear, and had an air of rakish gaiety that shocked her. The comedy seemed a gold mine, for he had always a guinea at command. He no longer allowed his daughter to fetch and carry between him and his employers. She must trapes no more along the familiar Strand to Fleet Street. He employed a messenger for this vulgar drudgery. He urged her to buy herself new hats and gowns, and to put her toilet on a handsome footing.

"Sure, so lovely a girl ought to set off her beauty," he said.

"Dear sir, I would rather see you save your money against sickness or——"

She was going to say "old age," but checked herself, with a tender delicacy.

"Hang saving! I had never a miser's temper. Davy shall take our next play. You had best stick to Spanish, and find me a plot in De Vega or Moratin, and not plague yourself about scraping a guinea or two."

'Twas heavenly fine weather and more than a year since Kilrush and Antonia first met at Mrs. Mandalay's ball; and the close friendship between the *blasé* worldling and the inexperienced girl had become a paramount influence in the life of each. The hours Antonia spent in his lordship's company were the happiest she had ever known, and the days when he did not come had a grey dulness that was a new sensation. The sound of his step on the stair put her in good spirits, and she was all smiles when he entered the room.

"I swear you have the happiest disposition," he said one day; "your face radiates sunshine."

"Oh, but I have my dull hours."

"Indeed! And when be they?"

"When you are not here."

Her bright and fearless outlook as she said the words showed him how far she was from divining a passion that had grown and strengthened in every hour of their companionship.

They talked of every subject under the sun. He had travelled much, as travelling went in those days; had read much, and had learnt still more from intercourse with the brightest minds of the age. He showed her the better side of his nature, the man he might have been had he never abandoned himself to the vices that the world calls pleasures. They talked often about religion; and though he had cast in his lot with the Deists before he left Oxford, it shocked him to find a young and innocent woman lost to all sense of natural piety. Her father had trained her to scorn all creeds, and to rank the Christian faith no higher than the most revolting or the most imbecile superstitions of India or the South Seas. She had read Voltaire before she read the gospel; and that inexorable pen had cast a blight over the sacred pages, and infused the poison of a malignant satire into the fountain of living waters. Kilrush praised her independence of spirit, and exulted in the thought that a woman who believed in nothing had nothing to lose outside the region of material advantages, and, convinced of this, felt sure that he could make her life happy.

And thus, seeing himself secure of her liking, he flung the fatal die and declared his love.

They were alone together in the June afternoon, as they so often were. He had met Thornton at the entrance to the court, trudging off to Adelphi Terrace, to wait upon Mr. Garrick; so he thought himself secure of an hour's *tête-à-tête*. She welcomed him with unconcealed pleasure, pushed aside her papers, took the bunch of roses that he carried her with her prettiest curtsey, and then busied herself in arranging the nosegay in a willow-pattern Worcester bowl, while he laid down his hat and cane, and took his accustomed seat by her writing-table. They were cabbage roses, and made a great mass of glowing pink above the dark blue of the bowl. She looked at them delightedly, handled them with delicate touch, fingers light as Titania's, and then stopped in the midst of her pleasant task, surprised at his silence.

"How pale your lordship looks! I hope you are not ill?"

He stretched out his hand and caught hers, wet and perfumed with the roses.

"Antonia, my love, my divinity, this comedy of friendship must end. Dear girl, do you not know that I adore you?"

She tried to draw her hand from his grasp, and looked at him with unutterable astonishment, but not in anger.

"You are surprised! Did you think that I could come here day after day, for a year—see you and hear you, be your friend and companion—and not love you? By Heaven, child, you must have thought me the dullest clay that ever held a human soul, if you could think so."

She looked at him still, mute and grave, deep blushes dyeing her cheeks, and her eyes darkly serious.

"Indeed, your lordship, I have never thought of you but as of a friend whose kindness honoured me beyond my deserts. Your rank, and the difference of our ages, prevented me from thinking of you as a suitor."

He started, and dropped her hand; and his face, which had flushed as he talked to her, grew pale again.

"Great God!" he thought, "she takes my avowal of love for an offer of marriage."

He would not have her deceived in his intentions for an instant. He had not always been fair and above-board in his dealings with women; but to this one he could not lie.

"Your suitor, in the vulgar sense of the word, I can never be, Antonia," he said gravely. "Twenty years ago, when my wife eloped with the friend I most trusted, and when I discovered that I had been a twelve-months' laughing-stock for the town—by one section supposed the complacent husband, by another the blind fool I really was—in that hateful hour I swore that I would never again give a woman the power of dishonouring my name. My heart might break from a jilt's ill-usage—but *that*, the name which belongs not to me only, but to all of my race who have borne it in the past or who will bear it in the future—that should be out of the power of woman's misconduct. And so to you whom I love with a passion more profound, more invincible than this heart ever felt for another since it began to beat, I cannot offer a legal tie; but I lay my adoring heart, my life, my fortune at your feet, and I swear to cleave to you and honour you with a constant and devoted affection which no husband upon this earth can surpass."

He tried to take her hand again, but she drew herself away from him with a superb gesture of mingled surprise and scorn.

"There was nothing further from my mind than that you could desire to marry me, except that you should wish to degrade me," she said in a voice graver than his own.

Her face was colourless, but she stood erect and firm, and had no look of swooning.

"Degrade you? Do you call it degradation to be the idol of my life, to be the beloved companion of a man who can lavish all this world knows of luxury and pleasure upon your lot, who will carry you to the fairest spots of earth, show you all that is noblest in art and nature, all that makes the bliss of intelligent beings, who will protect your interests by the most generous settlements ever made by a lover?"

"Oh, my lord, stop your inventory of temptation!" exclaimed Antonia. "The price you offer is extravagant, but I am not for sale. I thought you were my friend—indeed, for me you had become a dear and cherished friend. I was deceived, cruelly deceived! I shall know better another time when a man of your rank pretends to offer me the equality of friendship!"

There were tears in her eyes in spite of her courage, in which Roman virtue she far surpassed the average woman.

"Curse my rank!" he cried angrily. "It is myself I offer—myself and all that I hold of worldly advantages. What can my name matter to you—to you of all women, friendless and alone in the world, your existence unknown to more than some half-dozen people? *I* stand on a height where the arrows of ridicule fly thick and fast. Were I to marry a young woman—I who was deceived and deserted by a handsome wife before I was thirty—you cannot conceive what a storm of ridicule I should provoke, how Selwyn would coruscate with wit at my expense, and Horry Walpole scatter his contemptuous comments on my folly over half the continent of Europe. I suffered that kind of agony once—knew myself the target of all the wits and slanderers in London. I will not suffer it again!"

He was pacing the room, which was too small for the fever of his mind. To be refused without an instant's hesitation, as if he had tried to make a queen his mistress! To be scorned by Bill Thornton's daughter—Thornton, the old jail-bird whom he had helped to get out of prison—the fellow who had been sponging on him more or less for a score of years, most of all in this last year!

He looked back at his conquests of the past. How triumphant, how easy they were; and what trumpery victories they seemed, as he recalled them in the bitterness of his disappointment to-day.

Tonia stood by the open window, listening mechanically to the roll of wheels which rose and fell in the distance with a rhythmical monotony, like the sound of a summer sea. Kilrush stopped in his angry perambulation, saw her in tears, and flew to her side on the instant.

"My beloved girl, those tears inspire me with hope. If you were indifferent you would not weep."

"I weep for the death of our friendship," she answered sorrowfully.

"You should smile at the birth of our love. Great Heaven! what is there to stand between us and consummate bliss?"

"Your own resolve, my lord. You are determined to take no second wife; and I am determined to be no man's mistress. Be sure that in all our friendship I never thought of marriage, nor of courtship—I never angled for a noble husband. But when you profess yourself my lover, I must needs give you a plain answer."

"Tonia, surely your soul can rise above trivial prejudices! You who have boldly avowed your scorn of Churchmen and their creeds, who have neither hope of heaven nor fear of hell, can you think the tie between a man and woman who love as we do—yes, dearest, I protest you love me—can you believe that bond more sacred for being mumbled by a priest, or stronger for being scrawled in a parish register? By Heaven, I thought you had a spirit too lofty for vulgar superstitions!"

"There is one superstition I shall ever hold by—the belief that there are honest women in the world."

"Pshaw, child! Be but true to the man who adores you, and you will be the honestest of your sex. Fidelity to her lover is honour in woman; and she is the more virtuous who is constant without being bound. Nance Oldfield, the honestest woman I ever knew, never wore a wedding-ring."

"I think, sir," she began in a low and earnest voice that thrilled him, "there are two kinds of women—those who can suffer a life of shame, and those who cannot."

"Say rather, madam, that there are women with hearts and women without. You are of the latter species. Under the exquisite lines of the bosom I worship nature has placed a block of ice instead of a heart."

A street cry went wailing by like a dirge, "Strawberries, ripe strawberries. Who'll buy my strawberries?"

Kilrush wiped the cold dampness from his forehead, and resumed his pacing up and down, then stopped suddenly and surveyed the room, flinging up his hands in a passionate horror.

"Good God! that you should exist in such a hovel as this, while my great empty house waits for you, while my coach-and-six is ready to carry us on the road to an Italian paradise! There is a villa at Fiesole, on a hill above Florence. Oh, to have you there in the spring sunshine, among the spring

The Infidel | 59

flowers, all my own, my sweet companion, *animæ dimidium meæ*, the dearer half of my soul. Antonia, if you are obstinate and reject me, you will drive me mad!"

He dropped into a chair, with his head averted from her, and hid his face in his hands. She saw his whole frame shaken by his sobs. She had never seen a man cry before, and the spectacle unnerved her. If she could have yielded—if that stubborn pride of womanhood, which was her armour against the tempter, could have given way, it would have been at the sight of his tears. For a moment her lot trembled in the balance. She longed to kneel at his feet, to promise him anything he could ask rather than to see his distress; but pride came to the rescue.

Choking with tears, she rushed to the door.

"Farewell, sir," she sobbed; "farewell for ever."

She ran downstairs to the bottom of the house, and to Mrs. Potter's parlour behind the kitchen, empty at this hour, where she threw herself upon the narrow horsehair sofa, and sobbed heart-brokenly. Yet even in the midst of her weeping she listened for the familiar step upon the stairs above, and for the opening and shutting of the street door. It was at least ten minutes before she heard Kilrush leave the house, and then his footfall was so heavy that it sounded like a stranger's.

CHAPTER VII
PRIDE CONQUERS LOVE

Except the awful, the inexorable blank that Death leaves in the heart of the mourner, there is no vacancy of mind more agonizing than that which follows the defeat of a lover and the sudden cessation of an adored companionship. To Kilrush the whole world seemed of one dull grey after he had lost Antonia. The town, the company of which he had long been weary, now became actually hateful, and his only desire was to rush to some remote spot of earth where the very fact of distance might help him to forget the woman he loved. A man of a softer nature would have yielded to his charmer's objections, and sacrificed his pride to his love; but with Kilrush, pride—long-cherished pride of race and name—and a certain stubborn power of will prevailed over inclination. He suffered, but was resolute. He told himself that Antonia was cold and calculating, and unworthy of a generous passion like his. She counted, perhaps, on conquering his resolve, and making him marry her; and he took a vindictive pleasure in the thought of her vexation as the days went by without bringing him to her feet.

"Farewell for ever," she had cried, yet had hoped, perhaps, to see him return to her to-morrow, like some small country squire, who thinks all England will be outraged if he marry beneath his rural importance, yet yields to an irresistible love for the miller's daughter or the village barmaid.

"I have lived through too many fevers to die of this one," Kilrush thought, and braced his nerves to go on living, though all the colour seemed washed out of his life.

While his heart was being lacerated by anger and regret, he was surprised by the appearance of his cousin, the *ci-devant* captain of Dragoons, of whose existence he had taken no account since his afternoon visit to Clapham. He was in his library, a large room at the back of the house, looking into a small garden shadowed by an old brick wall, and overlooked by the back windows of Pall Mall, which looked down into it as into a green well. The room was lined with bookshelves from floor to ceiling, and the favourite calf binding of those days made a monotone of sombre brown, suggestive of gloom, even on a summer day, when the scent of stocks and mignonette was blown in through the open windows.

Kilrush received his kinsman with cold civility.

Not even in the splendour of his court uniform had George Stobart looked handsomer than to-day in his severely cut grey cloth coat and black silk waistcoat. There was a light in his eyes, a buoyant youthfulness in his aspect, which Kilrush observed with a pang of envy. Ah, had he been as young, Fate and Antonia might have been kinder.

George put down his hat, and took the chair his cousin indicated, chilled somewhat by so distant a greeting.

"I saw in *Lloyd's Evening Post* that your lordship intended starting for the Continent," he began, "and I thought it my duty to wait upon you before you left town."

"You are very good—and Lloyd is very impertinent—to take so much trouble about my movements. Yes, George, I am leaving England."

"Do you go far, sir?"

"Paris will be the first stage of my journey."

"And afterwards?"

"And afterwards? Kamschatka, perhaps, or—hell! I am fixed on nothing but to leave a town I loathe."

George looked inexpressibly shocked.

"I fear your lordship is out of health," he faltered.

"Fear nothing, hope nothing about me, sir; I am inclined to detest my fellow-men. If you take that for a symptom of sickness, why then I am indeed out of health."

"I am sorry I do not find you in happier spirits, sir, for I had a double motive in waiting on you."

"So have most men—in all they do. Well, sir?"

Kilrush threw himself back in his chair, and waited his cousin's communication with no more interest in his countenance or manner than if he were awaiting a petition from one of his footmen.

Nothing could be more marked than the contrast between the two men, though their features followed the same lines, and the hereditary mark of an ancient race was stamped indelibly on each. A life of passionate excitement, self-will, pride, had wasted the form and features of the elder, and made him look older than his actual years. Yet in those attenuated features there was such exquisite refinement, in that almost colourless complexion such a high-bred delicacy, that for most women the elder face would have been the more attractive. There was a pathetic appeal in the countenance of the man who had lived his life, who had emptied the cup of earthly joys, and for whom nothing remained but decay.

The young man's highest graces were his air of frankness and high courage, and his soldierly bearing, which three years among the Methodists had in no wise lessened. He had, indeed, in those years been still a soldier of the Church Militant, and had stood by John Wesley's side on more than one occasion when the missiles of a howling mob flew thick and fast around that hardy itinerant, and when riot threatened to end in murder.

"Well, sir, your second motive—your *arrière pensée?*" Kilrush exclaimed impatiently, the young man having taken up his hat again, and being engaged in smoothing the beaver with a hand that shook ever so slightly.

"You told me nearly a year ago, sir," he began, hardening himself for the encounter, "that you would never forgive me if I married my inferior— my inferior in the world's esteem, that is to say—an inferiority which I do not admit."

"Hang your admissions, sir! I perfectly remember what I said to you, and I hope you took warning by it, and that my aunt found another place for her housemaid."

"Your warning came too late. I had learnt to esteem Lucy Foreman at her just value. The housemaid, as your lordship is pleased to call her, is now my wife."

"Then, sir, since you know my ultimatum, what the devil brings you to this house?"

"I desired that you should hear what I have done from my lips, not from the public press."

"You are monstrous civil! Well, I am not going to waste angry words upon you, but your name will come out of my will before I sleep; and from to-day we are strangers. I can hold no intercourse with a man who disgraces his name by a beggarly marriage. By Heaven, sir, if I loved to distraction, if my happiness, my peace, my power to endure this wretched life, depended upon my winning the idol of my soul, I would not give my name to a woman of low birth or discreditable connections!"

He struck his clenched fist upon the table in front of him with a wild vehemence that took his cousin's breath away; then, recovering his composure, he asked coldly—

"Does your pious mother approve this folly, sir, and take your housemaid-wife to her heart?"

"My mother has shown a most unchristian temper. She has forbidden me her house, and swears to disinherit me. To have forfeited her affection will be ever my deep regret; but I can support the loss of her fortune."

"Indeed! Are you so vastly rich from other resources?"

"I have two hundred a year in India stock—my Uncle Matthew's bequest, and Lucy's good management promises to make this income enough for our home—a cottage near Richmond, where we have a garden and all the rustic things my Lucy loves."

"Having been reared in an alley near Moorfields! I wonder how long her love of the country will endure wet days and dark nights, and remoteness from shops and market? Oh, you are still in your honeymoon, sir, and your sky is all blue. You must wait a month or two before you will discover how much you are to be pitied, and that I was your true friend when I cautioned you against this madness. Good day to you, Mr. Stobart, and be good enough to forget that we have ever called each other cousins."

George rose, and bowed his farewell. The porter was in the hall ready to open the door for him. He looked round the great gloomy hall with a contemptuous smile as he passed out.

"John Wesley's house at the Foundery is more cheerful than this," he thought.

Kilrush sat with his elbows on the table and his hands clasped above his head in a melancholy silence.

"Which is the madman, he or I?" he asked himself.

The preparation for his continental journey occupied Lord Kilrush for a fortnight, during which time he waited with a passionate longing for some sign of relenting from Antonia; and in all those empty days his mind was torn by the strife between inclination and a stubborn resolve.

There were moments in which he asked himself why he did not make this woman his wife; that unfrocked priest, that tippling bookseller's hack, his father-in-law? Did anything in this world matter to a man so much as the joy of this present life, his instant happiness? In the hideous uncertainty of fate, were it not best to snatch the hour's gladness?

"What if I married her, and she turned wanton after a year of bliss?" he mused. "At least I should have had my day."

But then there came the dark suspicion that she had played him as the angler plays his fish, that she flung the glittering fly across his enraptured gaze, intent on landing a coronet; that her womanly candour, her almost childlike simplicity, were all so much play-acting. What could he expect of truth and honour from Thornton's daughter?

"If she had given herself to me generously, unquestioningly, I might believe she loved me," he thought. "But if I married her I must for ever suspect myself her dupe, the victim of a schemer's ambition, the sport of an artful coquette, to be betrayed at the first assault of a younger lover."

No token of relenting came from Antonia; but towards the end of the second week Mr. Thornton called to inquire about his lordship's health, and, being informed that his lordship was about to leave England for a considerable time, pressed for an interview, and was admitted to his dressing-room.

"I am in despair at the prospect of your lordship's departure," he said, on being bidden to seat himself. "I know not how my daughter and I will endure our lives in the absence of so valued a friend."

"I do not apprehend that *you* will suffer much from wanting my company, Thornton, since you have been generally out-of-doors during my visits. And as for your daughter, her interest in an elderly proser's conversation must have been exhausted long ago."

"On my soul, no! She has delighted in your society—as how could she do otherwise? She has an intellect vastly superior to her age and sex, and she had suffered a famine of intellectual conversation. I know that she has already begun to feel the loss of your company, for she has been strangely dispirited for the last ten days, and that indefatigable pen of hers now moves without her usual gusto."

"If she is ill, or drooping, I beg you to send for my physician, Sir Richard Maningham, who will attend her on my account."

"No, no—'tis no case for Æsculapius. She is out of spirits, but not ill. How far does your lordship design to extend your travels?"

"Oh, I have decided nothing. I shall stay at Fontainebleau till the cool season, and then go by easy stages to Italy. I may winter in Rome, and spend next spring in Florence."

"A year's absence! We shall sorely miss your lordship, and I am already too deeply in your debt to dare venture——"

"To ask me for a further loan," interrupted Kilrush. "We will have done with loans, and notes of hand"—Thornton turned pale—"I wish to help you. Above all, I want to prevent your making a slave of your daughter."

"A slave! My dear girl delights in literary work. She would be miserable if I refused her assistance."

The Infidel | 65

"Well, be sure she does not drudge for you. I hate to think of her solitary hours mewed in your miserable second-floor parlour, when she ought to be enjoying the summer air in some rural garden, idle and without a care. I want to strike a bargain with you, Thornton."

"I am your lordship's obedient——"

"Instead of these petty loans which degrade you and disgust me, I am willing to give you a small income—say, a hundred pounds a quarter——"

"My dear lord, this is undreamed-of munificence."

"On condition that you remove with your daughter to some pretty cottage in a rural neighbourhood—Fulham, Barnes, Hampstead, any rustic spot within reach of your booksellers and editors—and also that you provide your daughter with a suitable attendant, a woman of unblemished character, to wait upon her and accompany her in her walks—in a word, sir, that being the father of the loveliest woman I ever met, you do not ignore your responsibilities, and neglect her."

"Oh, sir, is this meant for a reproach, because I have suffered Antonia to receive you alone? Sure, 'twas the knowledge of her virtue and of your noble character that justified my confidence."

"True, sir, but there may be occasions when you should exercise a paternal supervision. I shall instruct my lawyer as to the payment of this allowance, and I expect that you will study your daughter's convenience and happiness in all your future arrangements. Should I hear you are neglecting that duty, your income will stop, on the instant. I must beg, also, that you keep the source of your means a secret from Miss Thornton, who has a haughtier spirit than yours, and might dislike being obliged by a friend. And now, as I have a hundred things to do before I leave town, I must bid you good morning."

"I go, my lord, but not till I have kissed this generous hand."

"Pshaw!"

Kilrush snatched his hand away impatiently, rang for his valet, and dismissed his grateful friend with a curt nod.

He left St. James's Square next day after his morning chocolate, in his coach and six, bound for Dover, determined not to return till he had learnt the lesson of forgetfulness and indifference.

CHAPTER VIII
THE LOVE THAT FOLLOWS THE DEAD

On his return to Rupert Buildings, William Thornton walked on air. An income, an assured income of a hundred pounds a quarter, was indeed an improvement upon those casual loans which he had begged of his patron from time to time, with somewhat more of boldness since Kilrush had shown so marked a liking for his daughter's society. He was elated by his patron's generosity; yet across his pleasant meditations in the short distance between St. James's Square and St. Martin's Lane, there was time for his thoughts to take a wider range, and for something of a cloud to fall across his sunshine.

He was puzzled, he was even troubled, by his lordship's generosity. What were the relations between that liberal patron and Antonia? Till a fortnight ago his daughter's happy frankness had assured him that all was well: that she was the kind of girl who may be trusted to take care of herself without paternal interference. But there had been a marked change in her manner after Kilrush's last visit. She had been languid and silent. She looked unhappy, and had been absent-minded when she talked of their literary projects—an essay for Cave—a story for the *Monthly Review*, or the possibility of Garrick's favour for an after-piece from the Italian of Goldoni.

Antonia waited upon him when he came in, helped him to change his laced coat for an old one that he wore in the house, brought him his slippers, and proceeded to prepare his tea; but there was no welcoming smile.

"My dearest girl, there is something amiss," Thornton said, after he had watched her for some time, while they sat opposite to each other with the tea-tray between them. "My Tonia is no longer the happy girl I have known so long. What ails my love? I have been with your friend Kilrush. He leaves England to-morrow. Is it the loss of his company distresses you?"

"No, no! It is best that he should come here no more."

"Why, dearest?"

"Because we could never more be friends. I was very happy in his friendship. I knew not how happy till we parted."

"Why should such a friendship end? Why did you part?"

She burst into tears.

"I cannot—cannot—cannot tell you."

"Nay, love, you should have no secrets from your father—an indulgent father, if sometimes a neglectful one. When have I ever scared you by a harsh word?"

"No, no; but it is very hard to tell you that the man I esteemed was unworthy of my friendship—that he came here with the vilest design—that he waited till he had won my regard—and then—and then—swore that he loved me passionately, devotedly—and offered to make me—his mistress."

Thornton heard her with a countenance that indicated more of thought than of horror.

"It would have been no disgrace to him to make you his wife," he said, "but the Delafields have ever pretended to a pride in excess of their rank. He did ill to offer you his affection upon those terms; yet I'll swear his vows of love were sincere. I have but just left him, and I never saw more distress of mind than I saw in his face to-day. When I told him that you had been drooping, he implored me to call in his own physician, at his charge."

"Oh, pray, sir, do not tell me how he looked or what he said!" cried Tonia, with a passionate impatience, drying her tears as she spoke, which broke out afresh before she had done. "I doubt he thinks money can heal every wound. He offered to lavish his fortune upon me, and marvelled that I could prefer this shabby parlour to a handsome house and dishonour."

"He did very ill," said Thornton, in a soothing voice, as if he were consoling a child in some childish trouble; "yet, my dearest Tonia, did you but know the world as well as I do, you would know that he made you what the world calls a handsome offer. To settle a fortune upon you—of course he would mean a *settlement:* anything else were unworthy of a thought—would be to give you the strongest pledge of his fidelity. Men who do not mean to be constant will not so engage their fortune. And if—if the foolish Delafield pride—that Irish pride, which counts a long line of ancestors as a sacred inheritance—stands in the way of marriage—I'll be hanged if I think you ought to have rejected him without the compliment of considering his offer and of consulting me."

"Father!"

She sprang up to her feet, and stood before him in all the dignity of her tall figure; and her face, with the tears streaming over it, was white with anger and contempt.

"My love, life is made up of compromises. Sure, I have tried to keep your mind clear of foolish prejudices; and, as a student of history, you must have seen the influences that govern the world. Beauty is one, and the most powerful, of those influences. Aspasia—Agnes Sorel—Madame de Pompadour. Need I multiply instances? But Beauty mewed up in a two-pair lodging is worthless to the possessor; while, with a fine establishment, a devoted protector, my dearest girl might command the highest company in the town."

"Father!" she cried again, with a voice that had a sharp ring of agony, "would you have had me say yes?"

"I would have had you consider your answer very seriously before you said no."

"You could have suffered your daughter to stoop to such humiliation; you would have had her listen to the proposal of a man who is free to marry any one he pleases—but will not marry *her*; who tells her in one breath that he loves her—and in the next that he will not make her his wife—oh, father, I did not think——"

"That I was a man of the world? My poor child, some of the greatest matches in England have begun with unfettered love; and be sure that, were your affection to consent to such a sacrifice, Kilrush would end by giving you his name."

"Pray, pray, sir, say no more—you are breaking my heart—I want to respect you still, if I can."

"Pshaw, child, after all we have read together! 'Tis a shock to hear such heroics! What is the true philosophy of life but to snatch all the comfort and happiness the hour offers? What is true morality but to do all the good we can to ourselves, and no harm to our neighbours? Will your fellow-creatures be any the better for your unkindness to Kilrush? With his fortune to deal with, you could do an infinitude of good."

"Oh, cease, I implore you!" she exclaimed distractedly. "If his tears could not conquer me, do you think your philosophy can shake my resolve?"

She left him, and took refuge in her garret, and sat staring blankly into space, heart-sick and disgusted with life. Her father! 'Twas the first time she had ever been ashamed of him. Her father to be the advocate of dishonour—to urge her to accept degradation! Her father, whom she had loved till this hour with a child's implicit belief in the wisdom and beneficence of a parent—was he no better than the wretches she had heard Patty talk about, the complacent husbands who flourished upon a wife's infidelity, the brothers who fawned upon a sister's protector? Was all the world made of the same base stuff; and did woman's virtue and man's honour live but in the dreams of genius?

She had accepted her father's dictum that religion and superstition were convertible terms. Her young mind had been steeped in the Voltairean philosophy before she was strong enough to form her own opinions or choose her own creed. She had read over and over again of the evil that religion had done in the world, and never of the good. Instead of the whole armour of righteousness, she had been shown the racks and thumb-screws of the Spanish Inquisition; and had been taught to associate the altar with the *auto da fé*. All she knew of piety was priestcraft; and though her heart melted with compassion for the martyrs of a mistaken belief, her mind scorned their credulity. But from her first hour of awakening reason she had never wavered in her ideas of right and wrong, honour and dishonour. As a child of twelve, newly entrusted with the expenditure of small sums, all her little dealings with Mrs. Potter had shown a scrupulous honesty, a delicacy and consideration, which the good woman had seldom met with in adult lodgers. The books that had made her an infidel had held before her high ideals of honour. And those other books—the books she most loved—her Shakespeare, her Spenser—had taught her all that is noblest in man and woman.

She thought of Shakespeare's Isabella, who, not to save the life of a beloved brother, would stoop to sin. She recalled her instinctive contempt for Claudio, who, to buy that worthless life, would have sold his sister to shame.

"My father is like Claudio," she thought; and then with a sudden compunction, "No, no, he is not selfish—he is only mistaken. It was of me he thought—and that if Kilrush loved me, and I loved him, I might be happy."

Her tears flowed afresh. Never till Kilrush threw off the mask had she known what it was to look along the dull vista of life and see no star, to feel the days a burden, the future a blank. She missed him. Oh, how she missed him! Day after day in the parlour below she had sat looking at his empty chair, listening unawares for a footstep she was never likely to hear again. She recalled his conversation, his opinions, his criticism of her favourite books, their arguments, their almost quarrels about abstract things. His face haunted her: those exquisitely refined features upon which the only effect of age was an increased delicacy of line and colouring; the depth of thought in the dark grey eyes; the grave smile with its so swift transition from satire to a tender melancholy. Was there ever such a man? His elegance, his dignity, his manner of entering a room or leaving it, the grace of every gesture, so careless yet so unerring—every trait of character, every charm of person, which she was unconscious of having noticed in their almost daily association, seemed now to have been burnt into her brain and to be written there for ever.

In the fortnight that had passed since they had parted, she had tried in vain to occupy herself with the work which had hitherto interested her so much as to make industry only another name for amusement. Her adaptation of Goldoni's *Villeggiatura* lay on her table, the pages soiled by exposure, sentence after sentence obliterated. The facile pen had lost its readiness. She found herself translating the lively Italian with a dull precision; she, who of old had so deftly turned every phrase into idiomatic English—who had lent so much of herself to her author.

Often in these sorrowful days she had pushed aside her manuscript to scribble her recollections of Kilrush's conversation upon a stray sheet of foolscap. Often again, in those saddest moments of all, she had recalled his words of impassioned love—his tears; and her own tears had fallen thick and fast upon the disfigured page.

Well, it was ended, that friendship which had been so sweet; and she had discovered the bitter truth that friendship between man and woman, when the woman is young and beautiful, is impossible.

The days, weeks, months went by; and the name of Kilrush was no more spoken by Thornton or his daughter. It was as if no such being had ever had any part in their lives, any influence over their fate. Yet Thornton was studiously obedient to his patron's wishes all the time.

Good Mrs. Potter, who was getting elderly, had for some years past groaned under the burden of the house in Rupert Buildings, with the double, or sometimes treble set of lodgers, who were needful to make the business remunerative. Servant girls were troublesome, even when paid as much as six pounds per annum, with a pound extra for tea and sugar; lodgers were not always punctual with the weekly rent, and sometimes left in her debt. Thornton paid her a low rent for his second floor and garret; but he stayed from year's end to year's end; and she valued him above the finer people who came and went in her bettermost rooms. So when he told her that he was going to remove to a rural neighbourhood, she opened her heart to him, and declared, firstly, that she was sick of London, and London husseys— otherwise domestic servants; secondly, that she could not live without Antonia; thirdly, that she had long had it in her mind to remove her goods and chattels to a countrified suburb, such as Highgate or Edmonton, and that could she be secure of one permanent lodger she would do so without loss of time.

"Choose a genteel house to the south-west of London, somewhere between Wandsworth and Barnes, and my daughter and I will share it with you," said Thornton; and Mrs. Potter, who had no particular leaning to north or east, agreed.

After this came a pleasant period of house-hunting, in which Antonia was by-and-by induced to take a languid interest, going in a hackney coach with Mrs. Potter and her daughter Sophy, who had served an apprenticeship to a dressmaker, and was very doubtful how to dispose of her talent now she was out of her time. After several suburban drives, through suburbs that were all garden and meadow, they discovered an old half-timbered cottage at Putney, whose casement windows looked across the Thames to the church and episcopal palace and gardens of Fulham. To Antonia, who had hardly known what it was to leave London since those distant childish years in Windsor Forest, the white walled cottage and garden seemed a heaven upon earth. Surely it must be a blissful thing to live beside that broad reach of Thames, to see willows dipping and reeds waving in the mild autumn wind, and the red sailed barges drifting slowly down stream, and to hear the rooks in the great elms yonder in the bishop's gardens, their clamorous chatter softened by the intervening river. She went back to London enchanted with Rosemary Bank, as the roomy old cottage called itself, and told her father that she thought she could be happy there.

"Then Potter shall take the cottage to-morrow," cried Thornton, in a rapture of eagerness; "for I'll be hanged if you have looked anything but miserable for the last six weeks. Just as our luck had turned too, my—my circumstances improved—and—and Garrick promising to put our little Italian play on the stage, and to give me a benefit if it runs twenty nights."

Tonia sighed, remembering the melancholy thoughts interwoven with every line of that lively two-act burletta which she had squeezed out of Goldoni's five-act comedy. Everybody was pleased with the neat little after-piece, most of all Patty Lester, who was to play the soubrette, in a short chintz petticoat, and high red heels to her shoes.

The theatre seemed a source of boundless wealth, for on Mrs. Potter— who dropped in sometimes at tea-time for a gossip; or, coming on a business errand, was invited to sit down and talk—complaining that she did not know what to do with her dressmaking daughter, Thornton offered to engage Mrs. Sophy as Antonia's "woman."

"She will have to accept a modest honorarium," he said, with his grand air, "but she will be getting her hand in to go out as waiting-woman to a lady of quality; and my Tonia will treat her more as a friend than a servant."

Mrs. Potter snapped at the offer, though she did not know the meaning of the word "honorarium." She guessed that it meant either wages or a present, and to find that idle slut of hers an occupation, and yet have her under the maternal eye, was an unspeakable advantage.

Antonia protested that she wanted no waiting-maid, though she loved Sophy.

"Indeed, sir, you are not rich enough to make a fine lady of me," she said.

"Nature has made you a lady, my love; and you are too sensible ever to become fine. When we are living in the country—and I have to come to London, occasionally, to look after my business—you will need a companion whose time will be always at your service."

And so, with no more discussion, Sophia Potter was engaged, at a salary of ten pounds per annum, paid quarterly.

At Rosemary Bank the changing seasons passed in a calm monotony; and it seemed to Antonia, during the second year of her life in the cottage by the Thames, as if she had never lived anywhere else. The London lodging, the Strand and Fleet Street, Miss Lester's rooms in the Piazza, receded in the distance of half-forgotten things; for the years of youth are long, and the passing of a year makes a great gap in time.

The link between Tonia and London seemed as completely broken as if she were living in Yorkshire or in Cornwall. There was a London coach that started from the King's Head at the bottom of Putney High Street every morning, for the Golden Cross, hard by Rupert Buildings; and this coach carried Mr. Thornton and his fortunes three or four times a week, and brought him home after dark. He had so much business that required his presence in the metropolis, and first and foremost the necessity of getting the latest news, which was always on tap at the Portico, where half a score of gutter wits and politicians settled the affairs of the nation, reviled Newcastle and the Pelhams, praised Pitt, canvassed the prospects of war in America or on the continent, and enlarged on the vices of the *beau monde*, every afternoon and evening.

Antonia accepted her father's absence as inevitable. Her own life was spent in a peaceful monotony. She had her books and her literary work for interest and occupation. She acquired some elementary knowledge of horticulture from an old man who came once a week to work in the garden; and, her love of flowers aiding her, she improved upon his instructions and became an expert in the delightful art. She and Sophy made the two-acre garden their pride. It was an old garden, and there was much of beauty ready to their hands; rustic arches overhung with roses and honeysuckle; espaliers of russet apples and jargonelle pears screening patches of useful vegetables; plots of old-established turf; long borders crowded with hardy perennials—a garden that had cost care and labour in days that were gone.

And then there was the river-bank between Putney and Kew, where Tonia found beauty and delight at all seasons; even in the long winter, when the snapping of thin ice rang through the still air as the barges moved slowly by, and the snow was piled in high ridges along the edge of the stream. Summer or winter, spring or autumn, Tonia loved that solitary shore, where the horses creeping along the towing-path were almost the only creatures that ever intruded on her privacy. She and Sophy were indefatigable pedestrians. They had indeed nothing else to do with themselves, Sophy told her mother, and must needs walk "to pass the time." Passing the time was the great problem in Sophia Potter's existence. To that end she waded through "Pamela" and "Clarissa," sitting in the garden, on sleepy summer afternoons. To that end she toiled at a piece of tambour work; and to that end she trudged, yawning dismally now and then, by Tonia's side from Putney to Barnes, from Barnes to Kew, while her young mistress's thoughts roamed in dreamland, following airy shadows, or sometimes perhaps following a distant traveller in cities and by lakes and mountains she knew not.

Often and often, in her peripatetic reveries, Antonia's fancies followed the image of Kilrush, whose continental wanderings were chronicled from time to time in *Lloyd's* or the *St. James's*. He was at Rome in the winter after their farewell; he was in Corsica in the following spring; he spent the summer at Aix in Savoy; moved to Montpelier in the late autumn; wintered at Florence. Tonia's thoughts followed him with a strange sadness, wherever he went. Youth cannot feed on regrets for ever, and the heartache of those first vacant days had been healed; but the thought that she might never see his face again hung like a cloud of sadness over the quiet of her life.

And now it was summer again, and the banks were all in flower, and the blue harebells trembled above the mossy hillocks on Barnes Common, and the long evenings were glorious with red and gold sunsets, and it was nearly two years since she had rushed from her lover's presence with a despairing farewell. Two years! Only two years! It seemed half a lifetime. Nothing was less likely than that they would ever meet again. Nothing, nothing, nothing! Yet there were daydreams, foolish dreams, in which she pictured his return—dreams that took their vividest colours on a lovely sunlit morning when the world seemed full of joy. He would appear before her suddenly at some turn of the river-bank. He would take her hand and seat himself by her side on such or such a fallen tree or rough rustic bench where she was wont to sit in her solitude. "I have come back," he would say, "come back to be your true friend, never more to wound you with words of love, but to be your friend always." The tears sprang to her eyes sometimes as imagination depicted that meeting. Surely he would come back! Could they, who had been such friends, be parted for ever?

But the quiet days went by, and her dream was not realized. No sign or token came to her from him who had been her friend, till one July evening, when she was startled by her father's unexpected return in a coach and four, which drove to the little garden gate with a rush and a clatter, as if those steaming horses had been winged dragons and were going to carry off the cottage and its inmates in a cloud of smoke and fire. Tonia ran to the gate in a sudden panic. What could have happened? Was her father being carried home to her hurt in some street accident—or dead? It was so unlike his accustomed arrival, on the stroke of eleven, walking quietly home from the last coach, which left the Golden Cross at a quarter-past nine, was due at the King's Head at half-past ten, and rarely kept its time.

Her father alighted from the carriage, sound of limb, but with an agitated countenance; and then she noticed for the first time that the postillions wore the Kilrush livery, and that his lordship's coat of arms was on the door.

"My love—my Tonia," cried Thornton, breathlessly, "you are to come with me, this instant—alas! there is not a moment to spare. Bring her hat and cloak," he called out to Sophy, who had followed at her lady's heels, and stood open-mouthed, devouring the wonder-vision of coach and postillions. "Run, girl, run!"

Tonia stared at her father in amazement.

"What has happened?" she asked. "Where am I to go?"

"Kilrush has sent me for you, Tonia. That good man—Kilrush—my friend—my benefactor—he who has made our lives so happy. I shall lose the best friend I ever had. Your cloak"—snatching a light cloth mantle from the breathless Sophy and wrapping it round Tonia. "Your hat. Come, get into the coach. I can tell you the rest as we drive to town."

He helped her into the carriage and took his seat beside her. She was looking at him in a grave wonder. In his flurry and agitation he had let her into a secret which had been carefully guarded hitherto.

"Is it to Lord Kilrush we owe our quiet lives here? Has his lordship given you money?" she asked gravely.

"Oh, he has helped—he has helped me, when our means ran low—as any rich friend would help a poor one. There is nothing strange in that, child," her father explained, with a deprecating air.

"Kilrush!" she repeated, deeply wounded. "It was his kindness changed our lives! I thought we were earning all our comforts—you and I. Why are you taking me to him, sir? I don't understand."

"I am taking you to his death-bed, Tonia. His doctors give him only a few hours of life, and he wants to see you before he dies, to bid you farewell."

The tears were rolling down Thornton's cheeks, but Antonia's eyes were tearless. She sat with her face turned to the village street, staring at the little rustic shops, the quaint gables and projecting beams, the dormer casements gilded by the sunset, Fairfax House, with its stout red walls, and massive stone mullions, and a garden full of roses and pinks, that perfumed the warm air as they drove by. She looked at all those familiar things in a stupor of wonder and regret.

"You often talk wildly," she said presently, in a toneless voice. "Is he really so ill? Is there no hope?"

The horses had swung round a corner, and they were driving by a lane that led to Wandsworth, where it joined the London road. At the rate at which they were going they would be at Westminster Bridge in less than half an hour.

"Alas, child, I have it from his doctor. 'Tis a hopeless case—has been hopeless for the last six months. He has been in a consumption since the beginning of the winter, has been sent from place to place, fighting with his malady. He came to London two days ago, from Geneva, as fast as he could travel—a journey that has hastened his end, the physician told me. Came to put his affairs in order, and to see you," Thornton concluded, after a pause.

"To see me! Ah, what am I that he should care?" cried Tonia.

To know that he was dying was to know that she had never ceased to love him. But she did not analyze her feelings. All that she knew of herself was a dull despair—the sense of a loss that engulfed everything she had ever valued in this world.

"What am I that he should care?" she repeated forlornly.

"You are all in all to him. He implored me to bring you—with tears, Antonia—he, my benefactor, the one friend who never turned a deaf ear to my necessities," said Thornton, too unhappy to control his speech.

"Shall we be there soon?" Tonia asked by-and-by, in a voice broken by sobs.

"In a quarter of an hour at the latest. God grant it may not be too late."

No other word was spoken till the coach stopped at the solemn old doorway in St. James's Square, a door through which Mrs. Arabella Churchill had passed in her day of pride, when the house was hers, and that handsome young soldier, her brother Jack, was a frequent visitor there.

Night had not fallen yet, and there were lingering splashes of red sunset upon the westward-facing windows of the Square; but on this side all was shadow, and the feeble oil-lamps made dots of yellow light on the cold greyness, and enhanced the melancholy of a summer twilight.

The door was opened as Thornton and Antonia alighted. Her father led her past the hall porter, across the spacious marble-paved vestibule that looked like a vault in the dimness of a solitary lamp which a footman was lighting as they entered. Huge imperials, portmanteaux and packing-cases filled one side of the hall; the bulk of his lordship's personal luggage, which no one had found time to carry upstairs, and the cases containing the pictures, porcelain, curios, which he had collected in his wanderings from city to city, and in which his interest had ceased so soon as the thing was bought. He had come home too ill for any one to give heed to these treasures. There would be time to unpack them after the funeral—that inevitable ceremony which the household had begun to discuss already. Would the dying man desire to be laid with his ancestors in the family vault under Limerick Cathedral, within sound of the Shannon?

Antonia followed her father up the dusky staircase, their footfall noiseless on the soft depth of an Indian carpet, followed him into a dark little ante-room, where two men in sombre attire sat at a table talking together by the light of two wax candles in tall Corinthian candlesticks. One of these was his lordship's family lawyer, the other his apothecary.

"Are we too late?" asked Thornton, breathlessly, with rapid glances from the attorney to the doctor—glances which included a folded paper lying on the table beside a silver standish.

"No, no; his lordship may last out the night," answered the doctor. "Pray be seated, madam. If my patient is asleep, we will wait his awakening. He does not sleep long. If he is awake you shall see him. He desired that you should be taken to him without delay."

He opened the door of the inner room almost noiselessly and looked in. A voice asked, "Is she here?"

It was the voice Tonia knew of old, but weaker. Her heart beat passionately. She did not wait for the doctor, but brushed past him on the threshold, and was scarce conscious of crossing the width of a larger room than she had ever seen. She had no eyes for the gloomy magnificence of the room, the high windows draped with dark red velvet, the panelled walls, the lofty bed, with its carved columns and ostrich plumes; she knew nothing, saw nothing, till she was on her knees by the bed, and the dying man was holding her hands in his.

"Go into the next room, both of you," he said, whereupon his valet and an elderly woman in a linen gown and apron, a piece of respectable incompetence, the best sick-nurse that his wealth and station could command, silently retired.

"Will you stop with me to the end, Tonia?"

"Yes, yes! But you are not going to die. I will not believe them. You must not die!"

"Would you be sorry? Would it make any difference?"

"It would break my heart. I did not know that I loved you till you had gone away. I did not know how dearly till to-night."

"And if I was to mend and be my own man again, and was to ask you the same question again, would you give me the same answer?"

"Yes," she answered slowly; "but you would not be so cruel."

"No, Tonia, no, I am wiser now; for I have come to understand that there is one woman in the world who would not forfeit her honour for love or happiness. Ah, my dearest, here, here, on the brink of death, I know there is nothing on this earth that a man should set above the woman he loves— no paltry thought of rank or station, no cowardly dread that she may prove unfaithful, no fear of the world's derision. If I could have my life again I should know how to use it. But 'tis past, and the only love I can ask for now is the love that follows the dead."

He paused, exhausted by the effort of speech. He spoke very slowly, and his voice was low and hoarse, but she could hear every word. She had risen from her knees, to be nearer him, and was sitting on the side of the bed, holding him in her arms. In her heart of hearts she had realized that death was near, though her soul rebelled against the inevitable. She was conscious of the coming darkness, conscious that she was holding him on the edge of an open grave.

"Do not talk so much, you are tiring yourself," she said gently, wiping his forehead with a cambric handkerchief that had lain among the heaped-up pillows. The odour of orange flower that it exhaled was in her mind years afterwards, associated with that bed of death.

He lay resting, with his eyelids half closed, his head leaning against her shoulder, her arm supporting him.

"I never thought to taste such ineffable bliss," he murmured. "You have made death euthanasia."

He lapsed into a half-sleeping state, which lasted for some minutes, while she sat as still as marble. Then he opened his eyes suddenly, and looked at her in an agitated way.

"Tonia, will you marry me?" he asked.

"Yes, yes, if you bid me, by-and-by, when you are well," she answered, humouring a dying man's fancy.

"Now, now! I have only a few hours to live. I sent for you to make you my wife. I want your love to follow me in death. I want you to bear my name—the name I refused you, the name that cost me half a lifetime of happiness. Tonia, swear that you will be true—that you will belong to me when I am dead, as you might have belonged to me in life."

She thought his mind was wandering. He had lifted himself from her arms, and was sitting up in bed, magnetized into new life by the intensity of his purpose.

"Ring that bell, dearest. Yes"—as she took up the handbell on his table—"all has been arranged. Death will be civil to the last Baron Kilrush, and will give me time for what I have to do."

His valet appeared at the door.

"Is his lordship's chaplain there?" Kilrush asked.

"Yes, my lord. The bishop has come with his chaplain."

"The bishop! My old friend is monstrous obliging. Show them in."

The valet ushered in a stately personage in full canonicals, accompanied by a young man in surplice and hood. The bishop came to the bedside, saluted Antonia courteously, and bent his portly form over Kilrush with an affectionate air.

"My dear friend, on so solemn an occasion I could not delegate my duty to another."

"You are very good. We are ready for you. My lawyer is in the next room—he has the license; and this"—pointing to a thin gold hoop worn with an antique intaglio ring on his little finger—"this was my mother's wedding ring—it will serve."

The bishop took the Prayer-book which his chaplain had opened at the Marriage Service, but paused with the book in his hand, looking at Antonia with a grave curiosity. Kilrush followed the look, and answered it as if it had been a question.

The Infidel | 79

"You understand, bishop, that this marriage is not an atonement," he said. "Miss Antonia Thornton is a lady of spotless reputation, who will do honour to the name I leave her."

"That is well, Kilrush. But I hope this marriage is not designed to injure any one belonging to you."

"No, I injure no one, for no one has any claim to be my heir."

The valet brought the candles from the further end of the room to a table near the bishop, and rearranged the pillows at his master's back. Antonia had risen from her seat on the edge of the bed, and stood watching Kilrush with the candlelight full upon her face.

The bishop looked at her with a shrewd scrutiny. He wanted to know what manner of woman she was, and what could be his old friend's motive for this death-bed folly. They had been at Eton and Oxford together; and though their paths had lain asunder since those early years, the bishop knew what kind of life Kilrush had led, and was disinclined to credit him with chivalrous or romantic impulses. He looked to the woman for the answer to the enigma. An artful adventuress, no doubt, who had worked upon the weaker will of a dying man. He scrutinized her with the keen glance of a man accustomed to read the secrets of the heart in the countenance, and his penetration was baffled by the tragic beauty of her face, as she gazed at Kilrush, with eyes which seemed incapable of seeing anything but him. He thought that no adventuress could conjure up that look of despairing love, that unconsciousness of external things, that supreme indifference to a ceremony which was to give her wealth and station for the rest of her life, indifference even to that episcopal dignity of purple and lawn which had rarely failed in its influence upon woman.

"Make your ceremony as brief as you can, bishop," said Kilrush. "I have something to say to my wife when 'tis over. Louis, call Mr. Thornton and Mr. Pegloss."

The valet opened the door, and admitted Thornton and the lawyer. The apothecary followed them, took up his position by his patient's pillow, and gave him a restorative draught.

The bishop began to read in his great deep voice—a voice which must have ensured a bishopric, but diminished from the thunder of his cathedral tones to a grave baritone, musical as the soughing of distant waves. The windows were open, and through the sultry air there came the cry of the watchman calling the hour, far off and at measured intervals—

"Past ten o'clock, and a cloudy night."

Tonia stood by the bed, holding her lover's hand.

"Who giveth this woman, etc."

Thornton was ready, trembling with excitement, dazed by the wonder of it all, and scarcely able to speak; and Tonia's voice was choked with tears when she made the bride's replies, slowly, stumblingly, prompted by the chaplain. The ceremony had no significance for her, except as a dying man's whim. Her only thought was of him. She could see his face more distinctly now, in the nearer light of the candles, and the awful change smote her heart with a pain she had never felt before. It was death, the dreadful, the inevitable, the end of all things. What meaning could marriage have in such an hour as this?

The chaplain read a final prayer. The ring had been put on. The marriage was complete.

The bishop knelt by the table, and began to read the prayers for the sick, Tonia standing by the bed, with Kilrush's hand in hers, heedless of the solemn voice. The bishop looked up at her in a shocked astonishment.

"It would be more becoming, madam, to kneel," he said in a loud whisper.

She sank on her knees beside the bed, and listened to the prayer that seemed to mock her with its supplications for health and healing, while Death, a palpable presence, hovered over the bed. To Antonia that ineffectual prayer seemed the last sentence—the sentence of doom.

"You are vastly civil, bishop," said Kilrush, opening his eyelids after one of his transient slumbers. "And now let Mr. Pegloss bring me the paper I have to sign."

The attorney came to the bedside on the instant, carrying a blotting-book which he arranged deftly, with a closely written sheet of foolscap spread upon it, in front of Kilrush, who had been raised again into a sitting position by the doctor and valet.

"This is my will, bishop," said Kilrush, as he wrote his name. "You and your chaplain can witness it. 'Twill give an odour of sanctity to my last act."

"Your lordship may command my services," said the bishop, taking the pen from his friend's hand.

It was something of a shock to have this service asked of him. A few hours ago there had been nothing he expected less than a legacy from his old schoolfellow; but after having been asked to send his chaplain to solemnize a death-bed marriage, after being as it were appealed to on the score of early friendship, and after having so cordially responded, it seemed to his episcopal mind that among the accumulated treasures of art which poor Kilrush was about to surrender, some small memento, were it but a diamond snuff-box, or an enamelled watch—should have come to him.

He wrote his stately signature with a flourish; the chaplain following.

Kilrush sank back among his pillows, supported by the arms he loved.

"Bishop, you are a connoisseur," he said, in his faint voice, looking up shrewdly at his schoolfellow's ample countenance, rosy with the rich hues of the Côte d'or. "That Raffaelle over the chimney-piece—'tis a replica of the Sposalizia at Milan. Some critics pronounce it the finer picture. Let it be a souvenir of your obliging goodness to-night. Louis, you will see the Raffaelle conveyed to his lordship's house immediately. Mr. Pegloss will assist you to take the picture down. And now good-night to you all."

"My dear Kilrush, you overpower me," murmured the bishop; and then he bent over the invalid, and whispered a solemn inquiry.

"No, no; I am not in a fit state of mind," Kilrush answered fretfully. "And my wife is not a believer."

"Not a believer!"

His lordship's eyebrows were elevated in unspeakable horror. He glanced with something of aversion at the lovely face hanging over the dying man with looks of all absorbing love. Not a believer! He would scarcely have been more horrified had she been a disciple of Wesley or Whitefield.

"My dear friend," he murmured, "'tis my bounden duty to urge——"

"Come to me to-morrow morning, bishop."

"Let it be so, then. At eight o'clock to-morrow morning."

"*A rivederci*," said Kilrush, with a mocking smile, waving an attenuated hand, as the churchman and his satellite withdrew.

Thornton and the lawyer followed, but only to the ante-room. The apothecary and valet remained. The physician had paid his last visit before Antonia arrived. There had been a consultation of three great men in the afternoon, and it had been decided that nothing more could be done for the patient than to make him as comfortable as his malady would permit, and for that the apothecary's art was sufficient.

"You can wait in the next room, Davis, within call," said Kilrush, as the grave elderly man, in a queer little chestnut wig, bent over him, looking anxiously in his face, and feeling his pulse.

The throb of life beat stronger than Davis had anticipated. A wonderful constitution that could so hold out against the ravages of disease! The breathing was laboured, but there was vigour enough left to last out the long night hours—to last for days and nights yet, the medico thought, as he left the room.

The valet was moving the candles from the table by the bed, when his master stopped him.

"Leave them there: I want to see my wife's face," he said.

The man obeyed, and followed the apothecary.

Husband and wife were alone.

"On your knees, Tonia—so, with your face towards the light," Kilrush said eagerly. "So, so, love. I want to see your eyes. You are my wife, Tonia, my wife for ever—in life and after life. This perishing clay will be hidden from your sight to-morrow—*this* Kilrush will cease to be—but—" striking his breast passionately, "there is something here that will live—the mind of the man who loved you—and who dies despairing—the martyr of his insensate pride."

He grasped her hands in both his own, looking into her eyes with a wild intensity that touched the boundary line of madness; but she did not shrink from him. That wasted countenance, leaden with the dull shadow of death, was for her the dearest thing on earth, the only thing she was conscious of in this last hour.

"Tonia, do you understand?" he gasped, struggling to recover breath. "I have married you to make you mine beyond the grave. It would be the agony of hell to die and leave you to another. You are mine by this bond. I have given you all a dying lover can give—my name, my fortune. Swear that you will be true to me, that you will never give yourself to another man. That you will be my wife—mine only—till the grave unites us, and that you will lie by my side when life is done, the vault by the Shannon your only wedding bed. Promise me never to bless another with your love."

"Never, never, never, upon my honour," she said, with a depth of earnestness that satisfied him.

"On your honour—yes, for your honour means something. If the spirits of the dead are free, I shall be near you. If you break your promise, I shall haunt you—an angry ghost, pitiless, cruel. As you hope for peace, do not cheat me."

In the unnatural strength of impassioned feeling he had exhausted that reserve of energy which the apothecary had noted, and in the rush of his passionate speech he was seized with a more violent fit of coughing than any that had attacked him since Antonia's coming. She was agonized at the sight of his suffering, and hung over him with despairing love, while the attenuated frame was convulsed with the struggle for breath. The fight ended suddenly. He flung his arms round her neck, and his head fell upon her bosom, in an appalling silence. A blood-vessel had burst in that last paroxysm, and in the red stream that poured from his lips, covering Tonia's gown with crimson splashes, his life ebbed away.

A piercing shriek startled the watchers in the ante-room. Doctor, nurse, valet, rushed to the bed-chamber, to find Antonia swooning on her knees beside the bed, the dead man's arms still clasped about her neck.

"Very sudden!" said the apothecary, as Thornton appeared at the door. "I thought his lordship would have held out longer."

When Antonia recovered her senses she found herself lying on a sofa in a room she had never seen before, with the respectable-incompetent in a linen apron holding a bottle of smelling-salts to her nostrils, and an odour of burnt feathers poisoning the atmosphere. Her father was sitting by her side, holding her hand, and patting it soothingly. Some one had taken off her gown, and her shoulders were wrapped in an old shawl, lent by the incompetent. The lofty room was a well of shadow, made visible by a single candle.

She lay in apathetic silence for some minutes, not knowing where she was, or what had happened, wondering whether it was evening or morning, summer or winter. It was only when her father talked to her that she began to remember.

"My sweet child, I implore you to compose yourself," he said. "My dear friend acted nobly. Alas, was there ever so fine, so generous a nature? My Tonia is one of the richest women in London, and with a name that may rank with the highest. My Tonia! How splendidly she will become her exalted station."

Antonia heard him unheeding.

"Let me go back to him," she said, rising to her feet.

"Not yet, madam," murmured the nurse. "To-morrow morning. Not to-night, dear lady. Let me help your ladyship to undress. The next room has been prepared fur your ladyship."

"Why can't I go to him?" asked Antonia, turning to her father. "I promised to stay with him till the end."

"Alas, love, thou wast with him till the last. His arms clasped thee in death. I doubt thou wilt never forget those moments, my poor wench. God! how he loved you! And he has made you a great lady."

She turned from him in disgust.

"You harp upon that," she said. "I loved him—I loved him. I loved him—and he is dead!"

The nurse had crept away to assist in the last sad duties. Father and daughter were alone, Antonia sitting speechless, staring into vacancy, Thornton babbling feebly every now and then, irrepressible in his exultation at so strange, so miraculous a turn of fortune's wheel.

"Kilrush's death would have beggared us, but for this," he thought.

A clock on the mantelpiece struck eleven. Only eleven o'clock! 'Twas but two hours since Antonia had entered the house, and her life before she crossed that threshold seemed to her far away in the dim distance of years that were gone.

He had loved her, and had repented his cruelty. There was comfort in that thought even in the despair of an eternal parting. Was it to be eternal? He had spoken of an after-life, a consciousness that was to follow and watch her. She, the Voltairean, who had been taught to smile at man's belief in immortality, the fairy-tale of faith, the myth of all ages and all nations—she, the unbeliever, hung upon those words of his for comfort.

"If his spirit can be with me, sure he will know how fondly I love him," she said; and the first tears she shed since his death flowed at the thought.

CHAPTER IX
THE SANDS RUN DOWN

The household in St. James's Square bowed themselves before the new Lady Kilrush, and made obeisance to her, as the wheat-sheaves bowed down to Joseph in his dream. The butler remembered his master's first wife, a pretty futile creature, always gadding, following the latest craze in modish dissipations, greedy of pleasure and excitement. It had been no surprise to him when she crept through the hall door in the summer gloaming, carrying her jewels in a handbag, to join the lover who was waiting in a coach and four round the corner. It was only her husband who had been blind—blind because he was indifferent.

To the household this strange marriage was a matter for profound satisfaction.

"Her ladyship desires to retain your services, and will make no changes except on your recommendation," Mr. Thornton told the late lord's house-steward and business manager, with a superb patronage; but without any authority from Antonia, who sat in a stony silence when he talked about plans for the future, and of all the pomps and pleasures that were waiting for his beloved girl after a year of mourning.

"Oh, why do you talk of servants, and horses, and things?" she exclaimed once, with an agonized look. "Can't you see—don't you understand—that I loved him?"

"I do understand. Yes, yes, my love. I can sympathize with your grief—your natural grief—for so noble a benefactor. But when your year of widowhood is past, my Tonia will awaken to the knowledge of her power. A beauty, a fortune, a peeress, and a young widow! By Heaven, you might aspire to be the bride of royalty! *And* a temper!" muttered Thornton, as his daughter rose suddenly from her chair and walked out of the room, before he had finished his harangue.

It was only when there was a question of the funeral that the new Lady Kilrush asserted herself.

"His lordship will be buried in the family vault at Limerick," she said decisively. "Be kind enough to make all needful arrangements, Mr. Goodwin. I shall travel with the funeral *cortège*."

"My dearest Tonia—so remote a spot, so wild and unsettled a country," pleaded Thornton. "Would it not be wiser to choose a nearer resting-place, among the sepulchres of the noble and distinguished; as, for instance, at St. Paul's, Covent Garden?"

Antonia did not answer, or appear to have heard, the paternal suggestion. Her father would scarcely let her out of his sight during these long days in the darkened house. She could only escape from him by withdrawing to her own room, where Sophy was in attendance upon her; the strange and stately bed-chamber with an amber satin bed, whose curtains had shaded the guilty dreams of the runaway wife.

The bishop made her a stately visit on the second day of her solitude, and tried to convert her to Anglican Christianity in an hour's affable conversation, addressing himself to her benighted mind in the simplest forms of speech, as if she had been an ignorant child. She heard him politely; but he could not lure her into an argument, and he knew that the good seed was falling on stony ground.

When he was leaving her she gave a heart-broken sigh, and said—

"I want to believe in a life after death, for then I should hope to see him again. But I cannot—I cannot! I have been trying ever since—that night"—speaking of it as if it were a long way off—"but I cannot—I cannot!"

The bishop sat down again, and quoted St. Paul to her for a quarter of an hour; but those sublime words could not convince her. The cynic's blighting sneer had withered all that womanhood has of instinctive piety—of upward-looking reverence for the Christian ideal. There is no fire so scathing, no poison so searching, as the light ridicule of a master-mind. The woman who had been educated by Voltaire could not find hope or comfort in the great apostle's argument for immortality. Was not Paul himself only *trying* to believe?

"Dear lady, if I send you Bishop Butler's 'Analogy'—the most convincing argument for that future life we all long for—will you promise me to read it?"

"I will read anything you please to send me, my lord; only I cannot promise to believe what I read."

The funeral train left St. James's Square in the cool grey of a summer dawn. It consisted of but three carriages: the hearse, with all its pompous decorations, and drawn by six post-horses, a coach and six for Antonia and her father, and a second coach for the steward, the valet, Louis, and Mrs. Sophia Potter, who tried to keep her countenance composed in a becoming sadness, but could not help considering the journey a treat, and occasionally forgetting that dismal carriage which led the procession.

They travelled by the Great Bath Road, halting at Hounslow for breakfast in the dust and dew of an exquisite morning; and it may be that Mr. Thornton, sitting at a well-furnished table by an open window overlooking all the bustle and gaiety of coaches and post-chaises arriving or departing, found it almost as hard a matter as Sophy did to maintain the proper dejection in voice and aspect, and not to enjoy himself too obviously.

It was not so much the unwonted luxury of his surroundings as the unwonted respect of his fellow-men that inspired him. To have innkeeper and waiters hanging about him, as if he had been a prince—he, whom mine host of the Red Lion had ever treated on terms of equality; or if the scale had turned either way 'twas mine host who gave himself the privilege of insolence to a customer who was often in his debt.

Antonia, shut in a room abovestairs with her maid, could not as yet taste the pleasures of her altered station. It was her father who derived enjoyment from her title, rolling it in his mouth with indescribable gusto—

"Tell her ladyship, my daughter, that her coach is at the door. Lady Kilrush desires to lose no time on the road. Louis, see that her ladyship's smelling-salts are in the coach-pocket, and that her ladyship's woman does not keep her waiting."

Louis, and Mr. Goodwin, the steward, had their little jests about Mr. Thornton; but Antonia had commanded their respect from the moment when she gave her instructions about the funeral. The capacity for command was hers, a quality that is in the character of man or woman, and which neither experience nor teaching can impart.

The journey to Bristol occupied four days, and Mr. Thornton enjoyed himself more and more at the great inns on the Great Bath Road, eating his dinner and his supper in the luxurious seclusion of a private sitting-room, tête-à-tête with an obsequious landlord or a loquacious head waiter, whose conversation kept him amused; and perhaps drinking somewhat deeper on account of Antonia's absence. Throughout the journey she had kept herself in strict seclusion, attended only by Sophy. All that the inn-servants saw of Lady Kilrush was a tall woman in deepest mourning who followed the head chambermaid to her room, and did not reappear till her coach was ready to start on the next stage.

From Bristol the dismal convoy crossed to Queenstown in a Government yacht, with a fair wind, and no ill-adventure. At Queenstown the monotonous road-journey was resumed in hired coaches; and late on the third evening the *cortège* drew up before Kilrush House, in the city of Limerick, a large red-brick house with its back to the river, hard by the bishop's palace, built before the battle of the Boyne.

Entering this melancholy mansion, which had been left in the care of a superannuated butler and his feeble old wife for nearly thirty years, Mr. Thornton's spirits sank to zero. He had been indisposed during the sea-voyage, nor had the accommodation at Irish inns satisfied a taste enervated by the luxuries of the Great Bath Road; but the Irish landlords had offered him cheerful society, and the Irish grog had sent him merrily to his bed. But, oh! the gloom of Kilrush House in the summer twilight; the horror of that closed chamber where the form of the coffin showed vaguely under the voluminous velvet of the pall; and where tall wax candles shed a pale light upon vacant walls and scanty furniture, all that there had been of beauty and value in the town house of the Lords of Kilrush having been removed to St. James's Square when the late lord married.

The funeral was solemnized on the following night, a torch-light procession, in which the lofty hearse, with its nodding plumes and pompous decoration of black velvet and silver, showed gigantic in the fitful flare of the torches, carried by a long train of horsemen who had assembled from far and near to do honour to the last Lord Kilrush.

He had been an absentee for the greater part of his life; but the name was held in high esteem, and perhaps his countrymen had more respect for him dead than they would have felt had he appeared among them living. The news of the funeral train journeying over sea and land, and of the beautiful bride accompanying her dead bridegroom, had gone through the South of Ireland, and men of rank and family had travelled long distances to assist in those last honours. It was half a century since such a funeral *cortège* had been seen in Limerick. And while the gentry came in hundreds to the ceremony, from the Irish town and the English town the rabble poured in throngs that must have been reckoned by thousands, Mr. Thornton thought, as he gazed from the coach window at a sea of faces: young women with streaming hair, spectral faces of old crones, their grey locks bound with red cotton handkerchiefs, rags, and semi-nakedness—all seeming phantasmagoric in the flickering light of the moving torches, all dreadful of aspect to the *habitué* of London streets.

But even more terrible than those wan faces and wild hair were the voices of that strange multitude, the wailing and sobbing of the women,

The Infidel | 89

the keening of the men, shrieks and lamentations, soul-freezing as the cry of the screech-owl or the howling of famished wolves. Thornton shrank shuddering into a corner of the mourning coach, which he shared with the chief mourner—that mute, motionless figure with shrouded face, in which he scarce recognized his daughter's familiar form.

The horror of the scene deepened when they entered the church, that wild crew pressing after them, thrust back from the door with difficulty by the funeral attendants. The distance to be traversed had been short, but the coaches had moved at a foot pace, with a halt every now and then, as the crowd became impassable. To Thornton the ceremony seemed to have lasted for half the night, and it surprised him to hear the church clock strike twelve as they left the vault where George Frederick Delafield, nineteenth Baron Kilrush, was laid with his ancestors.

It was over. Oh, the relief of it! This tedious business which had occupied nearly a fortnight was ended at last, and his daughter belonged to him again. He put his arm round her in the coach presently, and she sank weeping upon his breast. She had been tearless throughout the ceremony in the cathedral, and had maintained a statuesque composure of countenance, pale as marble against the flowing folds of a crape veil that draped her from brow to foot.

"Let us get back to London, love," he said. "The horrors of this place would kill us if we stopped here much longer."

"I want to see the house where he was born," she said.

"Well, 'tis a natural desire, perhaps, for 'tis your own house now, Kilrush Abbey. The Abbey is but a ruin, I doubt; but there is a fine stone mansion and a park—all my Antonia's property—but a deucedly expensive place to keep up, I'll warrant."

She did not tell him that her only interest in the Irish estate was on the dead man's account. Nothing she could say would check him in his jubilation at her change of fortune. It was best to let him enjoy himself in his own fashion. Their ages and places seemed reversed. It was she that had the gravity of mature years, the authority of a parent; while in him there was the inconsequence of a child, and the child's delight in trivial things.

She had seen the starved faces in the crowd, the grey hairs and scanty rags; and she went next day with Sophy on a voyage of discovery in the squalid alleys of the English and the Irish towns, scattering silver among the poverty-stricken creatures who crowded round her as she moved from door to door. What blessings, what an eloquence of grateful hearts, were poured upon her as she distributed handfuls of shillings, fat crown pieces, showers of sixpences that the children fought for in the gutters—an injudicious form of charity, perhaps, but it gave bread to the hungry, and some relief to her over-charged heart. She had never enjoyed the luxury of giving before. It was the first pleasure she had known since her marriage, the first distraction for a mind that had dwelt with agonizing intensity upon one image.

Mr. Goodwin, the late lord's steward, was one of those highly-trained servants who can render the thinking process a sinecure in the case of an indolent master. He had found thought and money for the funeral ceremony, and he showed himself equally capable in arranging Antonia's visit to the scene of her husband's birth and childhood, the cradle of her husband's race.

At Kilrush, as in Limerick, she found a deserted mansion, maintained with some show of decency by half a dozen servants. Over all there brooded that melancholy shadow which falls upon a house where the glad and moving life of a family is wanting. One spot only showed in the beauty and brightness of summer, a rose-garden in front of a small drawing-room, a garden of less than an acre, surrounded by tall ilex hedges, neatly clipped.

"'Tis the garden-parlour made for his lordship's mother when she came as a bride to Kilrush," Goodwin told Antonia, "and his lordship was very strict in his orders that everything should be maintained as her ladyship left it."

In those days of mourning and regret, Antonia preferred the picturesque seclusion of Kilrush to any home that could have been offered to her. The fine park, with its old timber and views over sea and river, pleased her. She loved the ruined abbey, dark with ages, and mantled with ivy of more than a century's growth. The spacious dwelling-house, with its long suites of rooms and shadowy corridors—a house built when Ormond was ruling in Ireland, and when the Delafields lived half the year at their country seat, and divided the other half-year between Limerick and Dublin—the old-fashioned furniture, the family portraits by painters whose fame had never travelled across the Irish Channel, and most of all the gardens, screened by a belt of sea-blown firs, pleased their new owner, and she proposed to remain there till winter.

"My dearest child, would you bury yourself alive in this desolate corner of the earth?" cried Thornton, whose nerves had hardly recovered from the horrors of the funeral, and who could not sleep without a rushlight for fear of the Delafield ghosts, who had indeed more than once in this shattered condition wished himself back in his two-pair chamber in Rupert Buildings. "Was there ever so unreasonable a fancy? You to seclude yourself from humanity! You who ought to be preparing yourself to shine in the *beau monde*, and who have still to acquire the accomplishments needful to your exalted station! The solid education, which it was my pride and delight to impart, might suffice for Miss Thornton; but Lady Kilrush cannot dispense with the elegant arts of a woman of fashion—the guitar, the harpsichord, to take part in a catch or a glee, or to walk a minuet, to play at faro, to ride, to drive a pair of ponies."

"Oh, pray stop, sir. I shall never be that kind of woman. You have taught me to find happiness in books, and have made me independent of trivial pleasures."

"Books are the paradise of the neglected and the poor, the solace of the prisoner for debt, the comfort of the hopeless invalid; but the accomplishments you call trivial are the serious business of people of rank and fortune, and to be without them is the stamp of the parvenu. My love, with your fortune, you ought to winter in Paris or Rome, to make the Grand Tour, like a young nobleman. Why should our sex have all the privileges of education?"

The word Rome acted like a spell. Antonia's childish dreams—while life in the future lay before her in a romantic light—had been of Italy. She had longed to see the home of her Italian mother.

"I should like to visit Italy by-and-by, sir," she said, "if you think you could bear so long a journey."

"My love, I am an old traveller. Nothing on the road comes amiss to me—Alps, Apennines, Italian inns, Italian post-chaises—so long as there is cash enough to pay the innkeeper."

"My dear father, I shall ever desire to do what pleases you," Antonia answered gently; "and though I love the quiet life here, I am ready to go wherever you wish to take me."

"For your own advantage, my beloved child, I consider foreign travel of the utmost consequence—*imprimis*, a winter in Paris."

"'Tis Italy I long for, sir."

"Paris for style and fashion is of more importance. We would move to Italy in the spring. Indeed, my love, you make no sacrifice in leaving Kilrush, for Goodwin assures me we should all be murdered here before Christmas."

"Mr. Goodwin hates the Irish. My heart goes out to my husband's people."

"You can engage your chairmen from this neighbourhood by-and-by, and even your running-footmen. There are fine-looking fellows among them that might take kindly to civilization; and they have admirable legs."

Having gained his point, Mr. Thornton did not rest till he carried his daughter back to London, where there was much to be done with the late lord's lawyers, who were surprised to discover a fine business capacity in this beautiful young woman whose marriage had so romantic a flavour.

"Whether she has dropped from the skies or risen from the gutter, she is the cleverest wench of her years I ever met with, as well as the handsomest," said the senior partner in the old-established firm of Hanfield and Bonham, conveyancers and attorneys. "The way in which she puts a question and grasps the particulars of her estate would do credit to a king's counsel."

Everything was settled before November, and good Mrs. Potter endowed with a pension which would enable her to live comfortably in the cottage at Putney without the labour of letting lodgings. Sophy was still to be Antonia's "woman;" but Mr. Thornton advised his daughter while in Paris to engage an accomplished Parisienne for the duties of the toilet.

"Sophy is well enough to fetch and carry for you," he said, "and as you have known her so long 'tis like enough you relish her company; but to dress your head and look after your gowns you need the skill and experience of a trained lady's-maid."

Thornton was enchanted at the idea of a winter in Paris. He had seen much of that gay city when he was a travelling tutor, and had loved all its works and ways. His sanguine mind had not considered the difference between twenty-five and the wrong side of fifty, and he hoped to taste all the pleasures of his youth with an unabated gusto. Alas! he found after a week in the Rue St. Honoré that the only pleasures which retained all their flavour—which had, indeed, gained by the passage of years—were the pleasures of the table. He could still enjoy a hand at faro or lansquenet; but he could no longer sit at cards half the night and grow more excited and intent as darkness drew nearer dawn. He could still admire a slim waist and a neat ankle, a *mignonne frimousse* under a black silk hood; but his heart beat no faster at the sight of joyous living beauty than at a picture by Greuze. In a word, he discovered that there is one thing wealth cannot buy for man or woman: the freshness of youth.

His daughter allowed him to draw upon her fortune with unquestioning liberality. It was a delight to her to think that he need toil no more, forgetting how much of their literary labours of late years had been performed by her, and how self-indulgent a life the easy-going Bill Thornton had led between Putney and St. Martin's Lane.

Antonia's desire in coming to Paris had been to lead a life of seclusion, seeing no one but the professors whom she might engage to complete her education; but a society in which beauty and wealth were ever potent was not likely to ignore the existence of the lovely Lady Kilrush, whose romantic marriage had been recorded in the *Parisian Gazette*, and whose establishment at a fashionable hotel in the Rue St. Honoré was duly announced in all the newspapers. Visits and invitations crowded upon her; and although she excused herself from all large assemblies and festive gatherings on account of her mourning, she was too much interested in the great minds of the age to deny herself to the Marquise du Deffant, in whose salon she met d'Alembert, Montesquieu, and Diderot, then at the summit of his renown, and an ardent admirer of English literature. With him she discussed Richardson, whose consummate romances she adored, and whose friendship she hoped to cultivate on her return to London. With him she talked of Voltaire, whose arcadian life at Crecy had come to a tragical close by the sudden death of Madame du Châtelet, and who, having quarrelled with his royal admirer, Frederick, was now a wanderer in Germany—forbidden to return to Paris, where his classic tragedies were being nightly illustrated by the genius of Lekain and Mdlle. Clairon.

To move in that refined and spiritual circle was a revelation of a new world to Thornton's daughter, a world in which everybody had some touch of that charm of mind and fancy which she had loved in Kilrush. The conversation of Parisian wits and philosophers reminded her of those vanished hours in the second-floor parlour above St. Martin's Church. Alas, how far away those lost hours seemed as she looked back at them, how infinitely sweeter than anything that Parisian society could give her!

The people whose conversation pleased her most were the men and women who had known her husband and would talk to her of him. It was this attraction which had drawn her to the clever lady whose life had been lately shadowed by the affliction of blindness, a calamity which she bore with admirable courage and resignation. Antonia loved to sit at Madame du Deffant's feet in the wintry dusk, they two alone in the modest salon which the widowed marquise occupied in the convent of St. Joseph, having given up her hotel soon after her husband's death. It pleased her to talk of the friends of her youth, and Kilrush, who was of her own age, had been an especial favourite.

"He was the most accomplished Englishman—except my young friend Walpole—that I ever knew," she said; "and although he had not all Walpole's wit, he had more than Walpole's charm. I look back along the vista of twenty troublesome years, and see him as if it were yesterday—a young man coming into my salon with a letter from the English ambassador. Dieu! how handsome he was then! That pale complexion, those classic features, and those dark grey eyes with black lashes—Irish eyes, I have heard them called! Thou shouldst be proud, child, to have been loved by such a man. And is it really true, now—thou needst have no reserve with an old woman—is it true that you and he had never been more than—friends, before that tragic hour in which the bishop joined your hands?"

"I am sorry, madame, that you can think it necessary to ask such a question."

"But, my dear, there was nothing in the world further from my thoughts than to wound you. Then I will put my question otherwise and again, between friends, in all candour. Are you not sorry, now that he is gone, now nothing that you can do could bring back one touch of his hand, one sound of his voice—does it not make you repent a little that Fate and you were not kinder to him?"

"No, madame, I cannot be sorry for having been guided by my own conscience."

There were tears in her voice, but the tone was steady.

"What! you have a conscience—you who believe no more in God than that audacious atheist, Diderot?"

"My conscience is a part of myself. It does not live in heaven."

"What a Roman you are! I swear you were born two thousand years too late, and should have been contemporary with Lucretia. Well, thou hadst a remarkable man for thy half-hour husband, and thou didst work a miracle in bringing such a *roué* to tie the knot; for I have heard him rail at marriage with withering cynicism, and swear that not for the greatest and loveliest princess in France would he wear matrimonial fetters."

"Nay, chère marquise, I pray you say no ill of him."

"Mon enfant, I am praising him. 'Twas but natural he should hate the marriage tie, having been so unlucky in his first wife. To have been handsome, accomplished, high-born, a prince among men, and to have been abandoned for a wretch in every way his inferior——"

"Did you know the lady, madame?"

"Yes, child, I saw her often in the first year of her marriage—a she-profligate, brimming over with a sensual beauty, like an over-ripe peach; a Rubens woman, white and red, and vapid and futile; conspicuous in every assembly by her gaudy dress, loud voice, and inane laughter."

"How could he have chosen such a wife?"

"'Twas she chose him. There are several versions of the story, but there is none that would not offend my Lucretia's modesty."

"He had the air of a man who had been unhappy," said Antonia, with a sigh.

"There is a kind of restless gaiety in your *roué* which is a sure sign of inward misery," replied the friend of philosophers. "Happiness tends ever to repose."

Mr. Thornton did not take kindly to the wits and philosophers of Madame du Deffant's circle. Perhaps he had an inward conviction that they saw through him, and measured his vices and weaknesses by a severe standard. The taint of the unforgotten jail hung about him, a humiliating sense of inferiority; while he was unfitted for the elegancies and refinements of modish society by those happy-go-lucky years in which he had lived in a kind of shabby luxury: the luxury of late hours, shirt-sleeves, clay pipes, and gin; the luxury of bad manners and self-indulgence.

After attending his daughter upon some of her early visits to the Convent of St. Joseph, he fell back upon a society more congenial, in the taverns and coffee-houses, where he consorted with noisy politicians and needy journalists and authors, furbished up his French, which was good, and picked up the philosophical jargon of the day, and was again a Socrates among companions whose drink he was ever ready to pay for.

Antonia devoted the greater part of her days and nights to self-improvement, practised the harpsichord under an eminent professor, and showed a marked capacity for music, though never hoping to do more than to amuse her lonely hours with the simpler sonatinas and variations of the composers she admired. She read Italian with one professor and Spanish with another; attended lectures on natural science, now the rage in Paris, where people raved about Buffon's "Théorie de la Terre." Her only relaxation was an occasional visit to the marquise, and to two other salons where a grave and cultured society held itself aloof from the frivolous pleasures of court and fashion; or an evening at the Comédie Française, where she saw Lekain in most of his famous *rôles*.

With the advent of spring she pleaded for the realization of her most cherished dream, and began to prepare for the journey to Italy, in spite of some reluctance on her father's part, whose free indulgence in the pleasures of French cookery and French wines had impaired a constitution that had thriven on Mrs. Potter's homely dishes, and had seemed impervious to gin. He looked older by ten years since he had lived as a rich man. He was nervous and irritable, he whose easy temper had passed for goodness of heart, and had won his daughter's affection. He was tormented by a restless impatience to realize all that wealth can yield of pleasure and luxury. He was miserable from the too ardent desire to be happy, and shortened his life by his eagerness to live. The theatres, the puppet-shows, the gambling-houses, the taverns where they danced—at every place where amusement was promised, he had been a visitor, and almost everywhere he had found satiety and disgust. How enchanting had been that Isle of Calypso, this Circean Cavern, when he first came to Paris, a tutor of five and twenty, the careless mentor of a lad of eighteen; how gross, how dull, how empty and foolish, to the man who was nearing his sixtieth birthday!

He had fallen back upon the monotony of the nightly rendezvous at the Café Procope, seeing the same faces, hearing the same talk—an assembly differing only in detail from his friends of "The Portico"—and it vexed him to discover that this was all his daughter's wealth could buy for him in the most wonderful city in the world.

"I am an old man," he told himself. "Money is very little use when one is past fifty. I fall asleep at the playhouse, for I hear but half the actors say. If I pay a neatly turned compliment to a handsome woman, she laughs at me. I am only fit to sit in a tavern, and rail at kings and ministers, with a pack of worn-out wretches like myself."

Mr. Thornton and his daughter started for Italy in the second week of April, with a sumptuosity that was but the customary style of persons of rank, but which delighted the Grub-Street hack, conscious of every detail in their altered circumstances. They travelled with a suite of six, consisting of Sophy and a French maid, provided by Madame du Deffant, and rejoicing in the name of Rodolphine. Mr. Thornton's personal attendant was the late lord's faithful Louis, who was excellent as valet and nurse, but who, being used to the quiet magnificence of Kilrush, had an ill-concealed contempt for a master who locked up his money, and was uneasy about the safety of his trinkets. With them went a young medical man whom Antonia had engaged to take charge of her father's health—a needless precaution, Mr. Thornton protested, but which was justified by the fact that he was often ailing, and was nervous and apprehensive about himself. A courier and a footman completed the party, which filled two large carriages, and required relays of eight horses.

Antonia delighted in the journey through strange places and picturesque scenery, with all the adventures of the road, and the variety of inns, where every style of entertainment, from splendour to squalor, was to be met with. Here for the first time she lost the aching sense of regret that had been with her ever since the death of Kilrush. The only drawback was her father's discontent, which increased with every stage of the journey, albeit the stages were shortened day after day to suit his humour, and he was allowed to stay as long as he liked at any inn where he pronounced the arrangements fairly comfortable. It was a wonder to his anxious daughter to see how he, who had been cheerful and good-humoured in his shabby parlour at Rupert Buildings, and had rarely grumbled at Mrs. Potter's homely cuisine, was now as difficult to please as the most patrician sybarite on the road. She bore with all his caprices, and indulged all his whims. She had seen a look in his face of late that chilled her, like the sound of a funeral bell. The time would come—soon perhaps—when she would look back and reproach herself for not having been kind enough.

They travelled by way of Mont Cenis and Turin, and so to Florence, where they arrived late in May, having spent nearly six weeks on the road. It grieved Antonia to see that her father was exhausted by his travels, in spite of the care that had been taken of him. He sank into his armchair with the air of a man who had come to the end of a journey that was to be final.

Florence was at its loveliest season, the streets full of flowers, and carriages, and well-dressed people rejoicing in the gaiety of balls and operas before retiring to the perfumed shades of their villa gardens among the wooded hills above the city. To Antonia the place was full of enchantment, but her anxiety about her father cast a shadow over the scene.

Her most eager desire in coming to Italy had been to see her mother's country, and to see something of her mother's kindred; but Thornton had hitherto evaded all her questions, putting her off with a fretful impatience.

"There is time enough to talk of them when we are in their neighbourhood, Tonia," he said. "Your mother had very few relations, and those who survive will have forgotten her. Why do you trouble yourself about them? They have never taken any trouble about you."

"I want to see some one who loved my mother, some one of her country and her kin. Can't you understand how I feel about her, sir, the mother whose face I cannot remember, but who loved me when I was unconscious of her love? Oh, to think that she held me in her arms and kissed me, and that I cared nothing, knew nothing! and now I would give ten years of my life for one of those kisses."

"Alas, my romantic child! Ah, Tonia, she was a lovely woman, the noblest, the sweetest of her sex. And you are like her. Take care of your beauty. Women in this country age early."

"You have never told me my mother's maiden name, or where she lived before you married her."

"Well, you shall visit her birthplace; 'tis a villa among the hills above the Lake of Como, a romantic spot. We will go there after Florence. I want to see Florence. 'Twas a place I enjoyed almost as much as Paris, when I was a young man. There were balls and assemblies every night, a regiment of handsome women, suppers and champagne. We were never abed till the morning, and never up till the afternoon."

Antonia returned to the subject after they had spent a fortnight in Florence, and when the weather was growing too hot for a continued residence there. Mr. Daniels, the young doctor, and an Italian physician, had agreed in consultation that the sooner Mr. Thornton removed to a cooler climate the better for his chance of improvement. Daniels suggested Vallombrosa, where the monks would accommodate them in the monastery. The physician advised the Baths of Lucca. The patient objected to both places. He wanted to go to Leghorn, and get back to London by sea.

"I am sick to death of Italy; and I believe a sea voyage would make me a strong man again. No man ought to be done for at my age."

Antonia was ready to do anything that medical science might suggest, but found it very difficult to please a patient who was seldom of the same mind two days running.

While doctors and patient debated, death threw the casting vote. Florentine sunshine is sometimes the treacherous ally of searching winds— those Italian winds which we know less by their poetical names than by their resemblance to a British north-easter. Mr. Thornton caught cold in a drive to Fiesole, and passed in a few hours to that region of half consciousness, the shadow-land betwixt life and death, where he could be no longer questioned as to the things he knew on earth.

He died after three days' fever, with his hand clasped in his daughter's, and he died without telling her the name of the villa where his Italian wife had lived, or the name she had borne before he married her.

Lady Kilrush mourned her father better than many a better man has been mourned. She laid him in an English graveyard outside the city walls; and then, being in love with this divine Italy whose daughter she considered herself, she retired to a convent near Fiesole, where the nuns were in the habit of taking English lodgers, and did not object to a wealthy heretic. Here in the shade of ancient cloisters, and in gardens older than Milton, she spent the summer, leaving only in the late autumn for Rome, where Louis had engaged a handsome apartment for her in the Corso, and where she lived in as much seclusion as she was allowed to enjoy till the following May, delighting in the city which had filled so large a place in her girlish daydreams.

"Never, never, never did I think to see those walls," she said, when her coach emerged from a narrow alley and she found herself in front of the Colosseum.

"'Tis a fine large building, but 'tis a pity the roof is off," said Sophy.

"What, child, did you think 'twas like Ranelagh, a covered place for dancing?"

"I don't know what else it could be good for, unless it was a market," retorted Sophy. "I never saw such a dirty town since I was born, and the stink of it is enough to poison a body."

Miss Potter lived through a Roman winter with her nose perpetually tilted in chronic disgust; but she was delighted with the carnival, and with the admiration her own neat little person evoked, as she tripped about the dirty streets, with her gown pinned high, and a petticoat short enough to show slim ankles in green silk stockings. She admitted that the churches were handsomer than any she had seen in London, but vowed they were all alike, and that she would not know St. Maria Marjorum from St. John Latterend.

In those days, when only the best and worst people travelled, and the humdrum classes had to stay at home, English society in Rome was aristocratic and exclusive; but Antonia's romantic story having got wind, she was called upon by several English women of rank who wished to cultivate the beautiful parvenu. Here, as in Paris, however, she excused herself from visiting on account of her mourning.

"My dear child, do you mean to wear weeds for ever?" cried the lovely Lady Diana Lestrange, on her honeymoon with a second husband, after being divorced from the first. "Sure his lordship is dead near two years."

"Does your ladyship think two years very long to mourn for a friend to whom I owe all I have ever known of love and friendship?"

"I think it a great deal too long for a fine woman to disguise herself in crape and bombazine, and mope alone of an evening in the pleasantest city in Europe. You must be dying of *ennui* for want of congenial society."

"I am too much occupied to be dull, madam. I am trying to carry on my education, so as to be more worthy the station to which my husband raised me."

"I swear you are a paragon! Well, we shall meet in town next winter, perhaps, if you do not join the blue-stocking circle, the Montagus and Carters, or turn religious, and spend all your evenings listening to a cushion-thumping Methodist at Lady Huntingdon's pious *soirées*. We have all sorts of diversions in town, Lady Kilrush, besides Ranelagh and Vauxhall."

"Your ladyship may be sure I shall prefer Ranelagh to the Oxford Methodists. I was not educated to love cant."

"Oh, the creatures are sincere, some of them, I believe; sincere fanatics. And the Wesleys have good blood. Their mother was an Annesley, Lord Valentia's great granddaughter. The Wesleys are gentlemen; and I doubt that is why people don't rave about them as they do about Whitefield, who was drawer in a Gloucester tavern."

Lady Kilrush went back to England in May, stopping at the Lake of Como on her way. She spent nearly a month on the shores of that lovely lake, visiting all the little towns along the coast, and exploring the white-walled villages upon the hills. She would have given so much to know in which of those villas whose gardens sloped to the blue water, or nestled in the wooded solitudes above the lake, had been her mother's birthplace.

Thornton had amused his daughter in her childhood by a romantic version of his marriage, in which his wife appeared as a lovely young patrician, whom he had stolen from her stately home. His fancy had expatiated upon a moonlit elopement, the escaping lovers pursued by an infuriated father. The romance had pleased the child, and he hardly meant to lie when he invented it. He let the lambent flame of his imagination play around common facts. 'Twas true that his wife was lovely, and that he had stolen her from an angry father, whose helping hand she had been from childhood. The patrician blood, the villa were but details, the airy adornment of the tutor's love-story.

Ignorant even of her mother's family name, it seemed hopeless for Antonia to discover the place of her birth; but it pleased her to linger in that lovely scene at the loveliest season of the year, to grow familiar with the country to which she belonged by reason of that maternal tie. She peered into the churches, thinking on the threshold of each that it was in such a temple her mother had worshipped in unquestioning piety, believing all the priests bade her believe.

"Perhaps it is happiest to believe in fables, and never to have learnt to reason or doubt," she thought, seeing the kneeling figures in the shadowy chapels, the heads reverently bent, the lips whispering devout supplications, as the beads of the rosary slipped through the sunburnt fingers—a prayer for every bead.

The house in St. James's Square had been prepared for its new mistress with a retinue in accordance with the statelier habits of the days of Walpole and Chesterfield, when a lady of rank and fortune required six running footmen to her chair, with a black page to walk in advance of it, and a mass of overfed flesh to sit in a hooded leather sentry-box in her hall and snub plebeian visitors.

Antonia had instructed her steward to keep all the old servants who were worthy of her confidence, and to engage as many new ones as might be necessary; and so the household had all the air of a long-settled establishment where the servants had nothing to learn, and where the measure of their own importance was their mistress's dignity, of which they would abate no jot or tittle. It is only the hireling of yesterday, the domestic nomad, who disparages his master or mistress.

Jewellers, milliners, mantua-makers, shoemakers, hairdressers flocked about Lady Kilrush the day after her arrival from Paris. All the harpies of Pall Mall and St. James's Street had been on the watch for her coming. Pictures, bronzes, porcelains, nodding mandarins, and Canton screens were brought for her inspection. The hall would have been like a fair but for the high-handed porter, whose fleshy person trembled with indignation at these assaults, and who sent fashionable shopmen to the rightabout as if they had been negro slaves. Thanks to his *savoir faire*, her ladyship was able to spend her morning in peace, and to see only the tradespeople who were necessary to her establishment. She gave her orders with a royal liberality, but she would have nothing forced upon her by officiousness.

"I would rather not hear about your London fashions, Mrs. Meddlebury," she told her respectable British dressmaker. "I have come straight from Paris, and know what the Dauphine is wearing. You will make my *negligés* and my sacques as I bid you; and be sure you send to Ireland for a tabinet and a poplin, as I desire sometimes to wear gowns of Irish manufacture."

CHAPTER X
A DUTY VISIT

Antonia's appearance at Leicester House was the occasion of a flight of newspaper paragraphs.

The *St. James's Evening Post* reminded its readers of the romantic marriage of a well-known Hibernian nobleman, "which we were the first to announce to the town, and of which full particulars were given in our columns; a freak of fancy on the part of the last Baron Kilrush, amply justified by the dazzling beauty of the young lady who made her curtsey to the Princess Dowager last week, sponsored by Lady Margaret Laroche, a connection of the late Lord Kilrush, and, as everybody knows, a star of the first magnitude in the *beau monde*." Here followed a description of the lady's personal appearance: her gown of white tabinet with a running pattern of shamrocks worked in silver, and the famous Kilrush pearls, which had not been seen for a quarter of a century.

Lloyd's was more piquant, and had recourse to initials. "It is not generally known that the lovely young widow who was the cynosure of neighbouring eyes at St. James's on his Majesty's birthday, began life in very humble circumstances. Her father, Mr. T— —n, was bred for the Church, but spent his youth as an itinerant tutor to lads of fashion, and did not prove an ornament to his sacred calling. He brought his clerical career to a hasty close by an ill-judged indulgence of the tender passion. His elopement with a buxom wench from a Lincolnshire homestead would have caused him less trouble had not his natural gallantry induced him to relieve his sweetheart of the burden of her father's cash-box, for which mistaken kindness he suffered two years' seclusion among highwaymen and pickpockets. The beautiful Lady K— —h was educated in the classics and in modern literature by this clever but unprincipled parent; and she is said to owe an independence of all religious dogma to the parental training. There is no such uncompromising infidel as an unfrocked priest."

The *Daily Journal* had its scraps of information. "A little bird has told us that the new beauty, whose appearance on the birthday so fluttered their dovecotes at St. James's Palace, spent her early youth in third-floor lodgings in a paved court adjoining St. Martin's Lane, where the young lady and her father drudged for the booksellers. 'Tis confidently asserted that this lovely *bas-bleu* had a considerable share in several comedies and burlettas produced by Mr. Garrick under the ostensible authorship of her father. 'Tis rarely that genius, beauty, and wealth are to be found united in a widow of three and twenty summers. How rich a quarry for our fops and fortune-hunters!"

The *St. James's* held forth again on the same theme. "Among the numerous motives which conjecture has put forward for the mysterious marriage in high life some two years ago—the most interesting particulars of which we alone were able to supply—the real reason has been entirely overlooked. Our more intimate knowledge of the *beau monde* enables us to hit the right nail on the head. By his deathbed union with the penniless daughter of a Grub-Street hack, Lord K—— was able to gratify his hatred of the young gentleman who ought to have been his heir. We are credibly informed that this unfortunate youth, first cousin of the brilliant but eccentric Irish peer, is now subsisting on a pittance in a labourer's cottage on a common near Richmond Park."

This last contribution to the literature of gossip seriously affected Antonia. She had read all the rest with a sublime indifference. She had been behind the scenes, and knew how such paragraphs were concocted—had, indeed, written a good deal of fashionable intelligence herself, collected by Mr. Thornton sometimes from the chairmen waiting at street corners, in those summer evening walks with his daughter, or in the grey autumn nights, when the town had a picturesque air in the long perspective of oil lamps that looked like strings of topazes hung upon the darkness. The Grub-Street hack had not thought it beneath him to converse in an affable humour with a chairman or a running footman, and so to discover how the most beautiful duchess in England was spending the evening, how much she lost at faro last night, and who it was handed her to her chair.

Antonia threw aside the papers with a contemptuous smile. They stabbed her to the heart when they maligned her dead father; but she was wise enough to refrain from any attempted refutation of a slander in which, alas! there might be a grain of truth. Her father was at rest. The malicious paragraph could not hurt him, and for her own part she had a virile stoicism which helped her to bear such attacks. She looked back at her journalistic work, and was thankful to remember that she had never written anything ill-natured, even when her father had urged her to give more point to a paragraph, and to insinuate that a lover had paid the duchess's losses at cards, or that there had been a curious shuffling of new-born babies in the ducal mansion. Her sprightliest lines had shone with a lambent flame that hurt nobody.

Her husband's rightful heir starving in a hovel! That was a concrete fact with which she could cope. But for the motive of that deathbed bond, she knew better than the hack scribbler; she knew that a passionate love, baulked and disappointed in life, had triumphed in the hour of death. He had bound her to himself to the end of her existence, in the sublime tyranny of that love which had not realized its strength till too late.

And that he should be supposed to have been actuated by a petty spite—an old man's hatred of a youthful heir!

"What reptiles these scribblers are!" she thought, "that will sell lies by the guinea's worth, and think themselves honest if they give full measure."

She sent for Goodwin.

"You must know all about his lordship's family," she said. "Can you tell me of any cousin whom he may be said to have disinherited?"

"There is no one who could be rightly called his lordship's heir, my lady; but there is a young gentleman, a cousin, only son to a sister of his lordship's father, who may at one time have expected to come into some of the property, the entail having expired, and there being no direct heir in existence."

"Had this gentleman offended his lordship?"

"Yes, my lady. He behaved very badly indeed, and his lordship forbade him the house."

"Was he dissipated—a spendthrift?"

"No, my lady. I don't think his lordship would have taken that so ill in a fine young man with a wealthy mother. It would have been only natural for him to be a man of pleasure. But Mr. Stobart's conduct was very bad indeed. He left the army ——"

"A coward?"

"No, my lady, I don't think we can call him that. He was singled out for his dash and spirit in the retreat at Fontenoy, where he saved the life of his superior officer at the risk of his own. But soon after his regiment came home he took up religion, left off powdering his hair, sold his commission, and gave the money to the building fund for Wesley's Chapel in the City Road."

"He must be a foolish fellow, I think," said Antonia, who was not fascinated by this description. "And was his lordship seriously offended by this conduct?"

"He didn't like the young gentleman turning Methodist, my lady; but that was not the worst."

"Indeed?"

"Mr. Stobart made a low marriage."

"What? Did he marry a woman of bad character?"

"I don't think there was anything against the young woman's *character*, my lady; but she was very low, a servant of Mrs. Stobart's, I believe, and a Methodist. John Wesley's influence was at the bottom of it all. There's no reckoning the harm those Oxford Methodists have done in high families. Well, there's Lady Huntingdon! There's no need to say more than that."

"But how comes this gentleman to be in poor circumstances, as the *St. James's Post* states, if his mother is rich?"

"Oh, my lady, the honourable Mrs. Stobart was quite as angry as his lordship, and she married Sir David Lanigan, an Irish baronet, who courted her when she was a girl at Kilrush Abbey. Your ladyship would notice her portrait in the long drawing-room at Kilrush."

"Yes, yes, I remember—a handsome face, with a look of his lordship. Then you have reason to believe that Mr. Stobart is living in poverty, as a consequence of his love-match?"

Her cheek crimsoned as she spoke, recalling that bitterest hour of her life in which Kilrush had told her that he could not marry her. That inexorable pride—the pride of the name-worshippers—had darkened this young man's existence, as it had darkened hers. But he, at least, had shaken off the fetters of caste, and had taken his own road to happiness.

"Thank you, Goodwin; that is all I want to know," she said.

An hour later she was being driven to Richmond in an open carriage, with the faithful Sophy seated opposite her, in the dazzling June sunshine. They stopped at Putney to spend half an hour with Mrs. Potter, and then drove on to the village of Sheen, and pulled up at a roadside inn, where Antonia inquired for Mr. Stobart's cottage, and was agreeably surprised at finding her question promptly answered.

"'Tis about a mile from here, your ladyship," said the landlord, who had run out of his bar-parlour to wait upon a lady in as fine a carriage as any that passed his door on a Saturday afternoon, when court and fashion drove to Richmond to air themselves in the Park and play cards at modish lodgings on the Green. "'Tis a white cottage facing the common—the first turning on the left hand will take you to it; but 'tis a bad road for carriages."

They drove along the high road for about a quarter of a mile, between market gardens, where the asparagus beds showed green and feathery, and where the strawberry banks were white with blossom, under the blue sky of early June. The hedges were full of hawthorn bloom and honeysuckle, dog-roses and red campion.

"Sure, the country's a sweet place to come to for an afternoon," said Sophy, as she sniffed the purer air; "but I'm glad we live in London."

The lane was narrow and full of ruts, so Antonia alighted at the turning and sent Sophy and the carriage back to the inn to wait for her. Sophy had a volume of a novel in her reticule, and would be able to amuse herself.

The walk gave Antonia time for quiet thought before she met the man who might receive her as an enemy. She was going to him with no high-flown ideas of restitution—of surrendering a fortune that she knew to be the bequest of love. She had accepted that heritage without compunction. She had given herself to the dead, and she thought it no wrong to receive the fortune that the dead had given to her. But if her husband's kinsman was in poor circumstances, it was her duty to share her riches with him. She had an instinctive dislike of all professors of religion; but she could but admire this young man for the humble marriage which had offended his cousin, and perhaps lost him a substantial part of his cousin's fortune.

The lane was a long one, between untrimmed hedges that breathed the delicate perfume of wild flowers, on one side a field of clover, a strawberry garden on the other. It was a relief to have left the dust of the high road, and the burden of Sophy's running commentary upon the houses and carriages and people on their way. Sheen Common lay before her at last, an undulating expanse carpeted with short sweet turf, where the lady's-slipper wrought a golden pattern on the greyish green, and where the yellow bloom of the gorse rose and fell over the hillocky ground in a dazzling perspective. Larks were singing in the midsummer blue, and behind the park wall, built when the first Charles was king, the rooks were calling amidst the darkness of forest trees. Close on her left hand as she came out of the lane, Antonia saw a cottage which she took for the labourer's hovel indicated in the *St. James's Evening Post*. It had been once a pair of cottages, with deeply sloping thatch and crow-step gables above end walls of red brick; but it was now one house in a flower-garden of about an acre, surrounded with a hedge of roses and lavender, inside a low white paling. The plastered porch, with its broad bench and little square window, was big enough for two or three people to sit in; the parlour casements were wide and low, and none of the rooms could have been above seven or eight feet high; but this humble dwelling, contemplated on the outside, had those charms of the picturesque and the rustic which are apt to make people forget that houses are meant to be lived in rather than to be looked at from over the way.

The garden was prettier than her own old garden at Putney, Tonia thought. Never had she seen so many flowers in so small a space. While she stood admiring this little paradise, out of range of the windows, she was startled by the sound of a voice close by; and then, for the first time, she became aware of a domestic group under an old crab-apple tree, which was big enough to spread a shade over a young man and woman sitting side by side on a garden bench, and a very juvenile nursemaid kneeling on the grass and supervising the movements of a crawling baby.

The young man was Mr. Stobart, no doubt; and the girl who sat sewing diligently, with bent head, and who looked hardly eighteen years of age, must be his wife; and the baby made the natural third in the domestic trio, the embodied grace and sanction of a virtuous marriage.

He was reading aloud from "Paradise Lost," the story of Adam and Eve before the coming of the Tempter. He had a fine baritone voice, and gave full effect to the music of Milton's verse, reading as a man who loves the thing he reads. In the restrictions which piety imposed upon the choice of books, he had been over the same ground much oftener than a more libertine student would have been; and this may have accounted for the young wife's appearance of being more interested in the hem of her baby's petticoat than in Milton's Eve.

"A simpleton," thought Tonia. "'Tis not every man would forfeit wealth and station for such a wife. But she looks sweet-tempered, and as free from earthly stain as a sea-nymph."

She went on to the low wooden gate, as white as if it had been painted yesterday, and rang a primitive kind of bell that hung on the gate-post.

The young woman laid down her sewing, and came to open the gate with the air of doing the most natural thing in the world; but on perceiving Antonia's splendour of silver-grey lute-string and plumed hat she stopped in confusion, dropping a low curtsey before she admitted the visitor.

Antonia thought her lovely. Those velvety brown eyes set off the delicacy of her complexion, while the bright auburn of her unpowdered hair, which fell about her forehead and hung upon her neck in natural curls, gave a vivid beauty to a face that without brilliant colouring would have meant very little. She had the exquisite freshness of creatures that do not think—almost without passions, quite without mind.

"I think you must be Mrs. Stobart," Tonia said gently. "I have come to see your husband, if he will be good enough to receive me. I am Lady Kilrush."

The timid sweetness of Mrs. Stobart's expression changed in a moment, and an angry red flamed over cheeks and brow.

"Then I'm sure I don't know what can be your ladyship's business here, unless you have come to crow over us," she said, "for I know you wasn't invited."

Stobart came to the gate in time to hear his wife's speech.

"Pray, my dear Lucy, let us have no ill-nature," he said, with grave displeasure, as he opened the gate. "You see, madam, my wife has not been bred in the school that teaches us how to hide our feelings. I hope your ladyship will excuse her for being too simple to be polite."

"I am sorry if she or you can think of me as an enemy," said Antonia, very coldly. She had been startled out of her friendly feeling by Mrs. Stobart's unexpected attack. "I only knew a few hours ago, from an insolent paragraph in a newspaper, that there was any one living who could think himself the worse for my marriage."

"Indeed, madam, I have never blamed you or Providence for that romantic incident. Will your ladyship sit under our favourite tree, where my wife and I have been sitting, or would you prefer to be within doors?"

"Oh, the garden by all means. I adore a garden; and yours is the prettiest for its size I have ever seen, except the rose-garden at Kilrush Abbey, which I dare swear you know."

"My aunt's garden? Yes. I was just old enough to remember her leading me by the hand among her rose trees. She died before my fourth birthday, and I have never seen Kilrush House since her death."

"'Tis vastly at your service, sir, with all it can offer of accommodation, if ever you and your lady care to occupy it for a season."

They were moving slowly towards the apple tree as they talked, Lucy Stobart hanging her head as she crept beside her husband, ashamed of her shrewish outburst, for which she expected a lecture by-and-by, and shedding a penitential tear or two behind a corner of her muslin apron.

"We shall not trespass on your ladyship's generosity. We have framed our lives upon a measure that would make Kilrush House out of the question."

"We are not rich enough to live in a great house," snapped Lucy, sinning again in the midst of her repentance.

"Say rather that we have done with the things that go with wealth and station, and have discovered the happiness that can be found in what fine people call poverty."

Nursemaid and baby had disappeared from the little lawn. Antonia took the seat Mr. Stobart indicated on the rustic bench; but her host and his wife remained standing, Lucy puzzled as to what she ought to do, George too much troubled in mind to know what he was doing.

"Mrs. Stobart, and you, sir, pray be seated. Let us be as friendly as we can," pleaded Antonia. "Be sure I came here in a friendly spirit. Pray be frank with me. I know nothing but what I read in the *St. James's Evening Post*. Is it true that you were once your cousin's acknowledged heir?"

"No, madam, it is not true. I was but his lordship's nearest relation."

"And he would have inherited his lordship's fortune if he had not married me," said Lucy, with irrepressible vehemence. "Sure you know 'twas so, George! And I can never forgive myself for having cost you a great fortune. And then Lord Kilrush must needs make a much lower marriage—on his death-bed, to spite you, for *my* father had never been——"

Her husband clapped his hand over her lips before she could finish the sentence. Antonia started up from the bench, pale with indignation.

"Lucy, I am ashamed of you," said George. "Go indoors and play with your baby. You do not know how to converse with a lady. I beg you to forgive her, madam, and to think of her as a pettish child, who will learn better behaviour in time."

"I can forgive much, but not to hear it said that Kilrush had any other motive than his love for me when he made me his wife. I loved him, sir—loved him too dearly to suffer that falsehood for an instant. No, Mrs. Stobart, don't go," as Lucy began to creep away, ashamed of her misconduct. "You must hear why I came, and what I have to say to your husband. I came as a friend, and I hoped to find a friendly welcome. I came to do justice, if justice can be done, but not to apologize for a marriage which was prompted by love, and love alone."

"Be patient with us, madam, and you may yet find us worthy of your friendship," said Stobart, gently. "But first of all be assured that we ask nothing from your generosity. We assert no claim to justice, not considering ourselves wronged."

"You think differently from your wife, Mr. Stobart."

"Oh, madam, cannot you see that my wife is a wayward child, who has never learnt to reason? To-night, on her knees at the foot of the Cross, she will shed penitential tears for her sins of pride and impatience."

"Pray, sir, do not talk of sin. 'Twas natural, perhaps, that your wife should think ill of me."

"Oh, madam, 'twas for his sake only that I was angry," protested Lucy, with streaming eyes. "Satan gets the better of me when I remember that he was disinherited for marrying me; and I thought you had come here to triumph over him. But, indeed, I covet nobody's fortune, and am content with this dear cottage, where I have been happier than I ever was in my life before."

"Let us be friends, then, Mrs. Stobart," Antonia said, with a graciousness that completely subjugated the contrite Lucy, whose murmured reply was inaudible, and who sat gazing at the visitor in a rapture of admiration.

Never had Lucy's eyes beheld so handsome a woman, or such a hat, with its black ostrich feathers, clasped at the side by a diamond buckle that flashed rainbow light in the sunshine. The glancing sheen of the pale grey gown, the long gloves drawn to the elbow under deep ruffles of Flemish lace, the diamond cross sparkling between the folds of Cyprus gauze that veiled the corsage, the *tout-ensemble* of a fine lady's toilette, filled Mrs. Stobart with wonder. Wholly unconscious of the impression she had made on the wife, Antonia addressed herself to the husband with an earnest countenance.

"I am thankful to find you do not accuse Lord Kilrush of injustice," she said. "But as his kinsman, you may naturally have expected to inherit some part of his wealth; and I therefore beg you to accept a fourth share of my income, which is reckoned at twenty thousand pounds. I hope that with five thousand a year your wife will be able to enjoy all the pleasures that fortune can give."

"Oh, Georgie!" exclaimed Lucy, breathless with a rapturous surprise.

Her husband laid his hand on hers with a caressing touch.

"Hush, my dearest," he said; and then in a graver tone, "Your offer is as unexpected as it is generous, madam; but I will not take advantage of an impulse which you might afterwards regret, and of which the world you live in would question the wisdom. Be sure I do not envy you my kinsman's fortune. If I ever stood in the place of his heir I lost that place two years before he died. He told me plainly that he meant to strike my name out of his will. I hoped for nothing, desired nothing from him."

"But sure, sir, nobody loves poverty. I have tasted it, and know what it means; and since I have enjoyed all the luxuries of wealth I own that it would distress me to go back to the two-pair parlour of which the evening papers love to remind me."

"True, madam; for in your world pleasure and money are inseparable ideas. When I left that world—at the call of religion—I renounced something far dearer to me than fortune. I gave up a soldier's career, and the hope to serve my country, and write my name upon her register of honourable deeds. Having made that sacrifice, I have nothing to lose, except the lives of those I love—nothing to desire for them or for myself, except that our present happiness may continue."

"But if I assure you that your acceptance of my offer would ease my conscience——"

"Nay, madam, your conscience may rest easy in the assurance that we are content——"

"I do not think your wife is content, Mr. Stobart. She received me just now as an enemy. Let me convince her that I am her friend."

"You can do that in a hundred ways, madam, without making her rich, which would be to be her enemy in disguise."

"Sure, your ladyship, I was full of sinfulness and pride when I spoke to you so uncivilly," Lucy said, in a contrite voice. "Mr. Stobart is a better judge of all serious matters than I am. I should never be clever if I lived to be a hundred, in spite of the pains he takes to teach me. And if he thinks we had best be poor, why, so do I; and this house is a palace compared with the hovel I lived in before he took me away from my father and mother."

"You hear, Lady Kilrush, my wife and I are of one mind. But to prove that 'tis for no stubborn pride that I reject your generous offer, I promise to appeal to your kindness at any hour of need, and, further, to call upon you once in a way for those charitable works in which the men I most honour are engaged. There is Mr. Whitefield's American Orphanage, for example——"

"Oh, command my purse, I pray you, sir. I rejoice in helping the poor—I who have known poverty. I will send you something for your orphans to-night. Let me assist all your good works."

"'Tis very generous of your ladyship to help us; for I doubt your own religious views scarcely tally with those of my friends."

"I have no religious views, Mr. Stobart. I have no religion except the love of my fellow-creatures."

"Great Heaven, madam, have the undermining influences of a corrupt society so early sapped your belief in Christ?"

"No, sir, society has not influenced me. I have never been a believer in Christianity as a creed, though I can admire Jesus of Nazareth as a philanthropist, and grieve for him as a martyr to the cruelty of man. I was taught to reason, where other children are taught to believe; to question and to think for myself, where other children are taught to be dumb and to stifle thought."

Stobart gazed at her with horror. Mrs. Stobart listened open-mouthed, astonished at the audacity which could give speech to such opinions.

"Oh, madam, 'tis sad to hear outspoken unbelief from the lips of youth. I doubt you have suffered the influence of that pernicious writer whose pen has peopled France with infidels."

"If, sir, you mean Voltaire, you do ill to condemn the apostle of toleration, to whom you and all other dissenters should be grateful."

"I scorn the championship of an infidel. I am no more a dissenter than the Wesleys or George Whitefield. I have not ceased to belong to the Church of England because I follow heaven-born teachers sent to startle that Church from a century of torpor. *They* have not ceased to be of the Church because bishops disapprove their ardour and parish priests exclude them from their pulpits."

"Oh, sir, I doubt not that you and those gentlemen are honest in your convictions. 'Tis my misfortune, perhaps, that I cannot think as you do."

"If you would condescend to hear those inspired preachers you would not long walk in the darkness that now encompasses you; for sure, madam, God meant you to be among the children of light, one of His elect, awaiting but His appointed hour for your redemption. Oh, after that new birth, how you will hate the life that lies behind! With what tears you will atone for your unbelief!"

His earnestness startled her. His strong voice trembled, his dark grey eyes were clouded with tears. Could any man so concern himself about the spiritual welfare of a stranger? She had grown up with a deep-rooted prejudice against professing Christians. She expected nothing from religious people but harshness and injustice, self-esteem and arrogance, masked under an assumption of humility. This man talked the jargon she hated, but she could not doubt his sincerity.

"Alas! madam, my heart aches for you, when I consider the peril of your soul. With youth and beauty, wealth, the world's esteem—all Satan's choicest lures—what safeguard, what defence have you?"

"Moi!" she answered, rising suddenly, and looking proud defiance at him, remembering that heroic monosyllable in Corneille's "Medea." "Oh, sir, it is on ourselves—on the light within, not the God in the sky—we must depend in the conflict between right and wrong. Do you think a creed can help a man in temptation, or that the Thirty-Nine Articles ever saved a sinner from falling?"

He was silent, lost in admiration at so much spirit and beauty, such boldness and pride. His own ideal of womanly grace was gentleness, obedience, an amiable nullity; but he must needs own the triumphant charms of this bold disputant, who was not afraid to confess an impiety that shocked him. He had known many Deists among his own sex; but the wickedest women he had met in his unregenerate days had been like the devils that believe and tremble.

"I have stayed over long," said Antonia, resuming the easy tone of trivial conversation, "and I have my woman waiting for me at the inn. Good day to you, Mrs. Stobart, and pray remember we are to be friends. I hope your husband will bring you to dine with me in St. James's Square."

"I know not if it would be wise to accept your ladyship's polite invitation," Stobart answered, "though we are grateful for the kindness that inspires it. I have an inward assurance that I am safest in keeping aloof from the world I once loved too well. My life here holds all that is good for my soul—all that my heart can desire."

"But is your religion but a passive piety, sir? Do you follow the doctrine of the Moravians, who abjure all active righteousness, and wait in stillness for the coming of faith? Do you do nothing for Christianity?"

"Indeed, madam, he works like a slave in doing good," protested Lucy, eagerly. "Mr. Wesley has given him a mission among the poorest wretches at Lambeth. He has set up a dispensary there, and schools for the children, and a night class for grown men. He toils among them for many hours three or four days a week. I tremble lest he should take some dreadful fever, and come home to me only to die. He goes to the prisons, and reads to the condemned creatures, and comes home broken-hearted at the cruelty of the law, at the sinfulness of mankind. What does he do for religion? He gives his life for it—almost as his Redeemer did!"

"You teach me to honour him, madam, and to honour you for so generously defending him against my impertinence. Pray forgive me, and you too, Mr. Stobart. I have allowed myself great freedom of speech; and if you do not return my visit I shall be sure you are offended."

"We shall not suffer you to think that, madam," Stobart answered gravely.

He insisted on escorting her to her carriage, and in the walk of nearly a mile they had time for conversation. He suffered himself for that brief span to acknowledge the existence of mundane things, and talked of Handel's oratorios, Richardson's novels, and even of Garrick and Shakespeare. He handed Lady Kilrush to her carriage, and saw her drive away from the inn door, a radiant vision in the afternoon light, before he went back to the cottage, and the adoring young wife, and the yearling baby, and a dish of tea, and the story of Eve and the Serpent.

The next day's post brought him an enclosure of two bank bills for five hundred pounds each, and one line in a strong and somewhat masculine penmanship.

"For your poor of Lambeth, and for Mr. Whitefield's orphans.

"ANTONIA KILRUSH."

CHAPTER XI
ANTONIA'S INITIATION

'Twas the close of the season when Antonia arrived in London, and she left St. James's Square two days after her interview with the Stobarts, on a visit to Lady Margaret Laroche at Bath, where that lady's drawing-rooms in Pulteney Street were open every evening to those worldlings who preferred whist and commerce to Whitefield, and the airy gossip of the *beau monde* to the heart-searchings of the aristocratic penitents who attended Lady Huntingdon's assemblies. Lady Margaret, familiarly known in the fashionable world as Lady Peggy, was one of those rare and delightful women who, without any desire to revolutionize, dare to think for themselves, and to arrange their lives in accord with their own tastes and inclinations, unshackled by the mode of the moment. Her circle was the most varied and the pleasantest in London and Bath, and she carried with her an atmosphere of easy gaiety which made her an element of cheerfulness in every house she visited. In a word, she had *esprit*, which, united with liberal ideas and far-reaching sympathies, made her the most delightful of companions as well as the staunchest of friends.

This lady—a distant cousin of Lord Kilrush's—had deemed it her duty to wait upon Antonia; and, finding as much intelligence as beauty, took the young widow under her wing and promised to make her the fashion.

"With so fine a house and so good an income you will like to see people," she said. "You had best spend a month with me at the Bath, where you will meet at least half the great world, and you will grow familiar with them there in less time than 'twould take you to be on curtseying terms in London, where the Court takes up so much of everybody's attention, and politics go before friendship. At the Bath we are all Jack and Peggy, my dear and my love. We eat badly cooked dinners in sweltering parlours, dance or gossip in a mixed mob at the Rooms every night, and simmer together in a witches' cauldron every morning; at least, other people do; but for my own part I abjure all such community in ailments."

At Bath Antonia found herself the rage in less than a fortnight, and had a crowd round her whenever she appeared among the morning dippers or at the evening dance. She was voted the most magnificent creature who had appeared since Lady Coventry began to go off in looks; and the men almost hustled each other for the privilege of handing her to her chair.

She accepted their attentions with a lofty indifference that enhanced her charms. Men talked of her "goddess air;" and in that age of *sobriquets* she was soon known as Juno and as Diana. She kept them all at an equal distance, yet was polite to all. Her sense of humour was tickled by the memory of those evening walks with her father in the West End streets, when she had caught stray glimpses of fashionable assemblies through open windows. "Was I as perfect a creature then as the woman they pretend to worship?" she questioned; "and, if I was, how strange that of all the men who passed me in the street, there was but one now and then, and he some hateful Silenus, that ever tried to pursue me. But I had not my white and silver gown then, nor the Kilrush jewels, nor my coach and six."

She had a supreme contempt for adulation which she ascribed to her fortune rather than to her charms; and Lady Margaret saw with satisfaction that her *protégée's* head was not one of those that the first-comer can turn.

"'Tis inevitable you should take a second husband," she said, "but I hope you will wait for a duke."

"There is no duke in England would tempt me, dear Lady Peggy. I shall carry my husband's name to the grave, where I hope to lie beside him."

"'Tis a graceful, romantic fancy you cherish, child; but be sure there will come a day when some warm living love will divert your thoughts from that icy rendezvous."

"Ah, madam, think how inimitable a lover I lost."

"I know he was an insinuating wretch whom women found irresistible; but you are too young to hang over an urn for the rest of your days, like a marble figure in Westminster Abbey. There is a long life before you that you must not spend in solitude."

"While I have so kind a friend as your ladyship I can never think myself alone."

"Alas! Antonia, I am an old woman. My friendship is like the fag end of a lease."

Lady Margaret was the widow of an admiral, with a handsome jointure, and a small neat house in Spring Gardens, where she was visited by all the best people in town, and by all the best-known painters, authors, and actors of the day, who were often to be found at four o'clock seated round her ladyship's dinner-table, and drinking her ladyship's admirable port and burgundy. Temperate herself as a sylph, Lady Peggy was a judge of wines, and always gave the best. She had a clever Scotchwoman for her cook, and a Frenchman for her major-domo, who kept her two Italian footmen in order, and did not think it beneath his dignity to compose a salmi, toss an omelet, or dress a salad on a special occasion, when a genius of the highest mark or a princess of the blood royal was to dine with his mistress.

With such a guide Antonia opened her house to the great world early in November, and her entertainments became at once the top of the fashion. Lady Margaret had instructed her in the whole science of party-giving, and especially whom to invite and whom to leave out.

"'Tis by the people who are *not* asked your parties will rank highest," she said.

"Sure, dear madam, I should not like to slight any one."

"Pshaw, woman, if you never slight any one you will confess yourself a parvenu. The first art a *grande dame* has to learn is how to be uncivil civilly. You must be gracious to every one you meet; but you cannot be too exclusive when it comes to inviting people."

"But if I am to look for spotless reputations my rooms will be empty;" and Antonia smiled at the thought of how small and dowdy a crew she could muster were stainless virtue the pass-word.

"You will invite nobody who has been found out—no woman who has thrown her cap over the mill, no man who has been *detected* cheating at cards. There are lots of 'em *do* it, but that don't count."

"But, dear Lady Margaret, among the actresses and authors you receive sure there must be some doubtful characters."

"Not doubtful, *chérie*; we know all about 'em. But *their* peccadillos don't count. We inquire no more about 'em than about the morals of a dancing bear. The creatures are there to amuse us, and we are not curious as how they behave in their garrets and back parlours. But 'twas not so much reputation I thought of when I urged you to be exclusive. 'Tis the ugly and the dull you must eliminate; the empty chatterers; the corpulent bores, who block doorways and crowd supper-rooms. There's your visiting list, *douce*," concluded Lady Peggy, handing her a closely written sheet of Bath post. "'Tis the salt of the earth, and if you ever introduce an unworthy name in it out of easy good nature, you deserve to lose all hope of fashion."

To be the fashion, to be one of the chosen few whom all foreigners and outsiders want to see; to be mobbed in the Park, stared at in the playhouse and at the opera; to be imitated in dress, gesture, speech; to introduce the latest mispronunciation and call Bristol "Bristo,"—is it not the highest prize in the lottery of woman's life? To be famous as painter, poet, actor? Alas! a fleeting renown. The new generation is at the door. The veteran must give way. But the empire of fashion is more enduring, and having won *that* crown, a woman must be a simpleton if she do not wear it all her life, and bring the best people in town to gape and whisper round her death-bed.

Antonia's first ball was a triumph. The lofty suites of rooms, the double staircase and surrounding gallery were thronged with rank and beauty; the clothes were finer than at the last birthday, the silver and gold brocades of dazzling splendour; the jewels, borrowed, hired, or owned, flashed prismatic colours across the softer candlelight. The newspapers expatiated on the entertainment, computed the candles by the thousand, the footmen by the score. Lady Kilrush was at once established as a woman of the highest *ton;* her drawing-rooms were crowded with morning visitors, her tea-table at six o'clock served as a rendezvous for all that was choicest in the world of fashion. Every day brought a series of engagements—breakfasts at Strawberry Hill, where Horace Walpole exercised his most delightful talents for the amusement of so charming a guest; great dinners where the Ministers and the Opposition drank their three bottles together in amity, the Duke of Newcastle and Mr. Pelham, Pitt and Fox, Granville and Pulteney,—a galaxy of ribbons and stars; parties at Syon House and at Osterley; excursions to Hampton Court and Windsor, braving the wintry roads in a coach and six, and with half a dozen out-riders as a guard against the hazards of the journey. Lady Kilrush had become one of the most popular women in London, and the only evil thing that was said of her was that she did not return visits as quickly as people expected.

Was she happy in the midst of it all, she who believed only in this brief life and the pleasure or the pain that it holds? Yes. She was too young, too beautiful and complete a creature not to be intoxicated by the brilliancy of her new existence, and the sense of unbounded power that wealth gave her. The novelty of the life was in itself enough for happiness. The London in which she moved to-day was as new to her as Rome had been, and more splendid, if less romantic. Operas, concerts, plays, auctions, picture-galleries, masquerades, ridottos, provided a series of pleasures that surpassed her dreams. Handel and the Italian singers offered inexhaustible delight. She might tire of all the rest—of Court balls and modish drums, of bidding for china monsters, buying toys of Mrs. Chenevix and trinkets of jeweller Deard in Pall Mall—but of music she could never tire, and the more she heard of Handel's oratorios the better she loved them.

CHAPTER XII
"SO RUN THAT YE MAY OBTAIN"

Mrs. Stobart, yawning by the neatly swept hearth in her cottage parlour, while her husband sat silent over a book, read an account of Antonia's party in a semi-religious newspaper, prefaced with a pious denunciation of the worldling's extravagant luxury. She insisted on reading the description to her husband, and as she was a slow reader, bored him to extinction.

"How fine it must have been!" she sighed at the end. "Oh, how I should love to have been there! What a pity you put her off with an excuse when she asked us to visit her!"

"My dear Lucy, what an idle thought! Your clothes for such a party would cost a hundred pounds; and how would you like to think that you carried on your person the money that would feed a score of orphan children for the winter?"

"Then is everybody wicked who gives such assemblies or goes to them? Sure if they all spent their superfluous wealth upon charity, instead of fine clothes and musicians and wax candles, there need be nobody starving or homeless in England."

"'Tis a problem the world has not solved yet, Lucy; but for my own part I think the man who squanders his fortune upon pomp and luxury can have no more appreciation of gospel truth than the heathen has who never heard of a Redeemer."

"Then you think Lady Kilrush is no better than a heathen?"

"Alas! poor wretch, did she not confess herself so in your hearing—an infidel, blind to the light of revelation, deaf to the message of pardon? We can but pity her, Lucy, and pray that God's hour may come for her as it came for you and me. She has a fine nature, and I cannot think she will be left in outer darkness."

"Unless she is one of those that were predestined to eternal perdition before they were born," said Lucy.

"You know I have never countenanced that gospel of despair, and I deplore that so fine a preacher as Mr. Whitefield should have taken up such gloomy views."

"She might have sent us a card for her ball," murmured Lucy. "'Twould have been civil, even though she guessed you would not take me."

The discontented sigh which followed the complaining speech showed George Stobart that his wife was still among the unregenerate. His religion was of a stern temper, and he could not suffer this unchristian peevishness to pass unreproved.

"Do you think, madam, that a journeyman printer's daughter would be in her place among dukes and duchesses at a fashionable assembly? 'Twas not for such a life I chose you."

Lucy, who always trembled at her husband's frown, though she never refrained from provoking his anger, replied with her accustomed argument of tears. George saw the slim shoulders shaken by suppressed sobs, flung his book aside in a rage, and began to pace the cottage parlour, whose narrow bounds he was not yet accustomed to. In mild weather the half-glass door stood ever open, and he could pass to the grass plot outside when his impatient mood was on; but with a November rain beating against the casement there was no escape, and he felt like a caged bear.

Finding her stifled sobs unregarded, Lucy began again, in the same complaining voice—

"I thought a gentleman's wife was fit company even for dukes and duchesses; and if it comes to fathers, I have less need to be ashamed of mine, though he starved and beat me, than Lady Kilrush has of hers, who was in jail for running away with a farmer's cash-box. 'Twas all in the evening paper when his lordship married her."

"Good God!" cried George, "are women by nature mean and petty? The first desire of a gentleman's wife, madam, should be to think and act like a lady, and to-day you do neither. I wish we had never seen Lady Kilrush, since an hour of her company has made you dissatisfied with a life for which I thought Heaven designed you. To sigh for balls and drums—you, who never danced a step in your life! And do you think when I left the army—the calling I loved—I meant to hang upon the skirts of fashion, stand in doorways, or elbow and shove in supper-rooms? I renounced all such idle pleasures when I left His Majesty's service and took up arms for Christ, whose soldier and servant I am."

Lucy, now entirely repentant, looked up at him with streaming eyes, shivering at his indignation, but admiring him.

"How handsome you are when you are angry!" she cried. "You are so good and noble, and I am so vile a sinner. 'Tis Satan tempting me. He makes me forget what a worm I am. He makes me proud and ungrateful — ungrateful to you, my dear, my honoured husband; ungrateful to God who gave me your love."

She slipped from her chair to the ground, and knelt there, weeping passionately, her pretty auburn hair falling over her face and neck, whose delicate whiteness showed like ivory between loose locks of burnished gold.

Her husband had recovered his self-command, lifted her tenderly from the ground, and held her against his breast. How pretty she was, how artless and childlike, and how brutal it was in him to be so angry at her poor little frivolous yearnings for fine clothes and fine company, music and candlelight! He kissed her on the forehead and lips in a gentle silence, led her to her chair, and then resumed his book.

"'Tis I am the sinner, Lucy," he said after a pause, during which her needle travelled slowly along the seam of the shirt she was making for him. "I did very ill to be so hot and impatient about a trifle. But these long empty days vex me. I hope I may be of the proper stuff for a Christian; but sure I should never have done for a hermit. I want to be up and doing."

"Indeed, George, you work too hard as it is. A long day at home should be a rest for you."

"I am not one of those who relish rest. Come, I will read to you, if you choose."

"I love to hear you read."

"Yes, and sit and dream of your baby, or your new tea-things, and scarce know whether I have been reading Milton or the Bible when I have done," he said gently, as he might have spoken to a child.

"You have such a beautiful voice. I love your voice better than the things you read. But let it be 'Pilgrim's Progress,' and I will listen to every word. I always think Christian is you. I can see you when I follow him with my thoughts."

Her husband smiled at the gentle flattery, and brought Bunyan's delightful story from the modest bookcase which held but some two score of classics and pious works — William Law, Dr. Watts, the writers loved and chosen by the followers of the New Light.

"Dost remember where we left your Christian?" he asked.

"'Twas when he was alone in the Valley of Humiliation, just before Apollyon met him," she answered quickly, though had the book been

"Paradise Lost," she would have hardly known whether 'twas before or after the fall when they left Adam and Eve. He read aloud till teatime, and read to himself after tea till the hour of evening prayer and Scripture exposition, to which the little nursemaid and a stout maid-of-all-work were summoned; and so the long day closed at an hour when West End London, from Wimpole Street to Whitehall, was alive with chairs and linkmen, French horns and dancing feet. In this cottage on the common there was a silence that made the chirp of the crickets a burden.

George Stobart was not a quietist. Religion unsupported by philanthropy would not have sufficed him for happiness. He could not spend half his life upon his knees in a rapture of self-humiliation—could not devote hours to searching his own heart. Once and for all he had been convinced of sin, assured that the road he had been travelling was a road that led to the gates of hell, and that in travelling it he had carried many weaker sinners along with him, and so had been a murderer of souls. Once and for all he had been assured of the free grace of God, and believed himself appointed to do good work—a brand snatched from the burning, whose duty it was to snatch other brands, to compel the lost sheep to come into the fold.

He loved to be up and doing. He had the soldier's temper, and must be fighting some one or something; nor could he keep in his chamber and wrestle with impalpable devils. He could not fight, like Luther, with the evil that was within him till he materialized the inward tempter, saw Satan standing before him, and flung his inkpot at a visible foe. Abstract piety could not satisfy George Stobart. He caught himself yawning over Law's "Serious Call," and "The Imitation of Christ."

In the beginning of the Great Revival, when the Oxford Methodists and the Moravian Christians had been as one brotherhood in the meeting-house by Fetter Lane, an enthusiast, by name Molther, had put forward a new way of salvation, which was to be "still." Those who desired to find faith were to give up the public means of grace. They were not even to pray or to read the Scriptures, nor to attempt to do any good works.

John Wesley's fine common sense had repudiated this doctrine, whereupon there had been confusion and falling away among the Fetter Lane society; and the great leader had withdrawn to a chapel and dwelling-house of his own creation, in a disused foundry for cannon, near Finsbury Square. It was here that George Stobart had found faith, and it was in Wesley's strong and active crusade against sin and suffering that he found satisfaction.

After somewhat reluctantly entering upon his career as an itinerant preacher, when the magnitude of the work, the multitudes eager to hear the

Word of God, revealed themselves to him, John Wesley, again reluctantly, enlisted the help of lay preachers. The Church had shut her doors upon him—that Anglican Church of which he had ever been a true and staunch apostle—and he had to do without the Church. He saw before him the people of England awakened from the torpor of a century of automatic religion, and saw that he needed more labourers in this vast vineyard than the Church could give him.

For the last two years George Stobart had been one of Wesley's favourite helpers, and had accompanied his chief in several of those itinerant journeys which made half England Wesleyan. He preached at Bristol, rode with Wesley, preaching at every stage of the journey, from Bristol to Falmouth, where he stood shoulder to shoulder with him in one of the worst riots the Christian hero ever faced. He was with him through the roughest encounters in Lancashire, stood beside him on the Market Cross at Bolton, when the great wild mob surged round them and stones flew thick and fast, and where, as if by a miracle, while many of the rabble were hurt, the preacher remained untouched.

In all this, in the effect of his own preaching, in the hazards and adventures of those long rides across the face of a country where most things were new, Stobart found unalloyed delight. He loved his mission in the streets and alleys of Lambeth, his visits to the London jails, for here he had to wrestle with the devils of ignorance and blasphemy, to preach cleanliness to men and women who had been born and reared in filth, to meet the wants of a multitude with a handful of silver, to give counsel, sympathy, compassion, where he could not give bread. This was work that pleased him. Here he felt himself the soldier and servant of Christ.

It was in the religion of the chamber that Stobart fell short of the mark. He loved the Word of God when God spoke by the lips of His Son; but he had not that reverent affection for the Old Testament which Wesley had urged upon him as essential to true religion. For the grandeur, the poetry of Holy Writ he had the highest appreciation; but there were many pages of the sacred volume in which he looked in vain for the light of inspiration. If he could have read his Bible in the same inquiring spirit that Samuel Coleridge brought to it, he might have been better satisfied with the book and with himself; but Wesley had forbidden any such liberal interpretation of the Scriptures. Every line, every word, every letter was to be accepted as the law of God.

He was dissatisfied with himself for his coldness, for wandering thoughts, for the dying out of that sacred fire which John Wesley's preaching had kindled in his soul at the time of his conversion. But he told himself that such a fire can burn but once in a lifetime. 'Tis like the burning bush in which Moses beheld his God. That stupendous vision comes once, and once only. It has done its purifying work, and burnt out sin. But between the starting-point of the converted penitent and the Christian's crown, how long and difficult the race! George Stobart had felt his footsteps flagging on the stony road. He had not lost courage. The dogged determination to win that eternal crown was still with him; but he had lost something of his first enthusiasm, that romantic temper in which it had pleased him to prove his sincerity by the sacrifice of fortune and station, and by a marriage which would have seemed impossible to him in his unregenerate days.

A week after Lady Kilrush had given her great entertainment there came a letter from her, addressed to Mrs. Stobart, and the very seal upon it was as precious in the sight of the printer's daughter as if it had been a jewel.

"Look, George, what a beautiful seal—a naked boy with a helmet, and two snakes twisted round his cane. Who can have written to me? Why, the name is signed outside, 'Townshend.' Sure I know nobody of that name."

"'Tis but the frank, child. The letter is from Lady Kilrush."

"How can you tell that?"

"I could swear to her hand among a hundred. Not the penmanship of one woman in a thousand shows such strength of will."

"Can one's writing show one's mind? I should never have thought it. I wonder if 'tis a card for her next assembly. Oh, George, don't be angry! I should like, once in my life, only once, to go to a party."

Her husband sighed as he patted her shoulder, with the gentle touch that only strong men have, and which always soothed her.

"Read your letter," he said; "'tis no card."

She took her scissors from her work-basket and carefully cut round the seal—loth to spoil anything so beautiful, though her heart beat fast with expectation. George read the letter aloud over her shoulder.

"St. James's Square, November 15th.

"DEAR MADAM,

"I hope that neither you nor Mr. Stobart have forgot your polite promise to visit me, and that you will do me the favour of dining with me at four o'clock next Monday, when Lady Margaret Laroche, the Duchess of Portland, Mr. Townshend, and some other of my most agreeable acquaintance, will be good enough to give me their company in the evening. As you live so far off, I shall venture to send my coach to fetch you before dark, and I shall be best pleased if you will spend the night in St. James's Square, and return home at your leisure and convenience on Tuesday. Knowing Mr. Stobart's serious mind, I did not presume to send you a card for my ball last week, as I should be sorry for any invitation of mine to seem an empty compliment.

"Pray persuade your husband, and my cousin by marriage, to gratify me by bidding you write 'Yes,' and believe me, with much respect,

"Your sincere friend and servant,

"ANTONIA KILRUSH."

"Must I say no, George?" Lucy asked, with a quivering lip, ready to burst into tears.

"Nay, child, I made you unhappy t'other day, and was miserable for two days after at the thought I had been a brute. If it would please you to visit her ladyship — —"

"Please me! I should feel as if I was flying over the moon."

"But you could not fly over the moon in a grogram gown. You need not vie with her Grace of Portland, but I doubt you have no clothes fit for company, and my purse is empty."

"But I have my wedding gown," she cried, clapping her hands—"the gown I bought at Clapham with the pocket-money your mother gave me, a crown piece at a time, and that I saved till it was over three guineas. And I bought a pearl grey silk, and your mother's woman helped me make it, and then when I told you what I had done you were vexed at my vanity, and would not let me wear it; so I was married in my old stuff gown, and the pearl grey silk has never been worn. The Duchess will not have a newer gown than mine, if you'll let me go."

"'When I was a child I thought as a child,'" quoted George. "Well, dearest, thou shalt have thy childish pleasure. To have seen how idle and empty a thing fine company is may make thee love our serious life better."

CHAPTER XIII
IN ST. JAMES'S SQUARE

On the afternoon when she was expecting Mr. and Mrs. Stobart, Lady Kilrush was surprised by a visit from an old friend whom she had almost forgotten. Her chair had just brought her from a round of visits, and she had not yet removed her hat and cloak, which Sophy was waiting to take from her, being ever jealous of her lady's French maid, when a visitor was announced —

"Mrs. Granger."

The room was the fourth and smallest of a suite of reception-rooms, which occupied the whole of the first floor, leaving space only for the wide central staircase, surrounded by a gallery that was a favourite resort of visitors at a crowded assembly, as a vantage-ground from which they could watch arrivals, look out for their particular friends, and criticize "clothes."

The room was half in dusk, and Antonia wondered who the little young lady in the cherry-coloured hood and satin petticoat of the same bright hue could be. It was not a colour favoured by people of taste at that time, and the little plump person in the high hoop had not the air of the Portland set, that *recherché* group of women among whom Antonia had been received on a friendly footing, on the strength of her own charms and Lady Peggy's popularity. Lady Peggy was of all the sets, best and worst, and exercised a commanding influence over all.

"My dear creature, sure you won't pretend you've forgot me?" cried the little woman, with broad, outspoken speech, after her first mincing salutation had been acknowledged by a stately curtsey and a "Your humble servant, madam."

"Why, 'tis Patty!" exclaimed Antonia, holding out both her hands.

"Yes, 'tis Patty—Mrs. Granger. Sure you remember old General Granger that you used to jeer at. I have been married to him over a year, and we have handsome lodgings in Leicester Square, and I keep my chair; and if he outlives his two elder brothers and three nephews, I shall be a peeress."

"My dear Patty, I am gladder than I can say to see your kind little face again. Sit down, child. You must stop and dine with me. I have some cousins coming to dinner, and some company afterwards."

"Well, I'm glad you're glad. I thought you was too proud to remember me, since you didn't send me a card for your ball t'other night, though all London was there."

"I did not know what had become of you. I have asked ever so many people who knew the theatres, and no one could say where Miss Lester had gone since her name vanished from the playbills."

"The General is a strait-laced old fool!" said Patty. "He doesn't like people to know I was an actress, though I flatter myself that nobody can hear me speak or see me curtsey without discovering it. There's an air of high comedy that nobody can mistake. Sure 'tis in the hope of catching it that fine ladies take up Kitty Clive."

"You mustn't call your husband a fool, Patty, especially if he's kind to you."

"Oh, he's kind enough, but he's very troublesome with his pussy-cats, and Minettes, and nonsense; though, to be sure, Minette is a prettier name than Martha, and genteeler than Patty. And he's very close with his money. I might have my coach as well as my chair if he wasn't a miser. I sometimes think I was a simpleton to leave the stage for a husband of seventy. Sure I might have been another Mrs. Cibber."

"You had been acting seven years, Patty. You gave your genius a fair chance."

"Pshaw, there's some that don't begin to hit the taste of the town till they've been at it three times seven. Look at old Colley, for instance. The managers kept him down half a lifetime. When I look at this house and think of my two parlours I feel I was a fool to marry the General. But there never was such a romance as your marriage."

"My marriage was a tragedy, Patty!"

"Ah, but you've got the comedy now. This fine house, and your hall porter—I never laid eyes on such a pompous creature—and your powdered footmen. You're a lucky devil, Tonia."

Antonia did not reprove her, being somewhat troubled in mind at the doubt of her own wisdom in bringing this free-and-easy young person in company with George Stobart and his wife. In her gladness at meeting the friend of her girlhood she had forgotten how strange such a mixture would be.

"If 'tis not convenient to dine with me to-day, Patty, I shall be just as pleased to see you to-morrow, or the first day that would suit you."

"Your ladyship—ladyship! oh, lord, ain't it droll?—your ladyship is vastly obleeging; but I came to stay if you'd have me. Granger is gone to Hounslow to dine with his old regiment, and I'm my own woman till ten o'clock. 'Twould be civil of you if you'd bid one of your footmen tell my chairmen to fetch me at a quarter to ten, and then we can sit by the fire and talk over old times. This is Mrs. Potter's girl, I doubt, she that waited upon us once when I took a dish of tea with you. How d'ye do, miss?"—holding out condescending finger-tips to Sophy, who had stood gazing at her since her entrance.

"Yes, this is Miss Potter, my friend and companion. You can take my hat and Mrs. Granger's hood, Sophy, and come back when Mr. and Mrs. Stobart are here."

When Sophy was gone, Lady Kilrush took Patty's plump cheeks between two caressing hands and contemplated her with a smile.

"You are as pretty as ever, child," she said, with an elder-sister air, as if she, instead of Patty, had been the senior by near a decade; "and I am glad to think you have left the playhouse and all its perils for a comfortable home with an honest man who loves you. Nay, I think you are prettier than you were in Covent Garden. The quiet life has freshened your looks. But you shouldn't wear cherry colour."

"Because of my red hair?"

"Because it is a cit's wife's colour, or a vain old woman's that wants to look young. 'Tis not the mode, Patty."

"My petticoat cost a pound a yard," said Patty, ruefully. "I thought the General would kill me when he saw the bill."

"Oh, 'tis pretty enough, and suits you well enough, *chérie*. I was half in jest. I have a kind friend who lectures me upon all such trifles, and so I thought I'd lecture you. And, my dearest Patty, as the cousin that's to dine with us is a very serious person, I should take it kindly of you not to talk of the playhouse, nor to abuse your husband."

"I hope I know how to behave in company," answered Patty, slightly huffed; and on Mr. and Mrs. Stobart being announced the next moment, she assumed a mincing stateliness which lasted the whole evening.

Stobart thought her an appalling personage, in spite of her reticence. Her cherry satin bodice was cut very low, and her ample bosom was spread with pearls and crosses like a jeweller's show-case. She made up for a paucity of diamonds by the size of her topazes and the profusion of her amethysts, and her Bristol paste buckles would have been big enough for the tallest of the Prussian king's grenadiers. Lucy Stobart, in her pearl-grey silk, made with a quaker-like simplicity, her pure complexion, golden-brown curls and slender shape, seemed all the lovelier by the contrast of Mrs. Granger's florid charms; but poor Patty behaved herself with an admirable reserve, and uttered no word that could offend.

Lucy looked at everything in a wondering rapture—the pictures, the marble busts on ebony and ormolu pedestals, the miniatures and jewels and toys scattered on tables, the glass cabinets displaying the most exquisite porcelain, the China monsters standing about the carpet, the confusion of beautiful objects which met her gaze on every side almost bewildered her. She looked about her like a child at a fair.

"And does your ladyship really live in this house?" she asked innocently. "'Tis not like a house to live in."

"Do you think it should he put under a glass case, or buried under burning ashes like Herculaneum, so that it may be found perfect and undisturbed two thousand years after we are all dead?" said Stobart, smiling at her.

He was pleased with her fresh young prettiness, which was not disgraced even by Antonia's imperial charms.

"You see, madam, how foolish I have been to indulge my wife with a sight of splendours which lie so far away from our lives," he said to Antonia, who accompanied them through the suite of drawing-rooms where clusters of candles had just been lighted in sconces on the walls, to show them the famous Gobelins tapestries that had once belonged to Madame de Montespan.

"I doubt, sir, Mrs. Stobart is too happy in her rural life ever to sigh for a large London house and its obligation to live in company," answered Antonia.

"I love our cottage dearly when my husband is at home, madam; but I have to spend weeks and months with no companion but my baby son, who can say but four words yet, while Mr. Stobart is wandering about the country with Mr. Wesley, and having sticks and stones aimed at him sometimes in the midst of his sermons. If your ladyship would persuade him to leave off field preaching I should be a happy woman."

"Nay, madam, I cannot come between a man and his conscience, however much our opinions may differ; and if Mr. Stobart thinks his sermons do good——"

"'Tis a question of living in light or darkness, madam. Those who carry the lamp John Wesley lighted know too well what need there is of their labours."

"You go among great sinners?"

"We go among the untaught savages of a civilized country, madam. If there is need of God's word anywhere upon this earth, it is needed where we go. Thousands of awakened souls answer for the usefulness of our labours."

"And you are content to pass your life in such work? You have not taken it up for a year or so, to abandon it when the fever of enthusiasm cools?"

"I have no such fever, madam. And to what should I go back if I took my hand from the plough? I have renounced the profession I loved, and have forfeited my mother's affection. She was my only near relation. My wife and I stand alone in the world; we have no friend but God, no profession but to serve Him."

"I wonder you do not go into the Church."

"The Church that has turned a cold shoulder upon Wesley and Whitefield is no church for me. I can do more good as a free man."

The door was flung open as the clock struck four, and Lady Margaret Laroche came fluttering in, almost before the butler could announce her.

"My matchless one, will you give me some dinner?" she demanded gaily. "I have been shopping in the city, hunting for feathers for my screen, and I know your hour. But I forgot you had visitors. Pray make us acquainted."

"My cousin, Mr. Stobart, Mrs. Stobart, Mrs. Granger." Lady Peggy sank to the floor in a curtsey, smiled benignantly at Lucy, and put up her glass to stare disapprovingly at Patty's cherry-coloured bodice.

Dinner was announced, and they went downstairs to that spacious dining-room, which had been so gloomy an apartment when Lord Kilrush dined there in his later years, generally alone. The room had seen wilder feasts than any that Lady Kilrush was likely to give there, when her late husband was in his pride of youth and folly, the boldest rake-hell in London.

The conversation at dinner was confined to Lady Margaret, Mr. Stobart, and Antonia; for Lucy had no more idea of talking than if she had been in church, and Mrs. Granger only opened her mouth when obliged by the business of the table, where two courses of eight dishes succeeded each other in the ponderous magnificence of silver and the substantiality of mock-turtle soup, turkey and chine, chicken pie, boiled rabbits, cod and oyster sauce, veal and ham, larded pheasants, with jellies and puddings, a bill of fare which, in its piling of Pelion upon Ossa, would be more likely to excite disgust than appetite in the modern *gourmet*. But in spite of such travelled wits as Bolingbroke, Walpole, Chesterfield, and Carteret, the antique Anglo-Saxon *menu* still obtained when George II. was king.

"You are the first Methodist I have ever dined with," said Lady Peggy, keenly interested in a new specimen of the varieties of mankind, "so I hope you will tell me all about this religious revival which has made such a stir among the lower classes, and sent Lady Huntingdon out of her wits."

"On my honour, madam, if but half the women of fashion in London were as sane as that noble lady, society would be in a much better way than it is."

"Oh, I grant you we have mad women enough. Nearly all the clever ones lean that way. But I doubt your religious mania is the worst; and a woman must be far gone who fills her house with a mixed rabble of crazy nobility and converted bricklayers. I am told Lady Huntingdon recognizes no distinctions of class among her followers."

"Nay, there you are wrong, Lady Peggy," cried Antonia, "for Mr. Whitefield preaches to the quality in her ladyship's drawing-room, but goes down to her kitchen to convert the rabble."

"Lady Huntingdon models her life upon the precepts of her Redeemer, madam," said Stobart, ignoring this interruption. "I hope you do not consider that an evidence of lunacy."

"There is a way of doing things, Mr. Stobart. God forbid I should blame anybody for being kind and condescending to the poor."

"Christians never condescend, madam. They have too acute a sense of their own lowness to consider any of their fellow-creatures beneath them. They are no more capable of condescending towards each other than the worms have that crawl in the same furrow."

"Ah, I see these Oxford Methodists have got you in their net. Well, sir, I admire an enthusiast, even if he is mistaken. Everybody in London is so much of a pattern that there are seasons when the wretch who fired the Ephesian dome would be a welcome figure in company—since any enthusiasm, right or wrong, is better than perpetual flatness."

"Lady Margaret has so active a mind that she tires of things sooner than most of us," said Antonia, smiling at the lively lady, whose hazel eyes twinkled almost as brightly as the few choice diamonds that sparkled in the folds of her Brussels neckerchief.

"I confess to being sick of feather-work and shell-work, and the women who can think of nothing else. And even the musical fanatics weary me with their everlasting babble about Handel and the Italian singers. There is not a spark of mind among the whole army of *conoscenti*. With a month's labour I'd teach the inhabitants of a parrot-house to jabber the same flummery."

And then Lady Peggy turned to Mr. Stobart and made him talk about his Methodists, as she called them, and listened with intelligent interest, and gave him no offence by her replies.

"Our cousin is a very pretty fellow, and the wife has not an ill figure," she said to Antonia after dinner, in a corner of the inner drawing-room, while Mrs. Stobart and Mrs. Granger sat side by side in the great saloon, looking at a portfolio of Italian prints; "but how, in the name of all that's odious, did you come by that cherry-coloured person?"

"She is my old friend, an actress at Drury Lane, but now retired from the stage and prosperously married."

"The creature has a pretty little face, but her clothes are execrable, and then the audacity of her shoulders! Such nakedness can only be suffered in a woman of the highest mode. Indecency with an ill-cut gown is unpardonable. Don't let her cross your threshold again, child."

"Dear Lady Peggy, you are too good a friend for me to disoblige you; but I will never be uncivil to one who was kind when I was poor."

"Well, well, you are a fine pig-headed creature, but if you must have such a friend, pray let your dressmaker clothe her. 'Twill cost you less than you will lose of credit by her appearance. Remember 'tis by your women friends you will be judged. 'Tis of little consequence what notorious gamblers and rakes pass in and out of your great assemblies, so long as they are men of fashion; but your women must be of the highest quality for birth, clothes, and breeding."

'Twas six o'clock, and a bevy of footmen were busied in setting out a tea and coffee table with Indian porcelain and silver urn, and the rooms began to be picturesquely sprinkled with elegant figures, like a canvas of Watteau's. It was a prettier scene than one of her ladyship's great assemblies, for the fine furniture, the priceless china and other ornaments were undisturbed, and there was enough space and atmosphere for people to admire the rooms and each other.

The Duchess of Portland and her chosen friend Mrs. Delany came sailing in, sparkling with gaiety, and tenderly embracing their matchless Orinda. Everybody of mark in those days had a nickname, and Mrs. Delany, who had a genius for finding nonsense names, had hit upon this one for Lady Kilrush; not because she was a poetess like the original Orinda, but because the epithet "matchless" seemed appropriate to so perfect a beauty and twenty thousand a year.

George Stobart stood in the curtained embrasure of a window, contemplating this elegant circle amidst which Antonia moved like a goddess, the loveliest where all had some claim to beauty, peerless among the *élite* of womankind. Her grace, her ease, her dignity would have become a throne, but every charm was natural, and a part of herself; not a modish demeanour acquired by an imitative faculty—the surface gloss of the low-born woman apt to mimic her betters. He could not withhold his admiration from charms that all the world admired, but the extravagance of the fashionable toilette disgusted him, and he looked with angry scorn at brocades of dazzling hues interwoven with gold and silver; court gowns of such elaborate decoration that a Spitalfields weaver might have worked half a lifetime upon a fabric where trees and flowers, garlands and classic temples, lakes and mountains were depicted in their natural colours on a ground of gold. He had been living among such people a few years ago, and had never questioned their right so to squander money; or, casually reckoning the cost of a woman's gala dress, or the wax candles burnt at a ball, he had approved such expenditure as a virtue in the rich, since it must needs be good for trade. To-night as he stood aloof, watching those radiant figures, his imagination conjured up the vision of an alley in which he had spent his morning hours, going from house to house, with a famished crowd hanging on his footsteps, a scene of sordid misery he could not remember without a shudder. Oh, those hungry faces, those gaunt and spectral forms, skeletons upon which the filthy rags hung loose; those faces of women that had once been fair, before vice, want, and the small-pox disfigured them; those villainous faces of men who had spent half their lives in jail, of women who had spent all their womanhood in infamy, and, mixed with these, the faces of little children still unmarked by the brand of sin, children whom he longed to gather up in his arms and carry out of that hell upon earth, had there been any refuge for such! His heart sickened as he looked at the splendour of clothes and jewels, pictures, statues, curios, and thought how many of God's creatures might be plucked from the furnace and set on the highway to heaven for the cost of all that finery.

He was not altogether a stranger in that scene, for he saw several old acquaintances among the company, but he felt himself out of touch with them, and tried to escape all greetings and inquiries. And later, when the tables had been opened, and half the assembly were seated at whist or commerce, while the other half pretended to listen to a *pot-pourri* from Handel's "Semele," arranged for fiddles and harpsichord, which was being performed in the saloon, he went to the inmost room where Lucy was sitting solitary beside the deserted tea-table.

"Come, child," he said curtly, "we have had enough of this. 'Tis a pleasure that leaves an ill taste in the mouth."

His wife rose with alacrity. She had crept away from the music-room, dazzled by the splendour of the scene, and too shy to remain among such magnificent people, who looked at her with a bland wonder through jewelled eye-glasses.

"I think there is to be a supper," she said hesitatingly.

"Do you wish to stay for it?"

"Nay, 'tis as you please."

"I have no pleasure but to escape from this herd."

Lucy saw that something had vexed him, and went hungry to bed, having been too much embarrassed by the unaccustomed attentions of splendid beings in livery to eat a good dinner.

There was nobody in the dining-room when Mr. and Mrs. Stobart went to breakfast at nine o'clock next morning. George, who had slept little, had been steeping himself in a grey fog in St. James's Park since eight; but Lucy had found it more difficult to dress herself, encumbered by the officious assistance of one of Antonia's women, than unaided in her own little bedchamber at Sheen.

"Her ladyship takes her chocolate in her dressing-room," the butler informed Mr. Stobart, "and desires that you and your lady will breakfast at your own hour," whereupon George and his wife seated themselves in the magnificent solitude of the dining-room, and ate moderately of a meal almost as abundant as the previous day's dinner, for what was less of substance upon the table was balanced by the cold joints, pies, and poultry of the "regalia," or sideboard display.

Lucy returned to her room directly after breakfast to pack her trunk, or rather to look on ruefully while her ladyship's woman packed it. Happily, all her garments were neat and in good condition, although of a quaker-like plainness.

George sat in the library, waiting till his wife should be ready for departure, and opened one book after another in a strange inability to fix his attention upon anything. How well he remembered that room, and his last interview with his cousin! This was the table on which Kilrush had struck his clenched fist, when he swore that not to secure a life of bliss would he marry beneath his rank. The mystery of his passionate words, his violent gesture, was clear enough now. To his pride of birth, to a foolish reverence for trivial things, he had sacrificed his earthly happiness. To the man who esteemed all things small in comparison with life eternal it seemed a paltry renunciation; yet there had been a kind of grandeur in it, a Roman stoicism that could suffer for an idea. And now that George Stobart knew the woman his cousin had loved, her charm, her beauty, he could better understand the pangs of unsatisfied love, the conflict between passion and pride.

There were hot-house flowers in a Nankin bowl on the table, and a fire of coal and logs burnt merrily in the wide basket grate. The room had a far more cheerful aspect on this November morning than on that sultry summer day, four years ago.

On a side table by the fireplace Stobart noticed a pile of books richly bound in crimson morocco—the newest edition of Voltaire.

"She reads and loves that arch mocker still, cherishes a writer who would laugh away her hope of heaven, her belief in the Physician of souls. Beset with temptation, the cynosure of profligates, she rejects the only rock that stands firm and high, a sure refuge when the waves of passion sweep over the drowning soul."

He remembered the world he lived in five years ago, a world that seemed as far away as if those years had been centuries. He knew that of the men who surrounded Lady Kilrush with the stately adulation courtiers offer to queens there was scarce one who was not at heart a seducer, who would not profit by the first hint of human weakness in their goddess. And she was alone, motherless, sisterless, without a friend of her own blood, alone among envious women and unprincipled men.

"Of all those fine gentlemen who prate of honour, and would rather commit murder than submit to a trumpery impertinence, I doubt if there is one who would scruple to act unfairly by a woman, or who would hold himself bound by the impassioned vows that cajoled her into sin," he thought.

He looked into the crimson-bound octavos, tossing them aside one by one. They were not all of them deadly, but the poison was there; in those satirical romances, in those "Questions sur l'Encyclopédie," in those notes upon ancient history, on page after page he might have found the same deadly mockery, the same insidious war against the Christian faith, l'Infâme.

The door was flung open by a footman, and Antonia appeared before him, radiant in the freshness of her morning beauty, unspoilt by eighteenth-century washes and pigments. She was dressed for walking, in a sea-green lute-string and a pink gauze hat, her elbow-sleeves and the bosom of her gown ruffled with the same pale pink, and she wore long loose straw-coloured Saxony gloves, wrinkled here and there from wrist to elbow. Her only jewels were diamond solitaire ear-rings and a diamond brooch with a pear-shaped pearl pendant, one of the famous Kilrush pearls, from the treasures of the Indian merchant, the spoil of kings and rajahs.

They shook hands, and she hoped he and Mrs. Stobart had breakfasted well.

"I take my own breakfast in my dressing-room with a book," she said apologetically, "because that is the only hour I can feel sure of being alone. Morning visits begin so early. I am deep in 'Sir Charles.' Incomparable man!"

"'Sir Charles?'" he faltered. "Oh, I understand. You are reading Richardson's new novel—a tedious, interminable book, I take it."

"Tedious! I tremble for the day when I finish it. The world will seem empty when I bid Harriet and Clementina farewell. But I shall return again and again to those dear creatures. I wish myself a bad memory for their sakes."

"Oh, madam, to be thus concerned about the flimsy creations of an old printer's idle brain!"

"Idle! Do you call genius idle? There was never another Richardson. I fear there never will be. A hundred years hence women will weep for Clarissa, and men will model themselves upon Grandison."

"It saddens me, madam, to see you as enthusiastic about a paltry fiction as I would have you about the truths of the gospel. And I see with pain that you still cherish the works of the most notorious blasphemer in Europe."

"The man who stands up like little David against the Goliath of intolerance; the man who has rescued the Calas family from undeserved infamy, cleared the name of that unhappy victim of a persecuting priesthood, condemned, not because it was clear that he was a murderer, but because it was certain that he was a Protestant."

"I own, madam, that in his fight for a dead man's honour, Monsieur de Voltaire acted handsomely. I am sorry that he who did so much for the love of his neighbour should spurn the gospel which instils that virtue."

"Voltaire loved his neighbour without being taught, or say rather that he can accept all that his reason approves in the teaching of Jesus of Nazareth, while he rejects the traditions of the Roman Church."

"Nay, did he stop *there* I were with him heart and soul. But he does more. He turns the Gospel light to darkness. Would to God, madam, that you could find a wiser guide for your footsteps through a world where Satan has spread his worst snares in the fairest places."

"Mr. Stobart," she said, looking at him gravely, her violet eyes darkened to black under the rosy shadow of her hat, "I sometimes wish I could believe in Christ the Saviour; but I would not if I must believe also in Satan. Let us argue no more upon theology; I only shock you. My coach is at the door, and I want to take Mrs. Stobart to an auction where I believe she will see the finest collection of Nankin monsters and willow-pattern tea-things that China has sent us since last winter. 'Tis the first sale of the season, and all the world will be there, and twenty who go to stare and chatter for one who means to buy."

"Your ladyship is vastly kind, but my wife and I must travel by the Richmond coach, which leaves the Golden Cross at noon. I have to thank you in her name and my own for your kind hospitality."

"Oh, sir, don't thank me. Only promise that you will come to see me again, and often. We will not talk about serious things, lest we should quarrel."

"Madam, if I come into this house again we must talk of serious things. Can I pretend to be your friend, see you living without God in the world—I who believe in His judgments as I believe in His mercies—and not try to save a beautiful soul that I see hovering above the pit of hell? Can I be your friend, and hold my peace?"

"Nay, sir, leave my soul to your God. If He is all you believe, He will not let me perish."

"If you are obstinate and deny Him He will cast you out. He has given you talents for which you have to render an account, intellect, force of will, wealth, and the power that goes with it. I will come to this house no more to see you wasting yourself upon insipid amusements, listening to idle flatteries, smiling upon sybarites and fops, moving from one to another, false alike to all, since all are your inferiors, and you can esteem none of them. Your coquetries, your friendships are alike hollow, as artificial as your swooning curtsey, taught by Serise, the dancing-master."

"Oh, sir, are all the Oxford Methodists as rude as you?"

"Forgive me, madam. I cannot stoop to that smooth lying that goes by the name of politeness. 'Now, now is the accepted time, now is the day of salvation.' My heart yearns to snatch a sinner from doom. Five years ago I should have been among your admirers, should have burnt the incense of vain adulation before you, as at the shrine of a goddess, should have been made happy with a smile, ineffably blessed by a civil word. But I have lived aloof from your *beau monde*, and I come back to discover what a Sodom it is. The company I once loved fills me with disgust and loathing. I see the flames of Tophet behind your galaxy of wax candles, the rags of lost sinners under your gold and silver brocade. I will come here no more."

He moved towards the door, she following him, holding out both her hands.

"Mr. Stobart, you make life a tragedy. I protest that some of my friends in gold and silver brocade are as good Christians as even your kindness could desire me to be. They are more fortunate than I am in never having been taught to question the creed that satisfied their fathers and grandfathers. I sometimes wish I had less of the doubting spirit. But pray do not let theological differences part us. You and your wife are a kind of relations, for you are of my dear husband's blood; I can never forget that. Come, sir, let us be reasonable," she exclaimed, seating herself at the table, and motioning him to the opposite chair.

She was sitting where Kilrush had sat during that last interview with his kinsman, in the same high-backed chair, the bright colouring of her face and hat shining against a background of black horsehair.

"What do you want me to do? Of what sins am I to repent?" she asked, smiling at him. "I try to help my fellow-creatures, to be honest and truthful and kind. What more can I do?"

"Sell all that thou hast, and distribute unto the poor."

"I cannot do that. I think I have a right to be happy. Fate has flung riches into my lap; and I love the things that money buys—this house, foreign travel, ease and splendour, pictures, music, the friends that wealth and station have brought round me. I love to mix with the salt of the earth. And you want me to renounce all these things, and to live as Jesus of Nazareth lived—Jesus, the Son of Joseph the carpenter."

"Jesus, the Son of God, who so lived His brief life on earth to be for all mankind an example."

"And are we all to be peasants?"

"Believe me, madam, there is only one perfect form of the Christian life, and that is the imitation of Christ."

"You would make this a hateful world if you had your way, Mr. Stobart."

"I would make it a Christian world if I could, Lady Kilrush."

"Well, sir, let me help you with your poor. I should like to do that, though I do not mean to sell this house, or the jewels that my husband's grandfather brought from the East Indies. I can spare a good deal for almsgiving, and yet sparkle at St. James's. Take me to see your poor people at Lambeth. Bring their sorrows nearer to my heart. I know I am leading a foolish, idle life, made up of gratified vanities and futile fevers, but 'tis such a pleasant life. I had my day of drudgery and petty cares, the struggle to make one shilling go as far as five, and my heart dances for joy sometimes among the pleasures and splendours in which I move to-day. But be sure I have a heart to pity the suffering. Let me go with you to Lambeth. I will buy no china dragons to-day; and the money I put in my purse to waste on toys shall be given to your poor. Take me to them to-day. You can go back to Sheen by a later coach."

He refused at first, protesting that the places to which he went were no fitting scenes for her. She would have to confront vice as well as poverty—revolting sights, hideous language, Lazarus with his sores, and a blaspheming Lazarus—things odious and things terrible.

"I am not afraid," she answered. "If there are such things we ought to know of them. I do know that vice and sin exist. I am not an ignorant girl. I was not born in the purple."

She was impetuous, resolute, insistent, and she overruled all his objections.

"You will be sorry that I let you have your way," he said at last, "and I am foolish so to humour a fine lady's whim."

"I am not a fine lady to-day. There is more than one side to my character."

"If you mean to come with me, you had best put on a plainer gown."

"I have none plainer than this. 'Tis no matter if I spoil it, for I am tired of the colour. Oh, here is Mrs. Stobart," she cried, as a servant ushered in Lucy, who entered timidly, looking for her husband.

"Your ladyship's servant," she murmured with a curtsey. "Is it time for us to go home, George?"

"Time for me to take you to the coach, Lucy. I shall spend the day among my people."

"And I am to go home alone," his wife said ruefully.

"I shall be with you by tea-time, and you will have your boy and a world of household cares to engage you till then."

She brightened at this, and smiled at him.

"I'll warrant Hannah will not have dusted the parlour," she said. "Oh, madam, we have such pretty mahogany furniture, and I do love to keep it bright. There's nothing like elbow-grease for a mahogany table."

"I know that by experience, child. I have used it myself," Antonia answered gaily.

She was pleased and excited at the idea of a plunge into the mysteries of outcast London. She had been poor herself, but had known only the shabby genteel poverty which keeps shoes to its feet and a weathertight roof over its head. With want and rags and filth she had never come in contact save in her brief glimpse of the Irish and English towns at Limerick; and looking back upon that experience of a brain overwrought with grief, it seemed to her like a fever-dream. To-day she would go among the abodes of misery with a mind quick to see and understand. Surely, surely she could do her part in the duty that the rich owe the poor without selling all that she had, without abrogating one iota of the sumptuous surroundings so dear to her romantic temper, to her innate love of the beautiful.

She kissed Mrs. Stobart at parting, and promised to visit her at Sheen the first day she was free of engagements.

George found her chariot at the door when he came back from despatching his wife in the Richmond stage.

"Come, come," she said, "let us hasten to your poor wretches. I am dying to give them the guineas I meant for my monsters."

"Faith, madam, you will find monsters enough where we are going, but not such as a fine lady could display on her china cupboard."

Mr. Stobart stopped the carriage on the south side of Westminster Bridge.

"If you are not averse to walking some little distance, it might be well to send your carriage home," he said. "I can take you back to your house in a hackney coach;" and on this the chariot was dismissed.

"You shall not go a yard out of your way on my account," she said. "I am not afraid of going about alone. The great ladies I know would swoon if they found themselves in a London street unattended; but I am not like them."

He gave her his arm, and they threaded their way through a labyrinth of streets and alleys that lay between the Thames and the waste spaces of Lambeth Marsh, a dreary region where the water lay in stagnant pools, receptacles for all unconsidered filth, exhaling putrid fever. Here and there above the forest of chimneys and chance medley of roofs and gables there rose the bulk of a pottery, for this was the chosen place of the potter's art; but for the rest the desolate region between Stangate and the New Cut was given over to poverty and crime. Fine old houses that had once stood in the midst of fair gardens had been divided into miserable tenements, and swarmed like anthills with half-starved humanity; alleys so narrow that the sunshine rarely visited them, covered and crowded the old garden ground; four-storied houses, built with a supreme neglect of such trifles as light and air, overshadowed the low hovels that had once been rustic cottages smiling across modest flower-gardens.

Mr. Stobart came to a halt in a lane leading to the river, where a row of rickety wooden houses hung over an expanse of malodorous mud. The tide was out, and a troop of half-naked children were chasing a starved dog, with a kettle tied to his tail, through the slime and slush of the foreshore.

"Oh, the poor dog!" cried Tonia, as they stood on a causeway at the end of the lane. "For pity's sake stop those little wretches!"

George called to them, but they only looked at him, and pursued their sport. Had he been alone he would have given the little demons chase, but he could not risk bespattering himself from head to foot in a lady's company.

"There is but one way to stop them," he said, "and that is to teach them better. We are trying to do that in our schools, but the task needs twenty-fold more men and more money than we can command. 'Twould shock you, no doubt, to see how the children of the poor amuse themselves; but I question if there is more cruelty to the brute creation among those unenlightened brats than among the children of our nobility, who are bred up to think a cock-fight or a stag-hunt the summit of earthly bliss. Jim Rednap," he shouted, as the chase doubled and came within earshot, "if you don't untie that kettle and let the dog go, I'll give you a flogging that will make you squall."

The biggest of the boys looked up at this address, recognized a well-known figure, and called to his companions to stop. They halted, their yells ceased, and the hunted cur scrambled up the slippery stone steps, at the top of which Antonia and Stobart were standing. He caught the dog, took off the kettle, and flung it into the river. The boy Rednap came slowly up the steps.

"'Twarn't me that begun it," he said sheepishly.

"'Twas you that should have stopped it. You're bigger and older than the others. You are twice as wicked, because you know better. What will your poor mother say when I tell her that you take pleasure in tormenting God's creatures?"

He was stooping to pat the half-starved mongrel as he spoke to the boy, and perhaps that tender touch of his hand and his countenance as he looked at the beast, was a better lesson than his spoken reproof.

"See," Antonia said, dropping a shilling into the boy's grimy palm. "Fetch me twopenn'orth of bread for the dog, and keep the change for yourself."

The boy stared, clutched the coin, and ran off.

"Will he come back?" asked Antonia.

"Yes; he's not as bad as he looks. His mother is one of the lost sheep that the Shepherd has found. Her season of repentance will be but brief, poor soul, since she is marked for death; but she leans on Him who never turned the light of His countenance from the penitent sinner."

"Is the boy's father living?"

George Stobart shrugged his shoulders.

"Who knows? She does not, poor wretch! He is dead for her. She has three children, and has toiled to keep them from starving till she has fallen under her burden."

"Let me provide for them! Let her know that they will be cared for when she is gone. It may make her last hours happy," said Antonia, impetuously.

"I will not hinder you in any work of beneficence; but among so many and in such pressing need of help it would be well to take time, and to consider how you can make your money go furthest."

"I will buy no more foolish things—trumpery that I forget or sicken of a few hours after 'tis bought. I will go to no more china auctions, squander no more guineas at Mrs. Chenevix's. Oh, Mr. Stobart, I know you despise me because I am like the young man in the gospel story. I am too rich not to be fond of riches. But indeed, sir, I do desire to help the poor."

"I believe it, madam, and that God will bless your desires. 'Tis not easy for a woman in the bloom of youth and beauty to take up the cross as Lady Huntingdon has done—to dedicate all she has of fortune and influence to the service of Christ. 'Twere cruel to reproach you for falling short of so rare a perfection."

"I have been told that Lady Huntingdon leaves it to doubters like me to feed the hungry and clothe the naked—since the cry of the destitute appeals to all alike—and that she devotes all her means to paying preachers, and providing chapels."

"That, madam, is her view of Christ's service; and I doubt she is right. When all mankind believe in Christ, there will be no more want and misery in this world; for the rich will remember that to refuse help to His poor is to deny Him."

The boy came back, breathless with running, and carrying a twopenny loaf in his grimy paw. He had gnawed off a corner crust as he ran.

"Dogs don't love crust," he remarked apologetically, as he knelt down in the dirt and fed the famished cur.

He went with them presently to his mother's garret, where Antonia sat by the woman's bed for half an hour, while Stobart read or talked to her. His tenderness to the sick woman and the reasonableness of all he said impressed even the unbeliever. His words touched her heart, though they left her mind unconvinced. The room showed an exceeding poverty, but was cleaner than Antonia had hoped to find it; and she could but smile upon discovering that Mr. Stobart had helped the three children to scrub the floor and clean the windows in the course of his last visit, and had made Jim, the eldest of the family, promise to brush the hearth and dust the room every morning, and had supplied him with a broom, and soap, and other materials for cleanliness. The boy was his mother's sick nurse, and was really helpful in his rough way. The other two children attended at an infant school which Stobart had set up in a room near, at a minimum cost for rent and fire. The teachers were three young women of the prosperous middle-classes, who each worked two days a week without remuneration.

After this quiet visit to the dying woman, Stobart led Lady Kilrush through crowded courts and alleys, where every object that her eyes rested on was a thing that revolted or pained her—brutal faces; famished faces; lowering viciousness; despairing want; brazen impudence that fixed her with a bold stare, and then burst into an angry laugh at her beauty, or pointed scornfully to the diamonds in her ears. Insolent remarks were flung after her; children in the gutters larded their speech with curses; obscene exclamations greeted the strange apparition of a woman so unlike the native womanhood. Had she been some freak of nature at a show in Bartholomew Fair, she could scarcely have been looked at with a more brutal curiosity.

Stobart held her arm fast in his, and hurried her through the filthy throng, hurried her past houses that he knew for dangerous—houses in which small-pox or jail fever had been raging, fever as terrible as that of the year '50, when half the bar at the Old Bailey had been stricken with death during the long hours of a famous trial for murder. Jail birds were common in these rotten dens where King George's poor had their abode, and they brought small-pox and putrid fever home with them, from King George's populous prisons, where the vile and the unfortunate, the poor debtor and the notorious felon, were herded cheek by jowl in a common misery. He was careful to take her only into the cleanest houses, to steer clear of vice and violence. He showed her his best cases—cases where gospel teaching had worked for good; the people he had helped into a decent way of life; industrious mothers; pious old women toiling for orphaned grandchildren; young women, redeemed from sin, maintaining themselves in a semi-starvation, content to drudge twelve hours a day just to keep off hunger.

Her heart melted with pity, and glowed with generous impulses. She clasped the women's hands; she vowed she would be their friend and helper, and showered her gold among them.

"Teach me how to help them," she said. "Oh, these martyrs of poverty! Show me how to make their lives happier."

"Be sure I shall not be slack to engage your ladyship in good works," he answered cordially. "If you will suffer me to be your counsellor you may do a world of good, and yet keep your fine house and your Indian jewels. Your influence should enlist others in the crusade against misery. It needs but the superfluous wealth of all the rich to save the lives and the souls of all the poor."

He was hurrying her towards a coach stand, through the deepening gloom of November. They had spent more than three hours in these haunts of wretchedness, and the brief day had closed upon them. The lights on Westminster Bridge and King Street seemed to belong to another world as the coach drove to St. James's Square. Stobart insisted on accompanying Antonia to her own door, and took leave of her on the threshold with much more of friendship than he had shown her hitherto. He seemed to her a changed being since they had walked through those wretched alleys together. Hitherto his manner with her had been stiff and constrained, with an underlying air of disapproval. But now that she had seen him beside a sick-bed, and had seen how he loved and understood the poor, and how he was loved and understood by them, she began to realize how good and generous a heart beat under that chilling exterior. The idea of a man in the flower of his youth flinging off a profession he loved, to devote his life to charity appealed to all her best feelings.

"I shall wait on your wife to-morrow morning," she said. "You will have time before I come to decide what I can do to help those poor wretches. Their white faces would haunt my dreams to-night if I did not know that I could do something to make them happier."

"Sleep sweetly," he answered gently. "You have a heart to pity the poor."

He bent over her gloved hand, touched it lightly with his lips, and vanished as she crossed her threshold, where the hall-porter and three pompous footmen gave a royal air to her entrance.

CHAPTER XIV
"ONE THREAD IN LIFE WORTH SPINNING"

Antonia spent the next morning, from twelve to two, in the cottage parlour at Sheen, where Stobart spread out his reports and calculations before her, showed her what he had done in the district John Wesley had allotted to him, and how much—how infinitely more than had been done— there remained to do!

"My own means are so narrow that I can give but little temporal help," he said. "I have to stand by with empty pockets and see suffering that a few shillings could relieve. I have even thought of appealing to my mother— who has not used me well—but she was married six months ago to an old admirer, Sir David Lanigan, an Irish soldier, and a fierce High Churchman, who hates the Wesleys; so I doubt 'twould be wasted humiliation to ask her for aid. I have not scrupled to beg of my rich friends, and have raised money to apprentice at least fifty lads who were in the way to become thieves and reprobates. I have ministered to the two ends of life—to childhood and old age. The middle period must fight for itself."

He read his notes of various hard cases. He had jotted down stern facts with a stern brevity; but the pathos in the facts themselves brought tears to Antonia's eyes more than once in the course of his reading. He showed her what good might be done by a few shillings a week to this family, in which there was a bedridden son—and to another where there was a consumptive daughter; how there was a little lad starving in the gutter who could be billeted upon a hard-working honest family—how for the cost of a room with fire and candle, and sixpence a day for a nurse, he could provide a nursery where the infants of the women-toilers could be kept during the day.

"I have heard of some nuns at Avignon who set up such a room for the women workers in the vineyards," he said. "I think they called it a *crèche*."

Mrs. Stobart sat by the window busy with her plain sewing, of which she had always enough to fill every leisure hour. She looked up now and then and listened, with a mild interest in her husband's work; but she was just a little tired of it, and the fervid enthusiasm of the time of her conversion seemed very far away. Staffordshire tea-things and copper tea-kettle, brass fender and mahogany bureau filled so large a place in her thoughts, after her husband and son, both of whom she loved with her utmost power of loving, which was not of a high order. She crept away at one o'clock to see her baby George eat his dinner. He was old enough to sit up in his high mahogany chair and feed himself, with many skirmishing movements of his spoon, which he brandished between the slow mouthfuls as if it were a tomahawk.

George and Antonia were so absorbed in their work that Mrs. Stobart had been gone nearly an hour before either of them knew she was absent. The maid came blundering in with a tray as the clock struck two, and began to lay the cloth. Antonia rose to take leave, and insisted on going at once. Her carriage had been waiting half an hour in a drizzling November rain. She left quickly, but not before she had seen that Mr. Stobart's dinner consisted of the somewhat scrimped remains of a shoulder of mutton, and a dish of potatoes boiled in their skins.

She knew some of the officers in his late regiment, and knew how they lived; and it shocked her a little to recall that squalid meal when she sat down at four o'clock, with a party of friends, at a table loaded with an extravagant profusion of the richest food her cook's inventive powers could bring together. She had seen the expensive French *chef* standing before her with pencil and bill of fare, racking his brains to devise something novel and costly.

That morning at Sheen was the beginning of a close alliance in the cause of charity between Mr. Stobart and Lady Kilrush. They were partners in a business of good works; and all questions of creed were for the most part ignored between them. He would have gladly spoken words in season, but she had a way of putting him off, and she had become to him so beneficent and divine a creature that it was difficult for him to remember that she was not a Christian.

The five thousand a year which she had so freely offered him for his own use she now set aside for his poor.

"I can spare as much," she said, "and yet be a fine lady. Some day, perhaps, when I am old and withered, like the hags that haunt Ranelagh, I may grow tired of finery; and then the poor shall have nearly all my money, and I will live as you do, in a cottage, at ten pounds a year, on a bone of cold mutton and a potato. But while I am young I doubt I shall go on caring for trumpery things. It is such a pleasant change, when I have been in one of your loathsome alleys, to find myself at Leicester House with the princess and her party of wits and *savants*, or at Carlisle House, dancing in a chain of dukes and duchesses, with a German Royal Highness for my partner."

The responsibilities that went with the administration of so large a fund made a change in George Stobart's life. His residence at Sheen had long been inconvenient, the journey to and fro wasting time for which he had better uses. Lucy loved her rustic home and garden in summer; but she was one of those people who love the country when the sun shines and the roses are in bloom. In the damp autumnal afternoons, when silvery mists veiled the common, her spirits sank, and she began to grow fretful at her husband's absence, and to reproach him if he were late in coming home.

He wanted his wife to be happy, and he wanted to be near the scene of his labours, and within half an hour's walk of St. James's Square. After a careful search he found a house on the south side of the Thames, a quarter of a mile from Westminster Bridge, in Crown Place, a modest terrace facing the river. The house was roomier and more convenient than his rustic cottage; but the long strip of garden between low walls was a sad falling off from the lawn and orchard at Sheen, and he feared that Lucy would regret the change.

Lucy had no regrets. The larger rooms at Lambeth, the dwarf cupboards on each side of the parlour fireplace, the convenient closets on the upper floor, the doorsteps and iron railings, and the view of the river, with the Abbey and Houses of Parliament, and the crowded roofs and chimneys of Westminster, filled her with delight. The cottage and garden had been enchanting while the glamour of newly wedded love shone upon them; but by the time her spirits had settled into a calm commonplace of domestic life Lucy had discovered that she hated the country, and smelt ghosts under the sloping ceilings of those quaint cottage garrets where generations of labouring men and women had been born and died. Not unseldom had she longed for the bustle of Moorfields, and the din and riot of Bartholomew Fair, the annual treat of her childhood.

She arranged her furniture in the new home with complacency, and thought her son's nursery and her best parlour the prettiest rooms in the world, much nicer to live in than her ladyship's suite of saloons, where the splendid spaciousness scared her. She had known few happier hours in her life than the February afternoon when Lady Kilrush and Sophy Potter came to tea, and were both full of compliments upon her parlour, which had been newly done up, with the panelled dado painted pink, and a wallpaper sprinkled with roses and butterflies.

Sophy Potter, who retired into the background of Antonia's life in St. James's Square, was often her companion in her visits to the poor, and took very kindly to the work. As it was hardly possible to avoid the peril of small-pox in such visits, Mr. Stobart prevailed upon mistress and maid to submit to the ordeal of inoculation. The operation in Sophy's case was succeeded by a mild form of the malady; but the virus had no effect upon Antonia, and her physician argued that the vigour of a constitution which resisted the artificial infection would ensure her immunity from the disease. Neither her husband's entreaties, nor the example of Lady Kilrush could induce Mrs. Stobart to brave the perils of inoculation. It was in vain that George pleaded, and set a doctor to argue with her. Her horror of the small-pox made her shrink with tears and trembling from the notion of the lightest attack produced artificially.

"If it kills me you will be sorry for having forced me to consent," she said, and George reluctantly submitted to her refusal. *She* never went among his poor, and had never expressed a desire to see them.

"I saw enough of such wretches round Moorfields," she said. "I never want to go near them again. And I have quite enough to do to keep my house clean, and look after my little boy. You would want another servant if I went trapesing about your lanes and alleys, when I ought to be washing the tea-things and polishing the furniture."

Could he be angry with her for being industrious and keeping his house a pattern of neatness? He had long ago come to understand the narrow range of her thoughts and feelings; but while she was pious and gentle and his devoted wife, he had no ground for thinking he had made a mistake in choosing a lowborn helpmeet.

From the hurried idleness of a fashionable life Antonia stole many hours for the dwellings of the poor. In most of her visits to those haunts of misery she was attended by Stobart; but she had a way of eluding his guardianship sometimes, and would set out alone, or with Miss Potter, on one of her visits of mercy.

As time went on he grew more apprehensive of danger in her explorations; for now that she was familiar with the class among which he worked, her intrepid spirit tempted her to plunge deeper into the dark abyss of guilty and unhappy lives.

The time came when he could no longer bear to think of the perils that surrounded her in the close and fetid alleys where typhus and small-pox were never wholly absent; and at the risk of offending her he assumed the voice of authority.

"You told me once that I was your only family connection," he said, "and I presume upon that slender tie to forbid you running such risks as you incur when you enter such a den of fever as the house where I found you yesterday."

"What, sir, *you* forbid me?—you whose clarion call startled me from my selfish pleasure; *you* who showed me my worthless life!"

"You have done much to redeem that worthlessness, by your sacrifice of income."

"Sacrifice! You know, sir, that in your heart of hearts you despise such paltering with charity. In your estimation, not to give all is to give nothing!"

"You paint me as a bigot, madam, and not as a Christian. Be sure that *He* who praised the Samaritan approves your charity, and that He who holds the seven stars in His right hand will open your eyes to the light of revelation. A soul so lofty will not be left for ever in darkness. But in the mean time there can be no good done by your presence in places where you hazard health and life. You have made me your almoner, and it is my duty to see that the uttermost good is done with the money you have entrusted to me. Your own presence in those perilous places is useless. You have no gospel to carry to the sick and dying."

"Oh, sir, I have sympathy and compassion to give them. I doubt they get enough of the gospel, and that the company of a woman who can feel for their sufferings and soothe them in their pain is not without use. There is no sick-bed that I have sat by where I have not been entreated to return. The poor creatures like to tell me their troubles, to expatiate on their miseries, and I listen, and never let them think I am tired."

"You scatter gold among them; you demoralize them by your reckless almsgiving."

"No, no, no! I feed them. If there come days when the larder is empty, they have at least the memory of a feast. Your gospel will not stop the pangs of hunger. That is but a hysterical devotion which goes famishing to bed to dream of the Golden City with jasper walls, and the angels standing round the throne. Dreams, dreams, only dreams! You stuff those suffering creatures with dreams."

"I strive to make them look beyond their sufferings here to the unspeakable bliss of the life hereafter," Stobart answered gravely; and then he entreated her to go no more into those alleys where he now worked every day, and from which he came to her two or three times a week to report progress.

He came to her after his work, in the hour before the six o'clock tea at which she was rarely without visitors. If he was told she had company he went away without seeing her; but between five and six was the likeliest hour for finding her alone, since her drawing-rooms were crowded with morning visitors, and her evenings were seasons of gaiety at home or abroad.

She received him always in the library, a room she loved, and where they had had their first serious conversation. Here, if he looked tired, she would order in the urn and tea-things, and would make tea for him, while he told her the story of the day. To sit in an easy-chair beside the wood fire and to have her minister to him made an oasis of rest in the desert of toil, and he soon began to look forward to this hour as the bright spot in his life, the recompense for every sacrifice of self.

The first thunder of a footman's double knock, the clatter of high heels and rustle of brocade in the hall, sent him away. He had made no second appearance among her modish visitors.

"Go and shine, and sparkle, and flutter your jewelled wings among other butterflies," he said. "I claim no part in your life in the world; but I am proud to know that there are hours in which you are something better than a woman of fashion."

The pleasures of the town and the assiduities of Antonia's friends and admirers became more absorbing as her influence in the great world increased. Her open-handed hospitality, the splendour of her house, and the success of her entertainments had placed her on a pinnacle of *ton*.

She held her own among the greatest ladies in London, and was on familiar terms with all the duchesses—Portland, Queensberry, Norfolk, Bedford, Hamilton—and nobody ever reminded her, by a shade of difference in their appreciation, that she had not been born in the purple.

She had more admirers than she took the trouble to count, and had refused offers of marriage that most women would have found irresistible. Charles Townshend had followed and courted her; and in spite of all she could do to discourage his addresses by a light gaiety of manner that proclaimed her indifference, he had found her alone one morning, and flung himself on his knees to sue for her hand.

Deeply hurt when she rejected him, he reproached her for having fooled him by her civility.

"Oh, sir, would you have me distant or sullen to the most brilliant man in London? I thought I let you see that, though I loved your company, my heart was disengaged, and that I had no preference for one man over another."

"I doubt, madam, you despise a plain mister, and will wait for the next marrying Duke. Wert not for the recent Marriage Act you might aspire to a prince of the blood royal. Your ambition would be justified by your beauty; and I believe your pride is equal to your charms."

"I shall never marry again, Mr. Townshend. I loved my husband; and the tragedy of our marriage made that love more sacred than the common affection of wives."

"Nay, madam, is there not something more potent than the memory of a departed husband, which makes you scorn my passion? I have several times met a certain grave gentleman in your hall, who seems privileged to enjoy your society when you have no other company, and who leaves you when your indifferent acquaintance are admitted."

"That gentleman is my dear lord's cousin, and a married man. He can have no influence upon my resolve against a second marriage."

She rang a bell, and made Mr. Townshend a curtsey which meant dismissal. He retired in silent displeasure, knowing that he had affronted her.

"'Tis deuced hard to be cut out by a sneaking Methodist," he muttered as he followed the footman downstairs.

He spent the evening at White's, played higher and drank deeper than usual, and was weak enough to mention the lady's name with a scornful anger which betrayed his mortification; and before the next night all the town knew that Townshend had been refused.

The rumour came to Stobart's knowledge a week later by means of a paragraph in the *Daily Journal*, with the usual initials and the usual stars. "Lady K., the beautiful widow, has fallen out with Mr. C. T., the aspiring politician, wit and trifler, whose eminent success as a lady-killer has made him unable to endure rejection at the hands of a beauty who, after all, belongs but to the lower ranks of the peerage, and cannot boast of a genteel ancestry."

Stobart read this stale news in a three-days'-old paper at the shabby coffee-house in the Borough, where he sometimes took a snack of bread and cheese and a glass of twopenny porter, instead of going home to dinner.

"I doubt she has many such offers," he thought, "for she hangs out every bait that can tempt a lover—beauty, parts, fortune. If she has refused Townshend 'tis, perhaps, only because there is some one else pleases her better. She will marry, and I shall lose her; for 'tis likely her husband will cut short her friendship for a follower of John Wesley, lest the Word of God should creep into his house unawares."

He left London early in April in Mr. Wesley's company, and rode with that indefatigable man through the rural English landscape, making from forty to fifty miles a day, and halting every day at some market cross, or on some heathy knoll on the outskirts of town or village, to preach the gospel to listening throngs. Their journey on this occasion took them through quiet agricultural communities and small market towns, where the ill-usage that Wesley had suffered at Bolton and at Falmouth was undreamt of among the congregations who hung upon his words and loved his presence. He was now in middle life, hale and wiry, a small, neatly built man, with an extraordinary capacity for enduring fatigue, and a serene temper which made light of scanty fare and rough quarters. He was an untiring rider, but had never troubled himself to acquire the art of horsemanship, and as he mostly read a book during his country rides, he had fallen into a slovenly, stooping attitude over the neck of his horse. He had been often thrown, but rarely hurt, and had a Spartan indifference to such disasters. He loved a good horse, but was willing to put up with any beast that would carry him to the spot where he was expected. He hated to break an appointment, and was the most punctual as well as the most polite of men.

He liked George Stobart, having assayed his mental and moral qualities at the beginning of their acquaintance, and having pronounced him true metal. He was a man of wide sympathies, and during this April journey through the heart of Hertfordshire, and then by the wooded pastures and wide grassy margins of the Warwickshire coach roads between Coventry and Stratford-on-Avon, he discovered that something was amiss with his helper.

"I hope you do not begin to tire of your work, Stobart," he said. "There are some young men I have seen put their hands to the plough in a fever of faith and piety, and drive their first furrow deep and straight, and then faith grows dim, and the line straggles, and my sorrowful heart tells me that the labourer is good for nothing. But I do not think you are of that kidney."

"I hope not, sir."

"But I see there is trouble of some sort on your mind. We passed a vista in that oak wood yonder, with the smiling sun showing like a disk of blood-red gold at the end of the clearing; and you, who have such an eye for landscape, stared at it with a vacant gaze. I'll vouch for it you have uneasy thoughts that come between you and God's beautiful world."

"I trouble myself without reason, sir, about a soul that I would fain win for Christ, and cannot."

"'Tis of your cousin's widow, Lady Kilrush, you are thinking," Wesley said, with a keen glance.

"Oh, sir, how did you divine that?"

"Because you told me of the lady's infidel opinions; and as I know how lavish she has been with her money in helping your work among the poor, I can understand that in sheer gratitude you would desire to bring her into the fold. I doubt you have tried, in all seriousness?"

"I have tried, sir; but not hard enough. My cousin is a strange creature— generous, impetuous, charitable; but she has a commanding temper, and a light way of putting me off in an argument, which make it hard to reason with her. And then I doubt Satan has ever the best of it, and that 'tis easier to argue on the evil side, easier to deny than to prove. When I am in my cousin's company, and we are both interested in the wretches she has saved from misery, I find myself forgetting that while she snatches the sick and famished from the jaws of death, her immortal soul is in danger of a worse death than the grave, and that in all the time we have been friends nothing has been done for her salvation."

"Mr. Stobart, I doubt you have thought too much of the woman and too little of the woman's unawakened soul," Wesley said, with grave reproof. "Her beauty has dazzled your senses; and conscience has been lulled to sleep. As your pastor and your friend I warn you that you do ill to cherish the company of a beautiful heathen, save with the sole intent of accomplishing her salvation."

"Oh, sir, can you think me so weak a wretch as to entertain one unworthy thought in relation to this lady, who has ever treated me with a sisterly friendship? The fact that she is exquisitely beautiful can make no difference in my concern for her. I would give half the years of my life to save her soul; and I see her carried along the flood-tide of modish pleasures, the mark for gamesters and spendthrifts, and I dread to hear that she has been won by the most audacious and the worst of the worthless crew."

"If you can keep your own conscience clear of evil, and win this woman from the toils of Satan, you will do well," said Wesley, "but tamper not with the truth; and if you fail in bringing her to a right way of thinking, part company with her for ever. You know that I am your friend, Stobart. My heart went out to you at the beginning of our acquaintance, when you told me of your marriage with a young woman so much your inferior in worldly rank, for your attachment to a girl of the servant class recalled my own experience. The woman I loved best, before I met Mrs. Wesley, was a woman who had been a domestic servant, but whose intellect and character fitted her for the highest place in the esteem of all good people. Circumstances prevented our union—and—I made another choice."

He concluded his speech with an involuntary sigh, and George Stobart knew that the great leader, who had many enthusiastic followers and helpers among the women of his flock, had not been fortunate in that one woman who ought to have been first in her sympathy with his work.

Stobart spent a month on the road with his chief, preaching at Bristol and to the Kingswood miners, and journeying from south to north with him, in company with one of Wesley's earliest and best lay preachers, a man of humble birth, but greatly gifted for his work among assemblies in which more than half of his hearers were heathens, to whom the Word of God was a new thing—souls dulled by the monotony of daily toil, and only to be aroused from the apathy of a brutish ignorance by an emotional preacher. Those who had stood by Whitefield's side when the tears rolled down the miners' blackened faces, knew how strong, how urgent, how pathetic must be the appeal, and how sure the result when that appeal is pitched in the right key.

The little band bore every hardship and inconvenience of a journey on horseback through all kinds of weather, with unvarying good humour; for Wesley's cheerful spirits set them so fine an example of Christian contentment that they who were his juniors would have been ashamed to complain.

In some of the towns on their route Mr. Wesley had friends who were eager to entertain the travellers, and in whose pious households they fared well. In other places they had to put up with the rough meals and hard beds of inns rarely frequented by gentlefolks; or sometimes, belated in desolate regions, had to take shelter in a roadside hovel, where they could scarce command a loaf of black bread for their supper, and a shakedown of straw for their couch.

May had begun when Wesley and his deacons arrived in London, after having preached to hundreds of thousands on their way. Stobart had been absent more than a month, and the time seemed much longer than it really was by reason of the distances traversed and the varieties of life encountered on the way. He had received a weekly letter from his wife, who told him of all her household cares, and of Georgie's daily growth in childish graces. He had answered all her letters, telling her of his adventures on the road, in which she took a keen interest, loving most of all to hear of the fine houses to which he was invited, the dishes at table, and the way they were served, the tea-things and tray, and if the urn were copper or silver, also the dress of the ladies, and whether they wore linen aprons in the morning. He knew her little weaknesses, and indulged her, and rarely returned from a journey without bringing her some trifling gift for her house, a cream-jug of some special ware, a damask table-cloth, or something he knew she loved.

Their union had been one of peace and a tranquil affection, which on Stobart's part outlived the brief fervour of a self-sacrificing love. The romantic feeling, the glow of religious enthusiasm which had led to his marriage, belonged to the past; but he told himself that he had done well to marry the printer's daughter, and that she was the fittest helpmeet he could have chosen, since she left him free to work out his salvation, and submitted with gentle obedience to the necessities of his spiritual life.

"Mr. Wesley would thank Providence for so placid a companion," he thought, having heard of his leader's sufferings from a virago who opened and destroyed his letters, insulted his friends, and tormented him with an unreasoning jealousy that made his home life a kind of martyrdom.

During that religious pilgrimage Stobart had written several times to Lady Kilrush—letters inspired by his intercourse with Wesley, and by the spiritual experiences of the day; letters written in the quiet of a sleeping household, and aflame with the ardent desire to save that one most precious soul from eternal condemnation. He had written with a vehement importunity which he had never ventured in his conversation; had wrestled with the infidel spirit as Jacob wrestled with the angel; had been moved even to tears by his own eloquence, carried away by the ardour of his feelings.

"Since I was last in your company I have seen multitudes won from Satan; have seen the roughest natures softened to penitent tears at the story of Calvary—the hardest hearts melted, reprobates and vagabonds laying down their burden of sins, and taking up the Cross. And I have thought of you, so gifted by nature, so rare a jewel for the crown of Christ—you whose inexhaustible treasures of love and compassion I have seen poured upon the most miserable of this world's outcasts, the very scum and refuse of debased humanity. You, so kind, so pitiful, so clear of brain and steadfast of purpose, can you for ever reject those Divine promises, that gift of eternal life by which alone we are better than the brutes that perish?"

"Alas! dear sir," Antonia wrote in her reply to this last letter, "can you not be content with so many victories, so great a multitude won from Satan, and leave one solitary sinner to work out her own destiny? If my mind could realize your kingdom of the saints, if I could believe that far off, in some vague region of this universe, whose vastness appals me, there is a world where I shall see the holy teacher of Nazareth, hear words of ineffable wisdom from living lips, and, most precious of all, see once again in a new and better life the husband who died in my arms, I would accept your creed with ecstatic joy. But I cannot. My father taught me to reason, not to dream; and I have no power to unlearn what I learnt from him, and from the books he put into my hands. Do not let us argue about spiritual things.

We shall never agree. Teach me to care for the poor and the wretched with a wise affection, and to use my fortune as a good woman, Pagan or Christian, ought to use riches, for the comfort of others, as well as for her own pleasure in the only world she believes in."

The London season, which in those days began and ended earlier than it does now, was growing more brilliant as it neared the close. When Mr. Stobart returned to town, Ranelagh, Vauxhall, the Italian Opera, Handel's Oratorios, the two patent theatres, and that little theatre in the Haymarket, where the malicious genius of Samuel Foote revelled in mimicry and caricature, were crowded nightly with the salt of the earth; and the ruinous pleasures of the St. James's Street clubs—White's, Arthur's, and the Cocoa Tree—were still in full swing, to the apprehension and horror of fathers and mothers, sisters, wives, and sweethearts, who might wake any morning to hear that son or husband, brother or lover, had been reduced to beggary between midnight and dawn. Losses at cards that ruined families, disputes that ended in blood, were the frequent tragedies that heightened the comedy of fashionable life by the zest of a poignant contrast.

George Stobart returned to London with Wesley's counsel in his mind. He had been told his duty as a Christian. He must hold no commune with a daughter of Belial, save in the hope of leading her into the fold. If his most strenuous endeavours failed to convert the unbeliever he must renounce her friendship and see her no more. He must not trifle with sacred things, honour her for a compassionate and generous disposition, admire her natural gifts, and forget that she was a daughter of perdition.

He recalled the hours he had spent in her company, hours in which all religious questions had been ignored while they discussed the means of feeding the hungry and clothing the naked. Surely they had been about the Master's work, though the Master's name had not been spoken. He remembered how, instead of being instant in season and out of season, he had kept silence about spiritual things, had even encouraged her to talk of those trivial pleasures she loved too well—the court, the opera, her patrician friends, her social triumphs. He recalled those romantic legends in which some pious knight, journeying towards the Holy Land, meets a lovely lady in distress, succours her, pities, and even loves her, only to discover the flames of hell in those luminous eyes, the fiery breath of Satan upon those alluring lips. He swore to be resolute with himself and inexorable to her, to accept no compromises, to reject even her gold, if he could not make her a Christian.

In his anxiety for her spiritual welfare it was a bitter disappointment to him not to find her at home when he called in St. James's Square on the day after his return. He called again next day, and was told that she was dining with the Duchess of Portland at Whitehall, and was to accompany her grace to the Duchess of Norfolk's ball in the evening.

He felt vexed and offended at this second repulse, yet he had reason to be grateful to her for her kindness to his wife during his absence. She, the fine lady, whose every hour was allotted in the mill-round of pleasure, had taken Lucy and the little boy to Hyde Park in her coach, and for long country drives to Chiswick and Kew, and had even accepted an occasional dish of tea in the parlour at Crown Place, had heard Georgie repeat one of Dr. Watts's hymns, and had brought him a present of toys from Mrs. Chevenix's, such as no Lambeth child had ever possessed.

He had been full of work since his return, visiting his schools and infant nurseries, and preaching in an old brewhouse which he had converted into a chapel, where he held a nightly service, consisting of one earnest prayer, a chapter of the New Testament, and a short sermon of friendly counsel, gentle reproof of evil habits and evil speech, and fervent exhortation to all sinners to lead a better life; and where he held, also, a class for adults who had never been taught to read or write, and for whom he laboured with unvarying patience and kindness.

He was more out of humour than a Christian should have been when, on his third visit to St. James's Square, he was told that her ladyship was confined to her room by a headache, and desired not to be disturbed, as she was going to the masquerade that evening.

The porter spoke of "the masquerade" with an assurance that no gentleman in London could fail to know all about so distinguished an entertainment.

Stobart left the door in a huff. It was six weeks since he had seen her face, and she valued his friendship so little that she cared not how many times he was sent away from her house. She would give herself no trouble to receive him.

Instead of going home to supper he wandered about the West End till nightfall, when streets and squares began to be alive with links and chairmen. At almost every door there was a coach or a chair, and the roll of wheels over the stones made an intermittent thunder. Everybody of any importance was going to the masquerade, which was a subscription dance at Ranelagh, given by a number of bachelor noblemen, and supposed to be accessible only to the choicest company; though 'twas odds that a week later it would be known that more than one notorious courtesan had stolen an entrance, and displayed her fine figure and her diamonds among the duchesses.

A fretful restlessness impelled Stobart to pursue his wanderings. The thought of the Lambeth parlour, with the sky shut out, and the tallow candles guttering in their brass candlesticks, oppressed him with an idea of imprisonment.

He walked at random, his nerves soothed by the cool night air, and presently, having turned into a main thoroughfare, found himself drifting the way the coaches and chairs were going, in a procession of lamps and torches, an undulating line of fire and light that flared and flickered with every waft of the south-west wind.

All the road between St. James's and Chelsea had a gala air to-night, for 'twas said the old king and the Duke of Cumberland would be at Ranelagh. People were standing in open doorways, groups were gathered at street corners, eager voices named the occupants of chariot or sedan, mostly wrong. The Duke of Newcastle was greeted with mingled cheers and hisses; Fox evoked a storm of applause; and young Mrs. Spencer's diamonds were looked at with gloating admiration by milliners' apprentices and half-starved shirt-makers.

Stobart went along with the coaches on the Chelsea Road to the entrance of Ranelagh, where a mob had assembled to see the company—a mob which seemed as lively and elated as if to stand and stare at beauty and jewels, fops and politicians, afforded almost as good an entertainment as the festivity under the dome. Having made his way with some elbowing to the front row, Stobart had a near view of the company, who had to traverse some paces between the spot where their coaches drew up and the Doric portico which opened into the rotunda, that magnificent pleasure-house which has been compared to the Pantheon at Rome for size and architectural dignity.

The portico was ablaze with strings and festoons of many-coloured lamps, and from within there came the inspiring sounds of dance music played by an orchestra of strings and brasses—sounds that mingled with the trampling of horses' hoofs, the cracking of whips, the oaths of coachmen, and the remonstrances of link-boys and footmen, trying to keep back the crowd.

"Oh, oh, oh!" cried the front row at the appearance of a tall woman, masked, and wearing a long pink satin cloak, which fell back as she descended from her chariot, revealing a magnificent form attired as Diana, in a white satin tunic which displayed more of a handsome leg than is often given to the public view, and a gauze drapery that made no envious screen between admiring eyes and an alabaster bust and shoulders.

"I'll wager her ladyship came out in such a hurry she forgot to put on her clothes," said one spectator.

The Infidel | 159

"I say, Sally," cried another, "if you or me was to come out such a figure, we should be in the stocks or the pillory before we went home."

"Sure 'tis a kindness in a great lady to show us that duchesses are made of flesh and blood like common folks, only finer."

Flashing eyes defied the crowd as the handsome duchess strode by, her silver buskins glittering in the rainbow light, her head held at an imperial level, admiring fops closing round her, with their hands on their sword-hilts, ready to repress or to punish insult.

"Sure, Charley, one would suppose these wretches had never seen a handsome woman till to-night," laughed the lady.

"I doubt they never have seen so much of one," answered the gentleman in a half-whisper, on which he was called "beast," and rebuked with a smart tap from Diana's fan.

A great many people had arrived, peeresses without number, and among them Katharine, Duchess of Queensberry, Prior's Kitty, made immortal by a verse. This lovely lady appeared in a studied simplicity of white lute-string, without a jewel—a beauty unadorned that had somewhat missed fire at the last birthday, against the magnificence of her rivals. The beautiful Duchess of Hamilton went by with her lovely sister, Lady Coventry, radiant in a complexion of white-lead which was said to be killing her. Starry creatures like goddesses passed in a glittering procession; the music, the babel of voices from within, made a tempest of sound; but *she* had not yet appeared, and Stobart waited to see her pass.

She came in her chariot, like Cinderella in the fairy tale. Hammer-cloth and liveries were a blaze of gold and blue. Three footmen hung behind, with powdered heads, sky-blue velvet coats, white breeches, pink stockings and gold garters—gorgeous creatures that leapt down to open the coach door and let down the steps, but were not suffered to come near her, for a bevy of her admirers had been watching for her arrival, and crowded about her carriage door, thrusting her lackeys aside.

She laughed at their eagerness.

"'Twas vastly kind of you to wait for me, Sir Joseph," she said to the foremost. "I should scarce have dared to plunge into the whirlpool of company unattended. Lady Margaret had a couple of young things to bring, who insisted upon coming here directly the room opened, so I let her come without me. I love a *fête* best at the flood-tide. Sure your lordship must think me monstrous troublesome if I have robbed you of a dance," she added, turning to a tall man in smoke-coloured velvet and silver.

"I think your ladyship knows that there is but one woman in Europe I love to dance with," said Lord Dunkeld, gravely.

He was a man of distinguished rank and fortune, distinguished merit also—a man whom Stobart had known and admired in his society days.

"Then 'tis some woman in Asia you are thinking of when I see you distrait or out of spirits," Antonia said lightly, as she took his arm.

"Alas! fair enslaver, you know too well your power to make me happy or wretched," he murmured in her ear.

"I hope everybody will be happy to-night," she said gaily, "or you subscribing gentlemen, who have taken so much trouble to please us, will be ill-paid for your pains. For my own part, I mean to think Ranelagh the seventh heaven, and not to refuse a dance."

She wore her velvet loup, with a filmy border of Brussels that clouded the carmine of her lips. Her white teeth flashed against the black lace, her smile was enchantingly gay.

Stobart heard her in a gloomy temper. What hope was there for such a woman—so given over to worldly pleasures, with no capacity for thought of serious things, no desire for immortality, finding her paradise in a masquerade, her happiness in the adulation of fools?

"How can I ever bring her nearer to God while she lives in a perpetual intoxication of earthly pleasures, while she so exults in her beauty and her power over the hearts of men?"

She wore a diamond tiara and necklace of matchless fire. Her gown was white and silver, the stomacher covered with coloured jewels that flashed between the opening of her long black silk domino, an ample garment with loose sleeves. She had arrayed herself in all her splendour for this much-talked-of masquerade, wishing to do honour to the gentlemen who gave the treat.

"Bid my servants fetch me at one o'clock, if you please, Sir Joseph," she said to the cavalier on her left.

"At one! Impossible! 'Tis nearly eleven already. I shall order them at three, and I'll wager they'll have to wait hours after that."

"You make very sure of your dance pleasing folks," she said. "I doubt I shall have yawned myself half dead before three o'clock; but you'll have to find me a seat in a dark corner where I can sleep behind my fan."

"There are no dark corners—except in the gallery for lovers and dowagers—and I pledge myself nobody under forty shall have any disposition for slumber," protested Sir Joseph, as he ran off to give her orders.

She passed under the lamp-lit portico on Lord Dunkeld's arm.

"*That* is the man she will marry," Stobart thought, as he walked away, hurrying from the crowd and the lights, and noise and laughter, and past a tavern a little way off, in front of which an army of footmen and links were gathered, and where they and the crowd were being served with beer and gin. He was glad to get into a dark lane that led towards Westminster Bridge, skirting the river, and to be able to think quietly.

She would marry Dunkeld. Was it not the best thing she could do—her best chance for the saving of that immortal soul which he had tried in vain to save? Dunkeld was no idle pleasure-lover, though he mixed in the diversions of his time. He was a politician, had written more than one pamphlet that had commanded the attention of the town. He was a good Churchman, a regular attendant at the Chapel Royal. He was rich enough to be above suspicion of mercenary views. He had never been a gambler or a profligate. He was seven and thirty, Antonia's senior by about twelve years. Assuredly she would be safer from the evil of the time as Dunkeld's wife than in her present unprotected position.

He repeated these arguments with unending iteration throughout his homeward walk. It was perhaps his duty to urge this union upon her. She had never spoken to him of Dunkeld, or in so casual a tone that he had suspected her of no uncommon friendship for that excellent man; yet he could hardly doubt that she favoured his suit. Dunkeld was handsome, accomplished, of an ancient Scottish family, had made his mark in the English House of Commons. Stobart could scarcely believe it possible that such a suitor had failed to engage Antonia's affections. At any rate, it was his duty—his duty as a friend, as a Christian—to persuade her to this marriage.

He found his wife sitting up for him, and the supper untouched, though it was midnight when he got home. The supper was but a frugal meal of bread and cheese, a spring salad, and small beer; but the table was neatly laid with a clean damask cloth, and adorned with a Lowestoft bowl of wallflowers. Lucy had a genius for small things, and was quick to learn any art that light hands and perseverance could accomplish.

"How late you are, George!" she exclaimed. "I was almost frightened. Have you been teaching your night class all these hours?"

"No, 'tis not a class night. I have been roaming the streets, full of thought, but idle of purpose. I let myself drift with the crowd, and went to stare at the fine people going into Ranelagh."

"You! Well, 'tis a wonder. But why didn't you take me? I should have loved to see the fancy dresses and masks and dominos. Indeed, I should have asked you many a time to let me see the quality going to Court, only I fancied you thought all such shows wicked."

"A wicked waste of time. I doubt I have been wickedly wasting my time to-night, Lucy; yet perhaps some good may come of my idleness. God can turn even our errors to profit."

"Oh, George, I have done very wrong," his wife said, with sudden seriousness. "I have forgotten something."

"Nay, child, 'tis not the first time. Thy genius never showed strongest in remembering things."

"But this was a serious thing, and you'll scold me when you know it."

"Be brief, dear, and I promise to be indulgent."

"You know Sally Dormer, the poor woman that's in a consumption, and that you and her ladyship are concerned about?"

"Yes."

"Her young brother called the day you came home, and told me the doctor had given her over, and she wanted to see you—she was pining and fretting because you was away; and she had been a terrible sinner, the boy said, and was afeared to meet her God. I meant to tell you the first minute I saw you, George; and then I was so glad to see you, and that put everything out of my head."

"And kept it out of your head for a week, Lucy—the prayer of a dying woman?"

"Ah, now you are angry with me."

"No, no; but I am sorry—very sorry. The poor soul is dead, perhaps. I might have been with her at the last hour, and might have given her hope and comfort. You should not forget such things as those, Lucy; your heart should serve instead of memory when a dying penitent's peace is in question."

"Oh, I am a hateful wretch, and I'd sooner you scolded me than not. But you had been away so long, and I had fretted about you, and was so glad to have you again."

She was in tears, and he held out his hand to her across the table.

"Don't cry, Lucy. Perhaps I do ill to leave you—even in God's service; but the call is strong."

He left his thought unspoken. He had been thinking that the man who gave himself to the service of Christ should have neither wife nor child. The earthly and the heavenly love were not compatible.

"I will go to Sally's garret the first thing to-morrow morning," he said. "Please God I may not be too late!"

He was silent for the rest of the meal, and his slumbers were brief and perturbed, his fitful sleep haunted by visions of splendour and beauty: the brazen duchess, erstwhile maid-of-honour, wife of two husbands, radiant and half-naked as the goddess of chastity, with a diamond crescent on her brow; and that other woman, whose modest bearing gave the grace of purity even to the splendour of her jewels and glittering silver gown. Dream faces followed him through the labyrinth of sleep, and his last dream was of the nightmare kind. He was in the retreat at Fontenoy, fighting at close quarters with a French dragoon, whom he knew of a sudden for the foul fiend in person, and that the stake for which he fought was Antonia's soul.

"He shall not have her," he cried. "I'd sooner see her another man's wife than the devil's prize."

He was awakened by his own voice, in a hoarse, gasping cry, and starting up in the broad light of a May morning, looked at his watch, and found it was half-past five. He rose quietly, so as not to disturb his sleeping wife, and made his morning toilet in a little back room that served as his dressing-closet—a Spartan chamber, in which an abundance of cold water was his only luxury. He left the house soon after six, and walked quickly through the quiet morning streets to the pestiferous alley where Sally Dormer lay dying or dead.

She was one of his penitents, a woman who was still young, and had once been beautiful, steeped in sin in the very morning of life, in the company of thieves and highwaymen, grown prematurely old in a profligate career, a courtesan's neglected offspring, and carrying the seeds of consumption from her cradle. Her mother had been dead ten years; her father had never been known to her; her only relative was a boy of eleven, her mother's sole legacy. A sermon of Whitefield's preached to thousands of hearers on Kennington Common, in the sultry stillness of an August night, had awakened her to the knowledge of sin. She was one of the many who went to hear the famous preacher, prompted by idle curiosity, and who left him changed and exalted, shuddering at the sins of the past, horrified at the perils of the future. That wave of penitent feeling might have ebbed as quickly as it rose but for George Stobart, who found the sinner while the effect of Whitefield's eloquence was new, and completed the work of conversion—a work more easily accomplished, perhaps, by reason of Sally Dormer's broken health.

She had been marked for death before that sultry night when she had stood under the summer stars, trembling at Whitefield's picture of the sinner's doom, pale to the lips as he dwelt on the terrors of hell, and God's curse upon the stubborn unbeliever. "All the curses of the law belong to you, oh, ye adamantine hearts, that melt not at the name of Jesus. Cursed are you when you go out; cursed are you when you come in; cursed are your thoughts; cursed are your words; cursed are your deeds! Everything you do, say, or think, from morning to night, is only one continued series of sin. Awake, awake, thou that sleepest, melt and tremble, heart of stone. Look to Him whom thou hast pierced! Look and love; look and mourn; look and praise. Though thou art stained with sin, and black with iniquity, thy God is yet thy God!"

Stobart had told Antonia of Sally Dormer's condition, and had provided by her means for the penitent's comfort in her lingering illness, the fatal end of which was obvious, however much her state varied from week to week. But he had opposed Antonia's desire to visit the invalid, shrinking with actual pain from the idea of any contact between the spotless woman and the castaway, who in her remorse for her past life was apt to expatiate upon vile experiences.

Five minutes' walk brought Mr. Stobart to a narrow street on the edge of the river, a street long given over to the dregs of humanity. The houses were old and dilapidated, and several of those on the water-side had been shored up at the back with timber supports, moss-grown and slimy from the river fog, yet a favourite climbing place for vagabond boys, as well as for a colony of starveling rats.

Sally's lodging was on the third story of a corner house, one of the oldest and most tumble-down, but also one of the most spacious, having formed part of a nobleman's mansion under the Tudor kings, when all the river-side was pleasaunce and garden.

The garret occupied the whole of the top floor, under a steeply sloping roof, and had two windows, one looking to the street, the other to the river. Here Sally had been slowly dying for near half a year, in charge of her little brother, and under the supervision of the dispensary doctor, who saw her daily.

The house was quiet in the summer morning. The men who had work to do had gone about it; the idlers were still in bed; the more respectable among the women were occupied with their children or their housework. Stobart met no one in the gloom of the rickety staircase, where the rotten boards offered numerous pitfalls for the unwary. He was used to ruin and decay in that water-side region, and trod carefully. The last flight was little better than a ladder, at the top of which he saw the garret door ajar, and heard a voice he knew speaking in tones so low and gentle that speech seemed a caress.

It was Antonia's voice. She was sitting by Sally Dormer's pillow, in all the splendour of white and silver brocade, diamond tiara and jewelled stomacher. Her right arm was round the sick woman, and Sally's dishevelled head leant against her shoulder.

"Great Heaven, what a change of scene!" he said, as he bent down and took Sally's hand. "'Tis not many hours since I saw you at Ranelagh."

"Were *you* at Ranelagh?"

"At the gate only. I do not enter such paradises. I went there last night, after your door was shut in my face for the third time. It seemed my only chance of seeing you; and the sight was worth a journey. But what madness to come here alone in your finery, to flash jewels worth a king's ransom before starving desperadoes! Sure 'twas wilfully to provoke danger."

"I am not afraid. My coach brought me to the end of the street, and my chair is to fetch me presently. I shall be taken care of, sir, be sure. This foolish Sally had set her heart on seeing me in my masquerade finery, so I came straight from Ranelagh; and I have been telling Sally about the ball and the beauties."

"An edifying discourse, truly!"

"Oh, you shall edify her to your heart's content when I am gone. I have been trying to amuse her. I stole those sweetmeats for Harry from the royal table"—smiling at the boy, who was sitting on the end of the bed, with his mouth full of bonbons. "I smuggled them into my pocket while the duke was talking to me."

"I was at Ranelagh once, your ladyship," said Sally, touching the gems on Antonia's stomacher one by one with her attenuated finger-tips, as if she were counting them, and as if their brilliancy gave her pleasure. "'Twas when I was young and lived like a lady. My first sweetheart took me there. He was a gentleman then. 'Twas before he took to the road. I dream of him often as he was in those days, seven years ago. He is changed now, and so am I. Sometimes I can scarce believe we are the same flesh and blood. 'Twas a handsome face, a dear face! I see it in my dreams every night."

"Sally, Sally, is this the spirit in which to remember your sins?" exclaimed Stobart, reprovingly. "See, madam, what mischief your mistaken kindness has done."

"No, no, no! My poor Sally is no less a true penitent because her thoughts turn for a few moments to the days that are gone. 'Tis a fault in your religion, sir, that it is all gloom. Your Master took a kinder view of life, and was indulgent to human affections as He was pitiful to human pains.

Sally has made her peace with God, and believes in a happy world where her sins will be forgiven, and she will wear the white robe of innocence, and hear the songs of angels round the heavenly throne."

"If thou hast indeed assurance of salvation, Sally, thou art happier than the great ones of the earth, who wilfully refuse their portion in Christ's atoning blood, who can neither realize their own iniquity, nor the Redeemer's power to take away their sins," Stobart said gravely.

"'Though your sins be as scarlet, they shall be as white as snow,'" murmured Sally, her fingers still wandering about Antonia's jewels, touching necklace and tiara, and the raven hair that fell in heavy curls about the full white throat.

"How beautiful you are!" she murmured. "If the angels are like you, and as kind, how dearly I shall love them! Poor hell-deserving me! *Will* they be kind, and never cast my sins in my face, nor draw their skirts away from me, and quicken their steps, as I have seen modest women do in the streets?"

"We are told that God's angels are much kinder than modest women, Sally," Antonia answered, smiling at her as she offered a cup of cooling drink to the parched lips.

She had been teaching the eleven-year-old Harry to make lemonade for his sick sister. One of the ladies from the infant nursery came in every day to make Sally's bed and clean her room, and for the rest the precocious little brother, reared in muddle, idleness, and intermittent starvation, was much more helpful than a happier child would have been.

"Shall I read to you, Sally?" Stobart asked in his grave voice, seating himself in an old rush-bottomed chair at the foot of the bed.

"Oh, sir, pray with me, pray for me! I would rather hear your prayers than the book. They do me more good."

Antonia gently withdrew her arm from the sick woman's waist, and arranged the pillows at her back—luxurious down pillows supplied from the *trop-plein* of St. James's Square—and rose from her seat by the bed.

"Good-bye, Sally," she said, putting on her black domino, which she had thrown off at the invalid's request, to exhibit the splendours beneath. "I shall come and see you soon again; and I leave you with a good friend."

"Oh, my lady, do stop for a bit. I love to have you by my bed; and, oh, I want you to hear his prayers. I want you to be justified by faith, you who have never sinned."

"Hush, hush, Sally!"

"Who know not sin—like mine. I want you to believe as I do. I want to meet you in heaven among the happy souls washed white in the blood of the Lamb. Stay and hear him pray."

"I'll stay for a little to please you, Sally; but indeed I am out of place here," Antonia said gravely, as she resumed her seat.

Stobart was kneeling at the foot of the bed, his face bent upon his clasped hands, and the women had been speaking in almost whispers, Sally's voice being weak from illness, and Antonia's lowered in sympathy. He looked up presently after a long silence and began his prayer. He had been struggling against earthly thoughts, striving for that detachment of mind and senses which he had found more and more difficult of late, striving to concentrate all his forces of heart and intellect upon the dying woman—the newly awakened soul hovering on the threshold of eternity. Could there be a more enthralling theme, a subject more removed from earthly desires and earthly temptations?

Antonia looked at him with something of awe in her gaze. She had never heard him pray. He had argued with her; he had striven his hardest to make her think as he thought; but he had never prayed for her. Into that holier region, that nearer approach to the God he worshipped, she had never passed. The temple doors were shut against so obstinate an unbeliever, so hardened a scorner.

His face seemed the face of a stranger, transfigured by that rapture of faith in the spirit world, made like to the angels in whose actual and everlasting existence this man—this rational, educated Englishman, of an over-civilized epoch—firmly believed. He believed, and was made happy by his belief. This present life was of no more value to him than the dull brown husk of the worm that knows it is to be a butterfly. To the Voltairean this thing was wonderful. The very strangeness of it fascinated her, and she listened with deepest interest to George Stobart's prayer.

His opening invocation had a formal tone. The words came slowly, and for some minutes his prayer was woven out of those familiar and moving texts he loved, while the thoughts and feelings of the man himself rose slowly from the depths of a heart that seemed ice-bound; but the man believed in Him to whom he prayed, and presently the ice melted, and the fire came, and the speaker forgot all surrounding things—the lovely eyes watching him in a grave wonder, the feelings and doubts and apprehensions of last night. The earthly fetters fell away from his liberated soul, and he was alone with his God, as much alone as Moses on the mountain, as Christ in the garden. Then, and then only, the man became eloquent. Moving words came from the heart so deeply moved, burning words from the spirit on fire with an exalted faith.

Sally Dormer sobbed upon Antonia's breast, the unbeliever looking down upon her with a tender pity, glad that the slow and painful passage to the grave should be soothed by beautiful fables, by dreams that took the sting from death.

Perhaps the thing that moved Antonia most was the unspeakable pity and compassion, the love that this man felt for the castaway. She had been told that the Oxford Methodists were a sanctimonious, pragmatical sect, whose heaven was an exclusive freehold, and who delighted in consigning their fellow-creatures to everlasting flames. But here she found sympathy with the sinner stronger than abhorrence of the sin. And her reason—that reason of which she was so proud—told her that with such a sinner none but an enthusiast could have prevailed. It needed the fiery speech of a Whitefield, the passionate appeal of an impassioned orator, to awaken a soul so dead.

"'Awake, thou that sleepest,'" cries the Church to the heathen; but if the Church that calls is a formal, unloving, half-somnolent Church, what chance of awakening?

The great Revival had been the work of a handful of young men—men whom the Church might have kept had her rulers been able to gauge their power, but who had been sent into the fields to carry on their work of conversion as their Master was sent before them.

Antonia was no nearer belief in Stobart's creed than she had been yesterday; but she was impressed by the sincerity of the man, the vitality of an unquestioning faith.

He was interrupted in the midst of an impassioned sentence by a startling appearance. The lattice facing the river had been left open to the balmy morning air. The casement rattled suddenly, and a pair of hands appeared clutching the sill, followed almost instantly by the vision of a ghastly face with starting eyeballs and panting mouth; and then a slenderly built man scrambled through the opening, and dropped head foremost into the room, breathless, and speechless for the moment.

George Stobart started to his feet.

"What are you doing here, fellow?" he exclaimed angrily.

The man took no notice of the question, but flung himself on his knees by the bed, and grasped Sally's hand. His clothes were torn and mud-stained, one of his coat-sleeves was ripped from wrist to shoulder. Great beads of sweat rolled down his ashen face.

"Hide me, hide me, Sally," he gasped hoarsely. "If ever you loved me, save me from the gallows. Hide me somewhere behind your bed—in your closet—anywhere. The constables are after me. It's a hanging business."

"Oh, Jack, I thought you was in Georgia—safe, and leading an honest life."

"I've come back. I'm one of them that can't be honest. They're after me. I gave them the slip on the bridge—ran for my life—climbed the old timbers. Hell, how slippery they are! They'll be round the corner directly. They'll search every house in the street."

He was looking about the room with strained eyes, searching for some hole to hide in. There was a curious kind of closet in the slope of the rafters, filling an acute angle. He was making for this, then stopped and ran to the window facing the river.

"Get out of this, fellow," said Stobart. "This woman has done with the companions of sin. Go!"

"No, no," cried Antonia; "you shall not give him over to those bloodhounds."

"What, madam, would you make yourself the abettor of crime—come between a felon and the law which protects honest people from thieves and murderers?"

"I hate your laws—your inexorable judges, your murdering laws, which will hang a child that never knew right from wrong for a stolen sixpence."

"They are round the corner; they are looking at the house," gasped the fugitive, moving from the window and looking round the room in a wild despair.

He had been caught in that very house years before, when he and Sally Dormer lodged there together, and when he was one of the luckiest professionals on the Dover road, with a couple of good horses, and a genius for getting clear off after a job. He had escaped by the skin of his teeth on that occasion, the witnesses for identification breaking down in the inquiry before the magistrate. He had saved his neck and some of the profits from an audacious attack on the Dover mail, and had gone to America in a shipload of mixed company, swearing to turn honest and cheat Jack Ketch. But he could as easily have turned wild Indian; and after a spirited career in Georgia he had got himself back to London, and being in low water, without means to buy himself a good horse, had sunk to the meaner status of foot-pad, and this morning had been concerned with three others in an attempt to stop a great lady's coach on the way from Ranelagh.

A chosen few among the most dissipated of the company had kept the ball going till seven o'clock, and had gone to breakfast and cards after seven—and it was one of these great ladies whose chariot had been stopped in the loneliest part of the road, between Chelsea and the Five Fields.

Antonia was looking out of the window that overhung the street. The thief made a rush towards the same window, and stopped midway, staring at this queen-like figure in mute surprise. Her beauty, her sumptuous dress and jewels made him almost think this dazzling appearance the hallucination of his own distraught brain. "Is it real?" he muttered, and then went back to the other casement, and looked out again.

"They are coming," he said in a dull voice. "'Tis no use to hide in that rat-hole. They'd have me out in a trice. The game's up, Sally. I shall dance upon nothing at Tyburn before the month is out."

He looked to the priming of a pair of pistols which he carried in a leather belt. They were ready for work. He took his stand behind the garret door. The first man who entered that room would be accounted for. They would not risk an ascent upon those slippery old beams which he had climbed for sport many a time in his boyhood; they would make their entrance from the street. Well, there was some hope of giving them trouble on the top flight of stairs, almost as steep as a ladder, and rotten enough to let them down headlong with a little extra impetus from above.

"They are not round yet," cried Antonia, snatching up her black silk domino from the chair where it hung. "Put on this, sir. So, so"—wrapping the voluminous cloak round the thief's thin frame. "Don't cry, Sally; we'll save him if we can, for your sake; and he'll turn honest for your sake. So; the cloak covers your feet. Why, I doubt I am the taller. Now for the mask," adjusting the little loup, which fastened with a spring, over the man's face, and the silk hood over his head.

"Come, Mr. Stobart, my chair is at the door," she said breathlessly. "Take this poor wretch downstairs, bundle him into the chair, and bid my servants carry him to my house, and hide him there. They can send a hackney coach to fetch me. Quick, quick!" she cried, stamping her foot; "quick, sir, if you would save a life."

Stobart looked from the masked figure to Antonia irresolutely, and then looked out of the river window. There was a mob hurrying along the muddy shore at the heels of three Bow Street runners, who were nearing the network of timbers below. There was no time for scruples. Five minutes would give the pursuers time to come round to the front of the house.

A wailing voice came from the bed—

"Oh, sir, save him, for Christ's sake! He was my first sweetheart; and he has always been kind to me. Give him this one chance."

The fugitive had not waited, but had scrambled downstairs in his strange disguise, stumbling every now and then when his feet caught in the trailing domino.

Antonia, watching from the window, saw him dash into the street, open the door of the sedan—'twas not the first he had opened as violently—and disappear inside it.

The chairmen stood dumbfounded; and had not Stobart appeared on the instant to give them their lady's orders, might have raised an alarm. Drilled to obedience, however, the men took up their load in prompt and orderly style, and the sedan, with two running footmen guarding it, turned one corner of the street a minute before the constables came round the other.

It was an unspeakable mortification for these gentlemen when they found their bird flown, how they knew not, or, indeed, whether he had ever been in the house, which they searched from cellar to garret, giving as much trouble as they could to all its inhabitants. It was in vain that they questioned Sally Dormer, who swore it was years since she had set eyes on her old friend Jack Parsons. It shocked Stobart to see that this brand plucked from the burning could be so ready with a lie, and that the two women rejoiced in the escape of Mr. Parsons almost as if he had been a Christian martyr saved from the lions.

"He is a man; and 'twas a life—a life like yours or mine—that we were saving," Antonia said by-and-by, when he expressed surprise at her conduct. "'Tis a thing a woman does instinctively. I think I would do as much to save a sheep from the slaughter-house. 'Twas a happy thought that brought the sedan to my mind. I remembered Lord Nithisdale's escape in '15."

"Lady Nithisdale was saving her husband's life by that stratagem."

"And I was saving a thief whose face I had never seen till five minutes before I fastened my mask upon it. But I saw a man trembling for his life, like a bird in a net; and I remembered how savage our law is, and how light judge and jury make of a fellow-creature's doom. I shall pack the rascal off to America again, and dare him to do ill there after his escape. You must help me to get him down the river this night, Mr. Stobart, and stowed away upon the first ship that sails from Gravesend."

"I must, must I?"

"If you refuse, I must employ Goodwin, and that might be dangerous."

"I cannot refuse you. Can you doubt that I admire your kindness, your generous sympathy with creatures that suffer? But I tremble at the thought of a nature so impulsive, a heart so easily melted."

"Oh, it can be hard on occasion," she said proudly, remembering the lovers who had sighed at her feet and been sent away despairing, since her reign in London had begun, her supremacy as a beauty and a fortune.

Having consented to help in her work of mercy, Stobart performed his task faithfully. He had allies among the vagabond classes whose honour he could rely on, and with the help of two stalwart boatmen he conveyed Jack Parsons to Erith, and saw him on board a trading vessel, carrying a score or so of emigrants and a freight of miscellaneous merchandise to Boston, which by good luck was to sail with the next favourable wind. He provided the fugitive with proper clothing and necessaries for the voyage, which might last months, and took pains to clothe him like a small tradesman's son; and as such he was shipped, with his passage paid, and the promise of a five-pound note, to be given him by the captain before he landed in America, to maintain him till he got work.

"If the lady who saved you from the gallows should hear of you by-and-by as leading an honest life, I dare say she will help you to better yourself out yonder; but if you fall back into sin you will deserve the worst that can happen to a hardened reprobate;" and with these words of counsel, a New Testament, and Charles Wesley's hymn book, Mr. Stobart took leave of Antonia's *protégé*, who sobbed out broken words of gratitude to him and to the good lady, which sounded as if they came from the heart.

"I had my chance before, sir, and I threw it away—but God's curse blight me if I forget what that woman did for me."

Stobart wrote to Lady Kilrush, with an account of what he had done, but it was some days before he saw her. He had to take up the thread of his mission work, and had to wait upon Mr. Wesley more than once—to discuss his philanthropic labours—at his house by the Foundery. He saw Sally Dormer every day, and was touched by the poor creature's adoration of Antonia, whom she now regarded as a heaven-sent angel.

"Oh, sir, you told me once that her ladyship was an infidel; but, indeed, sir, whatever she says, whatever she thinks, you cannot believe that such a creature will be shut out from heaven. Sure, sir, heaven must be full of women like her, and God must love them, because they are good."

"No, Sally, God cannot love those who deny Christ."

"But indeed she does not. While you was away, when I was so ill, I asked her to read the Bible to me, and she let me choose the chapters—the

Sermon on the Mount, and those chapters you love in St. John's Gospel—and she told me she loved Jesus—loved His words of kindness and mercy, His goodness to the sick and the poor, and to the little children."

"All that is no use, Sally, without faith in His atoning blood, without the conviction of sin, or the belief in saving grace. Yet I can scarce think that so good a woman as Lady Kilrush will be left for ever under the dominion of Satan. Faith will come to her some day—with the coming of sorrow."

"Yes, yes, it will come; and she will shine like a star in heaven. God cannot do without such angels round His throne."

Stobart reproved her gently for words that went too near blasphemy. He was melted by her affection for the generous friend who had done so much to brighten her declining days.

"She came to see me very often while you was away," Sally said; "and she paid the nurse-keeper to come every day, and sent me soups and jellies and all sorts of good things by a light-porter every morning. And she talks to me as if I was an honest woman. She never reminds me what a sinner I have been—or even that I'm not a lady."

It was more than a week after the scene in Sally Dormer's garret, and the ship that carried Mr. John Parsons was beating round the Start Point, when George Stobart called in St. James's Square early in the afternoon.

The dining-room door stood wide open as he crossed the hall, and he saw a long table strewed with roses and covered with gold plate, and the *débris* of a fashionable breakfast, chocolate-pots, champagne-glasses, carbonadoed hams, chickens and salads, jellies and junkets and creams.

"Her ladyship has been entertaining company," he said, with a sense of displeasure of which he felt ashamed, knowing how unreasonable it was. Had she not a right to live her own life, she who had never professed Christianity, least of all his kind of Christianity, which meant total renunciation of all self-indulgence, purple and fine linen, banquets and dances, splendid furniture and rich food?

"Yes, sir, her ladyship has been giving a breakfast-party to the Duke of Cumberland," replied the footman, swelling with pride. "Eight and twenty sat down—mostly dukes and duchesses—and Mr. Handel played on the 'arpsikon for an hour after breakfast. His royal 'ighness loves music," added the lackey, condescendingly, as he ushered Mr. Stobart into the library.

"Was Lord Dunkeld among the company?" Stobart asked.

"Yes, sir."

Stobart had come there charged with a mission, a self-imposed duty, which had been in his mind—paramount over all other considerations—ever since that night at Ranelagh, when he had seen Antonia and Lord Dunkeld together. Again and again he went over the same chain of reasoning, with always the same result. He saw her in the flower of youth, beautiful and impulsive, with a wild courage that scorned consequences, ready to break the law if her heart prompted; and he told himself that for such a woman marriage with a good man was the only safeguard from the innumerable perils of a woman's life. In her case marriage was inevitable. The worldlings would not cease from striving for so rich a prize. If she did not marry Dunkeld, she would marry some one else, his inferior, perhaps, in every virtue. It was his duty—his, as her friend, her earnest well-wisher—to persuade her to so suitable an alliance.

Having marked out this duty to be done, he was in a fever of anxiety to get his task accomplished. He was like a martyr, who knows death inevitable, and is eager for the faggot and the stake. That poignant eagerness was so strange a feeling—a fire of enthusiasm that was almost agony.

He walked up and down the library, agitated and impatient, his hands clasped above his head. He was wondering how she would receive his advice. She would be angry, perhaps; and would resent the impertinence of unsought counsel.

The windows were open, and the room was full of flowers and soft vernal air. A Kirkman harpsichord stood near the fireplace, scattered with loose sheets of music from the newest opera and oratorio. A guitar hung by a broad blue ribbon across an armchair. Light and trivial romances and modish magazines lay about the table; and another table was covered with baskets of shells and a half-finished picture-frame in shell-work. A white cockatoo cackled and screamed on his perch by a window. Nothing was wanting to mark the lady of fashion.

She came in, beaming with smiles, in the splendour of gala clothes, a sky-blue poplin sacque, covered with Irish lace, over a primrose satin petticoat powdered with silver shamrocks. Her hair was rolled back from her forehead, a little cap like a gauze butterfly was perched on the top of her head, and gauze lappets were crossed under her chin, and pinned with a single brilliant. The little cap gave a piquancy to her beauty, a dainty touch of the *soubrette*, which Boucher has immortalized in his portrait of the Pompadour.

"Well, sir," she cried gaily, making him a low curtsey, "we have broken the law between us, and I thank you heartily for your share in the offence against its majesty. Would to God that Admiral Byng could have been saved as easily!"

"You have a generous heart, madam—a heart too easily moved, perhaps, by human miseries, and I tremble for its impulses, while I admire its warmth and courage. You have never been absent from my thoughts since that morning in Sally's garret. Indeed, what man living could forget a scene so incongruous—yet—so beautiful?"

His voice faltered towards the end, and he leant against the late lord's tall armchair.

"You have not been kind in keeping away from me so long, when I was dying to give expression to my gratitude."

"Be sure my recompense was having obliged you. 'Twas superfluous to thank me. I have been very busy. I had arrears of work, and I knew all *your* hours were engaged."

"Sure there must always be something to do in a town full of people."

She was playing with the great white bird, smoothing his fluffy topknot, ruffling the soft saffron feathers round his neck, tempting him with the pink tips of taper fingers, flashing rose-coloured light from her diamond rings, whose splendour covered the slender hoop of gold with which Kilrush married her.

"You have been entertaining the Duke of Cumberland, I hear."

"Billy the Butcher! That's what my father and I used to call him, when we concocted Jacobite paragraphs for *Lloyd's Evening Post*. Yes, Mr. Stobart, I have been entertaining royalty for the first time in my life. The honour was not my own seeking either, for his royal highness challenged me to invite him."

"He would not be so much out of the fashion as not to be among your adorers."

"That is too prettily said for an Oxford Methodist. 'Tis a reminiscence of the soldier's manners. When the duke led me out for the second dance at the Duchess of Norfolk's ball he was pleased to compliment my housekeeping. 'I hear your ladyship's is the pleasantest house in town,' he said, 'but am I never to know more of it than hearsay?' On which I dropped my best curtsey, and told him that my house with all it contained was at his feet, and I had not finished my chocolate next morning before his royal highness's aide-de-camp was announced, who came to tell me his master would accept any invitation I was civil enough to send him."

"And this trivial conquest made you happy?"

"Sure it pleased me as any other toy would have done. 'Twas something to think about—whom I should invite—how I should dress my table.

I strewed it from end to end with cut roses, brought up from Essex this morning, with the dew on their petals. Their perfume had a flavour of the East—some valley in Cashmere—till a succession of smoking roasts polluted the atmosphere. I had a mind to imitate mediæval feasts, and give the prince a pie full of live singing birds, but one hardly knows how the birds might behave when the pie was cut."

"You had one sensible man among your guests, I doubt."

"*Merci du compliment—pour les autres*. Pray who was this paragon?"

"Lord Dunkeld."

"You know Lord Dunkeld?"

"He was my intimate friend some years ago."

"Before you left off having any friends but Methodists?"

"Before I knew that life was too serious a thing for trifling friendships."

"I am glad you approve of Dunkeld. Of all my modish friends he is the one I like best."

"Is it not something better than liking? Dear Lady Kilrush, accept the counsel of a friend whose heart is tortured by the consciousness of your unprotected position, the infinite perils that surround youth and beauty in a world given over to folly—a world which the most appalling convulsion of nature and the sudden death of thousands of unprepared sinners could not awaken from its dream of pleasure. I see you in your grace and loveliness, of a character too generous to suspect evil, hemmed round with profligates, the companion of unfaithful wives and damaged misses. And since I cannot win you for Christ, since you are deaf and cold to the Saviour's voice, I would at least see you guarded by a man of honour—a man who knows the world he lives in, and would know how to protect an adored wife from its worst dangers."

"I hardly follow the drift of this harangue, sir."

"Marry Dunkeld. You could not choose a better man, and I know that he adores you."

"You are vastly kind, sir, to interest yourself in my matrimonial projects. But there is more of the old woman—the spinster aunt—in this unasked advice than I expected from so serious a person as Mr. Stobart."

"I fear you are offended."

He had grown pale to the lips as he talked to her. His whole countenance, and the thrilling note in his voice betrayed the intensity of his feeling.

"No, I am only amused. But I regret that you should have wasted trouble on my affairs. It is true that Lord Dunkeld has honoured me with the offer of his hand on more than one occasion, but he has had his answer; and he is so sensible a man that in rejecting him as a lover I have not lost him as a friend."

"He will offer again, and you will accept him."

"Never!" she exclaimed with sudden energy, dropping her light, half-mocking tone, and looking at him with flashing eyes. "I shall never take a second husband, sir. You may be sure of that."

A crimson fire flashed across his pallid face, and slowly faded. He drew a deep breath, and there was a silence of moments that seemed long.

"You—you—must have some reason for such a strange resolve."

"Yes, I have my reason."

"May I know it?" he asked, trembling with emotion.

"No, sir, neither you nor any one else. 'Tis my own secret. And now let us talk of other matters. It was on your conscience to give me a spinster aunt's advice. You have done your duty very prettily, and your conscience can be at rest."

He stood looking at her in a strange silence. The beautiful face which had fired with a transient passion was now only pensive. She seated herself in her favourite chair by the open window, took up a tapestry-frame, and began to work in minute stitches that needed exquisite precision of eye and hand.

How much of his future life or earthly happiness he would have given to fathom her thoughts! He had come there to persuade her to marry; he had convinced himself that she ought to marry; and yet his heart was beating with a wild gladness. He felt like a wretch who had escaped the gallows. The rope had been round his neck when the reprieve came.

"Tell me about your night-school," she said, without looking up from her work. "Do the numbers go on increasing?"

"I—I—can't talk of the school to-day," he said. "I have a world of business on my hands. Good-bye."

He left her on the instant without offering his hand, hurried through the hall, and opened the great door before the porter, somnolent after the morning's bustle, could struggle out of his leathern chair.

"Never, never, never more must I cross that threshold," he told himself as he walked away.

He stopped on the other side of the road, and looked back at the great handsome house, so dull externally, with its long rows of uniform windows, its massive pediment and heavy iron railings, with the tall extinguishers on each side of the door in a flourish of hammered iron.

"If I ever enter that house again I shall deserve to perish everlastingly," he thought.

'Twas four o'clock, and the sun was blazing, a midsummer afternoon in early May. He walked to his house in Lambeth like a man in a dream, from which he seemed to wake with a startled air when his wife ran out into the passage to welcome him.

"How pale you look," she said. "Is it one of your old headaches?"

"No, no; 'tis nothing but the sudden heat. You are pale enough yourself, poor little woman! Come, Lucy, give me an early tea, and I'll take you and the boy for a jaunt up the river."

"Oh, George, how good you are! 'Tis near a year since you gave us a treat, or yourself a holiday."

"I have worked too hard, perhaps, and might have given you more pleasure. 'Tis difficult not to be selfish, even in trying to do good."

"I'll have tea ready in a jiffy, and Georgie dressed. I've been sitting at the window watching the boats, and wishing ever so to be on the river."

"Thou shalt have thy wish for this once, love," he said gently.

He was silent all through the simple meal, eating hardly anything, though 'twas the first food he had tasted since a seven-o'clock breakfast. He found himself wondering at the sunshine and the brightness of things, like a man who has come away from a newly filled grave—a grave where all his hopes and affections lie buried.

Lucy and her boy sat opposite him, and in the gaiety of their own prattle were unaware of his silence. The boy was three years old, and of an inexhaustible loquacity, having been encouraged to babble in Lucy's lonely hours. The sweet little voice ran on like a ripple of music, his mother hushing him every now and then, while Stobart sat with his head leaning on his hand, thinking, thinking, thinking.

They went up the river to Putney in a skiff, Stobart rowing, and it was one of the happiest evenings in Lucy's life. She had occupation enough for all the way in pointing out the houses and churches and gardens to Georgie, who asked incessant questions. She did not see the rower's pallid brow, with its look of infinite pain.

They landed at Fulham, moored the boat at the bottom of some wooden steps, and sat on a green bank, while Georgie picked the flowers off the blossoming sedges. Stobart sat with his elbows on his knees, gazing at the opposite shore, the rustic street climbing up the hill, and white cottages scattered far apart against a background of meadowland golden with marsh marigolds.

"Has rowing made your head worse, George?" his wife asked timidly.

"No, dear, no! There is nothing the matter"—holding out his hand to her. "Only I have been thinking—thinking of you and the boy, and of your lives in that dull house by the river. It is dull, I'm afraid."

"Never, when you are at home," she answered quickly. "You are very studious, and you don't talk much; but I am happy, quite happy, when you are sitting there. To have your company is all I desire."

"I have been a neglectful husband of late, Lucy. Those poor wretches in the Marsh have taken too much of my time and thought. Whatever a man's work in the world may be, he ought to remember his home."

"It is only when you are away—quite away, on those long journeys with Mr. Wesley."

"I will give up those journeys. Let the men who have neither wives nor children carry on *that* work. Would you like me to take Orders, Lucy?"

"Take Orders?"

"Enter the Church of England as an ordained priest. I might settle down then, get a London living. I have friends who could help me. It would not be to break with Wesley; he is a staunch Churchman."

"Yes, yes, I should love to see you in a real pulpit in a handsome black gown. I should love you to be a clergyman. All the town would flock to hear you, and people would talk of you as they do of Mr. Whitefield."

"No, no. I have not the metal to forge his thunderbolts. But we can think about it. I mean to be a kinder husband, Lucy. Yes, my poor girl, a kinder husband. Sure ours was a love match, was it not?"

"I loved you from the moment I heard your voice, that night at the Foundery Chapel, when I woke out of a swoon and heard you speaking to me. And in all those happy days at Clapham, when I used to tremble at the sound of your footstep, and when you taught me to read good books, an ignorant girl like me, and to behave like a lady. Oh, George, you have always, always been good to me."

The sun set, and the stars shone out of the deep serene as they went home, and a profound peace fell upon George Stobart's melancholy soul. To do his duty! That was the only thing that remained to be done. He understood John Wesley's warning better now. His soul had been in peril unspeakable. He loved her, he loved her, that queen among women—loved her with a passion measured by her own perfections. As she outshone every woman he had ever seen in loveliness, mental and physical, so his love for her surpassed any love he had ever imagined.

And to-day, when she had looked at him with so glorious a light in her eyes, when she had declared she would never marry, and confessed that she had a secret—a secret she would tell to none—he had trembled with an exquisite joy, an overpowering fear, as the conviction that she loved him flashed into his mind.

Why not? 'Twas hardly strange that the flame which had kindled in his breast had found a responsive warmth in hers. They had been so much to each other, had lived in such harmony of desires and hopes, each equally earnest in the endeavour to redress some of the manifold wrongs of the world. She had flung herself heart and soul into his philanthropic work, and here they had ever been at one. Her presence, her voice, her sweetness and grace had become the first necessity of his life, the one thing without which life was worthless. Was it strange if he had become more to her than a common friend? Was it strange if, after giving him her friendship, she had given him her heart?

But, oh, how deep a fall for the man who had set his hopes on high things, who had put on the whole armour of faith, had called himself a soldier and servant of Christ, who had looked back with loathing at the folly and the impiety of his boyhood and youth, and had set his face towards the City of the Saints, scorning earthly things! How deep a fall for the man who had cried with St. Paul, "For me to live is Christ, to die is gain"! How deep a fall to know himself the slave of a forbidden love, possessed heart and brain and in every fibre of his being by a passion stronger than any feeling of his unregenerate youth! Well, he had to fight the good fight, and to conquer man's most implacable enemy, sin. A year ago he had thought himself so safe, so far advanced on the narrow path, having only to reproach himself sometimes for a certain coldness in private prayer; successful in his mission work; happy in a humble marriage; having surrendered all things that worldlings care for in order to lead the Christian life, and having found a passionless peace as his reward.

Never more, of his free will, would he see this daughter of Babylon, this enchanting heathen, who had cast her fatal spell around his life. It might not be possible to avoid chance meetings in those miserable abodes where it was her whim to play the angel of pity; but doubtless that caprice of a fine lady would pass, and Lambeth Marsh would know her no more.

She wrote to him about a week after his last visit to St. James's Square.

"Why do you not come to take a dish of tea with me? My friends are leaving for their country seats, and I have been alone several afternoons, expecting you. Were you affronted with me for calling you a spinster aunt? Sure our friendship, and my esteem for your goodness, should excuse that careless impertinence. I enclose a bank bill which I pray you to spend as quickly as possible in buying clothing and shoes for the little ragged wretches I met coming out of your school yesterday. Ah, when will there be such schools all over England, in every city, in every village? Sure some day the country will take a lesson from such men as you and Mr. Wesley, and the poor will be better cared for than they are now."

The easy assurance of her letter surprised him. Every line indicated the woman of the world, the finished coquette. He replied coldly, thanking her for her bounty, and giving his absorbing occupations as a reason for not waiting upon her.

They met a week later in Sally Dormer's garret; but Antonia was leaving as he entered, and he did nothing to detain her. He had a brief vision of her beauty, more simply dressed than usual, in a black silk mantle and hood over a grey tabinet gown. He came upon her some days after in a shed at the back of the Vauxhall Pottery, entertaining a large party of pottery girls at supper, herself the merriest of the band. She had her woman Sophy to help her, and Mrs. Patty Granger, and he had never seen a more jovial feast. There was a long table upon trestles, loaded with joints and poultry, pies and puddings, and great copper tankards of small beer; at which feast two reluctant footmen, with disgusted countenances, assisted in undress livery, while an old blind fiddler sat in a corner playing the gayest tunes in his *répertoire*.

Antonia begged Mr. Stobart to stay and keep them company, but he declined. It was his class night, he told her, and he had his adult scholars waiting for him hard by. He carried away the vision of her radiant countenance, supremely happy in the happiness she had made for others. Was it possible better to realize the lessons of the Divine Altruist? And yet she was no more a Christian than the profligate Bolingbroke or the cynic Voltaire.

He was consistent and conscientious in his determination to avoid her, so far as possible without incivility. The town was beginning to thin, and he heard with relief that she was going on a visit to the Duchess of Portland at Bulstrode, near Maidenhead. In the autumn she was to be at Tunbridge Wells, to drink the waters, a business of six weeks.

"My physician orders it, though I swear I have nothing the matter with me," she told him, at one of their chance meetings in the Marsh. "'Tis good for my nerves to waste six weeks in a place where there is a dance every night, and where I shall spend every day in a crowd."

In another of these casual meetings she upbraided him for having deserted her.

"I have been more than usually busy," he said. "My schools are growing, and the dispensary is daily becoming a more serious business."

"Everything with you is serious; but you cannot be so seriously busy as not to have leisure for a dish of tea in St. James's Square once in a fortnight. Sure you know my heart is with you in all your good works, and that I like to hear about them."

"Indeed, madam, I am eternally grateful for your sympathy and your help; but of late I have had no leisure. My wife's spirits were suffering from a close London house, and I devote every hour I can steal from my work to giving her change of air."

"I am glad to hear it. Yes, Mrs. Stobart must miss your pretty garden at Sheen."

That month of May seemed to George Stobart to contain the longest and weariest days and hours he had ever known. The weather was close and oppressive, the rank odours of the Marsh were at their worst; jail fever, small-pox, putrid throats, all the most dreaded forms of infectious sickness hung heavy over the dwellers in that poverty-stricken settlement—the pottery hands, the glass-polishers, the lace-workers, the industrious and the idle, the honest and the criminal classes whom fate had herded together, unwilling neighbours in an equality of poverty.

He worked among the sick and the dying with unflagging zeal; he gave them the best of himself, all that he had of faith in God and Christ, sustaining their spirits in the last awful hours of consciousness by his own exaltation. He gave them inexhaustible pity and love, the compassion that is only possible to a man of keen imagination and quick sympathies. He understood their inarticulate sorrows, and was able to lift their minds above the actual to the unseen, and to convince them of an eternity of bliss that should pay them for a life of misery—promise more easy to believe now that all life's miseries belonged to the past, and the long agony of living was dwarfed by the nearness of death.

He followed Sally Dormer to her last resting-place in an obscure graveyard, and he provided for her brother's maintenance in the family of a hard-working carpenter, to whom the boy was to be apprenticed in due time. He had a more personal interest in this little lad than in his other scholars, remembering Antonia's interest in the dead woman, her almost sisterly affection for that fallen sister. The boy was intelligent, and took kindly to the simple tasks set him at Mr. Stobart's school, where the teaching went no further than reading, writing, and cyphering, and where the founder's sole ambition was to rear a generation of believing Christians, steeped, from the very dawn of intelligence, in the knowledge of Christ's life and example. He relied on those gospel lessons of universal charity and brotherly love, as an enduring influence over the minds and actions of his pupils, and hoped that from his school-rooms—some of them no better than an outhouse or a roomy garret, the humble predecessors of those ragged schools which were to begin their blessed work half a century later—the gospel light would radiate far and wide across the gloom of outcast lives and homes now ruled by Satan.

In his devotion to his mission work Mr. Stobart had not forgotten his promise to make his wife's life happier. He spent all the finest afternoons in rural airings with Lucy and little George; sometimes on the river, sometimes taking a little journey by coach as far as Sutton, or Ewell, or to Hampton Court; sometimes walking to Clapham Common, or as far as Dulwich, through lanes where the hedgerow oaks and elms hung a canopy of translucent green over the grassy path, and where they came every now and then on a patch of copse or a little wood, in which it was pleasant to sit and rest while the boy played about among the young fern in a rapture of delight.

He lavished kindness upon his wife and child. Never had there been a more indulgent father or a more attentive husband. Lucy, whose flower-like prettiness had faded a little in the smoke from the potteries and the Vauxhall glass-works, recovered her rose-and-lily tints in these excursions, and was full of grateful affection which touched her husband's heart. There was something pathetic in her accepting kindness as a favour which another woman would have claimed by the divine right of a wife. It pleased him to see her happy; and his conscience, which had been cruelly disturbed of late, was now at rest. But even that inward peace could not cure the dull aching of his heart, which ached he scarce knew why; or it might be that he stubbornly refused to know. He would have told himself, if he could, that the pain was physical, and that the weariness of life which followed him through every scene, and most of all in this sweet summer *idlesse*, was a question of bodily health, a lassitude for which a modish physician would have ordered "the Bath" or "the Wells."

Oh, the mental oppression of those May afternoons, the dull misery, vague, undefined, but intolerable, in which every sound jarred, even the silver-sweet of his child's joyous voice, in which every sight was steeped in gloom, even the lovely river, rose-flushed and smiling in the evening light!

He was miserable, and he tried to find the cause of his misery in things which lay remote from the one image he dared not contemplate. He told himself that the burden under which he ached was only the monotonous quiet of his days—the want of strong interests and active efforts such as kept John Wesley's mind in the freshness of a perpetual youth. *That* was the true fountain of Jouvence—action, progress, the consciousness of struggle and victory. He had tasted the joy of successful effort in his itinerant preaching—the uncouth mob crowding as to a show at a fair, the insulting assaults of semi-savages, the triumph when he had subjugated those rough natures, when by the mere force of his eloquence, by the magnetism of his own strong faith, he compelled the railers to listen, and saw ribald jokes change to eager interest, scorn give place to awe, and tears roll down the faces that sin had stained and blemished. All this had been to him as the wine of life; and this he had promised to renounce in order that he might do his duty as that commonplace domestic animal, a kind husband.

Sitting on the river bank in the summer quiet, in the rosy afterglow, amidst tall sedges and wild flowers that love the river, with his child prattling at his knee, playing with his watch-ribbon, asking questions that were never answered, and his wife seated at his side supremely content in having won him to give her so much of his company, George Stobart meditated upon the great mistake of his life—his marriage!

He remembered how lovely a creature the printer's daughter had seemed to him in her ecstasy of faith, how divine a thing the soul newly awakened to a sense of sin, and a desire for saving grace. His heart had gone out to her in an overwhelming wave of enthusiasm, a feeling so exalted, so different from any passion of his unregenerate years, that he had welcomed it as the one pure and perfect love of his life. He thought God had given him this friendless, ill-used girl to be his helpmeet, the sharer of all his aspirations, his lifelong labours in the service of Christ, as of that impassioned hour in Wesley's Chapel.

Soon, too soon, he had discovered the shallow nature behind that hysterical emotion, the tepid piety which alone remained after the fervour of newly awakened feelings. Too soon he had found that petty interests and trivial domestic cares and joys filled the measure of his wife's mind; that she thought more of her tea-trays and her sofa-covers than of thousands of Kingswood miners won from Satan to Christ; that he must never look to her for sympathy with his highest aspirations, hardly for interest in his everyday work among the poor.

When he suggested that she should help in his day nurseries or his infant schools, she refused with a shudder, lest she should bring home small-pox or scarlet fever to little Georgie. That fear of pestilence hung like a funeral pall over Lambeth Marsh; and all his efforts to popularize inoculation could do very little against dense ignorance, and terror of a preventive measure that seemed as bad as the disease.

"If I've got to have the small-pox anyhow, I'd sooner leave it to Providence," was the usual argument.

His marriage, so gravely resolved, with such generous disdain of worldly advantage, had not brought him happiness. The fellowship in thought and feeling, which is the soul of marriage, was wanting in a union that had yet every appearance of domestic affection, and which sufficed for the wife's content. She was happy, looking no deeper than the surface of things, and finding content in the calm prosperity of her life, the absence of poverty and ill-usage. His marriage was a mistake, and to the man who had taken upon himself, as he had done, the service of Christ's poor, any marriage must needs be a mistake. For the itinerant preacher, for the man with a suffering populace depending on his care, home ties were fetters that needs must gall. He could not serve two masters. He must be a half-hearted philanthropist or a neglectful husband; only an occasional preacher or a deserter of his home. He remembered the priests he had met and conversed with in France, men who had no claims, no interests outside their Church and their parish; and it seemed to him that he had bound himself with a servitude that made his service of Christ a dead letter.

His mission work must end if he was to do his duty at home. His career as John Wesley's helper had been the most absorbing episode in his life—a source of unbounded satisfaction to mind and conscience. He had gloried in the result of his labours, never questioning, in his own fervid faith, whether conversions so sudden would stand the test of time. He had counted every convert as a gain for ever, every flood of tears as a cleansing stream. But, precious though this work had been to him, conscience urged him to renounce it. His first duty was to make a home for the woman he had sworn to love and cherish. To this end he would try to become a priest of the Established Church, strive to obtain a London living, however small, and confine his service of Christ within a narrow radius, till fortune should widen his area of work. He had loved his freedom hitherto, the power to work for his own hand; but for Lucy's sake he would bend his shoulders to the Episcopal yoke, and enter on a phase of humble obedience to authority, prepared at any hour to be called to account for his opinions, and to be hampered and constrained in his gospel teaching. He would have to suffer, as others of the Oxford Methodists and their disciples had suffered, from the tyranny of ecclesiastical intolerance; but he would face all difficulties, submit to many restrictions, to make a home for his wife. And then there was always the hope that the Church of England would be swept from the great dismal swamp of formalism on the strong tide of the Great Revival, which ran higher and wider with every year of Wesley's and Whitefield's life. The teaching begun by Whitefield among the prisoners in Gloucester jail, by Wesley in the humble meeting-house in Fetter Lane, had spread over England, Scotland, and Ireland with an irresistible force, and must finally make its power felt in the Established Church.

From the market cross and the country side, from the colliers of Bristol and the miners of Cornwall, from the wild fervour of services and sermons under starlit skies, from congregations numbered by thousands, George Stobart was prepared to restrict the scope of his work to an obscure London pulpit or a poverty-stricken parish, content if in so doing his conscience could be at rest. But the outlook was dreary, and he began to measure the length of his earthly pilgrimage, and foresaw the long progress of eventless years, some little good done, perhaps, some souls gained for Christ, many small sorrows alleviated, but all his work shut within a narrow space, controlled by other people's opinions.

One agony which other men of deep religious feeling have suffered was spared to John Wesley's helper. His faith knew no shadow of change. His absolute belief in his God and his Saviour remained to him in the lowest depth of mental depression. He might feel himself a creature of sinful impulses, an outcast from God, but he never doubted the existence of that God, or the reality of that hereafter the hope of which lies at the root of all religion. The paradise of saints, the infinite joys of eternity, hung on the balance of good and evil, a stupendous stake, which most men played for with such wild recklessness, till the lights of this life began to fade, and the awful possibilities of that other life beyond the veil flashed on their troubled souls.

He was startled from the automatic monotony of his life by a letter whose superscription so agitated him that his shaking hand could scarcely break the seal. Indeed, he did not break it for some moments, but sat with the letter in his hand, staring at the familiar writing—Antonia's writing, a strong and firm penmanship, every letter definite and upright, somewhat resembling Joseph Addison's. Oh, how embued with sin, how trapped and entangled in Satan's net, must his soul be when only the sight of Antonia's writing could so move him!

He was alone. The letter had been brought him by the little maid-servant. His wife was upstairs, busy with her son, whose footsteps might be heard running across the floor above.

He broke the seal at last, and unfolded her letter.

"St. James's Square, Monday night.

"DEAR SIR,

"I believe it is near a month since you have honoured me with a visit, nor was I so fortunate as to meet you on Saturday afternoon, when I spent some hours among our poor friends in the Marsh, and went to look at Sally's grave in the Baptist burial-ground. I must impose on your goodness to order a neat headstone, with the dear creature's name and age, and one of those Scripture texts which so consoled her last hours. I doubt, since the afternoon was so fine, you were treating yourself to a rustic holiday with Mrs. Stobart, to whom I beg you to present my affectionate compliments.

"Well, sir, since you are too busy to visit me, I must needs thrust my company upon you, at the risk of being thought troublesome. In one of my conversations with Sally Dormer the poor soul entreated me, with tearful urgency, to hear the famous preacher who converted her, believing that even my stubborn mind must yield to his invincible arguments, must be touched and melted by his heavenly eloquence. To soothe her agitated spirits I promised to hear Mr. Whitefield preach, a promise which I gave the more readily as my curiosity had been aroused by the reports I had heard of his genius.

"I am told that he is to preach at Kennington Common to-morrow night, to a vaster audience than his new Tabernacle, large as it is, could contain, and I should like better to hear him under the starry vault of a June evening than in the sultry fustiness of a crowded meeting-house. I have ever been interested in your description of those open-air meetings where you yourself have been the preacher. There is something romantic and heart-stirring in your picture of the rugged heath, the throng of humanity huddled together under a wild night sky, seeing not each other's faces, but hearing the beating of each other's hearts, the quickened breath of agitated feeling, and in the midst of that listening silence the shrill cry of some overwrought creature falling to the ground in a transport of agitation, which you and Mr. Wesley take to be the visitation of a Divine Power.

"I have not courage to go alone to such a meeting, and I do not care to ask any of my modish friends to go with me, though there are several among my acquaintance who are admirers of Mr. Whitefield, and occasional attendants at Lady Huntingdon's pious assemblies. To them, did I express this desire, I might seem a hypocrite. You who have sounded the depths of my mind, and who know that although I am an unbeliever I have never been a scoffer, will think more indulgently of me.

"The service is to begin at ten o'clock. I shall call at your door at nine, and ask you to accompany me to Kennington in my coach.

"I remain, dear sir, with heartfelt respect,

"Your very sincere and humble servant,

"ANTONIA KILRUSH."

"What has happened, George?" asked his wife, who had come into the room unheard by him, while he was reading his letter. "You look as pleased as if you had come into a fortune."

He looked up at her with a bewildered air, and for the moment could not answer.

"What does she say, George? 'Tis from Lady Kilrush, I know, for her footman is waiting in the passage."

"Yes, 'tis from Lady Kilrush. She desires to hear Whitefield preach to-morrow night, and asks me to accompany her."

"What, is she coming round, after all? I doubt you will be monstrous proud if you convert her."

"I should be monstrous happy—but it will be God's work, not mine. My words have been like the idle wind. Whitefield's influence might do something; but, alas! I fear even he will fail to touch that proud heart, that resolute mind, so strong in the sense of intellectual power. Will you go with us to-morrow?"

"Mr. Whitefield's sermons are so long, and the heat at the Tabernacle always makes my head ache."

"'Tis not at the Tabernacle, but at Kennington, in the open air."

"And we may have to stand all the time. I think I'd rather stay at home with Georgie."

"Her ladyship will call for me at nine. The boy will be in bed and asleep hours before."

"I love to sit by his bed sewing. He wakes sometimes, and likes to find me there; and sometimes he has bad dreams, and wakes in a fright."

"And wants his mother's hand and voice to soothe his spirits. Happy child, who knows not the burden of sin, and has but shadowy fears that vanish at a word of comfort! Well, you must do as you please, Lucy; but there will be room for you in her ladyship's coach."

"Oh, she is always kind, and I should love the ride; but Mr. Whitefield's sermons are so long."

Stobart wrote briefly to assure Lady Kilrush of his pleasure in being her escort to Kennington, with the customary formal conclusion, protesting himself her ladyship's "most obliged and most devoted humble servant."

When his letter was despatched he went out to the Marsh, and walked for an hour in that waste region outside the streets and alleys where his work lay. His wife's parlour had grown too small for him. He felt stifled within those four walls.

He would see her again, spend some hours in her company, her trusted friend and protector, permitted to guard her amidst that rabble throng which was likely to assemble on the common. His heart beat with a fierce rapture at the thought of those coming hours. Only to stand by her side under the summer stars, hemmed round, half suffocated by the crowd; only to see her, and to hear the adored music of her voice, the voice which had so haunted him of late, that he had started up out of sleep sometimes, hearing her call his name. Vain delusion, that betrayed the drift of his dreams!

Her coach was at his door five minutes before the hour. The night was sultry, and the two parlour windows were wide open. He had been leaning with folded arms upon the window-sill watching for her, while Lucy sat at the table sewing by the light of two candles in tall brass candlesticks. She had thought the pair of tallow candles a mark of gentility in the beginning of her married life, when the remembrance of the slum near Moorfields was fresh; but she knew better now, having seen the splendours of St. James's Square, and wax candles reckoned by the hundred.

Her ladyship had four horses to her chariot, and a couple of postillions. The lamps flamed through the summer darkness.

"I may be late," Stobart said hurriedly. "Don't sit up for me, Lucy."

He saw Antonia's face at the coach door, and the sight of it so moved him that he could scarcely speak.

His wife ran to bid him good-bye, with her customary childlike kiss, standing on tip-toe to offer him her fresh young lips, but he waved her aside.

"We shall be late. Good-night."

His heart was beating furiously. On the threshold of his door he had half a mind to excuse himself to Antonia, and to go back. He felt as if the devil was tugging him into some dark labyrinth of doom. This man believed in the devil as firmly as he believed in God—believed in an actual omnipresent Satan, ubiquitous, ever on the watch to decoy sinners, ever eager to people hell with renegades from Christ. And he felt, with a thrill of agony, that he was in the devil's clutch to-night. Satan was spreading his choicest lure to catch the sinner's soul—a woman's ineffable beauty.

She was alone, and welcomed him with her sweetest smile.

"I am turning my back on Handel's new oratorio to hear your Mr. Whitefield," she said, as they shook hands; "but now the hour is approaching I feel as eager as if I were going to see a new Romeo as seducing as Spranger Barry."

"Ah, madam, dared I hope that Whitefield's eloquence could change this frivolous humour to a beginning of belief! Could your stubborn mind once bend itself to understand the mysteries of God's redeeming grace you would not long remain in darkness. Could but one ray of Divine truth stream in upon your soul, like the shaft of sunshine through Newton's shutter, you would soon be drowned in light, dazzled by the prismatic glory of the Heavenly Sun."

"And blinded, as I doubt you are, sir. I will not impose upon you. I do not go to Kennington to be assured of free grace, or to be convinced of sin; but first to keep a promise to the dead, and next to follow the fashion, which is to hear and criticize Mr. Whitefield. Some of my friends swear he is a finer orator than Mr. Pitt."

After this they remained silent for the greater part of the way, Antonia watching the road, where the houses were set back behind long gardens, and where the countrified inns had ample space in front for a horse-trough and rustic tables and benches, with here and there a row of fine elms. That sense of space and air which is so sadly wanting now in the mighty wilderness of brick and stone gave a rural charm to the suburbs when George II. was king. Ten minutes' walk took a man from town to country, from streets and alleys to meadow and cornfield, hedgerow and thicket. The perfume of summer flowers was in the air through which they drove, and the village that hemmed the fatal common, so recently a scene of ignominious death, was as rustic as a hamlet in Buckinghamshire.

The crowd had gathered thickly, and had spread itself over the greater part of the common when Lady Kilrush's chariot drew up on the outskirts of the assembly. Stobart alighted and went to reconnoitre. A platform had been erected about six feet from the ground, and on this there had been placed a row of chairs, and a table for the preacher, with a brass lantern standing on each side of the large quarto Bible. Whitefield was there, with one of his helpers, a member of Parliament, his devoted adherent, and two ladies, one of whom was the Countess of Yarmouth's daughter, Lady Chesterfield, dowered with the blood of the Guelfs, and a fine fortune from the royal coffers, Whitefield's most illustrious convert, and a shining light in Lady Huntingdon's saintly circle.

Stobart was on terms of friendship with the orator, and had no difficulty in obtaining a seat for Lady Kilrush. Indeed, her ladyship's name would have obtained the favour as easily had she sent it by her footman, for George Whitefield loved to melt patrician hearts, and draw tears from proud eyes. Enthusiast as he was, there is a something in his familiar letters which suggests that aristocratic converts counted double. They were the *écarté* kings, the trump-aces in the game he played against Satan.

Stobart brought Antonia through the crowd, and placed her in a chair at the end of the platform, farthest from the preacher, lest the thunder of his tremendous voice should sound too close to her ear.

There was a chair to spare for himself, and he took his seat at her side, in the silence of that vast audience, waiting for the giving out of the hymn with which these open-air services usually began.

Never before had Antonia seen so vast an assemblage hushed in a serious expectancy, with faces all turned to one point, that central spot above the heads of the crowd where the lanterns made an atmosphere of faint yellow light around George Whitefield's black figure standing beside the table, with one hand resting upon an open Bible, and the other uplifted to command silence and attention.

From the preacher's platform, almost to the edge of the common the crowd extended, black and dense, a company gathered from all over London, and compounded of classes so various that almost every Metropolitan type might be found there, from the Churchman of highest dignity, come to criticize and condemn, to the street-hawker, the professional mendicant, come to taste an excitement scarcely inferior to gin.

Whitefield's helper gave out the number of the hymn, and recited the first two lines in slow and distinct tones. Then, with a burst of sound loud as the stormy breakers rolling over a rock-bound beach, there rose the voices of a multitude that none could number, harsh and sweet, loud and low, soprano and contralto, bass and tenor, mingled in one vast chorus of praise. The effect was stupendous, and Antonia felt a catching of her breath, that was almost a sob. Did those words mean nothing, after all? Was that cry of a believing throng only empty air?

A short extempore prayer followed from the helper. George Whitefield's voice had not yet been heard. The influence of his presence was enough, and it may have been that his dramatic instinct led him to keep himself in reserve till that moment of hush and expectancy in which he pronounced the first words of his text.

He stood there, supreme in a force that is rare in the history of mankind, the force that rules multitudes. 'Twas no commanding grace of person that impressed this prodigious assembly. He stood there, the central point in that tremendous throng, a very common figure, short, fat, in a black gown with huge sleeves, and a ridiculous white wig, features without beauty or grandeur, eyes with a decided squint; and that vast concourse thrilled at his presence, as at a messenger from the throne of God. This was the heaven-born orator, the man who at two-and-twenty years of age had held assembled thousands spell-bound by his eloquence, the man gifted with a voice of surpassing beauty, and with a dramatic genius which enabled him to clothe abstract ideas with flesh and blood, and make them live and move before his awestruck hearers.

It was this dramatic genius that made Whitefield supreme over the masses. Those of his admirers who had leisure to read and weigh his published sermons might discover that he had no message to deliver, that those trumpet tones were but reverberations in the air, that of all who flocked to hear the famous preacher, none ever carried home a convincing and practicable scheme of religious life; yet none could doubt the power of the man to stir the feelings, to excite, awaken and alarm the ignorant and unenlightened, to melt and to startle even his superiors in education and refinement. None could deny that the man who began life as a pot-boy in a Gloucester tavern was the greatest preacher of his time.

Antonia watched and listened with a keen interest, enduring the heated atmosphere of the crowd as best she might. She had thrown off her mantle, and the starlight shone upon the marble of her throat and the diamond heart that fastened her gauze kerchief. One large ruby set in the midst of the diamonds enhanced their whiteness; and it seemed to Stobart as he looked at her that the vivid crimson spot symbolized his own heart's blood, always bleeding for her, drop by drop. Absorbed by her interest in the preacher, she was unconscious of those eyes that gazed at her with an unspeakable love, knew not that for this man it was happiness only to sit by her side, to watch every change in the lovely face, every grace of the perfect form, oblivious of the crowd, the orator, of everything upon earth except her.

To-night Whitefield was in one of his gloomy moods, the preacher of unmitigated Calvinism. It may be that his late quarrel with the Bishop of Bangor, and the persecution he had suffered at his West End chapel had soured him, and that he was unconsciously influenced by the hardness of a world in which a mighty hunter of souls was the mark for narrow-minded opposition and vulgar ridicule. His purpose to-night seemed rather to appal than to convince, to instil despair rather than hope.

His text from the Epistle of St. Jude was pronounced in solemn tones that reached wide across that closely packed mass of humanity—

"For there are certain men crept in unawares, who were before of old ordained to this condemnation, ungodly men, turning the grace of our God into lasciviousness, and denying the only Lord God, and our Lord Jesus Christ.... Clouds they are without water, carried about of winds; trees whose fruit withereth, without fruit, twice dead, plucked up by the roots; raging waves of the sea, foaming out their own shame; wandering stars, to whom is reserved the blackness of darkness for ever."

In an oration that lasted nearly two hours the preacher rang the changes on these tremendous words. Through every phase of sin, through every stage of the downward journey, his imagination followed the sinner, "of old ordained" to perish everlastingly. His vivid words described a soul inevitably lost; and again and again the melancholy music of those phrases, "raging waves of the sea, foaming out their own shame; wandering stars; clouds without water," rang out over the awe-stricken throng, moved by this picture of an imagined doom, with an emotion scarcely less intense than the thrill of agony that ran through the crowd at Tyburn when the doomed sinner swung into Eternity.

It was with the picture of Judas, his final example of sin and death, that the preacher closed his discourse.

"Let those who tell you there is no such thing as predestination turn their eyes upon Judas," he said, his voice falling to that grave note which preluded terror. "Let them consider the arch-apostate, the son of perdition. Oh, my brethren, had ever mortal man such opportunities of salvation as Judas had? Have the angels who stand about the throne of God, His worshippers and subordinates, half such privileges as Judas had? To be the friend and companion of his Saviour, in daily and familiar association with the Redeemer of souls; to walk by His side through the fields of Palestine; to sit at meat with Him; to be with Him in sadness and in joy, in prayer and praise; to journey over the wild sea with Him, and behold His power to still the tempest; to be His bosom friend; to live on an equality with God! Think of him, oh, you sinners who have never seen your Saviour's face, think of Judas! Think of those three years of sweet converse! Think of that Divine condescension which received sinful man in the brotherhood of friendship! Think of those journeys by the Lake of Gennesaret, those pilgrimages of prayer and praise, the daily, the hourly companionship with Divinity, the affectionate familiarity with Ineffable Wisdom!

"And, O God, great God of sinners, to think what came of such unutterable privileges! The disciple, the companion, bartered all that glory and delight, flung away those inestimable joys for a handful of silver. Which of you dare disbelieve in predestined damnation when he contemplates this hideous fall, when he sees the chosen brother of Jesus sink to the base huckstering of a Jonathan Wild, one of the sacred twelve reduced to the level of informers and thief-catchers, trucking his soul's salvation against thirty pieces of silver?

"'Twas the inexorable destiny of the foredoomed sinner, the appointed end to which those footsteps beside the lake, those footsteps across the mountain, those footsteps through the temple, and in the market-place, fast or slow, were always moving. God had sentenced this man to the most awful doom the mind can conceive, created to betray, the foredoomed destroyer of his Saviour. Who can question that he was marked for hell? How else account for such a fall? I despise that shallow reasoner who will tell you that the fall of Judas was a gradual descent, beginning in avarice, ending in murder. I laugh at that fond theorizer who will tell you that Judas was an ambitious dreamer, longing to behold the Kingdom of Christ triumphant on earth, and thinking to realize that dazzling dream by bringing about the conflict between his Master and earthly authority. I laugh at him who tells me that Judas expected to see the power of the Synagogue and the Forum shrivel like a burning scroll before the face of the Messiah; and that it was on the failure of that hope he rushed to the Field of Blood.

"No, dear sinners, a thousand and a thousand times no! Over that guilty head the fiat of the Eternal had gone forth, 'This is the son of perdition, this is he who shall betray the Son of God.'"

Then, after a long pause, sinking his mighty voice almost to a whisper, the preacher asked—

"Is there any son of perdition here to-night? Is there one among you whose stubborn heart answers not to his Saviour's call—a wretch in love with vice, who would rather have sensual pleasures on earth than everlasting bliss in heaven—a modern Judas who sells his Redeemer's love for thirty pieces of the devil's money, thirty profligate raptures, thirty vicious indulgences, thirty debauches in filthy taverns, thirty nights of riot and wantonness among gamesters and loose women?

"If there be any such, cast him from you. However near, however dear—father, brother, husband, son, flesh of your flesh and bone of your bone. Cast him out; oh, you who value your eternal happiness! You cannot mistake the mark of the lost soul. The son of perdition bears a brand of sin that no eye can fail to recognize. 'Tis Satan's broad-arrow, and stamps the wretch foredoomed to hell. You who would taste the joys of heaven, hold no fellowship with such on earth."

The great throng heard those concluding phrases in a profound silence. The heavy stillness of a sultry night, the muffled roll of distant thunder, the fitful lightning, now faint, now vivid, that flashed across the scene, intensified the dramatic effect of the sermon, and the crowds that had gathered noisily with much talk and some jeering, dwindled and melted away subdued and thoughtful.

Like many other of Whitefield's sermons which moved multitudes, there was little left after the last resonance of the mighty voice had sunk into silence. But the immediate effect of his oration was tremendous. Garrick had said that he would give a hundred pounds if he could say "Oh!" like Whitefield; and what Garrick could not do must have been something of exceptional power.

Antonia had given her whole mind to the preacher; yet for her his sermon was but a dramatic effort, and she went back to her coach full of wonder at that vast influence which a fine voice and a cultivated elocution had exercised over the multitude in England and America.

Upon George Stobart the preacher's influence was stronger.

"The man makes me believe against my own reason," he said, "which has ever striven against the idea of a fatal necessity. Come, Lady Kilrush, confess that his eloquence moved you."

"I confess as much with all my heart; and I am very glad to have heard him. He is a finer actor—an unconscious actor, of course—than Garrick; at least, he has a greater power to appal an ignorant crowd."

"I see you are as stubborn as ever."

"My mind is not a weather-cock, to be driven by changing winds. I doubt Mr. Whitefield may do good by such a discourse as we have heard to-night. He may scare feeble sinners, and teach them to believe that, weak and wicked as they are, God has marked them for salvation. But what of the sinner deeply sunk in guilt—will not he see only the hopelessness of any struggle to escape from Satan? 'So be it,' he will cry; 'if I am the son of perdition, let me drown my soul in sin, and forget the injustice of God.'"

George Stobart's only answer was a despairing sigh. "Let me drown my soul in sin, and forget God." Those awful words too well depicted the condition of his own mind to-night, sitting by her side in the roomy chariot, apart from her, with his face turned to the open window, his eyes looking into the summer stillness, unseeing, his heart beating with the fierce throb of passion held in check.

Was not Whitefield right, after all? Were there not men whose names were written in the Book of Doom, wretches not born to be judged, but judged before they were born? To-night that religion of despair seemed to him the only possible creed. He had looked back and remembered the sins of his youth—his life at Eton—his life in the Army. And he had believed the stain of those sins washed away in one ineffable hour of spiritual anguish and spiritual joy, the conviction of sin followed by the assurance of free grace. He had believed his past life annihilated, and himself made a new creature, pure as Adam before the fall. And in the years that had followed that day of grace he had walked with head erect, and eyes looking up to heaven, strong in his belief in Christ, but strongest in his reliance upon his own good works.

O God, what availed his labour in the service of humanity, his sacrifice of worldly gain, his preaching, his prayers, his faithful study of God's word? A wave of passion surged across his soul, and all of good that there had been in him was swept away. The original man, foredoomed to evil, appeared again. A soul drowned in sin! Her words, so carelessly spoken, had denounced him.

The silence lasted long, and they were nearing the lights of London when Antonia spoke.

"You are very silent, Mr. Stobart," she said; "I hope you have not any trouble on your mind to-night."

"No, no."

"Then 'tis that hideous doctrine troubles you."

"Perhaps. What if it be the only true key to God's mysteries? Yes, I believe there are souls given over to Satan."

"Oh, if you believe in Satan you can believe anything."

"Can you look round the world you live in and doubt the Power of Evil?"

"Of the evil within us, no. 'Tis in ourselves, in our own hearts and minds the devil lives. We have to fight him there. Oh, I believe in that devil, the devil of many names. Envy, hatred, malice, jealousy, vanity, self-love, discontent. I know the fiend under most of his aliases. But our part is to be stronger than our own evil inclinations. I am not afraid of the devil."

"He speaks for you in that arrogant speech, and his name is pride."

"Well, perhaps I spoke with too much assurance; but I believe pride is a virtue in women, as courage is in men. Or, perhaps, pride in women is only courage by another name."

He did not reply for some moments; and then an irrepressible impulse made him touch on a perilous subject.

"Have you changed your mind about Lord Dunkeld?"

"As how, sir?" she asked, with a chilling air.

"Have you resolved to accept him as a husband? Surely you could not be for ever adamant against so noble a suitor."

"You are vastly impertinent, to repeat a question that I answered some time ago. No, sir, I shall never accept Lord Dunkeld, nor any other suitor— had he the highest rank in the kingdom."

"You must have some strong reason."

"I have my reason, an all-sufficient reason; and now, sir, no more, I beg you. Indeed, I wonder that you can distress me by renewing this argument."

"Oh, madam, if you but knew the motive of my impertinence, the anguish of heart that speaks in those words! I would have you happily mated, Antonia. I—I—who adore you. Yes, though my jealous soul could scarce contemplate the image of your husband without the murderer's impulse—though to think of you belonging to another would be a torment worse than hell-fire. Could you know how I have wrestled with Satan; how when I urged you to marry Dunkeld every word I spoke was like a knife driven through my heart; how I longed to fling myself at your feet, to tell you, as I tell you now, at the peril of my salvation, that I love you, with all the strength of my soul, my soul drowned in sin, the unpardonable sin of loving you, the sin for which I must lose heaven and reckon with Satan, my darling sin, the sin unto death, never to be repented of."

He was on his knees, and his arms were about her, drawing her averted face towards his own with a wild violence, till her brow touched his, and his lips were pressed against her burning cheek. She felt the passion of his kiss, and his tears upon her face, before she wrenched herself from his arms, and dashed down the glass in front of her.

"Stop!" she called out to the postillions.

Startled at her authoritative cry, they pulled up their horses suddenly, with a loud clattering on the stones, a hundred yards from the bridge.

"You devil!" she said to Stobart, between her set teeth. "You that I took for a saint! I will not breathe the same air with you."

The carriage had hardly stopped when she opened the door and sprang out, not waiting for her footman to let down the steps. He had been asleep in the rumble, and only alighted a moment before his mistress.

She walked towards the bridge in a tumult of agitation, Stobart at her side, while her carriage and horses stood still, and her servants waited for orders, wondering at this strange caprice of their lady's.

"Hypocrite! hypocrite!" she repeated. "You—the Christian, the preacher who calls sinners to repentance; the man who sacrificed fortune to marry the girl he loved."

"I knew not what love meant."

"You chose a simple girl for your wife, and tired of her; pretended friendship for me, and under that mask of friendship nursed your profligate dreams; and now you dare insult me with your unholy love."

"I should not have so dared, madam—indeed, I believe I might have conquered my passion—so far as to remain for ever silent—if—if your own words——"

"My words? When have I ever spoken a word that could warrant such an affront?"

"When I advised you to accept Dunkeld—you refused with such impassioned vehemence—you confessed you had a reason."

"And you thought 'twas because I loved another woman's husband—that 'twas your saintly self I cared for? No, sir, 'twas because I swore to Kilrush on his death-bed that I would never belong to another, that our union, of but one tragical hour, should be all I would ever know of wedlock. I belong to him now as I belonged to him then. I love his memory now as I loved him then. That, sir, was my reason. Are you not ashamed of your fatuous self-esteem, which took it for a confession of love? Love for you, the Methodist preacher, the man of God!"

"Yes, I am ashamed—I am drinking the cup of shame."

"You have tricked me, sir. You have deceived me very cruelly. I trusted you—I thought that I had a friend—one man in the world who treated me like a woman of sense—who dared to disapprove, where all the world basely flattered me. And you are the worst of all—the snake in the grass. But do you think I fear you? I had a better man than you at my feet—the man I loved—my first love—a man with sovereign power over the hearts of women. Do you think I fear you? No, sir, 'twas then the tempter tried me. If there is a devil who assails women, I met him then, and vanquished him."

She trembled from head to foot in the excess of her feeling. She was leaning against the balustrade in one of the semicircular recesses on the bridge. He was sitting at the furthest end of the stone bench, his elbows on his knees, his face hidden.

"You have made me hate myself," he said. "'Tis useless to ask you to forgive me; but you can forget that so base a worm crawls upon this earth. *That* will cost you but a slight effort."

"Yes, I will try to forget you; and to forget how much I valued your friendship, or the friendship of the honourable man I took you for."

"I was that man, madam. Our friendship did not begin in treachery. I was your true and honourable friend—till—till the devil saw me in my foolish pride, my arrogant confidence in good works."

"Well, sir, 'tis a dream ended," she said, in those grave contralto tones that had ever been like music in his ear—the lower key to which her voice dropped when she was deeply moved; "and from to-night be good enough to remember that we are strangers."

"I shall not forget, madam, nor shall my presence make the future troublesome to you."

Something in his words scared her.

"You will do nothing violent—nothing desperately wicked?"

"No, madam, whatever the tempter whispers, however sweetly the river murmurs of rest and oblivion, I shall not kill myself. For me there is the 'something after death'!"

"Will you tell them to bring my coach?"

He rose and obeyed without a word, and stood by bareheaded till she drove away, not even offering to assist her as she stepped into the carriage, attended by her footman. Stobart stood watching till the chariot vanished in the darkness of the street beyond the bridge, then flung himself on the bench in the recess, and sat with his arms folded on the stone parapet, and his forehead leaning upon them, lost in despairing thoughts.

Judas, Judas, the companion of Christ, foredoomed to everlasting misery—Judas, the son of perdition! And what of him who six years ago gave himself to God—convinced of sin, sincerely repenting of the errors of his youth, resolved to lead a new life, to live in Christ and for Christ? How confident he had been, how happy in the assurance of grace—all his thoughts, all his desires in subjection to the Divine will, living not by the strict letter of Christ's law, but by every counsel of perfection, deeming no sacrifice of self too severe, no labour too exacting, in that heavenly service. And now, after that holy apprenticeship, after all those years of duty and obedience, after mounting so high upon the ladder of life, to find himself lying in the mire at the foot of it, caught in the toils of Satan, and again the slave of sin!

The slave of sin—yes—for though he hated the sin, he went on sinning. He loved her—he loved her with a passion that the Water of Life could not quench. How vain were those supplications for grace, those confessions of guilt which broke from his convulsed lips, while her image filled his heart. How vain his cry to Christ for help, while *her* voice sounded in his ears, and the thought of her indignation, her scorn, her icy indifference, reigned supreme in the fiery tumult of his brain.

Oh, how he loathed himself for his folly; how he writhed under a proud man's agony of humiliation at the thought of his fatuous self-delusion! Something in her look, something in her tone when she protested against a second marriage, had thrilled him with the conviction that his love had found its answer in her heart. When did that fatal love begin? He knew not how the insidious poison stole into his senses; but he could recall his first consciousness of that blissful slavery, his first lapse from honour. He could remember the hour and the moment, they two walking through the squalid street in the winter twilight, her gloved hand resting lightly on his arm, her eyes looking up at him, sapphire-blue under the long dark lashes, her low voice murmuring words of pity for the dying child that she had nursed in her lap, for the broken-hearted mother they had just left, and in his heart a wild rapture that was new and sweet.

"I love her, I love her," he had told himself in that moment. "But she will never know. It is as if I loved an angel. She is as far from me. My conscience can suffer no stain from so pure, so distant a love."

Self-deluded sinner! Hypocrite to himself! He knew now that this moment marked the beginning of apostasy, the law of sin warring against the inward light. He knew now that this woman—noble-minded, chaste, charitable, a creature of kindly impulses and generous acts, for him represented Antichrist, and that from the hour in which he proved her stubborn in unbelief, he should have renounced her friendship. He had paltered with truth, had tried to reconcile the kingdom of darkness with the kingdom of light, had been satisfied with the vague hope of a deferred conversion, and had made his bosom friend of the woman who denied his Master.

He loved her—with a love not to be repented of—a love that ran in his veins and moved his heart, and seemed as much a part of his being as the nerves and bones and flesh and blood that made him a man. He might lie in dust and ashes at the foot of the cross, scourge himself to death with the penitent's whip; but while the heart beat and the brain could think the wicked love would be there; and he would die adoring her, die and perish everlastingly, lost to salvation, cut off from Christ's compassion, by that unhallowed love.

There was the agony for him, the believer. To abhor sin, to believe in everlasting punishment, and to feel the impossibility of a saving repentance, to know himself a son of perdition; since what could avail the pangs of remorse for the man who went on sinning, whose whole life was coloured by a guilty passion?

The Divine Teacher's stern denunciation of such sin rang in his ears, as he crouched with folded arms on the stone parapet, alone in the summer darkness, an outcast from God.

"He that looketh upon a woman!" On his adulterous heart that sentence burnt like vitriol upon tender flesh. Only by ceasing to love her could he cease to sin; and, looking forward through the long vista of the coming years, he saw no possibility of change in his guilty heart, no hope of respite from yearning and regret. Six years of repentance for the sins and follies of his youth; six years of faithful service; six years of peace and self-approval; and now behold him thrust outside the gate, a soul more lost than in those unregenerate days when the consciousness of sin was first awakened in his mind, when remorse for a youthful intrigue, in which he had been the victim and sport of a vile woman, and for a duel that had ended fatally, first became intolerable. For him, the earnest believer, to whom religion was a terrible reality, the fall from a state of grace meant the loss of that great hope which alone can make life worth living, that "hope of eternal life, which God, that cannot lie, promised before the world began." For him sin unrepented of meant everlasting despair, the pains of hell, the companionship of devils.

He left the bridge, and wandered along the river bank, past his own house, past the Archbishop's Palace, to the dreary marshes between Lambeth and Battersea—wandered like a man hunted by evil spirits; and it was not till daylight that he turned his steps slowly homeward, dejected and forlorn.

CHAPTER XV
"MY LADY AND MY LOVE"

Antonia was wounded to the quick by a revelation that lost her the one friend whom she had counted as changeless amidst the fickle herd. She knew of how airy a substance the friendship of the many is made; and, pleasant as she found the polite world, she had as yet discovered no kindred spirit, no woman of her own age, and tastes, and inclinations, whom she could choose for her bosom friend. Lady Margaret Laroche was, indeed, her only intimate friend amidst the multitude of her admiring acquaintance. But in George Stobart, the man who dared to be uncivil, who gave her vinegar and wormwood when she was satiated with the honey and roses of modish society, she had found a closer sympathy, a quicker appreciation of her ideas and aspirations, than in any one she had known since those old days in Rupert Buildings, where she discussed every thought and every dream with Kilrush. And stormily as that former friendship had ended, she had never contemplated the possibility of evil passions here, in that stern ascetic, the man who had renounced the world, with all its pleasures, follies, and temptations. An infidel herself, she had honoured Stobart for his steadfast faith, his self-surrender.

She was troubled, shocked, distressed by the discovery that her friend was unworthy. His absence made a blank in her life, in spite of her innumerable distractions. The memory of his sin haunted her. She tried in vain to banish the offender's image from her mind, and the thought of him came upon her at strange seasons, and sometimes kept her awake at night, like the hot and cold fits of an Indian fever.

She was not the woman to cherish weak sentimentalism, vain regrets for an unworthy friend. She had lost him, and must endure her loss, knowing that henceforward friendship was impossible. She could never again admit him to her presence, never confide in him, never esteem and honour him. The man she had trusted was dead to her for ever. It was less than a week after the parting on Westminster Bridge when she received a letter which removed all fear of any chance encounter with the man who had offended her.

"The George Inn, Portsmouth.

"The wretch who writes these lines would scarce presume to address you were it not to bid a farewell that is to be eternal. I have gone back to my old trade of soldiering, and am to sail from this place at the first favourable wind, to serve in North America under General Amherst, with a company of grenadiers, mostly volunteers like myself. 'Tis beginning life again at the bottom of the ladder; but the lowest rank in his Majesty's service is too high for the deserter from Christ. The chances of savage warfare may bring me that peace which I can never know in this world, and should I fall I shall expire in the hope of salvation, trusting that the Great Judge will be merciful to a sinner who dies in the service of his King and country.

"If you ever think of me, madam, let it be with kindness, as of one tempted beyond his strength, and not a willing sinner.

"GEORGE STOBART."

She put the letter away in a secret drawer of her bureau, but she did not read it a second time. The lines were engraved upon her memory. She was angry with him. She was sorry for him.

The friend was lost, but the world remained; and Lady Kilrush flung herself with a new zest and eagerness into the modish whirlpool.

London was empty, but Tunbridge Wells was at the zenith. She took the handsomest lodging in the little town, a stone's throw from the Pantiles, with drawing-room windows looking over the Common, and commanding all the gaiety of the place. She invited Patty Granger and her General to spend the season with her, having an idea that her old friend's joyous trifling would help her to be light-hearted and prevent her brooding upon the past. She had not omitted Mrs. Granger's name last season when sending out cards for her drums and dances; but this invitation to Tunbridge was a more intimate thing, and Patty was overwhelmed by her kindness. In the cosmopolitan crowd at the Wells, in a company where German princes and English dukes rubbed shoulders with tradesmen's wives from Smock-alley, and pickpockets newly released from the Counter, Antonia's beauty and reckless expenditure secured her a numerous following, and made her conspicuous everywhere. She could not saunter across the Common with Mrs. Granger or Sophy Potter without attracting a crowd of acquaintance, who hung upon her steps like the court about the old King or the Princess of Wales.

Miss Potter declared that the Wells was like heaven. In London she saw very little fine company, and only went abroad with her mistress when her ladyship visited the poor, or drove on shopping expeditions to the city. But manners were less formal at the Wells; and Sophy went to picnics and frisked up and down the long perspective of country dances hand in hand with persons of quality.

Never had Sophy known her mistress so eager for amusement as during this particular season. She was ready to join in every festivity, however trivial, however foolish, and diversions that had a spice of eccentricity, like Lady Caroline Petersham's minced-chicken supper at Vauxhall, seemed to please her most. She entertained lavishly, gave breakfasts, picnics, dances, suppers—had a crowd at her tea-table every evening; and Mr. Pitt being at the Wells that year, she gave several entertainments in his honour, notably an excursion to Bayham Abbey, in a dozen coaches and four, and a picnic dinner among the ruins, at which the great minister—who had but lately grasped the sceptre of supreme power—flung off the burden of public care, forgot his gout and the dark cloud of war in Europe and America, Frederick's reverses, misfortunes in Canada, while he sunned himself in Antonia's beauty, and absorbed her claret and champagne.

"I could almost wish for another earthquake that would bury me under these antique walls," he said gaily. "Sure, madam, to expire at your feet were a death more illustrious than the Assyrian funeral pile."

"Sardanapalus was a worthless sybarite, sir, and the world could spare him. England without Mr. Pitt must cease to be a nation."

"Nay, but think how glad Newcastle would be, and how the old King would chuckle if a falling pillar despatched me. 'Twould be the one pleasing episode in my history. His Majesty would order me a public funeral, in his gratitude for my civility in dying. Death is a Prime Minister's ace of trumps, and his reputation with posterity sometimes hangs on that last card."

The minister's visit to Tunbridge was shortened by the news of the taking of Cape Breton and the siege of Louisbourg, the first substantial victory that English arms had won in America since Braddock's disastrous rout on the Monongahela. Amherst and his dragoons had landed on that storm-beaten coast in the nick of time. The aristocratic water-drinkers and the little shopkeepers at the Wells rejoiced as one man. Bonfires blazed on the Common, every window was illuminated, martial music was heard on every side, toasts were drunk, glasses broken, and a general flutter of excitement pervaded the Wells, while in London a train of French standards were being carried to Westminster Abbey, to the sound of trumpets and kettle-drums, and the wild huzzas of the populace.

Antonia wondered whether George Stobart had fallen among the English dragoons fighting in the trenches, of whose desperate courage old General Granger talked so glibly. She heard of heavy losses on both sides. She pictured him lying among the unconsidered dead, while the cross of St. George waved above the shattered ramparts, and the guns roared their triumphant thunder. She read the newspapers, half in hope, half in fear of finding Stobart's name; but it was not till General Amherst's despatches were made public some time later that her mind was set at rest, and she knew that he lived and had done well.

That little season at Tunbridge, where people had to stay six weeks for a water-cure, was a crowning triumph for Antonia as a woman of *ton*. Never till now had she so concentrated her thoughts upon the futilities of pleasure, never so studied every bill of fare, or so carefully planned every entertainment. Her originality and her lavish outlay made her the cynosure of that smaller great world at the Wells. Everybody applauded her taste, and anticipated her ruin.

"The woman has a genius for spending, which is much rarer than a genius for saving," said a distinguished gourmand, who dined twice a week at Antonia's lodgings. "A fool can waste money; but to scatter gold with both hands and make every guinea flash requires a great mind. I doubt Lady Kilrush will die a pauper; but she will have squandered her fortune like a gentlewoman."

Lady Peggy Laroche was at the Wells, and spent most of her leisure with Antonia. While approving her *protégée's* taste she urged the necessity of prudence.

"Prythee, child, do not fancy your income inexhaustible. Remember, there is a bottom to every well."

"Dear Lady Peggy, Goodwin could tell you that I am a woman of business, and have a head for figures. I am spending lavishly here, but when the season is over I shall go to Kilrush with Sophy and a footman, and mope through the winter with my books and my harpsichord; and if your ladyship would condescend to share my solitude I should need no more for happiness."

"You are vastly kind, child, to offer to bury me before my time; but I am too old to hibernate, and must make the most of my few remaining winters in London or Paris."

"If you knew the romance and wild grandeur of that granite coast."

"Bond Street is romantic enough for me, *ma douce*. I depend upon living faces, not granite rocks, for my amusement, and would rather have the trumpery gossip of St. James's than the roar of the Atlantic."

After having sparkled at the Wells and lived in a perpetual *va et vient* of modish company, Lady Kilrush found life on the shores of the Atlantic somewhat monotonous. Her nearest neighbours were ten miles off. Dean Delany's clever wife could find hourly diversions in a country seat near Dublin, where she could give a dance or a big dinner every week, and had all the Court people from the Castle running in upon her; but at Kilrush the solitude was only broken by visits from Irish squires and their wives, who had nothing in common with the mistress of the house. Antonia could have endured an unbroken isolation better than the strain of trying to please uninteresting acquaintance. She devoted a good deal of her leisure to visiting the cottagers on her own estate, and ministered to every case of distress that came within her knowledge, whether on her own soil or an absentee neighbour's. She took very kindly to the peasantry, accepted their redundant flattery with a smile, and lavished gifts on old and young. To the old, the *invalides du travail*, her heart went out with generous emotion. To have laboured for a lifetime, patient as a horse in the shafts, and to be satisfied with so little in the end; just the winter seat by the smouldering turf, by courtesy a fire; just to lie in front of the hut and bask in the summer sunshine; just not to die of starvation.

The Gaffers and Gammers fared well while Antonia was at Kilrush; and before leaving she arranged with her steward for tiny pensions to be paid regularly until her return.

"You are not to be worse off for my going to England," she told one of her old men, when she bade him good-bye.

"Sure, me lady, we should be the worse off for want of your beautiful face, if you was to lave us the Bank of Ireland," replied Gaffer.

She went back to London in December, in a Government yacht that narrowly escaped calamity, after waiting at Waterford over a week for favourable weather. But Antonia enjoyed the storm; it thrilled in every nerve, and set her pulses beating, and gave her something to think of, after the emptiness of a life too free from worldly cares.

She could return to her house in St. James's Square without fear of being troubled by the presence of the man who had made the word friendship a sound that sickened her. That traitor was far away.

Assured of his absence, she went back to the slums by Lambeth Marsh, where she was received with rapture. Her pensioners had not been forgotten while she was away, since she had provided for all the most pressing cases; but her return was like the coming of April warmth after a bitter winter. Everywhere she heard lamentations at Mr. Stobart's departure, although Wesley had filled his place with another of his helpers, an indefatigable worker, but a raw youth of unsympathetic manners and uncompromising doctrine. He was barely civil to Lady Kilrush when they happened to meet, having been told that she was an unbeliever, and did all in his power to discourage her ministrations among his people.

"If your ladyship came to them with the Bible in your hand they might be the better for your kindness," he said severely; "but the carnal comforts of food and drink, which your generosity provides for them, only serve to make them careless of everlasting bliss."

"What, sir, would you starve them into piety? Do you think 'tis only because they are miserable upon earth that Christians long for the joys of heaven? That is to hold the everlasting kingdom mighty cheap. Your great Exemplar had a broader philosophy, and did not disdain to feed as well as to teach His followers."

Antonia's heart was moved at the thought of the pretty young wife deserted by her husband, and living in solitude, without the distractions of fine company, or the delight in books and music which filled the blank spaces in her own life. Impelled by this compassionate feeling, she called on Mrs. Stobart one wintry afternoon, soon after her return from Ireland, and was received with gratification which was mainly due to the splendour of her coach, and the effect it would have on the neighbours.

"Your ladyship has doubtless heard that my husband has gone back to the army?" said Lucy, when her visitor was seated in the prim front parlour, where the mahogany furniture shone with an increased polish, and where there prevailed that chilling primness which marks a room that nobody uses. "It was a sad blow to me and to Mr. Wesley; but George always hankered after his old profession, though he knew it was Satan's choicest trade."

"Nay, Mrs. Stobart, I cannot think that Satan has any part in the calling of men who fight and die for their country. I doubt your husband's life in America will be as unselfish as his life in Lambeth."

"'He has taken his hand from the plough.' That is what Mr. Wesley said. 'He was the best of my helpers, and he has deserted me,' he said. And Mr. Wesley was sorry for my trouble in being forsaken by my husband."

She shed a few feeble tears as she dwelt upon her own dull life; but she did not seem deeply impressed by the thought of her husband's peril, or the chance that he might never come back to her.

"It was a cruel disappointment for me," she complained. "He had promised to join the Church of England, and then we might have had a vicarage, and he would have stayed at home, and only preached in his parish church. He had promised to be a kinder husband."

"Kinder? Oh, Mrs. Stobart, was he ever unkind?" exclaimed Antonia, kindling with the sense of injustice. She had noted his gentleness—his supreme patience with the unsympathetic wife; so inferior to him in mind and heart—a pink and white nullity.

"It was unkind to leave me while he went about the country preaching; it was unkind to go back to the army and leave me alone for years, more like a widow than a wife. And father comes and teases me for money now that George is away. He dursn't ask for more than his allowance while George was here."

"Your father is—a troublesome person?" inquired Antonia.

"I should think he was indeed. He kept himself tolerably sober while mother was alive. She used to spend every penny on drink, and he used to beat her for it, and both of them used to beat me. It was a miserable life. Mother died in the hospital three years ago; and when she was gone the thought of his unkindness to her seemed to prey upon father's mind, and he was always at the gin-shop, and lost his situation in the printing-office where he had worked half his life; and then he came to us with a pitiful story, and my husband gave him ten shillings a week, which was more than he could afford, without denying himself, only George never minded. I don't think he would have minded if he had been obliged to live like John the Baptist in the wilderness."

"And now Mr. Stobart is gone your father troubles you?"

"Indeed he does, madam. He comes for his money on a Saturday, looking such an object that I'm ashamed for the servant to see him; and then he comes again on Tuesday or Wednesday, and tells me he's starving, and sheds tears if I refuse to give him money. And I'm obliged to refuse him, or he wouldn't leave me a sixpence to keep the house. And then father goes down the steps abusing me, and using the wickedest language, on purpose for the neighbours to hear him. And he comes again and again, sometimes before the week is out."

The idea of this sordid trouble oppressed Antonia like a nightmare. She thought of her own father—so kind, so pleasant a comrade, yet unprincipled and self-indulgent. It needed perhaps only the lower grade to have made him as lost a creature.

"Let me give you some money for him," she said eagerly. "It will be a pleasure for me to help you."

"Oh, no, no, madam. I know how generous you are; but George would never forgive me if I took your ladyship's money. Besides, it would only do father harm. He would spend it upon drink. There's no help for it. Father is my cross, and I must just bear it. He has come to live in the Marsh, on purpose to be near me; and he makes believe that he's likely to get work as a book-keeper at the glass works. As if anybody would employ a man that's never sober! And he's a clever man too, your ladyship, and has read more books than most gentlemen. But he never went to a place of worship, and he never believed in anything but his own cleverness. And see where that has brought him! Sure I beg your ladyship's pardon," concluded Lucy, hastily, "I forgot that you was of father's way of thinking."

"You have at least the consolation of your son's affection, Mrs. Stobart, and it must be pleasant for you to watch the growth of his intelligence. Is he as healthy and as handsome as when I saw him last?"

"Handsomer, I think, your ladyship."

"Will he be home from school presently? I should love to see him."

"Nay, madam, that's impossible, for he is living at the Bath with his grandmother, Lady Lanigan. Mr. Stobart wrote to her before he left Portsmouth, a farewell letter that melted her hard heart. 'Twas after the news of the taking of Louisburg, when her ladyship came here in a terrible fantig, and almost swooned when she saw the boy, and swore he was the image of his father at the same age."

"And she carried him away with her on a visit?"

"Yes, madam. She begged so hard that I could not deny her. For you see, madam, he is her only grandson; and there's a fortune going begging, as you may say. His father was too proud to try and bring her round; but if Georgie behaves prettily, who knows but she may send him to Eton—where his father was bred—and leave him the whole of her fortune?"

"True, madam. No doubt you have done best for your boy. But I fear you must feel lonely without him."

"Oh, I missed him sadly for the first week or two, madam; but a child in a house, where there's but one servant, is a constant trouble. In and out, in and out with muddy shoes, morning, noon, and night. 'Tis clean, clean, clean after them all day long, and it makes one's girl cross and impudent. He has his grandma's own woman to wash and dress him, and a footman to change his shoes when he comes in from the street."

"Is the visit to last long?"

"That depends upon his behaviour, and if her ladyship cottons to him."

"Well, so long as you can do without him, of course 'tis best," said Antonia, in a dull voice.

Her mind was wandering to that exile whose name she would not pronounce. To have sacrificed station and fortune for such a wife as this—for a woman without heart or brains, who had not enough natural feeling to tremble for a husband in danger, or to grieve at the absence of an only child!

After a few visits to her Lambeth pensioners, Lady Kilrush wearied of the work, and allowed herself to be charitable by deputy. She hated the starched prig who had taken Stobart's place in the parish. She missed the quick sympathy, the strength and earnestness of the man who had helped her to understand the world's outcasts; and as her social engagements were more numerous than last winter, she abandoned the attempt to combine philanthropy with fashion, and made Sophy her deputy in the Marsh.

Sophy had a tender heart, and loved to distribute her ladyship's bounty. She liked the priggish Wesleyan, Mr. Samson Barker, who lectured and domineered over her, but who was a conscientious youth, and innocent of all evil, the outcome of nonconformist ancestors, a feeble specimen of humanity, with a high narrow forehead, pale protuberant eyes, and a receding chin. Impressed by his mental and moral superiority, Sophy, who began by ridiculing him, soon thought him beautiful, and held it one of her highest privileges to sit under his favourite preacher, Mr. William Romaine, at St. Olave's, Southwark, and to be allowed to invite Mr. Barker to Antonia's tea-table now and then, where his appearance was a source of amusement to the rest of the company, who declared that her ladyship was at heart a Methodist, though she read Tindal and Toland, and affected liberal ideas.

"Before next season we shall hear of you among the Lady Bettys and Lady Fannys who throng Lady Huntingdon's drawing-room, and intoxicate their senses with Whitefield's raving," said one of her adorers; "and then there will be no more dinners and suppers, no more dances and drums—only gruel and flannel petticoats for old women."

Lady Kilrush drained the cup of London pleasures that winter, and was a leader in every aristocratic dissipation, shining like a star in all the choicest assemblies, but so erratic in her movements as to win for herself the sobriquet of "the Comet."

"The last spot of earth where 'twould seem reasonable to expect you is the place where one is most likely to find you," Mr. Walpole told her one night, at a dinner of hard-drinking and hard-playing politicians, where Antonia, Lady Coventry, and a couple of duchesses were the only women in a party of twenty.

She had adorers of every age, from octogenarian peers, and generals who had fought under Marlborough, to beardless boys just of age and squandering their twenty thousands a year at White's and the Cocoa

Tree. The fact that she kept every admirer at the same distance made her irresistible. To be adamant where other women were wax; to receive the flatteries of trifling fops, the ardent worship of souls of flame, with the same goddess air, smiling at her victims, kind to all, but particular to none! That deliberate and stately North Briton, Lord Dunkeld, hung upon her footsteps with an untiring devotion that was the despair of a score of young women of quality, who wanted to marry him, and thought they had pretensions for the place.

'Twas a season of unusual gaiety, as if the thirst for pleasure were intensified by the news of the war, and the consciousness of fellow countrymen starving, perishing, massacred, scalped, or burnt alive, in the pathless forests across the Atlantic. The taking of Louisburg had set all England in a tumult of pride and delight, to the forgetfulness of the catastrophe at Ticonderoga, where there had been terrible losses under Abercromby, and of the death of Lord Howe, the young, the ardent, the born leader of men, slain by the enemy's first volley.

George Stobart's name figured in Amherst's despatches. He had fought in the trenches with his old regiment; he had been with Wolfe in the storming of Gallows Hill; and had been recommended for a commission on account of his gallant behaviour. People complimented Antonia about her "pious friend."

The King was near dying at the beginning of the winter, and the lion at the Tower happening to expire of old age, while his Majesty lay ill, the royal beast's dissolution was taken as a fatal augury, and his master was given over by the gossips. But King George recovered, and Sunday parties, drums and masquerades, auctions, ridottos, oratorios, operas, plays, and little suppers, went on again merrily all through the cold weather.

In the summer of 1759 Lady Kilrush carried out a long-cherished design of revisiting Italy. When last in that country her father's critical state of health had been a drag upon her movements. She would go there now a free agent, with ample leisure to explore the region in which she was most keenly interested, those romantic hills above the Lake of Como, where her mother's birthplace was to be found.

She took Sophy, her French maid, Rodolphine, and her first footman, who was an Italian, and travelled by Ostend and the Hague and the Rhine to Basle, then by Lucerne and Fluellen, to the rugged steeps of the St. Gothard, loitering on the road, and seeing all the churches and picture-galleries that were worth looking at, her travelling carriage half full of books, and her maid and footman following in a post-chaise with the luggage, which was a lighter load of trunks and imperials than a woman of *ton* might have been supposed to require, her ladyship's travelling toilette being of a severe simplicity.

When George II. was king there was a luxury of travelling, which made amends for the want of the *train de luxe* and the *wagon-lit*. It was the luxury of slowness; the delicious leisure of long days in the midst of exquisite scenery—by lake, and river, and mountain pass—that had time to grow into the mind and memory of the traveller; journeys in which there were long oases of rest; perfumed summer nights in quiet places, where the church bell was the only sound; mornings in obscure galleries where one picture in a catalogue of a hundred was a gem to be remembered ever after; glimpses of humble lives, saunterings in market-places, adventures, perils perhaps, an alarm of brigands, ears listening for a sudden shot ringing sharp among snow-clad hills—all the terrors, joys, chances, surprises of a difficult road; and at one's inn a warmth of welcome and a deferential service that in some wise atoned for bad cooking and ill-furnished rooms.

To Antonia that Italian journey offered a delicious repose from the fever of London pleasures. After George Stobart's departure for America there had been a jarring note in the harmony of life—a note that had to be drowned somehow; and hence had come that craving for excitement, that hastening from one trivial pleasure to another, which had made her so conspicuous a figure in the London of last winter.

In the solemn silence of everlasting hills, in a solitude that to Sophy seemed a thing of horror, Antonia thought of her last season; the crowded rooms, reeking with odours of pulvilio and melting wax, the painted faces, the atmosphere of heat and hair-powder, the diamonds; the haggard looks and burning eyes, round the tables where play ran high; the hatred and malice; the jests that wounded like daggers; the smiles that murdered reputations.

"Shall I ever go back to it all, and think a London season life's supreme felicity?" she wondered, standing in front of the Capuchins' Hospice, among the granite peaks of the St. Gothard, in the chill mountain air, while the mules were being saddled for the descent into Italy. They had ridden yesterday morning through the Urnerloch—that wonderful passage of two hundred feet through the solid rock, which had been made early in the century—by the green meadows of Andermatt, and across the Ursern valley; they had wound slowly upward through a wild and barren region to the friendly hospice where there was always welcome and shelter.

Lady Kilrush had left her English travelling carriage at Lucerne, and the journey from Airolo to Como would be made in an Italian post-chaise. Her footman was a native of Bellinzona, and was able to arrange all the details of their route.

At Como she hired one of the country boats, new from the builders, and engaged four stalwart Italian boatmen, who were to be in her service while she made a leisurely tour of the lake, stopping wherever the scene pleased her fancy, and putting up with the most primitive accommodation, provided the inn were clean, and the prospect beautiful.

That year of 1759, remarkable for the success of British arms in Europe, Hindostan, and America, the "great year," as Horace Walpole calls it, was also a year of golden weather, a summer of sunshine and cloudless skies, and Antonia revelled in the warmth and light of that lovely scene. It seemed as if every drop of blood in her veins rejoiced in the glory of her mother's birthplace. Here, in what spot she knew not, but somewhere along these sunlit hills that sloped gently to the lake, her mother's early years had been spent. She would have given much to find the spot; and in her long rambles with Sophy, or alone, she rarely passed a church without entering it, and if she could find the village priest rarely left him till he had searched the register of marriages for her father's name. But no such name appeared in those humble records; and she thought that her father might have carried his fugitive bride to Milan, or even into Switzerland, before the marriage ceremony was possible; the girl being under age, and the bridegroom a heretic. She looked with interest at every villa that sheltered a noble family, and questioned the peasants, and the people of the inn, about all the important inhabitants of their neighbourhood, hoping to hear in such or such a patrician family of a runaway marriage with a wandering Englishman. But the old people to whom she chiefly addressed herself had no memory of such an event.

It was the beginning of September, and the scene and atmosphere had lost nothing of their charm by familiarity, so having made the tour of the lake villages, and being somewhat tired of rough fare, ill-furnished rooms, and most of all of Sophy's repinings for the comforts of St. James's Square, Lady Kilrush hired a villa near the quaint little town of Bellagio, a villa perched almost at the point of the wooded promontory, with a garden that sloped to the water's edge. The villa belonged to one of Antonia's fashionable friends—a certain Lady Despard, a banker's widow, who gave herself more airs than an empress, and preferred Rome or Florence to London, because of the superior consequence her wealth gave her in cities where the measure of her rank was not too precisely known. This lady—after trying to imitate Lady Mary Wortley Montagu, and live among a peasant population—had wearied of her villa and the little town at her gates, the church bells, the voices of the fishermen, the feasts and processions, and lack of modish company; and her house was to be let furnished with all its amenities.

Antonia engaged the villa for a month, at a liberal rent, and established herself, with Giuseppe, the Italian footman, as her major-domo, and a modest household of his selection; not a household of much polish or experience, but of willing hands, smiling faces, eyes that sparkled and danced with the golden light of Italy. Antonia was at home and happy among these people, who served her as it were upon their knees, and whose voices had a note that was like a caress.

"I can understand how my mother loved her garden of roses, her chestnut woods, and long terraces where the vines make a roof of shade, and how she must have pined in a dull English village—a Lincolnshire village, dismal flats without a tree, straight roads, and church steeples, with the lead-coloured sea making a level line in the distance, that seems like the end of the world. Alas, to her eyes, accustomed to this golden land, these mountains climbing up to heaven, how heart-breaking it must all have been!"

Summer in Italy, summer on the Lake of Como. Never till now had Antonia known what summer means—that perfect glory of sunlight, that magical atmosphere, half golden light and half azure haze, in which earthly things put on the glory of a dream. Never before had she enjoyed the restfulness of a land where the atmosphere and the light are enough for happiness, a sensuous happiness, perhaps, but leaving the spirit wings free for flight. After the stress and tumult of a London winter, the strife of paltry ambitions, the malevolence that called itself wit, the aching sense of loneliness in a crowd, what bliss to loll at ease in the spacious country boat, under the arched awning, while the oars dipped, and the water rippled, and life went by like a sleep! She had almost left off remembering the days of the week, the passage of time. She only knew that the moon was waning. That great golden disk which had bathed the hills in light and tempted her to loiter on the lake till midnight, was no more. There was only a ragged crescent that rose in the dead of night and filled her with melancholy. She stood at her open window, in the dark hour before dawn, drinking the cool sweet air, and full of sorrowful thoughts.

Where was George Stobart under that dwindling moon? In what grim and frowning wilderness, amidst what desolate waste of mountains, in what wild scene of savage warfare, hemmed round by painted foes, deafened by war cries more hideous than the howling of the wolves in the midnight woods, done to death by the ingenious cruelties of human fiends, or dying of famine and neglected wounds, crawling on bleeding feet till the wearied body dropped across the narrow track that the tramp of soldiers had worn through the wilderness, dying forsaken and alone, perhaps, in the pitilessness of a panic flight.

Her heart ached as she thought of him. Alas, why had he been false to his own convictions, to his own faith? She knew that he had once been sincere, had once been strong in a hope that she could not share. When first she knew him he had been a good man. She looked back, and recalled the domestic picture—the rustic lawn basking in the June sunshine, the warm air perfumed with pinks and southernwood, and the husband seated in his garden reading to his wife. She had looked down at him from the proud height of her philosophy, had scorned his unquestioning belief in things unseen; but she had respected him for his renunciation of all the luxuries and pleasures the common herd love.

Of the progress of the American campaign since the victory at Cape Breton she knew very little. The posts between Italy and England were of a hopeless irregularity, and the newspapers which she had ordered to be sent her were more than half of them lost or stopped on the way, while an occasional gossiping letter from a fashionable friend told her more of the new clothes at the Birthday than the triumphs or reverses of British arms. The London papers were at this time more concerned about Prince Ferdinand's victory over the French at Minden, and Lord George Sackville's strange backwardness in following up the Prince's success, than about the fortunes of Amherst or Forbes, and the wild warfare of the West.

It was perhaps from the desire to be better informed that Antonia was glad to see Lord Dunkeld, who surprised her by alighting from a boat at the landing stage of her villa, in the first week of her residence. He found her sitting in her garden, dreaming over a book. He had arrived at Varenna on the previous evening, he told her, and meant to stop some time at the inn, which commanded a fine view of the two lakes, and had better accommodation than was usual in out-of-the-way places.

"May one ask what brings your lordship to Italy, when most of the fine gentlemen I know are shooting partridges in Norfolk?" Antonia asked, when they were seated on a marble bench in front of the lake.

There was a fountain on the lawn near them, and oleanders white and red, masses of blossom and delicate lance-shaped leaves, made a screen against wind and sun, and there were red roses trailing all along the marble balustrade above the lake, and poppies pink, and red, and white, and pale pink cyclamen, filled a circular bed at the base of a statue of Flora, and all the garden seemed alive with colour and light. A double flight of steps, broad and shallow, went down to the water, and Dunkeld's boat was moored there, with his two boatmen lounging under the awning, idle and contented. It is a stiff pull from Varenna to the point, when the wind is blowing from Lecco.

"Will your ladyship scorn me if I confess that I love better to sit in an Italian garden than to tramp over a Norfolk stubble? There is a delicate freshness in the scent of a turnip field at early morning; but I prefer roses, and the company of one woman in the world."

"Oh, my lord, keep your compliments for St. James's. They are out of harmony with my life here."

"Am I to have no license to say foolish things, after having crossed the Alps to see you?"

"Oh, sir, I am very credulous, but I cannot believe you have been so simple as to travel over a thousand miles for a pleasure that you could enjoy next month in London."

"I should have died of that other month. I bore your absence as long as I could, and questioned all your friends and your hall-porter to discover any hope of your return. But no one would satisfy me, and my heart sickened of uncertainty. So ten days ago I ordered my chaise for Dover, and have scarce drawn rein till last night at Varenna, where I heard of your ladyship. Nay, spare me that vexed look. I come as a friend, not as an importunate suitor. Do you suppose I forget that I am forbid all ecstatic hopes?"

She gave a troubled sigh, and rose from the bench, with an agitated air.

"Lady Kilrush, cannot you believe in friendship?" he asked, following her.

"Hardly. I have believed, and have had my confidence betrayed."

"When you told me that I could never be your husband, that a life's devotion, the adoration of the Indian for his God, could not move your heart to love me, I swore to school myself to indifference, thought it was possible to live contentedly without you. I have not learnt that lesson, madam; but I have taught myself to think of your merits, your perfections, as I might of a sister's; and I ask you to give me something of a sister's regard. You need not fear me, madam. Youth and the ardour of youth have gone by. I doubt you know that I was unhappy in an early attachment, and that the exquisite creature who was to have been my wife died in my arms in her father's park, struck by lightning. She was but eighteen, and I less than three years older. The stroke that should have taken us both, and sealed our love for eternity, left me to mourn her, and to doubt God's goodness, till time chastened my rebellious thoughts."

"I have heard that sad story, my lord, and have understood why you were more serious than other men of your age and circumstances. You have been happy in finding the consolations of religion."

"Alas, madam, to be without a fixed hope in a better world is to live in the midst of chaos. A Christian's faith is like a lamp burning at the end of a long dark passage. No matter if it seem but an infinitesimal point of light in the distance, 'twill serve to guide his footsteps through the gloom."

"Would not duty, honour, conscience do as much for him?"

"Perhaps, madam, since conscience is but another name for the fear of God. Be sure the time will come when a mind so superior as yours will be awakened to the truth; but I doubt the Christian religion has suffered in your esteem by your acquaintance with Mr. Stobart. The conversation of a fanatical Methodist, the jargon of Wesley and Whitefield, their unctuous cant repeated parrot-wise by a tyro, could but move your disgust."

"Indeed, my lord, you wrong my cousin, George Stobart," Antonia answered eagerly. "He is no canter—no parrot-echo of another man's words. His sacrifice of fortune and station should vouch for his sincerity."

"Oh, we will say he is of the stuff that makes martyrs, if your ladyship pleases; but 'tis a pity that a gentleman of birth and breeding—a soldier— should have taken up with the Methodist crew. Some one told me he has the gift of preaching. I doubt he expounds the doctrine of irresistible grace in Lady Huntingdon's kitchen, for the vulgar, while Whitefield thumps a cushion in her ladyship's drawing-room."

"My cousin has left off preaching for these two years last past, sir, and is fighting for his king in North America."

"Gad's life! Then he is a better man than I took him for, when his puritan countenance and grey suit passed me in your ladyship's hall. The American campaign is no child's play. Even our sturdy Highlanders have been panic-struck at the cruelties of those Indian fiends, whose war-whoops surpass the Scottish yell as a tiger outroars an ox."

"Can your lordship tell me the latest news of the war?"

"'Tis a tale of barren victories and heavy losses. Englishmen and colonials have fought like heroes, and endured like martyrs; but I doubt the end of the campaign is still far off. The effect of last year's victory at Louisburg, at which we in England made such an uproar, was weakened by Abercromby's defeat at Ticonderoga, and by Amherst's refusal to risk an immediate attack upon Quebec. Had he taken Wolfe's advice Canada would have been ours before now; but Amherst ever erred on the side of caution.

He is all for forts and block-houses, deliberation and defence—Wolfe all for the glorious hazards of attack."

"Then I doubt my cousin, Mr. Stobart, would sooner be with Wolfe than with Amherst."

"Is the gentleman such a fire-eater?"

"I believe he loves war, and would hate shilly-shally no less than Mr. Wolfe," Antonia answered, with a deep blush, and a sudden embarrassment.

The desperate mood in which Stobart left England had been in her mind as she spoke.

"Well, if he is with Amherst he has not seen much fighting since he left Cape Breton. Does he not write to you occasionally?"

"No, he writes only to his wife, and not often to her."

"'Tis not easy for a soldier on the march through a wilderness to despatch a letter—or even to write one," said Lord Dunkeld.

After this his lordship's boat was moored by the villa landing-stage in some hour of every day. His society was not unpleasant to Antonia in her Italian solitude. He had sworn to be her friend; and she thought she had at last discovered a man capable of friendship. She had no fear of being taken off her guard, shocked and insulted, as she had been by George Stobart. Here was no slumbering volcano, no snake in the grass, only a grave and dignified gentleman, of unimpeachable honour, and an old-fashioned piety, fully impressed by his own importance, who would fain have won her for his wife, but who, disappointed in that desire, wished to keep her for his friend.

He was six-and-thirty years of age, and that tragedy of his youth had exercised a sobering influence over all his after-life. He was a fine classical scholar, and had read much, and travelled much, but showed himself a true Briton by his ignorance of every living language except his own. A courier and a French valet saved him all communication with innkeepers and their kind, and a smile or a stately wave of the hand sufficed to make his wishes known to his Varenna boatmen. He loved Italy as a picture, without wanting to get any nearer the living figures in the foreground.

There was a festa at Bellagio on the Sunday after his arrival—a festa of thanksgiving for the fruits of the year, and he attended Antonia and Sophy to the church, where there was to be a solemn service, and the priestly benediction upon gifts provided by the faithful, which were afterwards to be sold by auction for the benefit of church and poor.

The piazza in front of the church was dazzling in the fierce afternoon sunshine when Antonia and Sophy climbed the steep street, and found themselves among the populace standing about the square, the women with babies in their arms, and little children at their knees, and the maimed and halt and blind and deaf and dumb, who seem to make up half the population of an Italian town on a Sunday afternoon.

The natives gazed in admiring wonder at the beautiful face under the broad Leghorn hat, with white ostrich feathers and diamond buckle, the tall figure in the straight simplicity of white muslin and a long blue sash, that almost touched the points of the blue kid shoes, the beautiful throat and pearl necklace showing above the modest muslin kerchief. Sophy was in white muslin also, but Sophy being low in figure, must needs affect a triple frilled skirt and a frilled muslin cape, which gave her the shape of a penwiper.

"Did I not know you superior to all petty arts I might say you dressed your waiting-woman to be a foil to your beauty," Lord Dunkeld told Antonia, when Sophy was out of earshot.

"Miss Potter chooses her own clothes, and I can never persuade her to wear anything but the latest fashion. She has but to see the picture of a new mode in the *Ladies' Magazine*, and she is miserable till she tries it on her own person."

They went into the church, where the hot sunlight was intensified by the pervading decoration, and the high altar glowed like a furnace. The marble pillars were covered with crimson brocade, and long crimson curtains hung from the roof, making a tent of warm rich red, the scarlet vestments of the acolytes striking a harsher note against the crimson glow.

Three priests in richly embroidered copes officiated at the altar, and between the rolling thunder of the organ came the sound of loud strident voices chanting without accompaniment, while children's treble pipes shrilled out alternate versicles. The congregation consisted mostly of women, wearing veils, white or black.

Antonia stood by a pillar near the door, enduring the heated atmosphere as long as she could, but she had to leave the church before the end of the service, followed by Sophy. Lord Dunkeld found them seated in the piazza, where they could wait for the procession, and watch the tributes of the pious being carried into the church by a side door—huge cakes, castles and temples in ornamental pastry, baskets of fruit, a dead hare, live fowls, birds in a cage, a fir tree with grapes and peaches tied to the branches, a family of white kittens mewing and struggling in a basket.

The train of priests and acolytes came pouring out into the sunshine, gorgeous in gold and brocade, the band playing a triumphal march. After the officiating priests came a procession of men in monkish robes, some struggling under the weight of massive crosses, the rest carrying tapers that burnt pale in the vivid light; some with upright form and raven hair, others the veterans of toil, with silvery locks and dark olive faces, strong and rugged features, withered hands seamed with the scars of labour; and following these came women of every age, from fifteen to ninety, their heads draped with white or black veils, but their faces uncovered.

Lord Dunkeld surveyed them with a critical eye. "Upon my soul, I did not think Italy could show so much ugliness," he said.

"Oh, but most of the girls are pretty."

"The girls, yes—but the women! They grow out of their good looks before they are thirty, and are hags and witches when an Englishwoman's mature charms are at the zenith. Stay, there is a pretty roguish face—and—look, look, madam, the girl next her—the tall girl—great Heaven, what a likeness!"

He ran forward a few paces to get a second look at a face that had startled him out of his Scottish phlegm—a face that was like Antonia's in feature and expression, though the colouring was darker and less delicate.

"Did you see that tall girl with the blue bead necklace?" Dunkeld asked Antonia, excitedly.

"I could not help seeing her, when you made such a fuss."

"She is your living image—she ought to be your younger sister."

"I have no sisters."

"Oh, 'tis a chance likeness, no doubt. Such resemblances are often stronger than any you can find in a gallery of family portraits."

Antonia turned to a little group of women close by, whom she had already questioned about the people in the procession. Did they know the girl in the blue necklace?

Yes, she was Francesca Bari. She lived with her grandfather, who had a little vineyard on the hill yonder, about a mile from the piazza where they were standing. The signorina had noticed her? She was accounted the prettiest girl in the district, and she was as good as she was pretty. Her mother and father were dead, and she worked hard to keep her grandfather's house in order, and to bring up her brother and sisters.

Dunkeld's interest in the girl began and ended in her likeness to the woman he loved; but Antonia was keenly interested, and early next morning was on her way to the hill above the Lecco lake, alone and on foot, to search for the dwelling of the Baris. She was ever on the alert to discover any trace of her mother's kindred; and it was possible that some branch of her race had sunk to the peasant class, and that the type which sometimes marks a long line of ancestry might be repeated here. Antonia was not going to shut her eyes to such a possibility, however humiliating it might be. Offshoots of the greatest families may be found in humble circumstances.

She passed a few scattered houses along the crest of the hill, and some women picking grapes in a vineyard close to the road told her the way to Bari's house. His vineyard was on the slope of the hill facing Lierna.

Less than half an hour's walk by steep and rugged paths, up and down hill, brought her to a house with bright ochre walls and dilapidated blue shutters, standing in a patch of garden, where great golden pumpkins sprawled between rows of cabbages and celery, under fig-trees covered with purple fruit, and apple and pear trees bent with age and the weight of their rosy and russet crop. A straggling hedge of roses and oleander divided the garden from the narrow lane, while beyond, the vines joined hands in green alleys along the terraced slope of the hill, sheltered by a little olive wood.

The girl with the blue necklace was digging in the garden. Antonia could see her across the red roses where the hedge was lowest. A child of three or four years old was sitting on a basket close by, and two older children were on their knees, weeding a cabbage bed. They were poorly clad, but they looked clean, healthy, and happy.

The girl heard the flutter of Antonia's muslin gown, and looked up, with her foot upon her spade. She wiped the perspiration from her forehead with a gaudy cotton handkerchief.

"May I take one of your roses?" Antonia asked, smiling at her across the gap in the hedge.

"Si, si," cried Francesca, "as many as the signorina likes. There are plenty of them."

She ran to the hedge and began to pluck the roses, in an eager hospitality. She was dazzled by the vision of the beautiful face, the yellow hat and snowy plumes, the diamond buckle flashing in the sun, and something in the smile that puzzled her. Without being conscious of the likeness between the stranger's face and that one she saw every morning unflatteringly reflected in the dusky little glass under her bedroom window, she had a feeling of familiarity with the violet eyes, the sunny smile.

Antonia thanked her for her roses, admired her garden, questioned her about her brother and sisters, and was at once on easy terms with her. Yes, they were motherless, and she had taken care of them ever since Etta, the baby, was a fortnight old. Yes, she worked hard every day; but she loved work, and when the vintage was good they were all happy. Grandfather had not been able to work for over a year; he was very old—"*vecchio vecchio*"—and very weak.

"I hope you have relations who help you," said Antonia, "distant relations, perhaps, who are richer than your grandfather?"

"No, there is no one. We had an aunt, but she is dead. She died before I was born. Grandfather says I am like her. It makes him cry sometimes to look at me, and to remember that he will never see her again! She was his favourite daughter."

"And was your grandfather always poor—always living here, on this little vineyard and garden?" Antonia asked, pale, and with an intent look in her eyes.

Had she found them, the kindred for whom she had been looking, in these simple peasants, these sons and daughters of toil, so humbly born, without a history, the very off-scouring of the earth? Was this the end of her father's fairy tale, this the lowly birthplace of the Italian bride, the daughter of a noble house, who had fled with the English tutor, who had stooped from her high estate to make a love match?

She remembered her father's reluctance to take her to her mother's home, or even to tell her the locality. She remembered how he had shuffled and prevaricated, and put off the subject, and she thought with bitter shame of his falsehoods, his sophistications. Alas, why had he feared to tell her the truth? Would she have thought less lovingly of her dead mother because of her humble lineage? Surely not! But she had been fooled by lies, had thought of herself as the daughter of a patrician race, and had cherished romantic dreams of a line of soldiers and statesmen, whose ambitions and aspirations, whose courage and genius, were in her blood.

The dilapidated walls yonder, the painted shutters rotten with age, the gaudy daub of Virgin and Child on the plastered façade, the garden of cabbages and pumpkins, and the patch of tall Indian corn! What a disillusion! How sorry an end of her dreams!

"Sicuro!" the girl answered, wondering at the fine lady's keen look. She had been questioned often about herself, often noticed by people of quality, on account of her beauty; but this lady had such an earnest air. "Si, si, signorina," she said; "grandfather has always lived here. He was born in our cottage. His father was gardener to the Marchese" (the grand seigneur of the district, name understood). "And he bought the vineyard with his savings when he was an old man. He was a very good gardener."

"May I see your grandfather?"

"Sicuro! He will be pleased to see the signorina," the girl answered readily, accustomed to be patronized by wandering strangers, and to receive little gifts from them.

Antonia followed her into the cottage. An old man was sitting in an armchair by the hearth, where an iron pot hung over a few smouldering sticks and a heap of grey ashes. He looked up at Antonia with eyes that saw all things dimly. The sunshine streamed into the room from the open door and window; but her face was in shadow as she went towards him with outstretched hand, Francesca explaining that the English lady wished to see him.

The patriarch tried to rise from his chair, but Antonia stopped him, seating herself by his side.

"I saw your grand-daughter at the festa," she said, "and I wanted to see more of her, if I could. Can you guess why I was anxious about her, and anxious to be her friend?"

She took off her hat, while the old man looked at her with a slow wonder, his worn-out eyes gradually realizing the lines in the splendid face.

"I have been told that your Francesca is like me," she said. "Can you see any resemblance?"

"Santo e santissimo! Si, si, the signorina is like Francesca, as two peaches side by side on the wall yonder; and she is like my daughter, my Tonia, my beloved, who died more than twenty years ago. But she is not dead to me—no, not to me. I see her face in my dreams. I hear her voice sometimes as I wake out of sleep, and then I look round, and call her, and she is not there; and I remember that I am an old man, and that she left me many, many years ago."

"You had a daughter called Antonia?"

"Si, signorina. It was her mother's name also. I called her Tonia. She was the handsomest girl between the two lakes. Everybody praised her, a good girl, as industrious as she was virtuous. A good and dutiful daughter till the Englishman stole her from us."

"Your Antonia married an Englishman?"

"Si, signorina! 'Twas thought a fine marriage for her. He wore a velvet coat, and he called himself a gentleman; but he was only a schoolmaster, and he came to Varenna in a coach and six with a young English milord."

"What was the tutor's name?"

"*Non posso pronunziar' il suo nome.* Tonton, Tonton, Guilliamo."

"Thornton! William Thornton?"

"*Ecco!*" cried the old man, nodding assent. "We had a dairy then, my wife and I," he continued, "and the young lord and his governor used to leave their boat and walk up the hill to get a drink of milk. They paid us handsomely, and we got to look for them every day, and they would stop and talk and laugh with my two girls. The governor could speak Italian almost like one of us; and the young milord was trying to learn; and they used all of them to laugh at his mistakes, and make a fool of him. Well, well, 'twas a merry time for us all."

"Did you consent to your daughter's marriage?"

"*Chi lo sa? Forse! Non diceva nè si nè no.* He was a gentleman, and I was proud that she should marry above her station. But he told me a bundle of lies. He pretended to be a rich man, and promised that he would bring her to Italy once a year. And then he took her away, in milord's coach, and they were married at Chiavenna, where he lied to the priest, as he had lied to me, and swore he was a good Catholic. He sent me the certificate of their marriage, so that I might know my daughter was an honest woman; but he never let me see her again."

He paused in a tearful mood.

"Perhaps it was not his own fault that he did not keep his promise," Antonia pleaded. "He may have been too poor to make such a journey."

"Yes, he was as poor as Job. Tonia wrote to me sometimes, and she told me they were very poor, and that she hated her English home, and pined for the garden and the vineyard, and the hills and lakes. She was afraid she would die without ever seeing us again. Her letters were full of sorrow. I could see her tears upon the page. And then there came a letter from him, with a great black seal. She was dead—*Ma non si muove foglia che Iddio non voglia.* 'Tis not for me to complain!"

The feeble frame was shaken by the old man's sobs. Antonia knelt on the brick floor by his chair, and soothed him with gentle touches and soft words. She was full of tender pity; but there was the feeling that she was stooping from her natural level to comfort a creature of a lower race, another order of being, with whom she could have no sympathy.

And he was her grandfather. His blood was in her veins. From him she inherited some of the qualities of her heart and brain: not from statesmen or heroes, but from a peasant, whose hands were gnarled and roughened by a lifetime's drudgery, whose thoughts and desires had never travelled beyond his vineyard and patch of Indian corn.

Her grandfather, living in this tumble-down old house, where the rotten shutters offered so poor a defence against foul weather, the floods and winds of autumn and winter, where the crumbling brick floor had sunk below the level of the soil outside: living as peasants live, and suffering all the deprivations and hardships of extreme poverty, while she, his own flesh and blood, had squandered thousands upon the caprices of a woman of fashion. And she found him worn out with toil, old and weak, on the brink of the grave perhaps. Her wealth could do but little for him.

She had no doubt of his identity. The story of his daughter's marriage was her mother's story.

There was no room for doubt, yet she shrank with a curious restraint from revealing the tie that bound her to him. She was full of generous pity for a long life that had known so few of this world's joys; but the feeling of caste was stronger than love or pity. She was ashamed of herself for feeling such bitter mortification, such a cruel disappointment. Oh, foolish pride which she had taken for an instinct of good birth! Because she was beautiful and admired, high-spirited and courageous, she must needs believe that she sprang from a noble line, and could claim all the honour due to race. Her father had lied to her, and she had believed the flattering fable. She could not reconcile herself to the humiliating truth so far as to claim her new-found kindred. But she was bent upon showing them all possible kindness short of that revelation. They were so poor, so humble, that she might safely play the part of benefactress. They had no pride to be crushed by her favours. She questioned the old man about his health, while the girl stood by the doorway listening, and the children's silvery voices sounded in the garden outside. Had he been ill long; did he suffer much; had he a doctor? He had been ailing a long time, but as for suffering, well, he had pains in his limbs, the house was damp in winter, but there was more weakness than suffering. "Also the ass when he is tired lies down in the middle of the road, and can go no farther," he said resignedly. As for a doctor; no, he had no need of one. The doctor would only bleed him; and he had too little blood as it was. One of his neighbours—an old woman that some folks counted a witch, but a good Catholic for all that—had given him medicine of her own making that had done him good.

"I think a doctor would do you more good, if you would see one. There is a doctor at Bellagio who came to see my woman the other day when she had a touch of fever. He seemed a clever man."

"*Si signorina, ma senza denari non si canta messa.* Clever men want to be paid. Your doctor would cost me the eyes of the head."

"You shall have as much money as ever you want," answered Antonia, pulling a long netted purse from her pocket.

The gold showed through the silken meshes, and the old man's eyes glittered with greed as he looked at it. She filled his tremulous hands with guineas, emptying both ends of the purse into his hollowed palms. He had never seen so much gold. The strangers who came to sit under his *pergola*, and drink great bowls of new milk from the fawn-coloured cows that were his best source of income, thought themselves generous if they gave him a *scudo* at parting: but here was a visitor from fairyland raining gold into his hands.

"They are English guineas, and you will gain by the exchange," she said, "so you can have the physician to see you every day. He will not want to bleed you when he sees how weak you are."

The old man shook his head doubtfully. They were so ready with the lancet, those doctors! His eyes were fixed on the guineas, as he tried to reckon them. The coins lay in too close a heap to be counted easily.

He broke into a rapture of gratitude, invoking every saint in the calendar, and Antonia shivered with pain at the exaggeration of his acknowledgments. He thanked her as a wayside beggar would have done. His benedictions were the same as the professional mendicants, the maimed and halt and blind, gave her when she dropped a coin into a basket or a hat. He belonged to the race which is accustomed to taking favours from strangers. He belonged to the sons of bondage, poverty's hereditary slaves.

She appealed to Francesca.

"Would it not be better for your grandfather if he lived at Bellagio, where he would have a comfortable house in a street, and plenty of neighbours?" she asked.

"I don't think he would like to leave the vineyard, Signorina; though it would be very pleasant to live in the town," answered Francesca.

Her dark eyes sparkled at the thought. It was lonely on the hill, where she had only the children to talk to, and her grandfather, whose conversation was one long lamentation.

The old man looked up with a scared expression.

The Infidel | 227

"Ohime! Non posso!" he exclaimed, "I could not leave the villino. I shall die as I have lived, in the villino!"

"Well, you must do what is best pleasing to yourself," Antonia said. "All I desire is that you should be happy, and enjoy every comfort that money can buy."

She bent down and kissed the sunburnt forehead, so wrinkled and weather-beaten after the long life of toil. She asked Francesca to walk a little way with her; and they went out into the lane together.

"Your house looks comfortless even in sunshine," Antonia said. "It must be worse in winter!"

"*Si, signorina.* It is very cold in bad weather, but grandfather loves the villino."

"You might get a carpenter to mend the windows and put new hinges on the shutters. They look as if they would hardly shut."

"Indeed, signorina, 'tis long since our shutters have been shut. Grandfather is too poor to pay a carpenter. Nothing in the house has been mended since I can remember."

"But you have your cows and your vineyard. How is it that he is so poor?"

The girl shrugged her shoulders. She knew nothing.

"Is it you who keeps the purse?"

"No, no, *signorina, non so niente.* Grandfather gives me money to pay the baker— —"

"And the butcher?"

"We do not buy meat. I kill a fowl sometimes, or a rabbit; but for the most part we have cabbage soup and polenta."

"Well, you will have plenty of money in future. I shall see to that; and you must take care that your grandfather has good food every day, and a doctor when he is ailing, and warm blankets for winter. I want you both to be happy and well cared for. And you must get a man to dig in the garden and carry water for you. I don't like to see a girl work as you do."

Francesca stared at the beautiful lady in open wonder. She was doubtless mad as a March hare, la Poverina; but what a delightful form her madness had taken. It might be that the Blessed Virgin had inspired this madness, and sent this lovely lunatic wandering from house to house among the deserving poor, scattering gold wherever she found want and piety. It was almost a miracle. Indeed, who could be sure that this benign lady was not the Blessed One herself, who could appear in any manner she pleased, even arrayed in the latest fashion of plumed hats and India muslin *négligées?*

Antonia left the girl a little way from the villino, and walked slowly down the hill to Bellagio, deep in thought. Alas, alas, to have found her mother's kindred, and to feel no thrill of love, no yearning to take them to her heart, only the same kind of pity she had felt for those poor wretches in Lambeth Marsh, only an eager desire to make their lot happier, to give them all good things that money can buy.

"Should I grow to love that old man if I knew him better?" she wondered. "Is there some dormant affection in my heart, some hereditary love that needs but to be warmed into life by time and custom? God knows what I am made of. I do not feel as if I could ever care for that poor old man as grandfathers are cared for. My mother's father, and he loved her dearly! It is base ingratitude in me not to love him."

She recalled the greedy look that came into the withered old face at sight of the gold. A painter need have asked no better model for Harpagon. She would have given much not to have seen that look.

She would visit them often, she thought, and would win him to softer moods. She would question him about her mother's girlhood, beguile him into fond memories of the long-lost daughter, memories of his younger days, before grinding poverty had made him so eager for gold. She would make herself familiar with Bari and his granddaughter, find out all their wants, all their desires, and provide for the welfare of the old life that was waning, and the young life with a long future before it. She would make age and youth happy, if it were possible. But she would not tell them of the relationship that made it her duty to care for them. She would let them remember her as the eccentric stranger, who had found them in poverty, and left them in easy circumstances; the benefactress dropped from the clouds.

To what end should she tell them of kinship if she could not give them a kinswoman's love? And she could not. The girl was a beautiful creature, kindly, gentle, caressing; but she was a peasant, a peasant whose thoughts had never travelled beyond the narrow circle of her hills, whose rough knuckles and thick fingers told of years of toil, who had not one feeling in common with the cousin bred upon books, and plunged in the morning of youth into the most enlightened society in Christendom, the London of Walpoles and Herveys, Carterets and St. Johns, Pitts and Foxes.

She would not tell them. She could not imagine her lips framing the words. She could not say to Francesca, "We are first cousins, the next thing to sisters." But she could make them happy. That was possible. She could take all needful measures to provide them with a substantial income; a competence which should enable them to rebuild the rotten old villa, and spend the rest of their days in ease and plenty.

Lord Dunkeld called on her in the evening, and took a dish of tea with the two ladies in their garden betwixt sunset and moonrise. He found Antonia looking pale and tired.

"She started on one of her solitary rambles early this morning," Sophy said; "as if any one ought to walk in this climate, and she was as white as her muslin gown when she came home. She had much better have idled with me in the boat."

"I did not go far," Antonia said, "but I found some interesting people— only peasants. The girl your lordship noticed yesterday in the procession."

"The girl who is so like you?" exclaimed Dunkeld. "I thought your ladyship was a stranger to at least one of the deadly sins, and knew no touch of vanity. But I find you are mortal, and that you had a fancy to see a face like your own."

"Yes, I had a fancy to see the girl. And now I want to help her, if I can. She is desperately poor."

"Is anybody poor in Italy? I have always thought that Italian peasants live upon sunshine and a few ripe figs, and have no use for money."

"They are very poor. The grandfather is old, and ailing. Can you find me an honest lawyer here, or at Varenna?"

"For your ladyship I would attempt miracles. I will do my best."

"And as quickly as you can, my lord, for I want to go back to England."

"Grant me the felicity of escorting you when you go, and make me your slave in the mean time; though, as I am always that, madam, 'tis a one-sided bargain."

"Oh, pray come in our coach with us, my lord," cried Sophy. "I was in a panic all the way here, on account of the brigands."

"Heavens! Was your coach attacked?"

"No, no, sir," said Antonia, laughing. "The brigands came no nearer than a vague rumour that some of their calling had been heard of above Andermatt."

"But who knows what may happen when we are going home, now that the days are so much shorter?" protested Sophy.

"If one strong arm and a pair of pistols can help you, Miss Potter——"

"Oh, I shall feel ever so much safer with your lordship in our coach. I know if those wretches came—with black masks, perhaps—Giuseppe would run away."

Giuseppe was the Italian footman, whom Sophy suspected of being a poor-spirited creature, in spite of a figure which would have delighted the late King of Prussia.

Antonia went to the villino on the following afternoon, and being unable to shake off Lord Dunkeld, allowed him to accompany her. She liked his conversation, which diverted her thoughts from brooding upon the past, and on George Stobart's peril in the wild world across the Atlantic. He filled the place of that brilliant society which had been her anodyne for every grief; and she was grateful to him for a steadfastness in friendship which promised to last for a lifetime. His colder temperament had allowed him to put off the lover and assume the friend. He had been strong as a granite pillar where George Stobart had proved a broken reed.

They found the girl tying up the vine branches in a long berceau, and the old man sitting by the smouldering ashes as he had sat yesterday, in a monotony of idleness. The windows had not been mended, and the shutters still hung forlornly upon broken hinges.

Antonia asked the girl if she had not been able to find a carpenter to do the work.

"Grandfather would not let a carpenter come. He is afraid of the noise."

"And when bad weather comes the rain will come in."

"*Si, signorina;* the rain always comes in."

"And your broken shutters cannot keep out the cold winds."

"No, signorina; the wind almost blows grandfather out of his chair sometimes."

"Then he really ought to let a carpenter come."

The old man was listening intently, and Dunkeld was watching his face.

"They are brigands, those carpenters," he said. "'Tis a waste of money to employ them. I don't mind the wind, signorina. Francia can hang up a curtain."

"Oh, grandfather, the curtain is an old rag! And the signorina gave you money to pay the carpenter."

"*Andiamo adagio, carissima.* I am not going to waste the signorina's money on idlers and cheats, nor yet upon doctors. I hate doctors! They are knaves, bloodthirsty rogues that want to be paid for sticking a knife into a man as if he were a pig!"

Antonia did not argue the point, and left the old man after a few kindly words. She was disgusted at his obstinacy, which made it so hard a matter to improve his circumstances. She walked some way in silence, Dunkeld at her side.

"I fear your new *protégé* is a troublesome subject," he said, "and that you will find a difficulty in helping him."

"I cannot understand his objection to having that wretched old barn made wind and weather tight."

"I can. The man is a miser. You have given him money, and he wants to keep it, to hide it under his mattress, perhaps, and gloat over it in the dead of the night. The miser has a keener joy in the touch of a guinea than in any indulgence of meat or drink, warmth and comfort, that money can buy."

"I fear your lordship has guessed the riddle," Antonia answered, wounded to the quick. "I gave him all the gold in my purse yesterday. 'Twas at least twenty guineas. Well, I must take other means. I will send a carpenter to do all the work that is wanted, and take the Bellagio doctor to the villino to-morrow morning."

"Will your ladyship be offended if I presume to advise?"

"Offended! I shall think you vastly kind."

"Leave these people alone. The old man is unworthy of your protection. The girl is happy in present condition. Your bounty will but administer to her grandfather's avarice, and will not better her life."

"But I must help them—I must, I must," Antonia protested. "It is my duty. I cannot let them suffer the ills of poverty while I am rich. I must find some way to make their lives easy."

Dunkeld wondered at her vehemence, and pursued the argument no further. This passion of charity was but an instinct of her generous nature, the desire to share fortune's gifts with the unfortunate.

She returned from this second visit dispirited and unhappy. Was she doomed never to be able to esteem those whom she was bound to love? She had loved her father fondly, though she had known him unprincipled and shifty; but what affection could she feel for this old man against whom her class instinct revolted, unless she could find in him humble virtues that could atone for humble birth? And she found him sordid, untruthful, avaricious.

She called on the local doctor next morning, and went with him to the villino, where he diagnosed the old man's ailments as only old age, the weakness induced by poor food, and the rheumatic symptoms that were the natural result of living in a draughty house. He recommended warmth and a generous diet, and promised to call once a week through the coming winter, his fee for each visit being something less than an English shilling.

After he had gone Antonia sat in the garden with Baptisto Bari and his granddaughter for an hour. She had his chair carried into the sunshine, and out of the way of the noise, while a couple of workmen mended the windows and shutters. She had found a builder in Bellagio, and had instructed him to do all that could be done to make the house comfortable before winter. He was to get the work done with the least possible inconvenience to the family.

Sitting in the quiet garden, while Francesca gathered beans for the soup, and while the children sprawled in the sun, playing with some toys Antonia had brought them, Bari was easily lured into talking of the past, and of the daughter he had loved. All that was best in his nature revealed itself when he talked of his sorrow; and Antonia thought that the miser's despicable passion had only grown upon him after the loss that had, perhaps, blighted his life. And then, when he was an old man, death had taken his remaining daughter; and he had been left, lonely and heart-broken, with his orphan grandchildren. He had begun to scrape and pinch for their support, most likely; and then the miser's insane love of money had grown upon him, like some insidious disease.

Antonia tried to interest him, and to make excuses for him, and she spoke to him very plainly upon the money question. She appealed even to his selfishness.

"When I give you money, it is that you may have all the good things that money can buy," she said; "good wine and strengthening food, warm clothes, a comfortable bed. What is the use of a few guineas in a cracked teacup, or hidden in a corner of your mattress?" —Baptisto almost jumped out of his chair, and she knew she had hit upon the place of his treasure. "What is the use of hoarding money that other people will spend and waste, perhaps, when you are dead?"

"No, no, she will not waste it. *Che Diavolo!* She will give me a handsome funeral, and spend all the rest on masses for the good of my soul. That is what she will have to do."

"You need not save money for that. If you live comfortably your life will be prolonged, most likely; and I promise that you shall have a handsome funeral, and the—the masses."

She went again next day, and on the day after, always alone; and the old man became more and more at his ease with her; but all that she did was done for duty's sake, and she found it harder work to talk to him than it had been to talk with poor dying Sally Dormer, by whose bedside she had spent many quiet hours. The abyss between them was wider. But she felt more affectionately towards Francesca, who adored her almost as if she were indeed the celestial lady whose miraculous presence every good Catholic is prepared to meet at any solemn crisis of life.

Antonia did not rest till, with the assistance of a banker and lawyer at Varenna, she had settled an income of three hundred pounds a year upon Baptisto, with reversion to his grandchildren, she herself acting as trustee in conjunction with the banker, who was partner in an old-established banking house at Milan, of which the Varenna bank—in a pavilion in an angle of a garden wall—was a branch.

This done, her mind was at ease, and she prepared for her journey to England. She would return, as she had come, by the Low Countries, avoiding France on account of the war.

Lord Dunkeld had advised and assisted her in making the settlement on the Baris, but she knew that he thought her foolish and quixotic in her determination to provide for this particular family.

"I could find you a score of claimants for your bounty, far more pathetic cases than Baptisto, if you are so set upon playing the good angel," he said. "'Tis a mercy you do not want to provide for the whole pauper population upon the same magnificent scale. Three hundred a year for an Italian peasant! But a woman's charity is ever a romantic impulse; and one can but admire her tenderness, though one may question her discretion."

"I may have a reason you cannot fathom," Antonia said gravely.

"Oh, 'tis the heart moves you to this act, not the reason! This world would be happier if all women were as unreasonable."

She despised herself for suppressing the motive of her bounty. To be praised for generosity, while she was ashamed to acknowledge her own kindred, ashamed of her own lowly origin! What could be meaner or more degrading? But she thought of Dunkeld's thousand years' pedigree, the pride of birth, the instinct of race, which he had so often revealed unconsciously in their familiar talk; and it was difficult to sink her own pride before so proud a man.

The last day came, and he insisted on accompanying her in her farewell visit. She had given him the privileges of a trusted friend, and had no excuse for refusing his company.

She told Baptisto Bari what she had done for him.

"You will have seventy-five pounds paid you every quarter," she said; "and all you have to do is to spend your money freely, and let Francesca buy everything that is wanted for you, and the children, and herself. I shall come back next year, and I shall be very sorry and very angry if I do not find you living in comfort, and the villino looking as handsome as a nobleman's villa."

The old man protested his gratitude, with tears. Yes, he would spend his money. He had been spending it. See, there was the magnificent new curtain; and he had a pillow for his bed; and a barrel of oil for the lamp. They had the lamp lighted every night. And he had coffee—a dish of coffee on Sunday—and they had been drinking their milk, and making butter for themselves, instead of selling all the milk to the *negozio* in Bellagio. Indeed, he had discovered that money was a very useful thing when one spent it; though it was also useful to keep it against the day of misfortune or death.

"True, m'amico; but it is bad economy to keep your money under your pillow, and let your house fall over your ears for want of mending," answered Antonia; and then she bade him good-bye—good-bye till next year, and bent down to kiss the withered forehead, above white pent-house eyebrows.

The keen old eyes clouded over with tears as her lips touched him, and the tremulous old hands were joined in prayer that God and the Saints might reward her piety.

She opened her arms to Francesca, who fell upon her breast, sobbing.

"Ah, sweetest lady, had the poor ever such a friend, ever such a benefactor? Heaven sent you to us. We pray for you night and day, for your happiness on earth, for your soul's bliss in heaven," cried the girl, in her melodious Italian.

Antonia could scarcely drag herself away from the clinging arms, the tears and benedictions; but she left Francesca at the garden gate, and amid all those tears and kisses had not revealed herself to her kindred.

She crossed the hill in silence, Dunkeld at her side, watching her thoughtful countenance, and perplexed by its almost tragic gloom.

"You are a wonderful woman," he said lightly, by-and-by, to break the spell of silence. "You take these Italian peasants to your heart as if they were your own flesh and blood. Is it the Italian blood in your veins that opens your heart to beings of so different a race?"

"Perhaps."

"I could understand your letting the girl hug you—a creature so lovely, and in the bloom and freshness of youth. But that wrinkled old miser! Well, 'twas a divine charity that moved you to squander a kiss upon that parchment brow."

Antonia turned to him in a sudden tumult of feeling, remorse, shame, self-disparagement.

"Oh, stop, stop!" she cried. "Your words scald me like molten lead. Divine charity! Why, I am the most despicable of women. I hate myself for my paltry pride. I can bear the shame of it no longer. 'Twill be your lordship's turn to scorn me as I scorn myself. That old man is my mother's father. I came to Italy to hunt for her kindred, to find in what palace she was reared, from what princely race I inherited my haughty spirit. And a chance, the chance likeness between Francesca and me, resulted in the discovery that I came of a long line of peasants, servants, the tillers of the ground, the race that lives by submissive toil, that has never known independence. And I was ashamed of them—bitterly ashamed. It was anguish to me to know that I sprang from that humble stock, most of all when I thought of you, your warriors, and statesmen, bishops, judges—all the long line of rulers and master minds, stretching back into the dark night of history, part of yourself; for if they had never lived you could not be what you are."

"Oh, madam, you own a more noble lineage than Scottish Thanes can boast of. The seaborn Venus had no ancestors, but was queen of the earth by the divine right of beauty. You are a daughter of the gods, and may easily dispense with a parchment pedigree."

"Oh, pray, sir, no idle compliments! I would rather suffer your contempt than your mocking praise. I can scarcely be more despicable in your esteem than I am in my own."

"I could never think ill of you, my sweet friend; never doubt the nobility of your heart and mind. The test has been a severe one; for to a woman the death of a romantic dream means much; but the gold rings true. You had a right to keep this secret from me if you pleased."

"And from them?"

"That is a nicer question. I doubt it is your duty to make them happier by the knowledge that they have a legitimate claim to your bounty. I think you would do well to disclose your relationship to them before you leave Italy. The old man may not live till your return; and the thought that pride had come between you and one so near in blood might be a lasting regret."

"Yes, yes, your lordship is right. I will see them again this evening. I will tell my grandfather who and what I am. Yes, it was odious of me to play the Lady Bountiful, to let him praise me for generosity—me, his daughter's child. Sure I am glad I made my confession to you, for now I know that you are my true friend."

"I will never advise you ill, if I can help it, madam," he said, stooping to kiss her hand. "And doubt not that you can trust me with every secret of your heart and mind, for there can exist no feeling or thought in either that is not common to generous natures."

Lady Kilrush spent the sunset hour with her kindred, and was touched by the old man's delight when he clasped to his heart the child of that daughter he had loved and mourned. She knelt beside him with uncovered head as she told him the story of her childhood, her love for the mother she had lost before memory began. He turned her face to the sunset glow, and gazed at her with eyes drowned in tears. He was no longer the money-grubber, keenly expectant of a stranger's bounty. The whole nature of the man seemed changed by the awakening of an unforgotten love.

"Yes, it is Tonia's face," he cried. "I knew you were beautiful; I knew you were like her; but not how like. Your brow has the same lines, your lips have the same curves. Yes, now, as you smile at me, I see my beloved one again."

There was nothing sordid or vulgar in the peasant now. His countenance shone with the pure light of love, and Antonia's heart went out to him with some touch of filial affection.

Before they parted he gave her a letter—the ink dim with age—her mother's last letter, written from the Lincolnshire homestead where she died; and Antonia read of the love that had hung over her cradle, that tender maternal love she had been fated never to know.

She deferred her journey for a few days, at her grandfather's entreaty, and spent many hours at the villino. She encouraged Baptisto and Francesca to talk to her of all the details of their lives. She drew nearer to them in thought and feeling, and made new plans for their happiness, promising to come to Bellagio every autumn, and offering to build them a new house next year at the other end of their garden where the view was finer. But the old man protested that the villino would last his time, and that he would never like any house as well.

"Then the new house must be built for Francesca when she marries," Antonia told him gaily. "We will wait till she has a suitor she loves."

CHAPTER XVI
DEATH AND VICTORY

It was late in October when Lady Kilrush arrived at her house in St. James's Square. What a gloomy splendour, what an unromantic luxury the spacious mansion presented after the lake and mountains, the chestnut woods and rose gardens of Lombardy. Yet this old English comfort within doors, while the grey mists of autumn brooded over the square where the oil lamps made spots of quivering golden light amidst the deepening gloom, had a certain charm, and Antonia was not ill pleased to find herself taking a dish of tea by the fire in the library with her old friend Patty Granger, who brought her the news of the town, the weddings and elopements, the duels and law-suits, the beauties who had lost their looks, and the prodigals who had anticipated their majority and ruined an estate by a single cast at hazard.

"And so Lord Dunkeld travelled all the way from Como with you and Mrs. Potter?" said Patty, when she had emptied her budget. "You must have been vastly tired of him by the time you got home, after being boxed in a travelling chariot for over a se'nnight."

"There are people of whose company one does not easily tire, Patty."

"Then my old General ain't one of 'em; for I yawn till my jaws ache whenever we spend an evening together, and he sits and proses over Marlborough's wars and the two chargers he had shot under him at Malplaquet. Sure I knew all his stories by heart long before we were married; and 'tain't likely I'll listen to 'em now. But if you can relish Lord Dunkeld's conversation for a week in a chaise, perhaps you'll be able to endure it from year's end to year's end when you're his wife."

"What are you thinking of, child? I am not going to marry Lord Dunkeld, or any other man living."

"Then I think you ought to have put the poor wretch out of his pain a year ago, and not let him dance attendance on you half over Europe."

"His lordship has known my mind for a long time, and is pleased to honour me with his friendship."

"Ah, you have a knack of turning lovers into friends. You was friends with Mr. Stobart till you quarrelled with him and sent him off to the wars. And I doubt he's killed by this time, if he was with Wolfe; for the General tells me our soldiers haven't a chance against the French."

"Does the General say that, Patty?" Antonia asked anxiously.

She had read all the newspapers on her home-coming. There was no fresh news from America; but the tone about the war was despondent. Wolfe's army before Quebec was but nine thousand, the enemy's force nearly double. Amherst was at a distance, winter approaching, the outlook of a universal blackness.

"The General has hardly any hopes," said Patty. "He has seen Wolfe's last letter, such a down-hearted letter; and the poor man is fitter to lie a-bed in a hospital than to storm a city. He has always been a sickly wretch; never could abide the sea, and suffers more on a voyage than a delicate young woman."

Antonia lay awake half that night, despondent and uneasy, and in her troubled morning sleep dreamt of George Stobart, in a grenadier's uniform, with an ashen countenance, the blood streaming from a sabre cut on his forehead. He looked at her with fading eyes, and reproached her for her cruelty. 'Twas her unkindness had sent him to his doom.

She woke out of this nightmare vision to hear news-boys yelling in the square. "Taking of Quebec. A glorious victory. Death of General Wolfe. Death of General Montcalm." She sprang from her bed, threw up a window, and looked down into the square. It was hardly light. The news-boys were bawling as if they were mad, and street doors and area gates were opening, and eager hands were stretched out to snatch the papers. A ragamuffin crowd was following the news-boys, the crowd that is afoot at all hours, and comes from nowhere. "Great English victory—Slaughter of the enemy. Death of General Wolfe on the field of battle. Death of General Montcalm. Destruction of the French. Quebec taken."

Mr. Pitt had received the news late last night, and this morning 'twas in all the papers. The shouting of the news-vendors made a confusion of harsh noises, each trying to bawl louder than his fellows. And then came the sound of trumpet and drum in Pall Mall, as the guard marched to the Palace, and anon loud hurrahs from the excited crowd in the square, in Pall Mall, everywhere, filling the air with vociferous exultation.

Death and victory! The words reached Antonia's ear together. Victory purchased at what cost of blood, what sacrifice of lives that were dear? She had met old General Wolfe and his handsome wife, now a widow, the hero's proud mother; and it was sad to think of that lady's agony to-day, while all England was rejoicing, all who had not lost their dearest as she had.

Both generals slain! And how many of those they led to battle? Were George Stobart's bones lying on the heights of Abraham, the prey of eagles and wolves, or buried hastily by some friendly hand, hidden for ever under that far-off soil, which the winter snow would soon cover? Her heart ached at the thought that she would see him no more, she who had desired, or thought she desired, never to look upon his face.

She sent her woman for the newspapers, and turned them over with trembling hands, standing by the open window in the chill autumnal air, too much discomposed even to sit down. The *Daily Advertiser* had a letter with a description of the siege; all the wonder of it; the boats creeping up the river under the midnight stars; the ascent of that grim height through the darkness, the soldiers clambering with uncertain foothold, clutching at bushes, struggling through trees, their muskets slung at their backs, the *qui vive?* of the French sentinel above, the courage, the address, the presence of mind of leaders and men. There had been great losses; but there was no list of the killed; and Stobart might be among them.

She ordered her coach to be at the door in an hour, and waited only to dress and take a cup of chocolate before she went to see Mrs. Stobart, who, if her husband had survived the siege, might have had a letter by the ship that brought England the news from Quebec.

A stranger opened the door at Crown Place. Instead of Mrs. Stobart's handmaiden, in white apron and mob cap, Antonia saw an old woman, of dejected aspect, who stared at the footman and coach as at some appalling vision.

Yes, Mrs. Stobart was at home, but she was very ill, the woman said, and it might be dangerous for the lady to see her.

The lady, who had alighted at the opening of the door, took no heed of this warning. The wife was ill, struck down perhaps by the shock of fatal news. Antonia instantly associated Lucy's illness with the fate of her husband.

"Where is she?" she asked, and ran upstairs without waiting to be answered. In an eight-roomed house it was not difficult to find the mistress's chamber. She opened the door of the front room softly, and found herself in darkness, an obscurity made horrible by the stifling heat of the room, where the red cinders of what had been a fierce fire made a lurid glow behind the high brass fender. The dimity curtains were closed round the bed. Antonia drew one of them aside and looked at the sick woman. She was asleep, and breathing heavily, her forehead bound with a linen cloth, and the hand lying on the coverlet burnt like a hot coal under Antonia's touch.

The old woman came panting up the stairs, and after stopping to recover her normal breathing power, which was but feeble, she addressed the visitor in a voice of alarm.

"Oh, madam, you had best come away from the bed. 'Tis the small-pox, a bad case, and if you have never had the disease——"

"I have been inoculated. I am not afraid," Antonia answered quickly, thinking only of the patient. Alas, poor soul, to be seized with that hateful sickness, which she so feared. "How did she come by this horrible malady, ma'am?"

"She caught it from an old gentleman, my lady—I believe he was a relation—who died in the house. She was taken ill the night after his funeral, a fortnight ago. 'Tis the worst kind of small-pox. She was quite sensible two days ago, and then the fever came back, the secondary fever, the doctor calls it. Even if she gets over it she will be disfigured for life, poor lady, and may lose her eyesight. 'Tis as bad a case as I ever nursed, and if your honour hadn't been inoculated——"

"But I have, woman, and I have no fear. Pray tell me where is this lady's son? Was he in the house when she was taken ill?"

"No, my lady. The little master is living with his gran'ma, the servant girl told me."

"That is fortunate. Are you Mrs. Stobart's only nurse?"

"Yes, my lady."

"And at night when you are asleep, who attends upon her?"

"I am a very light sleeper, ma'am. I mostly hears her when she calls me, if she calls loud enough."

"She must have two nurses. I will get another woman to help you, and I shall come every day to see that she is attended properly. Pray, who is her doctor?"

The woman named a humble apothecary in Lambeth, called Morton, whom Antonia had often met in her visits to the poor, a meek elderly man in whose skill and kindness she had confidence, in spite of his rusty coat and breeches, coarse cotton stockings and grubby hands.

"I will send a physician to see her. Tell Mr. Morton that I shall send Dr. Heberden, who will confer with him. Do you know if Mrs. Stobart has had any trouble on her mind lately, any anxiety?"

"Only about her house, my lady. Her slut of a maid ran away directly she heard 'twas small-pox."

The apothecary came in while Antonia was standing by the bed, and was aghast at the spectacle.

"Does your ladyship know what risk you run here? Oh, madam, for God's sake, leave this infected air."

"I am not afraid. I did not take the disease when the doctors tried to inoculate me. I doubt I am proof against the poison."

"Nay, madam, you must not count on that. I implore you to leave this room instantly, and never to re-enter it. 'Tis a bad case of confluent small-pox, and I fear 'twill be fatal."

"And this poor lady is alone, her husband fighting in America, killed in the late battle, perhaps. At whatever risk I shall do all I can for her. And I hope we may save her, sir, with care and good nursing."

"Your ladyship may be sure I will do my best," said Morton.

"I will go out into the air while you see to your patient. This room is stifling. You will find me below, waiting to talk to you."

She walked on the footpath by the river till the apothecary came to her, and then gave him her instructions. Dr. Heberden was to see the patient that afternoon, if possible. Antonia would wait upon him and persuade him to do so. And Mr. Morton was to be at hand to receive his instructions. And a nurse was to be found, more serviceable than the old woman on the premises, who seemed civil and obliging, and could be kept to help her.

"And I shall see the patient every day," concluded Antonia.

"I must warn your ladyship once more, that you will do so at the peril of your life."

"My good Mr. Morton, there are situations in which that hazard hardly counts. This poor lady's husband, for instance, has he not risked his life a hundred times in America? Risked and lost it, perhaps!"

There was a catch in her voice like a stifled sob, as she spoke the last sentence.

"That is a vastly different matter, your ladyship," said Morton gravely; but he ventured no farther remonstrance.

Antonia saw the physician, and obtained his promise to see Mrs. Stobart that afternoon. She drove through streets that were in a tumult of rejoicing at the success of British arms. No one thought of the general who had fallen, the soldiers who had died. Victory was on every lip, exultation in every mind. 'Twas all the coachman could do to steer horses and chariot through the crowd.

Arrived at home safely, Lady Kilrush told the hall porter to deny her to all visitors, which would not be difficult, since her arrival in London had not been recorded in the newspapers, and Lord Dunkeld was on the road to Scotland, to shoot grouse on his own moors. She ordered her chair for six o'clock, and in the meanwhile shut herself in her dressing-room, where Sophy found her, to whom she related her morning's work.

"If you are frightened don't come near me," she said.

"I am frightened for you, madam, not for myself. I suppose after having had such a bout when I was inoculated I am safe to escape the small-pox for the rest of my life. Sure I carry the marks on my face and neck, though they mayn't be so bad as to make me hideous."

"Then if you are not afraid, you can keep me company in this room of an evening, till Mrs. Stobart is well enough to be sent into the country; and you can drive and walk with me. I will admit no visitors, for I must see her every day if I would be sure that her nurses do their duty. Poor soul, she is alone, and in great danger."

Sophy implored her mistress to run no such hazard, besought her with tears, and with the importunity of a warm affection. In her ladyship's case inoculation had been a failure. She would be mad to re-enter that infected house. Sophy would herself visit Mrs. Stobart, and see that she was properly nursed.

"No, child, no, it is I who must go. It is my duty."

"Why, I never knew you was so fond of her—a pretty simpleton, with scarce a word to say for herself."

"Don't argue with me, Sophy. It is useless. If there is any risk, I have run it," Antonia answered.

She shivered as she recalled that darkened chamber, the tainted atmosphere, the oppressive heat of a fire that had been burning day and night through the mild October weather. She knew that there was poison in that pestilential air, and that she had inhaled it, knew and did not care.

Her eyes were shining with a feverish light. Her heart ached with remorseful pity for the deserted wife, deserted by the man who had fled from his country, flung himself into a service of danger, flung away his life perhaps. It was because she had been unwise, had encouraged a close friendship that was but a mask for love, that yonder poor woman was lying on her sick bed deserted by her natural protector. He had sacrificed every tie, renounced every duty, on account of that guilty love. She hated herself when she thought that she had lured him from his home, had made him her friend and counsellor, at the expense of his young wife. Every hour he had spent with her in St. James's Square had been stolen from Lucy and her boy. It was the wife who had a right to his thoughts, his counsels, his leisure; and she had filched them from her. He had lingered by the fireside in her library, reluctant to leave her, when he should have been brightening Lucy's monotonous existence, elevating her mind by his conversation, continuing that education of heart and intellect in which he had been engaged before he lost himself in a fatal friendship. She had driven him from her with anger and contempt, driven him into exile and danger; but had she not as much need to be angry with herself, remembering her pleasure in his company, her forgetfulness of his wife's claims?

This one thing remained for her to do, to watch over the lonely wife in her day of peril, to win her back to life and health if it were possible. This atoning act would ease her conscience, perhaps, and bring her peace of mind. If George Stobart lived to come back to England he would know that she had done her duty, and, although not a Christian, had fulfilled the Christian's mission of mercy and love.

And if that ghastly distemper struck her down—a possible result, though she did not apprehend it—what then? She had no keen love of life, and would not much regret to lay down the load of days that had lost their savour. She had tasted all the pleasures that the world, the flesh, and the devil can offer a beautiful woman, all the luxuries that gold can buy, all the homage that rank can claim, the adulation of high-born profligates, the envy of rival beauties, and every trivial diversion that Satan can put into the minds of the idle rich. She had struck every note in the gamut of elegant pleasures; and had arrived at that period of satiety in which some women take to vice as the natural crescendo in the scale of emotion. What sacrifice would it be to die for her who feared no hereafter, had no account to render?

She visited Mrs. Stobart every day, questioned nurses and doctors, and took infinite trouble to secure the patient's comfort. She sat by the sick-bed, endured the fetid atmosphere of a room carefully shut against the air of heaven, she listened to Lucy's delirious ravings, her frantic appeals to her husband to come back to her. She, who in her right senses had seemed to grieve so little at his absence, in her wanderings was for ever recalling the happy hours of their courtship, acting over again that simple story of a girl's first love for a sweetheart of superior station.

Antonia listened with an aching heart. The love was there then; the woman was not the pink-and-white automaton she had once thought her.

And she had come between George Stobart and this idyllic affection, had spoiled two lives, unwittingly, but not without guilt. She had absorbed him, suffered him to squander all his leisure upon her company, sought his counsel, invited his sympathy, made herself a part of his life, as no woman has the right to do with another woman's husband.

And now, sitting by what might be the bed of death, she could not forgive herself for that friendship which she had cherished without thought of the cost. She had courted his company, and reproached him when he absented himself. He had been her most cherished companion; those days had been blank on which they had not met. All the feverish pleasures of the great world had not been enough to make up for one lost hour of his society. Their talk beside the firelit hearth, in the darkening twilight, their meetings in poverty-stricken garrets and loathsome alleys, had been more to her than all the rest of her life.

"If she should die before he comes back to her it will be on my conscience for ever that I was the wretch who parted them," she thought.

The doctors were not hopeful of Mrs. Stobart's recovery. She had very little strength, they told Lady Kilrush, very little power to fight against the disease, which had attacked her in its most virulent form. Should she recover, she would be disfigured for life, and possibly blind.

Oh, the horror of it! If he came home to find the pretty childish face, the lily and rose complexion, so cruelly transformed! Was not death almost better for the victim than such a resurrection?

Heaven was kinder to this weak soul than to spare her for such a cruel fate. After Antonia had been visiting her for over a week, in which time there had been no improvement in the symptoms, there came a rally with some hours of consciousness; but this was only the prelude of approaching death.

Lucy recognized Antonia, spoke of her husband and her son in a sage and matter-of-fact tone which was quite unlike her talk in delirium, was glad that the boy was safely out of the way when she was seized with the malady.

"My father came here one night, in a raging fever," she told Antonia. "I was frightened; but I hadn't the heart to drive him out of the house. He looked like a dying man. It was the small-pox. He had sent the disease inward by getting up from his bed and going out into the streets in the rain. He lay ill over a week, and I got an old woman to nurse him. I never went near him after I knew. But the infection was in the house, I suppose. I remember the night of his funeral, and my aching bones, and my burning head. I knew I was going to be ill. And then I remember nothing more—nothing more. Was it last night—the funeral?"

She spoke in a weak voice, in broken sentences, with long pauses between, Antonia holding her hand as she talked. The poor wasted hand was icy cold now; the fever was gone—gone with the life of the patient.

"You'll give Mr. Stobart my love," she said, "and please tell him I was very unhappy after he went to America. It was very kind of you to come to me; but then you like visiting sick people. I don't. Mr. Stobart used to tell me I was no Dorcas."

She lingered for a day and a night after this return of consciousness; but her last hours were passed in a stupor, and she died in her sleep, so quietly that the nurse who kept watch by her bed knew not the moment of her last sigh.

CHAPTER XVII
SWORD AND BIBLE

Lady Kilrush wrote to Lady Lanigan at the Circus, Bath, to inform her of her daughter-in-law's death. She had written some days before to acquaint that lady with poor Lucy's sad condition; but there had been as yet no reply to the first letter, and there was no time to wait for an answer to the second, so she made all arrangements for the funeral, and chose Lucy's last resting-place in the rural churchyard at Mortlake, not very far from the cottage where she had first seen the Methodist and his young wife. She was suffering from a chill and a touch of fever on the morning of the funeral, but bore up long enough to see George Stobart's wife laid in earth, since there was no one else but the doctor and the nurse to perform that last office. She engaged the old woman whom she had found on the premises to remain in the house as caretaker, till Mr. Stobart's return.

She had hardly strength to drag her aching limbs upstairs when her task was over; and, as the evening wore on, her illness increased, and although she made light of her symptoms to Sophy, she could hardly doubt their dire significance.

She stood in front of her glass for some minutes before she took to her bed. Her head ached, and her throat was parched and swollen, but she was in full beauty still. A hectic crimson burned on her cheeks, and her eyes were bright with fever. Her hair, dark as midnight, fell in natural curls over the marble whiteness of a throat and bust that had been sung by a score of modish rhymesters, and declared to excel the charms of every Venus in the Vatican. Would she ever see that face again, she wondered, after she lay down on yonder bed? Would some strange disfigured image look at her from that familiar glass—the long cheval glass before which she had stood so often in her trivial moods to study the set of a mantua, the hang of a petticoat, a dazzling figure in a splendour of gold and silver, and colour that mocked the glory of an autumn sunset, or for a whim, perhaps, in back velvet, sable from head to foot, a sombre background for her tiara and rivière of diamonds, and her famous pearl necklace.

She burst into a wild laugh as she thought of those gems. Would she ever again wear pearls or diamonds on her neck? Disfigured—blind, perhaps, a creature upon whose hideous form fine clothes and flashing jewels would seem more appalling than a shroud!

"Good-bye, beautiful Lady Kilrush," she said, making a low curtsey to the figure in the glass; and then all grew dim, and she could only totter to the bell-pull and ring for help.

Sophy came to her. The French maid had been banished after her mistress's first visit to Mrs. Stobart, Antonia having taken pains to lessen the risk of contagion for her household. Sophy had waited upon her, and had been her only means of communication with the servants.

Dr. Heberden saw her next morning, and recognized the tokens of a disease not much less terrible than the plague. He was careful not to alarm the patient, but gave his instructions to Miss Potter, and promised to send a capable nurse.

"If I am going to be ill let me have the little Lambeth apothecary to attend me," Antonia said to the physician. "I have seen him by the sick-beds of the poor, and I know what a kind soul it is."

"Let it be so, dear lady. He will make a good watch-dog. I shall see you every day till you are well."

"That will not be for a long time, sir. I know what I have to expect," she answered calmly. "But if I am likely to be hideous, for pity's sake, don't try to save my life."

"I protest, your ladyship takes alarm too soon. Your sickness may be no more than a chill, with a touch of fever."

"Oh, I know, I know," she answered, her eyes searching his countenance. "You cannot deceive me, sir. I was prepared for this. I did not think it would come. I thought I was too strong. I hardly feared it; but I knew it was possible. I did what I had to do without counting the cost."

She was in a high fever, but still in her right senses. She lay in a half stupor for the rest of the day, and her nurses, a comfortable looking middle-aged woman sent by Dr. Heberden, and Sophy Potter, had nothing to do but watch her and give her a cooling drink from time to time.

It was growing dusk, and Sophy and Mrs. Ball, the nurse, were taking tea in the dressing-room, when the door was opened and a lady appeared, struggling with a sheet steeped in vinegar that had been hung over the door by Mr. Morton's order. The intruder was Mrs. Granger, modishly dressed in a chintz silk tucked up over a black satin petticoat.

"Drat your vinegar," she cried. "I'll wager my new silk is done for."

"Oh, madam, you oughtn't to have come here," cried Sophy, starting up in a fright. "Her ladyship is taken with— —"

"Yes, I know. I've had it, Miss Potter—had it rather bad when I was a child. You might have seen some marks on my forehead and chin if you'd ever looked close at me. I should have been marked much worse, and I should never have been Mrs. General Granger, if mother hadn't sat by the bed and held my hands day and night to stop me doing myself a mischief. And I'm going to keep watch over Antonia, and save her beauty, if it's in human power to do it."

"I am the nurse engaged for the case," said Mrs. Ball, rising from the tea-board with a stately air, "and your ladyship's services will not be required."

"That's for my ladyship to judge, not you. Lady Kilrush and me was close friends before we married; and I'm not going to leave her at the mercy of any nurse in London, not if she was nurse to the Princess of Wales."

"I think Dr. Heberden's favourite nurse may be trusted, madam," said Mrs. Ball, with growing indignation.

Sophy had gone back to the sick-room.

"I wonder her ladyship's hall porter should have let you come upstairs, madam, when he had positive orders to admit nobody," continued Mrs. Ball.

"I didn't wait for his permission when I had got the truth out of him. Lions and tigers wouldn't have kept me from my friend, much less hired nurses and hall porters."

She took off her hat and flung it on the sofa, and went into the next room with so resolute an air that Mrs. Ball could only stand staring at her.

Antonia looked up as she approached the bed, and held out her hand to her.

"Oh, Patty, how glad I am to see you. Your face always brings back my youth. But no, no, no, don't come near me. Tell her, Sophy—tell her! Oh, what a racking headache."

Her head fell back upon the pillow. It was impossible to hold it up with that insufferable pain.

Patty reminded her friend of the pock marks on her temple and chin, and that she ran no risk in being with her; and from that moment till the peril was past, through a fortnight of keen anxiety, General Granger's wife remained at Antonia's bedside, watching over her with a devotion that never wearied. It was useless for Mrs. Ball to protest, or for Sophy Potter to show signs of jealousy.

"I'm going to save her beautiful face for her," Patty declared. "She shan't get up from her sick-bed to find herself a fright. She's the handsomest woman in London, and beauty like hers is worth fighting for."

Dr. Heberden heard her, and approved. He had seen her clever management, her tender care of Antonia, when the fever was raging, and the delirious sufferer would have done herself mischief in an agony of irritation. The famous doctor was vastly polite to this volunteer nurse, and complimented her on her skill and courage.

"As for my courage, sir, 'tis nothing to boast of," Patty answered frankly. "Poor as my face is, I wouldn't have risked spoiling it, and shouldn't be here if I had not had the distemper when I was a child."

Lady Kilrush passed safely through the malady that had been fatal to Lucy Stobart; but her convalescence was very slow, and she suffered a depression of spirits from which neither her devoted Sophy Potter nor her lively friend Patty could rouse her. She came back to life unwillingly, and felt as if she had nothing to live for.

On the very first day that she was able to leave her bed for an hour or two, Patty led her to the great cheval glass.

"There!" she cried, "look at yourself as close as you please. You are not pitted as much as I am even. Why, Lord bless the woman! Aren't you pleased with yourself, Tonia? You stare as if you saw a ghost."

"'Tis a ghost I am looking at, Patty, the ghost of my old self. Oh, you have been an angel of goodness, dear; and it is a mercy not to be loathsome; but the past is past, and I shall never be the beautiful Lady Kilrush again. I hope I was not too proud of my kingdom while I had it. 'Tis gone from me for ever."

"Why, you simpleton! All this fuss because you are hollow-cheeked and pale—and your beautiful hair has been cut off."

"A wreck, Patty! A haggard ghost! Don't think I am going to weep for the loss of a complexion. I had grown tired of the world before I fell ill. It will give me little pain to leave it altogether—only there is nothing else—nothing left but to sit by the fire with a book, and wait for the slow years to roll by. And the years are so slow. It seems a century since I came into this house for the first time, and found the man I loved lying on his death-bed."

"Oh, how foolish this sadness is! If I was a peeress, with such jewels as yours, a young widow, my own mistress, free to do what I liked for the rest of my days, or to pick and choose a new tyrant if I liked—I should jump for joy. You will be as handsome as ever you was after six weeks at the Wells. And you ought to marry a duke, like your friend Miss Gunning that was, who would never have been thought your equal for looks if there had not been two of her."

"Dear Patty, I have done with vanities. But never doubt my gratitude for the kindness that saved me from being a hideous spectacle."

"Nay, 'tis but the lion and the mouse over again. You took me in hand and made a lady of me, and how could I do less than jump at the first chance of making a return? I used to be a little bit envious of your handsome face once, Tonia, when you used to come to my lodgings in the piazza, in your shabby clothes, so careless and so lovely."

Lady Kilrush would see no one after her illness, putting off all visitors with polite little notes of apology, protesting that she was not yet in health to receive visits, and must defer the pleasures of friendship till she was stronger. On this the rumour went about that the disease had disfigured her beyond recognition, and all the envious women of her acquaintance were loud in their compassion.

"'Tis vastly sad to think she is too ugly to let anybody see her," said one. "I'm told she wears a thick veil even in her own house, for fear of frightening her footmen."

"They say she offered a thousand pounds to any one who would invent a wash that would hide the spots," said another.

"Spots, my dear! 'Tis vastly fine to talk of spots. The poor wretch has holes in her face as deep as your thimble."

"And is as blind as Samson Agonistes," said a fourth.

"And oh, dear, we are all so sorry for her," said the chorus, with sighs and uplifted hands; and then the fiddles began a country dance, and everybody was curtseying and simpering and setting to partners, down the long perspective of fine clothes and powdered heads, and Lady Kilrush was forgotten.

Not by Lord Dunkeld, who started post-haste for London directly he heard of her illness, and being informed that she was out of danger, and sitting up in her dressing-room every afternoon, pleaded hard to be admitted, but was resolutely refused.

Sophy wrote to him at her mistress's dictation, assuring him of her lady's unchanging esteem, but adding that she was too much out of spirits to see even her most valued friends.

"Most valued! I wonder what value she sets upon me?" questioned Dunkeld, cruelly disappointed. "'Tis the parson-soldier, or the soldier-parson she values. Perhaps the loss of her beauty moves her most because she will be less fair in his eyes. I doubt that it is always of one man only that a woman thinks, when she rejoices in her beauty. It is for *his* sake; to please *his* eye! The fellow may be a Caliban, perhaps, and yet he is the shrine at which she offers her charms."

He tried to picture that glorious beauty changed to ugliness, tried and could not; for he could not banish her image as he had seen her in Italy. Her beauty sparkled and shone before him; and imagination could not conjure up the tragic transformation.

"There is no change that could lessen my love," he thought. "She has grown into my heart, and is a part of my life. I may be appalled when I see her, may suffer tortures at a sight so piteous; but she will be dearer to me in her ruined beauty than the handsomest woman in London."

He thought of one of the handsomest, the exquisite Lady Coventry, the younger of the Gunning sisters, whose brief reign was hastening towards its melancholy close: a butterfly creature, inferior to Antonia in all mental qualities, but with much grace and sparkle, and an Irishwoman's high spirits. The Ring in Hyde Park, the Rotunda at Ranelagh, the Opera House and the Pantheon, would be poorer for the loss of that brilliant figure.

"And if Antonia appears there no more 'twill be two stars dropped out of our firmament," thought Dunkeld.

It was in vain that Patty urged her friend to try the waters of Bath or Bristol, as Dr. Heberden had advised, seeing that his patient was slow to recover her strength. Antonia refused to leave St. James's Square.

"If I went to drink the waters I should have a host of trivial acquaintants buzzing round me," she told Patty. "And I have taken a hatred of all company, but yours and Sophy's. Indeed, I think I hate the world. Here I am as safe as in a prison; for my fine friends will think the house infected, and will be afraid to trust their beauty in it."

"Sure there has been pains enough taken to drive away the contagion," said Sophy, who had suffered some inconvenience from the stringent measures Lady Kilrush had insisted upon after her recovery.

"But my friends do not know that, and till they forget my illness this house is my castle."

Mrs. Granger dropped in at teatime two or three times a week, and brought the gossip of the town, and exercised all her wit to enliven her friend; but Antonia seemed sunk in a hopeless languor and melancholy, and only affected an interest in the outside world to please her visitor.

"I'll swear you are not listening, and have scarce heard a word of it," Patty would exclaim, stopping midway in her account of the last event that had startled the town. A rich old Mrs. Somebody who was going to marry a boy; or a high-born Iphigenia sacrificed to an octogenarian bridegroom.

Antonia had left off caring what people did, or what became of them.

Even the doings of her duchesses had ceased to interest. They had sent affectionate notes and messages, and she had responded civilly. The Duke of Cumberland had sent an equerry with his card, and tender inquiries. The Princess had sent one of her ladies. And all that Antonia desired in her present mood was to be forgotten. She was glad that Lady Margaret Laroche, whom she liked best of all of her fashionable friends, was spending the winter in Paris; since she could hardly have denied herself where she was under so many obligations.

She read the papers every day, wondering whether she would ever come upon George Stobart's name in the news from America; but the name had not appeared, nor had Mr. Stobart been heard of at his own house at the beginning of the year, when she sent a servant to inquire of the woman in charge there. It was a bitter cold winter; but London was full of movement and gaiety while Antonia sat alone in the library at the back of the great solemn house, where the shutting of one of the massive doors reverberated from cellar to roof-tree in the silence. Never had there been a gayer season. It seemed as if the noise of all the crackers and squibs that had been burnt after the news from Quebec was still in the air. The cold weather killed a good many old people, and there were the usual number of putrid sore throats and typhus fevers in the fine West End mansions; but the herd went on their way rejoicing and illuminating, and praising God for the triumph of English arms on land and sea, since the victories of the great year '59 were being briskly followed up in the year that had just begun—the thirty-third of his Majesty's illustrious reign. His Majesty was waxing old and feeble, and the hero of Dettingen was soon to follow that other old lion in the Tower; and most people's eyes were turned to the mild effulgence of the rising star, the young Prince of Wales, or to the Prince's mother, and his guardian, my Lord Bute, who might be supposed to direct that youthful mind. Soon, very soon, the great bell would be tolling, the muffled drums beating, and the pomp of a royal funeral would fill the night with torches and solemn music.

That bitter winter was over, and the river was running gaily under April skies, when George Stobart came up the Thames to the Pool of London. What an insignificant river it seemed after the St. Lawrence! what a poor little flat world lay all around him, as his eyes looked out upon his native land—melancholy eyes, that found no joy in anything, no pleasure in that aspect of familiar scenes which delights most wanderers in their home-coming. Duty brought him home, while inclination would have kept him in Georgia, whither he had made his way by a difficult and perilous journey, from the snow-fields and frozen rivers of Canada to the orange groves and sunny sea of the South, after a weary time in the hospital at Quebec. There had been much for him to see in the little colony established by the philanthropic Oglethorpe five-and-twenty years before, a refuge and a home for poor debtors from the English prisons. He had preached several times in one of the school-rooms at Savannah; and the fire and fervour of his exhortations had won him a numerous following, black and white. He had gone among Whitefield's slaves; but although he found them for the most part well-used and contented, he loathed a condition which Whitefield justified, and against which Wesley had never lifted up his voice. To Stobart this buying and selling of humanity was intolerable. True that in these pious communities the African was better off than many a slave of toil in Spitalfields or Whitechapel; but he lived under the fear of the lash, and he knew not when it might suit his owner's convenience to sell him into a worse bondage.

It was with a willing heart that the soldier-priest laid down the sword and took up the Bible. In his hours of despair, in all the longing and regret of a hopeless love, his faith had remained unshaken. There was still the terror, and there was still the hope: the fear of everlasting condemnation, the hope of life eternal. Among the ignorant throng whom the great evangelist awakened to a sense of sin and a yearning for pardon, there were numerous backsliders; but the men of education and enlightenment who followed John Wesley seldom fell away. To them the things unseen, the promise and the hope, were more real than the bustle and strife of the world that hemmed them round. They walked the streets of the city with their eyes looking afar off, their thoughts full of that heavenly kingdom where life would put on a loveliness unthinkable here below. Sickening at the horrors of a world in which there were such things as the gallows at Tyburn, with its batch of victims ten or a dozen at a time—men, women, boys and girls, children almost; the Fleet prison; Bedlam, with its manacles and scourges, and Sunday promenades for the idle curious; Bridewell, Newgate. Sickening at such a world as this, the Methodist turned his ecstatic gaze towards that Kingdom of Christ the Lord, where there should be no more tears, no more war, no more oppression, no more grinding poverty or foul disease, and where all the redeemed should be equals in one brotherhood of heavenly love.

George Stobart went back to his mission work as faithful a believer as in the day of his conversion. He had not been an idle servant while he was with his regiment. He had preached the gospel wherever he could find hearers, had been instant in season and out of season; but his persistence had not been of a noisy kind, and although his superior officers were disposed to docket him as a religious monomaniac, after the manner of Methodists, they had never found him troublesome or insubordinate.

"Mr. Stobart is a gentleman," said the major. "And if expounding the Scriptures to a parcel of unbelieving rascals can console him for short rations, and keep him warm in a temperature ten degrees below zero—why, who the deuce would deny him that luxury? If he's a saint at his prayers, he's a devil in a *mêlée*; and he saved my scalp from the redskins when we were fighting in the dark in the marshes before Louisburg."

Stobart landed at the docks, had his luggage put on a hackney coach, and drove to his house at Lambeth, without a shadow of doubt that he would find all things as he had left them more than two years ago. Lucy's last letter had been written in a cheerful spirit. She was elated at Georgie's good luck in pleasing his grandmamma, and she prophesied that he would inherit Lady Lanigan's fortune and become a person of importance. Her father's drunken habits and persecuting visits were her only trouble. Her health was good, and her last maidservant was the best she had found since she began housekeeping. True that this letter had been written more than half a year ago; but the idea of change or misfortune in the quiet life at home hardly entered into the mind of the man who had so lately passed through all the perils of the siege of Quebec, from the first disastrous attack on the heights of the Montmorenci to the daring escalade and the battle on the Plains of Abraham, to say nothing of minor dangers and adventures which had made his life of the last two years a series of hairbreadth escapes. He counted on his wife's smiling welcome; and in the tediousness of the voyage he had been schooling himself to his duty as a husband, to give love for love with liberal measure, to make his wife's future years happy.

"Poor Wesley's only mistake in life is to have made an unfortunate marriage, and not to be able to make the best of a bad bargain," he thought. "But my Lucy is no such termagant as Mrs. John; and I must be a wretch if I cannot live contentedly with her. She was fair, and gentle, and loving; and I chose her for the companion of my life. I must stand by my choice."

In long, wakeful nights, when the ship was rolling in a stormy sea, he had ample leisure to travel again and again over the same ground, to make the same resolutions, to repeat the same prayers for strength within and guidance from above.

There was one name he never breathed to himself, one face he tried to shut out of his memory; but such names and such faces have the sleeper at their mercy; and his dreams were often haunted by an image that his waking thoughts ever strove to banish.

The spring afternoon was grey and cheerless; a fine rain was falling; and the narrow streets, muddy gutters, and smoky atmosphere of London were not attractive after the clear air and bright white light of Georgia.

He felt in worse spirits than before he left the ship—his prison of near six weeks—and the journey seemed interminable; but the coach rolled over Westminster Bridge at last, and drew up in front of his house. The outside shutters were closed over the parlour windows, though it was only five o'clock and broad daylight. Lucy must be away from home; with his mother, perhaps, who, having melted to the grandson, might have made a further concession and extended her kindness to the daughter-in-law—her meek *protégée* of days gone by. The suggestion seemed reasonable; but the aspect of those closed shutters chilled him.

He knocked loudly at first; and knocked a second time before the door was opened by a decent old woman in clean white cap and apron.

"Is your mistress away from home?"

The explanation was slow, disjointed, on the woman's part. His questioning was quick, impassioned, horror-stricken; but the story was told at last, the woman sparing him no ghastly particulars: the patient's sufferings; the disfiguring malady which had afterwards seized Lady Kilrush, who had come through it worse than Mrs. Stobart, and was said to be a terrible "objick." Poor Lady Kilrush! who had been so kind, and had visited Mrs. Stobart at the risk of her life, although the doctors had warned her of her danger times and often. And now she was shut up in her house and would see no one, not even her own servants, without the black velvet mask which she wore day and night.

Stobart had gone into the parlour while they were talking. The grey day came in through the holes in the shutters, and made a twilight in the familiar room. Everything was the same as when his wife used to dust and polish the furniture with indefatigable care, and place every chair and table with a prim correctness of line that had often irritated him. There was the bureau at which he used to write; and the little Pembroke table was in its own place between the windows, with the big Bible laid upon a patchwork mat.

And she for whom he had made the home was lying yonder in Mortlake churchyard, the place of rustic graves through which he had passed so often, crossing the meadows between Sheen and the church, on his way to the river. She was gone! and all his schemes for making her life happy, all his remorseful thoughts of her, had been in vain. She was gone! His last irrevocable act had been an act of unkindness. He had left her to die alone.

For his sins against God he might atone, and might feel the assurance of pardon; but for his sin against this weak mortal who had loved him, and whom he had sworn to cherish, there was no possibility of atonement.

"Not to *her*, not to *her*," he thought. "I may repent in sackcloth and ashes—I may rip the flesh from my bones with the penitent's scourge, like Henry Plantagenet. But could he make amends to the martyr Becket? Can I make amends to her? 'O God! O God! that it were possible to undo things done; to call back yesterday!'" he thought, recalling a passage in an old play that had burnt itself into his brain, by many a pang of regret for acts ill done or duties neglected.

He wandered from room to room in the familiar house which seemed so strange in its blank emptiness, looking at everything with brooding gaze—the parlour where he had spent so many solitary hours in study and in prayer. His books were on the shelves as he had left them—the old Puritan writers he loved—Baxter, Charnock, Howe, Bunyan. He had taken only three books on his voyage: his Bible, a pocket Milton, and Charles Wesley's Hymns. His study looked as if he had left it yesterday. The trees and shrubs were budding in the long slip of garden, where he had paced the narrow pathway so often in troubled thought.

He went upstairs, and stood beside the bed where his wife had lain in her last sleep. The curtains had been stripped from the tent-bedstead, the carpet taken up, and every scrap of drapery removed from the windows when the house was disinfected. The room looked poverty-stricken and grim.

The caretaker followed him from room to room, praising herself for the cleanliness of the house, and keeping up a continuous stream of talk to which he gave the scantiest attention. In the bedchamber she was reminded of Lady Kilrush and her goodness, and began to dilate upon that theme.

Was there ever such a noble lady? She had thought of everything. He might make himself quite happy about his poor dear lady. Never had a patient been better nursed. Her ladyship never missed a day, and saw with her own eyes that everything was being done. And she was with his lady a long time on that last day when the fever left her and she was able to talk sensibly. And his lady was quite happy at the last—oh, so happy! And the old woman clasped her hands in a kind of ecstasy. "Quite blind," she said, "and with a handkerchief bound over her poor eyes—but oh, so happy!"

He left the house, heavy-hearted, and walked across the bridge and by Whitehall to St. James's Square. He could not exist in uncertainty about Antonia's fate. He must discover if there were any truth in what the woman had told him, if that resplendent beauty, Nature's choicest dower given to one woman among thousands, had indeed been sacrificed. So great a sacrifice made by an Infidel! a woman who had no hope in an everlasting reward for the renunciation of happiness here. He recalled the exquisite face that had lured him to sin, and pictured it scarred and blemished—as he had seen so many faces,—changed by that fatal disease which leaves ruin where it spares life. He shuddered and sickened at the vision his imagination evoked. Would he honour her less, adore her less, so disfigured? He had told himself sometimes in his guilty reveries, when Satan had got the better of him, that he would love her if she were a leper; that it was the soul, the noble, the daring, the generous nature of the woman that he idolized; that he was scarcely a sinner for loving the most perfect creature God had ever made.

If she hid her blemished face from the world, would she consent to see him? Or would he find his sin still unpardoned? Would she hold him at a distance for ever because of one fatal hour in his life? She could scarcely forget their last parting, when she had prayed never to look upon his face again; but time might have mitigated her wrath, and she might have forgiven him.

Her ladyship saw no visitors, the porter told him, and was about to shut the door in his face; but Mr. Stobart pushed his way in, and scribbled a note at a writing-table in the hall.

"Pray be so kind as to see me. I want to thank you for your goodness to my wife. I landed in London two hours ago on my arrival from America."

He walked up and down the hall while a footman carried the note to his mistress. His heart beat heavily, tortured with the anticipation of horror; to look upon the altered face; to have to tell himself that *this* was Antonia.

The man came back, solemn and slow, in his rich livery and powdered head. Her ladyship would see Mr. Stobart.

She was sitting in a large armchair by the fire, her face showing dimly in the twilight. He could distinguish nothing but her pallor and the difference in the style of her hair. The flowing curls that he had admired were gone. He felt thankful for the darkness which spared him the immediate sight of her changed aspect.

"I am glad you are back in England, Mr. Stobart, and have escaped the perils of that dreadful war," she said, in a low, grave voice. "But you have had a sorrowful welcome home."

"Yes, it was a heavy blow."

"I hope you had received Lady Lanigan's letter, and that the blow was softened by foreknowledge."

"No, I had no letter; I came home expecting to find all things as I left them. My mind was full of schemes for making my wife happier than I had made her in the past. But I doubt sins of omission are irrevocable. A man may sometimes undo what he has done, but he cannot make amends for what he has left undone."

There was a silence. The shadows deepened. The wood fire burnt low and gave no light.

"I have no words to thank you for your goodness to my wife," he said. "That you should go to her in her loneliness, that you should so brave all perils, be so compassionate, so self-sacrificing! What can I say to you? There is nothing nobler in the lives of the saints. There was never Christian living more worthy to be called Christ's disciple."

"Oh, sir, there needed no Gospel light to show me so plain a course. Your wife was alone, while you were fighting for your country. I promised years ago to be her friend. Could there be any question as to my duty?"

"'Twill need all my future life to prove my gratitude."

"You have left the army?"

"Yes. I resigned my commission after Quebec."

"You were at the taking of Quebec, then? I thought you were with Amherst when he recovered Ticonderoga."

"So I was, madam. But after we took the fort I was entrusted to carry a letter for General Wolfe conveying General Amherst's plans. 'Twas a difficult journey, by a circuitous route, and I was more than a month on the way; but I was in time to be in the escalade and the battle. It was glorious—a glorious tragedy. England and France lost two of the finest leaders that ever soldier followed—Montcalm and Wolfe. Alas! shall I ever forget James Wolfe's spectral face in the grey of that fatal morning? He was fitter to be lying on a sick-bed than to be commanding an army. He looked a ghost, and fought like the god of war."

"Shall you go back to your work with Mr. Wesley?"

"If he will have me—and, indeed, I think he will, for he needs helpers. 'Tis in his army—the evangelical army—I shall fight henceforward. I stand alone in the world now, for my son's welfare could scarce be better assured than with his grandmother, who offers to provide his education, and is likely to make him her heir. My experience in Georgia renewed my self-confidence, and I doubt I may yet be of some use to my fellow-creatures."

"You could scarce fail in that," she answered gently. "I remember how those poor wretches at Lambeth loved you."

Her voice was unaltered. It had all that grave music he remembered of old, when she spoke of serious things. It soothed him to sit in the darkness and hear her talk, and he dreaded the coming of light that would break the spell.

Did he love her as he had loved her before those slow years of severance? Yes. Her lightest word thrilled him. He thought of the change in her with unspeakable dread; but he knew that it would not change his heart. Lovely or unlovely she would still be Antonia, the woman he adored. A footman came in to light the candles.

"This half darkness is very pleasant, madam," Stobart said hurriedly. "Do you desire more light?"

"I am expecting a friend to take tea with me, and I can hardly receive her in the dark. You may light the candles, Robert."

There were six candles in each of two bronze candelabra on the mantelpiece, and two more in tall silver candlesticks on the writing-table. Stobart sat looking down at the fading embers, and did not lift his eyes till the servant had left the room. Then, as the door shut, he looked up and saw Antonia watching him in the bright candlelight.

He gave a sudden cry, in uncontrollable emotion, and burst into tears. "You—you are not changed!" he cried, as soon as he could control his speech. "Oh, madam, I beseech you not to despise me for these unmanly tears! but—but I was told——"

"You were told that the disease had used me very cruelly; that I should be better dead than such a horrid spectacle," she said. "I know that has been the talk of the town—and I let them talk. I have done with the town." ·

"Thank God!" he exclaimed, starting up from his chair and walking about the room in a tumult of emotion. "Thank God, it was a lie that old woman told me. It would have broken my heart to know that your divine charity had cost you the loss of your beauty."

His eyes shone with wonder and delight as he looked at her. She was greatly changed, but in his sight not less lovely. Her bloom was gone. She could no longer dazzle the mob in Hyde Park by her vivid beauty. She was very pale, and her cheeks were hollow and thin. Her eyes looked unnaturally large, and her hair, once so luxuriant, was clustered in short curls under a little lace cap.

"Oh, so far as that goes, sir, I renounce any claim I ever had to rank among beauties," she said, amused at his surprise. "Through the devoted care of a friend I was spared the worst kind of disfigurement; but as I have lost my complexion, my figure, and my hair, I can no longer hope to take any place among the Waldegraves and Hamiltons. And I have done with the great world and its vanities."

"Then you will give yourself to that better world—the world of the true believer; you will be among the saved?"

"Alas, sir, I am no nearer the heavenly kingdom than I was before I sickened of the earthly one. I am very tired of the pomps and vanities, but I cannot entertain the hope of finding an alternative pleasure in sermons and long prayers, or the pious company Lady Huntingdon assembles every Thursday evening."

"If you have renounced the world of pleasure—the rest will follow."

"You think a woman must live in some kind of fever? I own that Lady Fanny Shirley seems always as busy and full of engagements as if she were at the top of the *ton*. She flies from one end of London to the other to hear a new preacher, and makes more fuss about the opening of some poor little chapel in the suburbs, than the Duchess of Buccleuch makes about an *al fresco* ball that costs thousands. There is the chairman's knock. Perhaps you will scarce care to meet my lively friend, Mrs. Granger, in your sad circumstances."

"Not for the world. Adieu, madam. I shall go to Mortlake to-morrow to look at my poor Lucy's resting-place, and shall start the next day for Bath to see my son; and thence to Bristol, where I hope to find Mr. Wesley."

He bent down to kiss her hand, so thin and so alabaster white, and said in a low voice, with his head still bent—

"Dare I hope that my madness of the past is pardoned?"

"The past is past," she answered coldly. "The world has changed for both of us. Adieu."

He left her, passing Mrs. Granger in the hall.

"You have admitted a sneaking Methodist," cried Patty, "after denying yourself to all the people of fashion in London."

Mr. Wesley received the returning prodigal with kindness. In that vast enterprise of one who said "My parish is the world," loyal adherents were of unspeakable value. The few churchmen who served under his banner were but a sprinkling compared with his lay itinerants; and Stobart was among the best of these. He was too manly a man to think the worse of his helper for having changed gown for sword during a troubled interval of his life; for he divined that Stobart must have been in some bitter strait before he went back to the soldier's trade.

He listened with interest to Stobart's American adventures, and congratulated him upon having been with Wolfe at Quebec.

"'Twas a glorious victory," he said; "but I doubt the French may yet prove too strong for us in Canada, and that we are still far from a peaceful settlement."

"They are strong in numbers, sir, but weak in leaders. Lévis is a poor substitute for Montcalm, and, if the Governor Vaudreuil harasses him and ties his hands, as he harassed the late marquis, whom he hated, his work will be difficult. I should not have left the regiment while there was a chance of more fighting, if I had not been disabled by my wounds."

"You were badly wounded?"

"I had a bullet through my ribs that looked like making an end of me; and I walk lame still from a ball in my left hip. I spent eight weeks in the general hospital at Quebec, where the nuns tended me with an angelic kindness; and I was still but a feeble specimen of humanity when I set out on the journey to Georgia, through a country beset by Indians."

"I honour those good women for their charity, Stobart; but I hope you did not let them instil their pernicious doctrine into your mind while it was enfeebled by sickness."

"No, sir. Yet there was one pious enthusiast whom I could not silence; and be not offended if I say that her fervent discourse about spiritual things reminded me of your own teaching."

"Surely that's not possible!"

"Extremes meet, sir; and, I doubt, had you not been a high-church Methodist you would have been a Roman Catholic of the most exalted type."

Stobart accompanied Mr. Wesley from Bristol to St. Ives, then back to Bristol by a different route, taking the south coast of Cornwall and Devonshire. From Bristol they crossed to Ireland; and returned by Milford Haven through Wales to London, a tour that lasted till the first days of October.

Wesley was then fifty-seven years of age, in the zenith of his renown as the founder of a sect that had spread itself abroad with amazing power since the day when a handful of young men at Oxford, poor, obscure, unpretending, had met together in each other's rooms to pray and expound the Scriptures, and by their orderly habits, and the method with which they

EPILOGUE

Thirty years later, on the anniversary of Antonia's death, George Stobart, Bishop of Northborough—the fighting bishop, as some of his admirers called him, a profound scholar, a fiery controversialist, a celibate and an ascetic, once famous as a Methodist field-preacher, and now the leader of the extreme High Church party—sat by the fireside in his library in the episcopal Palace, a lofty and spacious room, where a pair of wax candles on the writing-table served but to accentuate the darkness. He sat leaning forward in the candlelight, with one elbow on the arm of his chair, looking at a long dark ringlet that lay in his open hand, bound with a black ribbon to which was attached a label in Wesley's writing—

"Antonia's hair, cut after death by her sorrowing friend, J. W."

"Only a woman's hair," murmured the bishop. "'Tis said that Swift spoke those words in pure cynicism over a ringlet of his ill-used Stella. Only a woman's hair! And for me the memorial of a life's love, the one earthly relic which reminds the priest that he was once a man. Oh, thou who wert the idol of this heart, dost thou in some undiscovered region still live to pity thy desolate lover? Shall we meet and know each other again, where there is neither marrying nor giving in marriage? Or is it all a dream, nothing but a dream?"

"I had been kneeling by her bedside in silent prayer for some time, her marble hand clasped in mine, when she cried out suddenly, 'Husband, I have kept my vow,' and, looking upward with a seraphic smile, her spirit passed into eternity. I assisted in the funeral service, and saw her mortal remains laid in the family vault, where her coffin was placed beside that of the last Lord Kilrush.

"Yours in sorrow and affection,

"JOHN WESLEY."